The Dog's Bollocks

Previously titled:
*The Valentine Present
and Other Diabolical Liberties*

A romantic comedy by
Lynda Renham

About the Author

Lynda lives in Oxford, UK. She has appeared on BBC radio discussion programmes and is a prolific blogger, Twitter and Facebook contributor. She is author of the best-selling romantic comedy novels including *Croissants and Jam*, *Coconuts and Wonderbras* and *Pink Wellies and Flat Caps*.

This book is dedicated to fellow stutterers. I also suffered from a stammer when a little younger and know the frustration. As with all things, laughter is the best medicine.

Lynda Renham

The right of Lynda Renham to be identified as the author of the work has been asserted by her in accordance with the Copyright, Designs and Patents Act 1988.

ISBN 978-0-9927874-0-0

first edition

Cover Illustration by Gracie Klumpp
www.gracieklumpp.com

Printed for Raucous Publishing in Great Britain by
SRP (Exeter)

Chapter One

Don't you just hate people who are always on time? Even worse are those people who aren't only on time but fifteen minutes early. Totally unexpected buggers aren't they? There you are in the middle of a quickie and they turn up on your doorstep, and you're staring at them with that post orgasmic flush on your face as you accept their bunch of carnations and bottle of plonk. Not that Julian and I often have quickies before people come to dinner you understand, just in case you think we do, but you know what I mean. The only quickie you'll catch us doing fifteen minutes before guests arrive is sieving lumps out of the cheese sauce. Lumpy cheese sauce is a speciality of mine. As for me, I am late for just about everything. I just can't seem to get anywhere on time no matter how hard I try, and believe me, I try. I'm trying pretty hard right now. Julian, however, is one of those people who is always on time and I imagine he is well on his way to the church by now.

'I'll meet you at the church. Try not to be late,' he had said with a wink, knowing full well I would be.

Meanwhile, I'm desperately trying to bungle Celia Blakely out of the laundrette where I work so I can finish my shift, change, and get to my friend, Silvia's, wedding.

'So, I said to Mr Newman, you know Mr Newman don't you?'
I don't know Mr Newman in the least and I am beginning to wonder if I actually want to.

'He lives just up the road. His wife was ...'
She leans closer and I shift slightly so I can hear her while continuing to unload the dryer.

'Having *it* with Mr Douglas from number thirty-three.'

'Oh,' I say, folding the towels and placing them into her laundry bag.

'She went to the Isle of Dogs with him. Well, I said to Mr Newman she can go to the dogs a woman like that. We don't want the likes of her here in Battersea do we?'

I shake my head and glance at the clock. I'm going to be so late. I find myself wondering if Julian and I might have *it* later. A wedding always gets you in the mood doesn't it? Lots of slow dances and champagne, and Julian in a nice fresh smelling shirt and I can see myself getting quite turned on. After all it seems like ages since we have.

'Where's this wedding you're going to?'

'St John's Wood, it's a bit of a posh one. My mum used to clean at their house when I was little and I used to play with their girl. I've got to get the bus when I clock off here.'

She grabs the washing bag and hands me ten pounds.

'Here's a little extra. Get a taxi. I know you're struggling with that café and your studies.'

Café? God, Julian would have a hundred canary fits if he heard the restaurant being called a café.

'Oh no, I couldn't Celia.'

'Don't argue, just take it. It's your birthday soon, ain't it?'

'Yeah, tomorrow actually. Thanks Celia, I'll pay you back. Honest.' She tuts.

'I wouldn't want it back.'

I see her to the door and rush to the back room to change, tapping Julian's number into my mobile as I go. It rings and rings and finally goes to voicemail. Shit, he is probably at the church already. I pull off my stripy laundrette overall and study myself in the cracked back room mirror and slip on my new scarlet satin dress. It's not strictly new of course. I bought it at Oxfam, but it's perfect. I expect Alistair will quip something about *The Waltons* when he sees it. A quick shake of my shaggy blonde hair and a stroke of mascara transform me. I look critically at my reflection and sigh. Not enough time to achieve my normal Kate Moss look. Who I am I kidding? I clip a diamante slide into my hair and swipe Sugar Kiss Red lipstick over my full lips and stroke Rosy Red blusher onto my cheeks and sigh. Not bad I suppose. Of course, I'm sure I could look sensational if I had that Bobbi Brown stuff that Fiona uses. I'm so knackered. The last thing I need is a wedding, and a posh one at that. I slip on my trainers, as they are easier for running, and throw my red satin sling backs into a carrier bag. Clutching my woollen shawl, I open the door.

'Bye Maud,' I shout to my boss.

My mobile trills and I fumble in my bag. It's Sid, my landlord.

'Harriet, I hate to phone you darling. I've tried Julian but I'm not getting an answer. I'm sure it's a silly mistake. Just a bloody oversight but as it happened last month I just thought I should check all is okay.'

What happened last month? I look down the street for a taxi.

'Sorry, what's that Sid?'

'Julian's bank isn't paying the standing order for the rent. I'm sure it's a mix up again, like last month.'

I feel my stomach lurch.

'Last month?' I say my voice rising.

I sense his embarrassment.

'Not to worry babe, I'll try him again. We'll get it sorted. He said he would settle last month's rent and this month by the end of last week, but I think he must have used the wrong account again. Not to worry huh?'

'I'll speak to him. We're at a wedding today. But I'll get him to sort it tomorrow for you. I'm sure it's just a mix up like you say.'

I hang up and push the conversation to the back of my mind. Sid's right I'm sure. It's just a silly mix up. Right, all I need now is to hail a taxi and that's no mean feat. I'll probably have to flash them. Oh well, there's a first time for everything.

* * *

'This is it,' I tell the taxi driver as I slip on my new Shoezone stilettos.

'That's twenty quid darling.'

'What? You've got to be kidding. That's bleeding extortion more like,' I quip fumbling in my purse. 'What a liberty.'

I reluctantly hand over the money and dash through the church gates, struggling with the strap of one of my sandals as I go. That will teach me to buy cheap. I wobble on one foot and fiddle with the strap when I feel a hand on my arm.

'Can I help with this?'

I turn to the voice and come face to face with a very striking man. In fact, he is so good looking he sends an ache through me. He's wearing a dinner suit and his white shirt complements his tanned skin. His warm hazel eyes twinkle with amusement and a small smile flickers over his face. His voice is soft but clear and seems to have a hint of laughter in it. Is he mocking me, or is it just his manner? He holds out his arm and I lean gently on it and adjust my shoe strap while trying to ignore the fact that my breathing has quickened. His arm feels warm and sends a tingle down my spine.

'Ta very much,' I say gratefully, removing my hand as quickly as possible before I end up ripping off his shirt.

Blimey, I haven't felt this randy in months. He nods towards the church where the organ is playing softly.

'I think they've started,' he says in his soft cultured voice.

I do believe I have lost the power of speech, bloody hell, that's a first.

'Shall we?' he asks, heading towards the church.

Ooh, I'd love to but I'm not so sure a church is an appropriate place. For a split second I imagine him without that white shirt and feel myself go weak at the knees. I follow meekly, slipping in quietly at the back. I spot Fiona and Alistair but Julian is not with them, and I can see no sign of him. I love the smell of churches. I couldn't tell you why. They are kind of sweet and musty all together. Although right now this church smells of Chanel perfume, Pierre Cardin aftershave and rose petals. There is also a faint smell of baby vomit which I am trying to ignore. I love weddings too. I don't care where they are, I just like the atmosphere. Church weddings are best of course. The atmosphere in a registry office is nowhere near as holy is it? I'd like to get married in a church, not that Julian and I have ever talked about marriage even though we've been together for three years. And let's face it, we can barely afford to eat at the moment, let alone plan a wedding. We never seem to have time to discuss our relationship. Either I'm dashing out to work, or panicking to finish a study assignment and you don't normally bring up the subject of marriage as you're tumbling out of bed or flying through the kitchen waving a piece of Marmite-smeared toast. Julian is working hard getting his restaurant going and if we are both home at the same time we are so knackered that we barely exchange more than twenty words. When it's time for bed we are normally out for the count in seconds. Our sex life isn't riveting but then whose is after three years? Mind you, my sister Caron and her boyfriend are at it nine to the dozen, or so she would have me believe, and they've been together for four years. It would be exciting though, I don't mean going at it nine to the dozen, although that would be pretty exciting if I could just get up the energy. No, I mean getting married would be exciting. I look down at my dress and feel my head again to check the diamante slide is still there. All the other women are wearing huge hats and fabulous dresses and I feel just a touch underdressed. I'm not good at top hat and tails weddings. I love my friends but I feel so out of place with some of them. I bet these guests didn't buy their outfits from Oxfam. I pull the dress gently from my newly pierced navel and adjust my bra slightly. I love Oxfam. I don't know what I would do without it, not that I want people to continually starve, I mean that obviously goes without saying, but charity shops are a godsend to people like me. It's just a shame they don't sell cheap food.

The wedding march roaring from the organ snaps me out of my daydream. I turn to see the bride enter, but am acutely aware of the good-looking man beside me and the fresh clean smell that comes from him. I gasp as Silvia glides down the aisle in her beautiful Vera Wang wedding dress.

'She looks amazing,' I sigh.

'She looks okay,' says the man beside me.

I gape at him.

'You're kidding, that's a Vera Wang dress. I'd die for a Vera Wang dress.'

Oh God, I sound so shallow. I give him a sideways glance and try to guess his age. I've never been good with ages but at a guess I'd say he was early thirties. I wonder if his wife/girlfriend and Julian are stuck somewhere together. There is absolutely no way this sex god is single.

'I like *your* dress,' he says softly, looking into my eyes.

'You do?' I say surprised. 'It was a fiver in Oxfam ...' I bite my lip. What am I saying? I don't need any help in making a bad impression do I?

'Alistair always thinks I look like crap. He's dead embarrassed to be seen with me,' I whisper.

'Is Alistair your boyfriend?'

'Heavens no, I'd rather slash my wrists ...'

He must think me so common.

'He's my friend's partner,' I say, pointing at Fiona a few rows ahead, 'but he's a bit rude. My boyfriend Julian hasn't arrived yet,' I say quickly, although I'm not sure why.

'I'm Brice Edmunds by the way.'

Brice? I should have known he would have a sexy name.

'Harriet Lawson,' I reply, wishing it were something much grander.

There is a hushed silence as the vicar begins the service. It is so unlike Julian to be late. Forty-five minutes later and it is all over and we are applauding Silvia and Hugh as they leave the church. I make my way outside and wait for Fi and Alistair while searching for Julian. Brice passes me and smiles. He could stop hearts with that smile. I spot Fiona and Alistair and head towards them. My God, his flies are undone. I'm so preoccupied with Alistair's trousers that I send myself sprawling as my heel tangles in my dress. Fiona catches me and wraps me in a tight embrace. Thank God for a familiar face, although it would have been much nicer had it been Julian's.

'On time as always,' Alistair quips sarcastically. 'There is something c-c-comforting about your consistent lateness.'

'Hello Alistair, you look nice, like the Y-fronts.'

Fiona follows my eyes to Alistair's zipper.

'Christ Alistair, your flies are undone. Do something before that Jeremy guy sees you.'

'What Jeremy guy?' Alistair asks while fumbling with the zipper.

'Over there. He's a Lord or Sir or something. Anyway, zip your flies up for Christ's sake.'

I peer at the man.

'I don't think he is,' I say.

'Are you sure? He looks familiar,' she says.

'That's because he's the parking attendant at Homebase,' sighs Alistair.

I narrow my eyes.

'He's right you know,' I say.

'Are you sure? What's he doing here?'

'P-p-parking cars,' huffs Alistair. 'I wish you would wear your contact lenses. Honestly you'll be curtsying to parking attendants before we know where we are.'

'I do wear them. I'm just so tired and they make my eyes sore. I was sure my glasses were in my bag. I feel like I'm jet lagged. You know, that 'when you're not here' feeling?'

'I'm rather wishing I wasn't. I feel like a sodding wallflower,' I say looking around desperately for Julian.

'A scarlet w-w-wallflower,' sneers Alistair. 'It's a w-w-wedding you know, not a b-b-bloody period drama.'

What a cheek, some people just don't appreciate individualism do they?

'Bloody things,' he mumbles yanking the zip up.

'You look lovely,' Fiona assures me. 'I love the snap pearl buttons on that dress.'

'You don't think it's a bit, you know, *Little House on the Prairie?*' I say feeling self-conscious.

'A little bit?' sneers Alistair. 'That's an understatement.'

'Ignore him, he wouldn't know style if it bit him on the arse,' Fiona says glaring at Alistair.

'Have you seen Julian?' I ask. 'He should have been here ages ago. I'm sure he left well before I did. You know how he likes to be on time.'

'Most people like to be on time,' says Alistair.

'I can't see anybody without my contacts,' moans Fiona, 'let alone Julian. He's probably got held up at the restaurant.'
I shake my head sending a pearl drop earring flying.

'I've tried the restaurant, and his mobile, and he isn't answering either. I've only brought a cheap card with me. He's supposed to be bringing the present.'

'I imagine he's still bombing it down the A40 in your Mini,' says Alistair casually.
I stare at him.

'What?'

'That's just the thing. Alistair swears he saw Julian bombing it down the A40 in your Mini. I said that's not possible. It's completely the wrong way, and your Mini won't do more than forty,' says Fiona.

'Not with an empty tank it won't. That's why I got a taxi here. I forgot about petrol. I don't mean I forgot that the car takes petrol, of course. I'm not that dippy.'

'That's a relief,' quips Alistair.
I shoot him a dirty look.

'I just forgot I was on the red and I'm flat broke. Bombing it down the A40, are you sure he was in the Pooch? The thing will blow up.'

'I don't think it is p-p-possible to mistake your Mini. You know that distinctive whining sound that says *Harriet's Mini?*'
Why on earth would Julian be ragging the Pooch down the A40 when he's got his new van? I hope the wheels weren't nicked from it. That's all we need. The past nine months have been shit. Every single penny going into Julian's dream of setting up a French

restaurant which, so far, has not done very well at all. If it wasn't for our friends eating there we wouldn't have broken even. I've seriously started considering selling a kidney. Julian's obviously, not mine. I'm not that crazy. After all, we could survive on three between the two of us. In fact, maybe I could sell off bits of Julian's body until he has the restaurant up and running and I have all my studies paid for. Although, strictly speaking, not all our money has gone into the venture. I have been secretly squirrelling away some of my earnings. I decided from the start that one of us needed to put a little by and I'm so glad I did. I need to pay for the next part of my tuition fees as I am not planning to work in a laundrette all my life. I can't help worrying though, what earthly reason would Julian have for racing down the A40 in my Mini? Come to think of it why is he ragging it down the A40 at all when the church is the opposite way? Still, Julian always did have a terrible sense of direction. All the same, it's a bit odd. Julian would never be late unless there was a good reason.

'It's not like Julian to be late,' I say voicing my concerns.

'There's a f-f-first time for everything,' says Alistair.

'It's dead posh this wedding isn't it?' says Fiona, breaking into my thoughts. 'There are Lords and MPs and everything. It's a real high-class do isn't it? They're all big knobs.'

'Is that a fact? Perhaps you should keep an eye on that zip Alistair. You don't want people making comparisons,' I laugh.

Fiona snorts and quickly turns away. Alistair scowls and storms off.

'God, what's wrong with him?'

'He's tired. He's putting a lot of hours in at the office. We both are. Honestly, what with the rent and food ...'

'What's food?' I quip.

'Oh come on Harriet, things aren't that bad surely.'

I sigh.

'No, that's true. There are my mum's scraps after all.'

'C-c-come on,' calls Alistair.

'He's not stammering much today, that's good isn't it?'

'He's taken a Valium,' she says with a sigh and grabs my arm. 'Come on, lead me to the reception. I can't see a sodding thing beyond my hand without my contacts, and you know how I hate wearing glasses.'

Chapter Two

'Oh no, you're not on our table are you?' Alistair mumbles as he studies the table plan.

'Do you need another Valium?' asks Fiona helpfully.

'Of c-c-c-course not,' he stutters. 'I'm not a b-b-b-bloody drug addict.'

'Right, just trying to help. You don't mind if I have one do you?'

Before he can reply she has popped a little yellow pill into her mouth and downed it with champagne.

'Blimey, am I that bad to sit with that you need tranquillising?' I say hurtfully.

She hugs me.

'Of course not. I'm always tense at weddings.'

I'm getting worried about Julian. He is not answering his phone and has not returned my texts. It is so unlike him. I sometimes wonder if Julian really loves me. Of course, I'm sure he does, it's just sometimes I wonder. He's always saying how grateful he is but that isn't the same is it?

'I really appreciate you working double shifts to help with the restaurant Harry, I really do.'

But that isn't exactly saying *I love you* is it? And he only moved in with me when his rent went up. *Two can live cheaper than one* he had said. Not quite the declaration of love I had been waiting for.

'I hate line ups,' Fiona moans, heading awkwardly towards the bride and groom, patting her neat bun as she goes.

'Do your flies up.'

'Buggery things,' Alistair groans. 'There's something wrong with the zip on these t-t-trousers.'

I fumble in my clutch bag for the card and totter behind Fiona, trying to avoid a vomiting baby that is screaming behind me.

'Well done, well done,' bellows a man. 'Where's the Bollingers? You're looking dandy my dear. I love the scarlet woman look. Sir Alfred Marcham at your service.'

He drapes an arm around my shoulder and leans his hand down to cup my breast while his other hand gropes my bum. Fiona takes a sharp breath. I smile at him politely.

'Everyone's entitled to be stupid, but you're abusing the privilege don't you think? Please remove your hands.'
He squeezes my breast.

'I'm just being friendly my dear,' he grins.

'Well, I would much prefer it if you'd be a little less friendly,' I say, leaning across him.

'Now, remove your grubby knighted hand from my breast this second you pompous pervert or I'll knee your groin so hard, your cock will fly out of your mouth,' I whisper in his ear.

'Just a little fun my dear,' he responds, giving my bum another squeeze.

'I think that's enough fun for one day Sir Alfred, don't you?' says a familiar voice. I turn to see the gallant helper is my partner from the back pew. He removes Sir Alfred's hand, accidentally brushing my breast with his own as he does so. I blush and lower my eyes.

'Steady on Brice old man,' says Sir Alfred, holding up his hands. 'I never would have had her down as your type,' he adds with a smirk.
What a cheeky bleeder. Brice avoids my eyes, gives a little nod and walks away.

'You're a lively little filly,' grins Sir Alfred. 'I like that.'

'Don't get any ideas about mounting me,' I hiss before stepping on his foot with my heel. At the same moment the vomiting baby coughs, projecting vomit at his shirt. Fiona looks at the child with disgust.

'Why she doesn't stick that monster on her tit I'll never know. At least he'd shut up.'

'Be quiet,' hisses Alistair.

'Do you think if you stick Alistair on yours he'll shut up,' I snigger.

'No, but I'd clear the hall. I hate these sorts of weddings,' she moans. 'Who was that?' she says nodding to Brice. 'He's bloody gorgeous.'

'Just someone who arrived late like me, we crept into church together.'

'Sounds like the beginning of a great romance,' she laughs. 'Right, let's get through this line up. Don't you just hate these things?'

'Let's just drink plenty of Bollingers,' I laugh.

'Would you be a darling and let me dive in front of you? It's just that if I don't get him on the breast soon I swear he'll turn into the Antichrist,' says the harassed mother.

Turn into? I thought he already was. We step aside and she pushes forward.

'Silvia,' Fiona squeals on reaching the bride, 'you look spectacular and the dress ...'

'What's that smell?' mumbles Alistair.

'What?' Silvia snaps.

'Alistair asked is it Chanel?' I say, quickly handing her the card. 'You look fab, congratulations.'

I peck Hugh on each cheek.

'Lovely wedding Hugh.'

'Yah, classic so far,' he grins, seemingly unaware of the stink surrounding him.

'No it's not Chanel,' says Alistair, seemingly in a world of his own. 'More like v-v-v- ...'

'Versace,' squeals Fiona, kicking Alistair in the shin. 'Yes, I think it's more Versace too. Anyway the dress is gorgeous.'

Even if it does smell to high heaven.

'Dior actually, Mummy is wearing Chanel,' says a sour-faced Silvia.

'Oh, I ...'

'Mark,' yells Silvia to a man behind us, pushing Fiona out of the way so roughly that she narrowly escapes falling into Silvia's father's arms.

'Sloshed already?' he laughs.

Fiona forces a laugh.

'Yes that's weddings for you, never been sober at one yet. Congratulations. It's a lovely wedding.'

'Fuck,' she mumbles as Alistair joins us.

'Did you smell that bloody dress? It stinks of vomit.'

'Most likely the Antichrist,' I say.

'How bloody awful,' groans Fiona.

I check my mobile again. Oh God, what if Julian has had an accident on the way here? It really isn't like him not to text. I grab a glass of champagne from a passing waiter.

'To the Ladies, come on,' says Fiona. 'What an awful wedding, it's all bank managers and toffs. Have you seen the best man? What a ponce. The vicar is pretty gorgeous though.'

Fiona grins at me through the mirror and I think how fabulous she looks. My closest friend and confidante and a brilliant accountant to boot. I've known her since uni. We shared a love of Sylvia Plath and erotic novels. Sylvia Plath got forgotten over the years but the erotic novel lives on. She's horse crazy though, which is something we don't share. Fiona's family always had horses, whereas we only ever had budgies. Still, we can't all have everything can we? She's as vain as they come of course, and blind as a bat. I've stopped her on more than one occasion from walking into a door and all because she will not wear her glasses, and contact lenses just don't suit her. But do you think she'll give up on them? A bit like her relationship with stuttering Alistair, who I so wish she would dump. She is much too good for him. I have always envied her deep chestnut hair. It's wonderfully thick, shiny and naturally wavy. I drop my head forwards and fluff up my honey blonde hair before clipping the diamante slide back in.

'I swear I've aged since Julian opened the restaurant,' I groan. 'Do you think I look my age?' I ask Fiona anxiously.

She looks dubious.

'I hate answering questions like that,' she says wrinkling up her face.

'Oh no,' I sigh. 'I knew it. I'm twenty-eight and prematurely aging. I'm like that woman in the Facebook advert with *her shocking $3 trick to a wrinkle free face* who looks ninety if she's a day. I'll have to get that cream, and I don't believe it will be just three dollars. Damn it.'

'It's because I don't have my contacts in,' she says, attempting to comfort me while spraying Issey Floral everywhere. 'I'm sure you look about twenty.'

'Now I know you're lying.'

'Don't let me flirt with anyone hideous will you. You know what I'm like after a few drinks. That's the trouble with being blind as a bat. I'll probably end up either flirting with Sir Alfred or the vicar,' she says, popping on her glasses to see her reflection.

'I thought you forgot your glasses.'

'Of course not, that's just what I tell Alistair. I wouldn't be seen dead in them in a place like this.'

Ten minutes later and we are back in the hall where the smell of baby vomit is distinctly noticeable. There is still no sign of Julian.

'Is that the gorgeous vicar on our table?' hisses Fiona.

I nod.

'And several ponces,' I groan. 'As long as they don't think my scarlet dress entitles them to a quick grope.'

The men scrape back their chairs and stand up. Alistair quickly follows and our eyes go to his flies.

'We must seem desperate looking at his crotch,' whispers Fiona. 'Not that I can see it from here. Nothing's hanging out is it?'

'We must seem desperate just looking at Alistair, period,' I quip. 'No, nothing is hanging out, at least nothing worth looking at.'

'Thanks a lot,' retorts Fiona, fumbling in her bag and producing the bottle of Valium.

'One more won't hurt,' she mumbles.

'Ladies,' says one of the men in an upper-crust voice as he pulls back a chair.

'Ta very much,' I say, sitting down and smiling at the vicar who sits next to me.

'Where have you been?' snaps Alistair.

'I've been snorting coke in the loo and having sex with a waiter,' Fiona slurs, taking a sip of Merlot. 'I thought it might ease my tension.'

'Good afternoon,' says a pompous looking man opposite me, holding out his hand. 'I'm Duncan, otherwise known as the government chief whip,' he adds proudly.

'Ooh, I should have brought my leathers,' I smile.

'I thought your performance in church was excellent,' I tell the vicar. 'In a non-kinky way of course.'

He coughs uncomfortably.

'Thank you very much but it's all in a day's work.'

I stare fascinated at his dog collar. Fiona fights back a giggle. There is a tapping sound from the mike and a deep booming voice bellows from the PA.

'My lords, ladies and gentlemen, please stand for Mr and Mrs Hugh Cramphorn-Williams.'

'Oh shit,' mumbles Fiona.

'Don't you mean puke?' I say, discreetly removing a small Febreze spray from my clutch bag.

Silvia wafts along the grand hall, leaving a wake of baby vomit fragrance as she goes. I madly pump at the spray as she passes. Alistair lifts his hand to his nose but Fiona stops him.

'It's rude,' she tells him.

'It's bloody rude swanning by us in a vomit smelling wedding dress too,' groans Alistair.

I have to agree with him.

'Oh no, really?' says the vicar.

I nod.

'It was the Antichrist,' I say and bite my lip. Honestly, talk about opening my mouth and putting my foot in it. 'Although I'm sure you get it all the time. Not the Antichrist vomiting all over you, obviously. Crikey that would be a bit like the Exorcist wouldn't it? I mean babies vomiting on you, obviously. Not the other ...'

You know that feeling when you're just in too deep? He smiles warmly.

'Indeed. Babies tend to puke over me a lot I'm afraid, especially at christenings.'

'Downside of the job I suppose. You'd think God would protect you really,' I say, looking around for Julian.

'I expect he has bigger fish to fry.'

I nod thoughtfully.

'Yes, I'm quite sure he has. I can't imagine why he would want to be here today with all these posh pricks. Far more people needing his attention I would think. Although there are a few perverts here I imagine.'

Good heavens, is he blushing? Oh dear, I hope he doesn't think I mean him.

'You know, in the government,' I say attempting to remove the foot from my mouth.

I turn to the man the other side of me and fight back a gasp. God, he's so handsome, perhaps just a little too handsome if there could be such a thing. I need to come to these kinds of weddings more often. His sensuous eyes sparkle and I feel my legs weaken. Shame about his arrogance, which seems to emanate from him even more than his aftershave. His full mouth widens in a smile and he clasps my hand in his. He is immaculately dressed and I know for certain that his clothes aren't off the peg from the local charity shop. I self-consciously pull the strap of my dress back onto my shoulder and check the diamante slide is still in place.

'Hello, I'm Hamilton Lancaster,' he says in a manner that presumes I already knew that. I can't say I do, although the name sounds vaguely familiar even if it does sound like a cigar.

'The Hamilton Lancaster,' Alistair yells, wagging a finger at me.
Who the bonking hell is Hamilton Lancaster when he's at home?

'He's only one of the richest men in England,' Fiona whispers in
my ear.

'An honour to meet you Mr Lancaster, I am pr-pr-pr-pr-pr- ...'
says Alistair.

'A prick,' whispers Fiona.

'Privileged,' gasps Alistair eventually.

I stifle a giggle and Fiona slurps some wine.

'Thank you, but ...'

'I f-f-f-follow all that you do. I'd like to start my own b-b-b- ...'

'Brothel?' mumbles Fiona.

'Business,' he blurts out, grabbing an orange juice.

'Faggot?' says a waiter, leaning over Alistair.

Alistair blanches.

'How d-d-d- ...'

'Divine,' finishes Fiona.

'Dare you,' explodes Alistair.

'Or traditional Haggis sir?'

'He'll have the faggot,' laughs Fiona.

I realise I am still holding on to the Hamilton Lancaster's hand.

'Hi, I'm the Harriet Lawson,' I say.

'That's some grip you have there,' he says, pulling his hand away.

'So, what do you do Harriet?'

Shit. I consider lying but change my mind.

'I work in a laundrette,' I say proudly.

'But she's studying health and social care. She wants to work
with the underprivileged,' slurs Fiona.

'Because it will make her feel more at home,' Alistair smirks.

'A laundrette?' he repeats, making it sound like a strip club.

'That's right,' I reply primly, dropping my serviette into my lap.

He nods thoughtfully.

'How long have you owned a laundrette?'

Alistair scoffs.

'Harriet doesn't own her own b-b-brain, let alone anything else.'

'Oh b-b-b-bugger off,' I snap.

'Do you want a Valium?' Fiona asks.

'No, I don't,' I fume, wiping my mouth with a serviette. 'I don't
own the laundrette. Meet the poorest woman in England. I don't
own anything actually. I wasn't born with a silver spoon in my mouth

like you. I expect you own half the country if you're anything like that Richard Branson bloke. Is Hamilton your real name?'

'I'm afraid it is, and I suppose I am a bit like that Branson bloke but without the balloon.'

'Your ego is inflated enough is it?'

'Christ,' moans Alistair. 'She's a bl-bl-bloody embarrassment.'

'It could always do with a bit more inflating if you're offering,' Hamilton says seductively. 'But you may find me a little out of your league.'

What a rotter, trying to make me feel stupid. I move my chair towards the vicar and turn my head from Hamilton Lancaster. I hate people who think they are better than everyone else. I'll be happier when Julian gets here. I discreetly glance at my phone but there is still nothing from him. To think we've got to put up with this stink for hours. Alistair leans towards Hamilton and a button pops from his waistcoat and lands in Hamilton's champagne glass.

'When I get married I will hire a classy p-p-p- ...'

'Prostitute?' I query. 'Do you think Hamilton may know one?' Alistair glares at me.

'Pub,' he finishes. 'There would be lots of tit-tit-tit- ...'

'Christ,' moans Fiona.

'I'm not even going to try to help him on that one,' I say.

'Tit-titbits. Nothing formal like this w-w-w- ...'

'Wanker,' Fiona mumbles.

I glance at the poker-faced waiter.

'Sorry about this,' I say. 'He can't help it, runs in the family you know.'

'Harry shut up,' hisses Fiona.

'Wedding,' finishes Alistair.

'I'll sue this bloody hire company,' he moans as Hamilton fishes the button from his glass.

'Is there any danger of you being naked by the time we get to dessert?' I ask. 'It's just I would prefer not to be around.'

'Oh dear,' moans Fiona. 'I think I've drunk too much.'

I stand up and edge my way through the tables. I make my way to the foyer to see if there is any sign of Julian. This is ridiculous, is he bleeding walking here? Come to think of it, he most likely is if he was bombing it down the A40 in the Pooch. No way is my little car going to survive that thrashing. I try his phone again but it goes straight to voicemail.

'Sorry,' I say to Fiona, as I reluctantly return to my table. 'I was desperate to phone Julian. I can't think where he can be.'

'Talking of desperation, Alistair tells me that money is a bit tight for you at the moment,' pipes up Hamilton.

'Excuse me?' I say.

What a git. Alistair, that is. I can't turn my back for five minutes. Although this Hamilton is turning out to be a bit of one too isn't he?

'I could maybe help with that. I've got a proposition I'd like to offer that would be beneficial to both of us.'

Well I never. My eyes widen and for a second I am at a loss for words, and let me tell you in the world of Harriet Lawson that rarely happens. I've never been propositioned by a millionaire in my life and I'm not starting now. Honestly these aristocrats, what bloody arrogance they have.

'Thanks very much but I'm sure that whatever you have in your pants pales in comparison to the variety of battery operated boyfriends I have in my drawer at home, but thanks all the same.'

He places his hand on my arm.

'It's not what you think.'

'It never is. Amazing wedding this isn't it? There seems to be a staggeringly high number of wankers present. Anyway, if you'll excuse me I need to get back to my mansion where, amazingly, there will be another wanker awaiting me.'

'I'm off,' I say loudly.

'I w-w-wondered what that smell was,' says Alistair. 'W-w-we all thought it was the bride.'

He laughs at his own joke.

'Why did you tell Hamilton-bloody-Lancaster that I was strapped for cash?' I hiss.

'I thought you c-c-c-could use the money.'

'He just propositioned me,' I say, glaring at Hamilton.

'God Alistair,' Fiona snarls, 'what's wrong with you these days?'

'He needs a w-w-w- ...'

'Yes, well I don't care how much he needs a wank I'm not giving it to him, no matter how much he's offering. I'm leaving,' I say, standing up.

'Just a minute ...' says Hamilton, trying to grab my arm. I push his hand off and begin walking to the foyer.

'Christ,' gasps Fiona, 'we'll drive you home Harriet, won't we Alistair?'

Buggeration. I will murder Julian for not being here. What the hell is he playing at?

Chapter Three

Five Hours Earlier

Julian slams the door of his Mercedes van, juggling a freshly iced birthday cake in one hand and a card in the other. He pauses for a moment to admire his new vehicle. Spotting a tiny mark on the bonnet he rubs it with the sleeve of his jacket and, after satisfying himself that the mark has gone, rushes to the communal door of the flats. God, he's so late. Not even time for a shower. He lets himself in and places the cake onto the kitchen table. That will please her. He will hide it on the top shelf of the cupboard and present it to her on her birthday. He saunters into the bedroom and smiles when he sees the morning suit laid out on the bed for him. He is just about to pop on the bow tie when he hears the front door open. Thinking it is his girlfriend he strolls out of the bedroom beaming.

'I thought we were meeting at the ch ...'

He stops instantly. The smile freezes on his face and his mouth opens and closes several times with nothing emanating from it. Two burly men stand in his living room. The room normally looks small but now it seems miniature. A smartly dressed man walks between the two men and smiles at Julian. Julian's eyes lower to the man's left hand and the missing little finger.

'Ello Julian, 'appy Valentine's Day,' says Jack Diamond. 'I've come to deliver your Valentine's present,' he smiles, revealing a gold tooth.

'Yeah, and it ain't a Valentine's card either,' says one of the younger men.

'Ow rude of me,' continues Jack. 'Where's me manners? I didn't introduce me lads, Babyface Jack and Mad Jack Junior.'

He smiles while slapping his hand on the shoulder of each son in turn.

'But it's not Valentine's Day,' says Julian.

'I like to be early,' smiles Diamond.

'Yeah, I like to be early,' repeats Babyface Jack.

'You needn't have worried,' mutters Julian.

'Cat got your tongue Julian?' asks Jack as he winks at Mad Jack Junior.

'Of course, we could arrange for you to lose your tongue,' says Mad Jack.

Julian struggles to lick his lips, not wanting to expose his tongue for too long so as not to draw attention to it. Oh God, this is a nightmare. His mobile rings and he tries to ignore it but it continues incessantly.

'Someone loves yer,' laughs Jack Diamond.

'Yeah, someone loves yer,' repeats Babyface Jack.

'It's been three months Julian, and you ain't given me nothin'.'

'Yeah, it's been three months,' echoes Babyface Jack, 'and you ain't given me nothin'.'

'You're taking a diabolical liberty you are,' says Diamond.

'Yeah, a diabolical liberty,' repeats Babyface Jack.

'It's just I haven't had it to give to you Jack …' Julian looks from one Jack to the other, unsure of which Jack he should be addressing. Christ, how can they all have the same bloody name?

'The restaurant has only just opened and things have been difficult,' he apologises.

'And yet I still make an effort to come 'ere and give you a present. With Valentine's Day coming up, 'ow could I not? But I thinks you wanna give me your present first don't yer Jules?' says Diamond menacingly with a twitch of his shoulders. Julian cringes.

'I, well … The thing is …' begins Julian, his mouth growing drier.

'That cake looks a bit of awright. Is that for me? I'm touched.'

Julian nods dumbly. Jack sighs.

'Shall I remind yer what your little present should be? And it ain't a frigging iced cake.'

He beckons to Babyface.

'Yeah, shall we remind yer what your little present should be,' says Babyface, giving Jack the note.

'Will you stop frigging repeating everything I say,' growls Diamond.

'I'm not frigging repeating everything you say.'

Jack sighs.

'So Julian, it's been three months now and …'

'I'm only behind with one month,' breaks in Julian.

The three Jacks stare at him menacingly.

'You disagreeing with me mate?'

Julian shakes his head,

'So, you owes me, with interest ...' He glances at the piece of paper and Julian holds his breath as Jack reads from the note.

'Two chicken breasts, a tin of tomatoes and a pint of milk?'

Julian looks up questioningly.

'What the hell is this Babyface?' demands Jack.

'Sorry, that's Mum's shopping list, she said ...'

'I don't give a toss what she said.'

Jack slaps him across the head and the man whimpers. Julian winces and takes another step back. They all wait while Babyface Jack composes himself and produces the right note.

'Kids, you see how I indulge 'em? Now, you owes me twenty grand plus interest, which is?' he looks again at Babyface.

'I dunno but I bet it's a lot,' says Babyface, turning to Julian. 'You scumbag, we should cut off your ear and send it to your mother for not paying us.'

Jack Diamond grunts.

'I'll cut off *your* sodding ear and send it to *your* bleedin' mother if you don't give me those sodding figures,' he snarls at Babyface.

Babyface Jack pulls a mobile from his pocket and punches numbers into a calculator. Jack Diamond fidgets uncomfortably while they wait and Julian wonders if he can make a run for it.

'Well?' asks Jack.

Babyface wrinkles his forehead in concentration.

'The creep owes us, with interest, thirty thousand quid and ten pence.'

'We should smash your skull in you tight-fisted loser,' says Mad Jack, kicking over the coffee table.

Jack Diamond sighs.

'Ave some respect Mad Jack, now pick that up. Sorry about that Jules. I blame their mother. You should see 'er in a temper. It's bleedin' worse than an 'orror film.'

'That can't be right,' says Julian. 'There is no way it's that much even with the interest. You've calculated it wrong.'

There is silence.

'What I mean is, I don't owe the ten pence,' Julian adds quickly.

'You saying you owe us less, you pilchard,' snarls Babyface. 'You saying my phone don't know 'ow to add up?'

'You saying my son's an idiot? No one calls my son an idiot, Julian.'

'You do Dad,' argues Babyface Jack.

'Shut up,' snarls Jack, clipping him round the ear. 'That's different.'

Mad Jack Junior sniggers as Jack Diamond pulls a penknife from his pocket. Julian swallows.

'I'm not calling him an idiot,' Julian adds frantically, 'in fact, I think he is a genius.'

'You do, do yer,' says Babyface, pulling his shoulders back. 'You got a death wish or something?'

Jack pushes Julian back against the wall and holds the knife to his throat.

'No one calls my son a genius, do you understand? Not even me. And Christ knows if he was one I'd know. So, don't insult my intelligence.'

'Bloody hell,' groans Julian quietly. They're fucking lunatics. He begins to move and Diamond grabs him again.

'I'm giving you twenty-four 'ours Julian. But I need a present now.'

'Oh God, not my ear, please don't send my ear to my mother.'

'I was thinking more of that nice shiny motor you've got outside and we'll see what else we can find in this lovely little flat of yours shall we?'

He turns to his sons.

'Trash the joint.'

Mad Jack opens a gym bag and removes a baseball bat.

'Oh Christ,' groans Julian.

He lifts it high into the air and is about to bring it down onto the glass coffee table.

'Aven't you forgotten something?' Jack asks exasperated

'No, I don't think so,' replies Mad Jack.

'We don't wanna upset the neighbours do we?'

'You want me to slit their throats first?' suggests Mad Jack Junior.

'Oh God,' groans Julian.

'No, I want you to put on some music so no one will 'ear you doing the 'ousework.'

Mad Jack nods as Diamond pulls a shaky Julian into the kitchen.

'How about a nice cuppa and a piece of that cake you made me Jules? Did I ever tell yer about the nice tea party I 'ad with Fat Tessie when he owed me money?'
The booming strains of Lady Gaga drown out Jack Diamond's words but Julian hears enough to groan *Oh God* one more time.

Chapter Four

The closer we get to Marlborough Mansions the more my stomach knots. I had tried Julian's mobile almost continuously since we left the reception but all I get is his voicemail. We are just a few minutes from the Mansions now. It sounds posh doesn't it, *Marlborough Mansions*, but I can assure you that the only posh thing about Marlborough Mansions is the name. Our street isn't the roughest in the area but it's in the top five. I cringe as we turn into Marlborough Terrace. Fiona and Alistair have a lovely semi just fifteen minutes away. Fi is always in Ikea or John Lewis, buying lovely shabby chic stuff to hang in the rooms. You know the kind of thing, white painted hearts and photo frames that dangle from silk ribbons, and pretty beaded curtains that separate the rooms and have been known to separate me from my body parts before now. Their house should carry a public health warning. I was practically garrotted on the damn beaded curtains when my necklace got tangled in one once. Luckily, after a frantic search for the scissors, I was saved in the nick of time. I have no idea what I expect when we turn the corner into Marlborough Terrace but I am convinced it will be something horrific and sigh with relief as everything looks perfectly normal. There are the yobs in hoodies snorting cocaine in their usual spot by the garages, Indian rap music blaring from the flats opposite, and the youngsters kicking around a football. Everything seems perfectly normal. No blue flashing lights, or cordoned-off buildings, no ambulance or neighbours standing anxiously outside the Mansions. There is no sign of anything amiss. In fact, there is no sign of my little Pooch, or Alistair's new white van, come to that. He can't possibly be driving both at the same time can he? I look at my nails and the *Scarlet Vamp* chipped nail polish.

'The Pooch has gone,' says Fiona, stating the bloody obvious as only Fiona can. I look at the graffiti-streaked building that is my home and force myself out of the car.

'You don't need us to come in too, do you?' asks Alistair while leaving the engine running.

'For God's sake, what's wrong with you Alistair?' snaps Fiona. 'Anyone would think you were in the East End of London. It's not like the place is full of gangsters.'

He looks disdainfully at the cracked glass in the communal door.

'A football,' I say by way of explanation.

'Of course we're coming in,' says Fiona while glaring at Alistair, 'It's quite safe.'

'Famous last w-w-w-words,' mumbles Alistair.

'Take another Valium,' Fiona snaps.

'I'm not a bloody drug addict.'

I pull a face and drape my shawl around me as one of the hoodies walks towards us.

'Oh great,' mumbles Alistair, 'now we're in *West Side Story*.'

'Ya wanna go out then darlin'? 'ave a good time?' shouts one of the lads with bulging eyes.

'Thank you very much but I'm already going out this evening,' replies Fiona politely.

I roll my eyes.

'Piss off wanker. She's used to real men,' I say dismissively, heading to the entrance.

'I bet she ain't seen one like mine,' laughs the youth, unzipping his fly.

'No, she's seen better,' I say nodding to Alistair's undone flies. 'And far superior underpants.'

'Alistair,' hisses Fiona, 'zip up for God's sake. What's wrong with you? There's a school playground opposite. You'll end up on a list.'

'It's these b-b-b-bloody trousers.'

'No need to show off mate,' laughs the other youth.

'What about you darlin'? Gonna let me treat you to a kebab and a bottle of cider. I could die for you babe,' he says sidling close to me.

'Oh really, can you prove it? I'll lend you a knife.'

'Bitch.'

'How can you live here?' asks Fiona.

'Easily, I can't afford anywhere else.'

I look up at the window of our flat and cock my ear. I'm not sure what I'm expecting to hear but everything sounds fine. I enter the tatty hallway and bypass the out of service lift and climb the stairs with Fiona and Alistair following, stepping around empty sweet wrappers and discarded cigarette butts as we go. Mrs Mollard appears in her doorway, her paisley scarf knotted tightly at her throat.

'You're a wee scunner girlie. I'm going ta skelp yer wee behind I am. I'm not canty. Bucking music.'

Fiona looks at me with a puzzled expression.

'Is she foreign?' she whispers while nodding pleasantly to Mrs Mollard.

'She hasn't got her teeth in and can't say her 'f's, and yes, she's Scottish.'

'For God's sake,' groans Alistair.

I'm starting to think that all Alistair can do is moan and groan, and I'm thinking he does that very well.

'Bucking pervert', says Mrs Mollard with her eyes lowered to Alistair's crotch.

Fiona yanks up his flies and he yelps.

'I'm so sorry Mrs Mollard, what music was that?'

'Bucking racket,' she repeats. 'Yer deaf are yer?'

'Have you seen Julian?' I ask.

''ooligan, what 'ooligan?'

'No, Julian,' I shout. 'Have you seen Julian?'

'He went oot with th' motor.'

'Oh thanks so much Mrs Mollard.'

I bounce up the next flight of stairs hearing Fiona's heels clattering behind me and Alistair's heavy panting, sounding every bit like a *bucking pervert*. When I reach my door I see it is ajar.

'Your door is open,' says Fiona in a breathless raspy voice.

'I know,' I say

'That's not right is it?' she whispers.

'Why do you keep stating the bloody obvious?' I hiss.

'Sorry,' she mumbles.

Okay, I must calm down. There is absolutely no need to panic. Just think of all the obvious sensible things that most people would think when faced with their front door ajar and both their cars gone, not to mention a missing boyfriend. Oh God, I can't think of one sensible thing. Julian said he was coming home early to get changed, that explains why he was home this afternoon and playing music. He probably hurried and rushed out. Yes, that must be it. Good theory, whispers a voice in my head, but how do you explain him driving two cars at the same time? And he must have been in one hell of a rush to not even close the front door, let alone lock it. I sigh, oh well it was a good theory while it lasted. I decide that now is the time to panic.

'I think we've been burgled,' I whisper.

'I bet it was those buggers downstairs,' says Alistair shakily. 'They'd probably slit our throats for our mobile phones.'

'This isn't Africa,' hisses Fiona.

'Feels like it.'

'Don't be racist.'

'How is that racist?'

I take a step towards the door and am about to push it open when Fiona says,

'Nothing makes sense. If you've been burgled then why has Julian gone, and why has he taken your car and why hasn't he phoned you?'

'Maybe he panicked,' I say lamely.

Or maybe he didn't take your car, whispers that inner voice again. Perhaps it wasn't Julian. Perhaps Alistair is right and they have slit his throat for his phone and that's why he hasn't called.

'I think we should call the p-p-police,' whispers Alistair.

'Why?' I say feeling panic turning into hysteria.

'B-b-because I'd feel safer.'

I push the door open and gingerly step inside.

'Julian,' I whisper, peeking around the door with one eye closed and the other squinted. The living room door is also ajar. I fling it open, deciding I may as well get the vision of Julian's mangled body over and done with, as frankly the reality can't be any worse than what I'm imagining.

'Oh my God,' gasps Fiona, putting on her glasses.

'Holy f-f-fuck,' says Alistair.

I stare at my ransacked living room and feel myself wobble. The coffee table has been turned over and the contents of the bedroom drawers have been slung all around the room. I stupidly find myself hoping that Alistair doesn't notice my holey knickers, and worse still, my dual-pleasure vibrator that is lying on the couch along with the *Bound To Tease Suede Flogger*. I can't very well call Alistair a bucking pervert now, not with that lot strewn all over the place can I? Not that Julian and I are into bondage you understand. He bought it as a Christmas present, just for a bit of fun, but I giggled so much every time he produced it that we didn't get round to all that much flogging, although right now I could flog him well and proper. What is the bugger thinking of arsing if off down the A40?

'What's that?' Alistair asks nervously.

'It's for swatting flies,' I lie.

My mobile rings and both Fiona and I scream. I pull the phone from my bag and see it is Julian. Thank God.

'Julian where the hell are you, and what's happened, the flat is is is …'

'The flat's fucked,' finishes Alistair, walking out of the bedroom. 'The whole p-p-place is wrecked.'

'Do you want your Valium?' Fiona asks, pulling the bottle from her handbag with shaky hands.

'Of c-c-course not, I'm not a drug addict.'

'You don't mind if I have another one do you?' she says throwing two into her mouth and shuddering.

'I'm sorry Harry. I would have phoned but I've been terrified to stop. I wanted to get as far away as possible.'

In my Mini I wouldn't think that could be further than Clapham.

'Jesus, they're bloody psychopaths Harry. They were going to cut off my ear and send it to my mother.'

'Shit. I never imagined they could be that aggressive,' I say, picturing the youths downstairs, while remembering what Alistair had said about them slitting out throats.

'I should never have taken out that bloody loan. Oh Christ, I only missed one payment.'

Loan, what is he talking about? The buggers downstairs are more likely to nick money off us than lend it? I can hear the whine from my little Mini and grieve for it. My scrambled brain tries to make some sense of what he is saying. We only have one loan. No, that can't possibly be right.

'Barclays threatened to cut off your ear and send it to your mum? But that's disgraceful,' I say. 'I thought we consolidated our debts with the easy payment terms. That's what the man said. He seemed very nice. Not the kind of person who would make threats like that.'

I can picture the man now. He was terribly sweet and went out of his way to get us the best deal possible. I can't believe that lovely ginger-haired young man would ever cut off anyone's ear. Mind you, my mum always said you couldn't trust a man with ginger hair.

'Start a Twitter campaign, that always works,' says Fi helpfully.

'Or Facebook, name and shame,' adds Alistair. 'After all with their big bonuses it is disgraceful. Thuggish b-b-b-behaviour. I'm glad I'm with Lloyds.'

Fiona shivers.

'God, what will they do to me? My credit card is totally maxed out,' she moans, wringing her hands.

'What the hell has Barclays got to do with anything?' shouts Julian over the whining engine.

'I'm not being difficult Julian, but have you got the Pooch in fourth gear? She never whines like that in fifth.'

'I didn't know there was a fifth on this bloody car.'

Oh no.

'Jesus Julian, It all seems a bit over the top for seven thousand pounds.'

'B-b-bastards', growls Alistair. 'Just look at this place.'

'Harry, don't be so bloody ridiculous. You surely didn't for one minute think we were doing that well did you? The restaurant has been losing money from day one. I've been borrowing money left, right and centre, and now Jack Diamond wants his pound of flesh. He's taken my van. God Harry, I really thought they were going to cut out my tongue.'

'Your tongue? But I thought it was your ear?' I say and find myself thinking how useful it would have been if it had been his kidney. At least we could have sold that. Oh that's terrible, what am I thinking?

'And who the hell is Jack Diamond?' I ask.

He sounds like something out of *The Krays*.

'They were going to do both. Jack Diamond is a nutter. I didn't know he was a bloody East End gangster when I took out the loan. Oh Christ Harry, they want thirty thousand pounds in twenty-four hours.'

I stop breathing. I can barely raise thirty pounds in twenty-four hours, let alone thirty thousand.

'How much? For God's sake Julian, what were you thinking of borrowing money from loan sharks. I don't believe this. What are we going to do?' I say, falling onto the couch and accidentally clicking on the vibrator.

'Shit,' I mumble, fumbling to turn it off with shaky hands. Any other time the bloody thing won't work. Isn't it just Sod's Law?

However, I don't think with Julian's body parts being under extreme threat it is quite the time for an earth-shattering orgasm. I sigh, realising my attempts to switch the damn thing off are only making it vibrate faster.

'I can't come home yet can I? Unless you *want* them to cut off my ear,' he says petulantly. 'And I'm never going to be able to raise that kind of cash in twenty-four hours.'

'Of course I don't want that. I like your ears. What will we do then? What about the restaurant?'

'I need to sort things out. Don't worry. They won't hurt you, some gangster code of honour they told me.'

Oh well, that's comforting. They don't mind smashing up my home and going through my undies drawers or threatening to cut off bits of my boyfriend's body parts but they'll leave me alone. I wince at the sound of gears crunching. What does he mean, don't worry? Is he serious? My flat is totally wrecked. I have men threatening to cut off bits of my boyfriend's body and they're not even offering to pay for them. The Pooch is being throttled to death and my best friend is overdosing on Valium as we speak. I'm totally broke, apart from my tuition savings of course. Oh God, the savings. I drop the mobile with a clatter and dive into the kitchen, stepping over bits of broken crockery. A birthday cake sits on the table, a huge slice out of it and what looks like a shopping list at the side of it. I pull the lid off the biscuit tin and stare into the empty barrel. The bastards have taken my savings and eaten my birthday cake. I snatch up the shopping list and read it.

Two chicken breasts, a tin of tomatoes and a pint of milk.

What the hell? If Julian thinks he can leave a bleeding shopping list before buggering off then he can think again. I turn it over and feel my blood curdle as I read the words in red ink.

'24 hours punk, and I'm not talking the TV series.'

I pick up the mobile miserably but Julian has gone.

'They've eaten my birthday cake,' I say tearfully, 'and they've taken the money for my studies, and they're threatening to cut off his tongue and his ear.'

Fiona gasps.

'Zip your bloody flies up Alistair for Christ's sake, who knows what they'll chop off if they come back.'

I sit holding the buzzing vibrator and wonder what on earth I am going to do. I feel like I'm in *The Valentine's Day Massacre*. I don't think I can ever watch that film again, or *The Krays* come to that. My mobile bleeps. It is a text from Mum. Just when I thought things couldn't get any worse.

'*Darling I'm sending over some thugs for your birthday.*'
I sigh. A few seconds later it rings.

'Did you get my text?' she asks.

'Yes, I did and the thugs have been and gone. Thanks for that.'

'I meant *things* sweetheart. Bleeding predictive thingy. They should arrive tomorrow. What do you mean they've been and gone?'

'A man called Jack Diamond came and smashed up the flat and he is going to cut off Julian's ear because Julian owes him money. Everywhere is a mess and Fiona is here and she's taking Alistair's Valium and we don't know if they'll come back and cut off Alistair's cock. They also took the savings for my studies,' I say in a rush, finally adding, 'and I think I'm in shock.'

'I d-d-don't know why we-we-we're staying,' mutters Alistair.
I wipe my face and try to steady my voice. There is silence for a few seconds.

'What's that buzzing noise?' asks Mum.

'My vibrator,' I say, exhaling heavily.

'Your what?'

'My vibrator,' I repeat, massaging my temples.

'Harriet love,' she says sternly, 'I hardly think this is the time for that. Your dad and I are on our way.'

Chapter Five

Ten Days Earlier

Margarita surveys her family. Couldn't her grandson sit up straight for God's sake? His laziness was becoming legendary and she was tired of it. She blames Sebastian for spoiling his son. Too much money and not enough sense was his problem. Her eyes travel to her son. His bent head reveals a bald patch at the top. She's never noticed that before. He doesn't get that from his father she thinks proudly. He had a full head of hair when he died aged eighty-nine and all of his own teeth. Melanie fidgets with her Stella McCartney handbag, her new diamond ring sparkling brightly. I'm probably keeping her from some society lunch Margarita thinks gleefully. This is the most time my son and daughter-in-law have spent with me in three years. She snorts and everyone looks up expectantly. The buggers thought I was dying. She hides her mirth behind tight lips. They're wondering how much longer they have to sit here before they can make an excuse to leave. She takes a shuddering breath and Sebastian jumps up and leans across the sterile white sheets.

'Mother, do you need something?'

'Sit me up,' she barks.

He gestures to his son and meeting his vacant stare she sighs.

'Help me up you useless lump,' she barks.

He jumps from his chair and fumbles under her armpits. Melanie plumps the pillows in an ungainly fashion.

'You won't chip a nail fluffing pillows you silly woman,' Margarita growls.

The smell of Melanie's Chanel perfume is suffocating. There is silence in the room and all that can be heard is the droning of a lawnmower outside.

'I've got a few things I want to say,' Margarita says evenly.

Oh yes, as soon as they think I'm going to discuss money they're all interested. She snorts with derision and turns her attention to the lawnmower. Her gnarled hands grasp the bed linen and she pulls herself up.

'I've got about six months left … maybe less; the damn doctors won't commit themselves.'

Sebastian jumps from his seat and fiddles with the curtains.

'Don't be silly …'

'Sit down,' she snaps, 'and don't tell your eighty-five-year-old mother not to be silly. You might be Sir Sebastian in everyone else's eyes but you're still my son. If you've been doing your maths, which I'm sure you have, then you'll know what you'll be getting when I'm dead …'

'Mother …'

'Let Grandmother speak.'

Her eyes fall onto her grandson and he fidgets uncomfortably. You've bucked up she thinks. It must be that magic word *money* that did it.

'I'm the majority shareholder in our company and I've had to think long and hard about those shares and what happens to them when I'm dead. Your father worked hard to build up this company and I'm not prepared to let it go to the dogs just because you lot can't get your act together.'

They all hold their breath.

'I've decided not to leave them to you, Sebastian.'

He opens his mouth to protest.

'I'm leaving them to my grandsons.'

Sebastian's shoulders relax slightly and she sees Melanie's hands twitch in her lap.

'On certain conditions,' she adds slowly.

'Conditions?' echoes Sebastian, glancing at his son.

An evil grin crosses her face so quickly that for a moment they all wonder if they actually saw it.

'The company has become a laughing stock, Sebastian. Your father would turn in his grave, if he was in one. Anyway,' she adds wearily, 'no one in this family is responsible enough to take over the family business. Look at you,' she points to her grandson. 'You probably don't even know what the business does. Well, do you …?'

A small fluttering in her chest causes her to lay a hand on her heart and breathe deeply for a few seconds. They all lean over her attentively and she waves a hand.

'I'm not dying yet you will be sorry to hear. But if I am, then it is from inhaling Melanie's atrocious perfume. Well do you?' she asks again of her grandson.

He looks embarrassed.

'Exactly, and as for your cousin, he has a good heart but no interest whatsoever in the business, which is a shame as he has good financial sense. No, I've made up my mind: unless one of you can show me that you have every intention of settling down, carrying on the family name and making the family business respectable once again then I'll have no choice but to sell my shares to Lord Wilmington and accept his takeover bid.'

'But you can't, Pa would never forgive you,' gasps Sebastian.

'You burnt him remember, so I doubt he'll know little about it.'

'He *was* already dead,' snaps Melanie. 'Anyone would think we burnt him at the stake the way you talk.'

'Oh, so his being dead entitled you, did it?' barks Margarita. 'There's a clause in my will so you can't burn me. I'm coming back to haunt you.'

Sebastian sighs. Christ, why does she always make it sound like they had a funeral pyre instead of a cremation?

'It's called cremation Mother.'

'God give me strength,' mumbles Melanie. 'She's out of her mind.'

Her handsome grandson leans towards her.

'But I am thinking of settling down Grandma ...'

She scoffs loudly and gestures agitatedly to a bottle of water by the bed.

'Don't raise my blood pressure boy. If you're talking about Phoebe Montague then you'll be making the biggest mistake of your life. I will never endorse such a marriage.'

'But she ...' begins Melanie.

'Is a gold-digger and so is that father of hers. He has no business sense whatsoever. What man with an ounce of sense bankrupts himself not once, but twice? Of course he wants to see our families connected. You're a fool, just like your father.'

She shakes her head.

'Montague enterprises are doing very well,' says Melanie, sticking up for her son. 'I personally think Phoebe would make a lovely daughter-in-law. Her fashion business is ...'

'Your opinion is of little interest to me Melanie. Now, marry Phoebe if you wish but you'll inherit nothing from me if you do.'

'It's not Phoebe. I've actually met someone. I think you'll like her Grandma. I've known her for a few months now and ...'

'What?' snaps Melanie. 'You never said anything?'

'The boy doesn't have to tell you everything does he?' snaps Margarita. 'Now, I suppose my daughter knows I'm ill. Too busy in Florida no doubt. Does her son know I'm in hospital?'

'Victoria is making every effort to get here,' says Melanie, 'and we've emailed *him* but he is in a remote location, you know how difficult it is ...'

'Yes well, I don't want to hear any more excuses. I'm sure he'll be back once he gets the email. Why he wants to be in the damn jungle I'll never understand. Now, I'll be coming home. Melanie, I want you to get rid of those baroque chairs in the west wing, and those ghastly silk curtains ...'

'But Laurence Llewelyn-Bowen ...'

'I don't care if Lawrence of Arabia hung them. I want them gone. I'm moving back to Hepworth Hall ...'

'But they were a hundred pounds a yard and ...'

'I couldn't give a fig. I don't want some queer's curtains in my wing anyway ...'

'It's not politically correct to use the word queer mater,' says Sebastian, hunching his shoulders. 'One refers to them as gay now.'

'Laurence Llewelyn isn't gay,' says Melanie.

'I know, but ...' says Sebastian with a sigh.

'I don't care if he's miserable; get his curtains out of the west wing and that ridiculous Hungarian painting that hangs in the hallway. I also want my chaise longue from the London apartment. You'll need to organise a room for Lionel too.'

Melanie turns her eyes pleadingly towards Margarita.

'But the east wing is much nicer and more paisley, and that's where you usually stay when you come to the house.'

Margarita glares at her.

'Do I look like I'm a fan of paisley? And besides, this is not a holiday. I'm giving up the London apartment.'

There is a guilty silence.

'I have organised a chairlift to be fitted and Sebastian, you will collect me on Friday. Lionel will organise my things.'

She reclines back onto the pillows.

'Right, that's all settled then. It's time for us all to go to Glenwood. I need some Scottish air, and bring this new girlfriend. I want to meet her. You can all leave me now.'

They look at each other and like obedient children leave the exclusive hospital room.

'My God,' mutters Melanie. 'She's losing her mind. We'll have to move everything around to accommodate her.'

Sebastian looks at his son.

'I don't know what you're playing at but you'd better do something before we go to Glenwood. God help you if you come alone.'

Hamilton Lancaster looks at his new Testoni shoes and wonders where he can find a future wife who will meet his grandmother's standards. Time is not on his side.

Chapter Six

I hold my breath while Fiona tots up the figures. We're sitting in her warm cosy lounge which rather resembles a Laura Ashley showroom. I lean back onto her poppy-red cushions and drop another rum truffle into my mouth. It's all so decadent and lovely that I could easily convince myself that the whole thing with Julian is just a bad dream. It has been five days since the Valentine's Day catastrophe. My birthday has been and gone and there has not been a single word from Julian. I've been overwhelmed with demands for money from people I didn't even know existed. The staff at the restaurant hadn't been paid, and I'd found a carrier bag under the bed full of bills. Each day had just got worse. I'm now on first name terms with the bank manager and by that I don't mean we're dating. Apparently, the rent hasn't been paid for two months. Yesterday a man came to cut off the gas and it is only a matter of time before the phone is disconnected too. If the weather doesn't start to warm up I may well have to stay at my mums, or work twenty-four seven at the laundrette. At least it is warm there. To add insult to injury it now transpires that Julian took the loan out for the new van in my name. I can't even give the van back as Jack Diamond has it. I'm so cross with Julian for dumping all this on me. I gave up a perfectly good nursing career for him when we started living together all because he didn't like me working nights. It's all so unfair and one sided. My dream is to help those less privileged than myself and I am halfway through an Open University degree for that, but with all my savings gone I'm going to have to chuck that in too.

'You just wait until the restaurant is flourishing. We'll be able to go wherever we want and whenever we want and you can do as much charity work as you like then. We just need to build up the business,' he had assured me. Or should I say lied to me.

'Well?' I say impatiently.

She chews her lip.

'Do you want another truffle?' she asks.

'I've already eaten six.'

'It may comfort you,' she says with a small tremor in her voice.

Oh shit, I don't think a rum truffle is going to soften the blow. A bottle of rum maybe, but a rum truffle, I think not.

'Okay, you've got to tell me sometime,' I say, stuffing another truffle into my mouth. Well it's worth a try and I need some fortifying.

'Okay, ready ...'

I nod. She pops a truffle into her own mouth and I wonder if I should nip out and buy some more, but before I can suggest it she drops her bombshell.

'Fifty-three thousand pounds, and that's just what we know about.'

I grab the arm of the couch for support and reel. If someone had dropped a nuclear bomb on me I couldn't have been more shell-shocked. She can't be serious. She must have tapped an extra nought in somewhere. I mean, it's easily done isn't it?

'That ...' I begin hoarsely. God, I'm in a state of shock. I can't speak. 'Can't possibly be right,' I say finally, in a high-pitched voice.

'Do you need a Valium?' she offers.

I put my head in my hands.

'A razor blade would be better.'

'Alistair uses an electric razor.'

Right Fiona, as if I was serious. This is a disaster. I mean a *real* disaster. On the disaster scale of one to ten it must rate eleven.

'Honestly, I gave up a promising nursing career for him so we could spend more time together and he does this to me.'

She purses her lips.

'I did tell you not to.'

'Well, he said once the restaurant was booming I could go back.'

Mind you, he said a lot of things.

'Yes, well booming is the right word. It is likely to go boom if Jack whats-is-face doesn't get his money.'

'Are you sure it's that much? How can it be? How can anyone spend that much money?'

She shuffles the bills around on the coffee table.

'Well, there is the rent for a start. He hasn't paid it for two months so that's nearly two thousand. He has a Barclaycard bill of eight thousand. Then there is the loan of twenty he took out at the bank ...'

'Twenty!' I shriek. 'But I thought it was seven.'

'You must have signed the papers,' she says gently.

Christ, how could I have been such a fool? I just signed where Julian told me. I believed him when he said it was for seven thousand. She pulls a face.

'But obviously the loan agreement you signed was not the loan he told you about.'

The little bastard, wait till I get my hands on him.

'Not to mention the staff at the restaurant who weren't paid last month, and then there is the finance on the van and I'm only counting the monthly payment, and that is definitely in your name. Something else you signed without realising it.'

'God Fiona, how could I have been so stupid?' I say, pushing two more rum truffles into my mouth.

'Plus there are the overdue electricity bill and gas bill plus the phone bill of course. There's another credit card too. Looks like he was entertaining like bloody Elton John ...'

'Well he wasn't buying me flowers like Elton bleeding John,' I snap.

'Okay, don't take it out on me.'

I sigh.

'Sorry.'

'And there's the rent on the restaurant premises from last month, and a John Lewis store card which is sky high and ...'

'Okay okay, enough torture. There aren't enough rum truffles for me to hear any more.'

How am I ever going to be able to pay back fifty thousand pounds? I'd need a dozen kidneys to sort this lot out.

'Of course that's not taking into account whatever he owed the loan sharks,' Fiona adds quickly. 'Sorry, just thought I should mention that.'

Holy shit.

'But, you are only liable for the bills that are in your name and of course the rent if you want to stay there and the phone bills and ...'

'Which is?' I say, holding my breath.

'About thirty-eight thousand, that's if you pay the staff and the rent on the restaurant and the full finance on the van.'

I groan.

'Are you sure you don't have any razor blades? What the hell am I going to do? I've got my studies to pay for too.'

'Tea,' says Fiona jumping up, scattering the bills. 'Tea is liquid wisdom.'

'Oh really, can I have a pint then, with a chaser of three truffles.'

I'll bloody kill Julian if Jack Diamond doesn't get to him before I do.

Chapter Seven

'Harriet Dolly, you'd know I'd help you out if I could but I've got a wife and kids. If I let everyone stay here rent free, I'd be out on the streets myself.'

'I could move into your house then,' I joke, handing him his laundry.

'Very funny Harriet. What do we owe you, and don't say the usual.'

'Oh nothing Sid, honestly, it's just a bit of washing powder. The machines are on the go all day anyway.'
He shakes his head.

'Just give me another week, Sid. I'm going to try and get a refund on my studies ...'
He raises his hand.

'No, now don't you stop your studies. You've got a future there. Move in with your parents for a time. You might feel safer as well.'

'They've only just thrown out my grandmother and forced her kicking and screaming into a nursing home, so I don't think they would relish having me there. In fact, I would not feel in the least bit safe. If I move in with my mum I'll be cutting my own ear off before I know where I am.'

'Well, there's no rush darling. Let's talk about it again in a week, okay?'

'Ta anyway Sid,' I say gratefully, hitting the lift button. 'I'll sell my ovaries. I never did want kids, not really.'

'Don't you make me feel guilty now, and that thing is still buggered,' he nods at the lift.

'Right,' I sigh, heading for the stairs. Maybe I'll have a heart attack halfway. That will solve everything.

'Oh yeah, I nearly forgot. You had a visitor.'
My heart seems to stop there and then. It looks like I may well have a heart attack before I even reach the first stair. Oh Christ, now what? Not Jack Diamond coming to collect more ears I hope.

'He didn't mention body parts by any chance did he?' I say shuddering.

'Not that I recall. He said something about making you an offer you can't refuse and he'll pop back later.'

Oh my God. I don't want an offer I can't refuse, not unless it is to clear my debts, but I don't think that is the offer Jack Diamond has in mind. It is more likely to involve someone's ear or tongue, or God forbid, some other appendage. Oh dear, awful visions of rushing into A and E carrying an appendage of Julian's and pleading with them to sew it back on are too gruesome to bear. Unless of course it is one we can sell, that's something different altogether.

'Nice chap,' Sid said. 'Smartly dressed and nicely spoken, your bank manager no doubt.'

That doesn't bode well, does it? Not when the bank manager makes house calls with offers you can't refuse. I sprint up the stairs faster than I have ever done in my life. I look wildly around the flat. The half-eaten birthday cake sits on the counter. I suppose they'll want to finish that, the bastards. I dash into the bedroom and fumble amongst my shoes and grasp my trainers. My mobile trills and I stick it under my chin as I tie the laces.

'I have good news,' cries Mum.

I wish I did.

'I can't talk Mum, I ...'

'Caron and Gary's offer on that lovely semi was accepted. We're going to Ikea tomorrow to look at furniture. *Ikea!* You can't get better than that. And Gary said she can use his Barclaycard Platinum. He's very generous isn't he love? Now, that's the type of man you want,' she affirms.

Blimey, is this shaved head, tattooed Gary, we're talking about? It's a far cry from when Gary was nothing less than a blood-sucking psychopathic vampire, resembling a character out of *True Blood*, who was obviously leading Caron into deviant sexual acts. Come to think of it maybe I do need a man like Gary.

'A man with a Barclaycard Platinum, right got it. I'll advertise for one tomorrow. Now, I have to dash ...'

'You are eating aren't you?'

'Yes, I'm just off to raid the dustbins as we speak. Can I ring you back?'

'Oh dear, now I'm worried,' she says in a whiney voice. 'I'll have to take my blood pressure. The doctor said all this anxiety over you is sending me into a depression.'

I know the feeling.

'It was 140 over 80 earlier,' she says anxiously.

'That's good then isn't it?'

'Of course not,' she snaps.

'Right,' I say, checking the time. I've been here ten minutes and my blood pressure is probably off the scale.

'If only you were like your sister Caron and had a nice boyfriend like Gary ... Anyway your dad and I have been talking and we have enough savings. After all we don't really need a holiday this year. Your dad said there is so much to do in the garden anyway and ...'

Oh no.

'Mum, I can't take your savings, and besides it would never be enough ...'

'But it would help sweetheart wouldn't it? Oh dear, I do worry what will happen to you. I don't want you on the streets.'

'Mum, I assure you prostitution would be my last resort.'

She gasps.

'My giddy aunt, I meant living on them, not walking them. Besides, you could never do that. A woman needs to be glamorous to do that kind of thing.'

Wonderful. Why is it whenever my mum and I have a nice conversation she always manages to end it by insulting me?

'Well, ta very much for that vote of confidence.'

'Of course, you could come and live with us for a time,' she says reluctantly.

There is a rapping at the door and fear clutches my stomach.

'I'll call you later,' I whisper.

My heart is thumping so fast I feel sure it will burst. Next time Mum asks me for birthday ideas I'll ask for a panic room. There is another thump and I bite my lip.

'Hello Harriet, it's Hamilton Lancaster.'

Hamilton Lancaster? *The* Hamilton Lancaster? What on earth is he doing here? I push my eye against the peep hole and see that it most certainly is Hamilton Lancaster, and he looks none too comfortable either. This is a bit fishy if you ask me. I've only met the guy once and he mistook me for a prostitute. A quick glance in the mirror reveals flushed cheeks and wide eyes. My hair is a bit wild. Mind you, I'm looking a bit wild in general these days.

'Did you come earlier?' I shout through the door.

'I beg your pardon?'

I suppose on reflection that didn't sound too good did it?

'Did you visit earlier?'

'Yes I did.'

What on earth for?

'What do you want?'

'To come in would be nice. I've driven around three times and almost got arrested for kerb crawling.'

Ah, knowing him he probably was. I open the door to see him looking red faced and uncomfortable. He's wearing a black overcoat and an expensive silk scarf. He gives a weak smile. Once inside he looks around warily, fidgeting with his scarf. He thrusts a bunch of tulips at me.

'I understand it was your birthday a few days ago.'

I take the tulips. Blimey, Julian never buys me flowers.

'Do you want me to take your clothes?' I say and blush. That came out all wrong. I sound like I'm anyone's for a bunch of tulips.

'What?' he asks, stepping back.

'I meant your coat and scarf,' I say quickly.

'Oh right, yes of course. I'll keep it on if that's all right. It's a bit chilly in here.'

I nod.

'They cut off the gas. I use a snuggie and hot water bottle now.'

I begin pricking the tulips with a pin. He looks at me curiously.

'It stops them drooping if you give them a prick.'

Christ, why is everything coming out wrong.

'Oh,' he says, 'I never knew that.'

'It only works on tulips, not everything that droops.'

I think it would be better if I just shut up. His eyes fall on the birthday cake.

'Oh, would you like some? I've not actually had any myself so I can't tell you what it's like.'

'They really did trash your place didn't they?' he says looking around.

'I've actually cleaned up,' I say bristling.

What a cheek, and how the hell did he know about that anyway?

'Oh,' he says, raising his eyebrows, 'I thought ...'

'Why are you here?' I say, 'And how did you know where I lived?'
He fidgets and I feel my face turning red. I fill the kettle. Maybe if I
do something normal we will both stop thinking about the offer he's
going to make. I hope it's not sex related. What if he is one of those
rich toffs who likes to do weird kinky stuff, you know the kind of
thing. Then again maybe you don't and I'm not even sure I do.
Anyway, whatever it is it must be so kinky if he can't get anyone else
to do it. Maybe he wants me to tie him up and whip him. Pity Julian
isn't making me this offer. I'd happily tie Julian up and whip him. Not
that I know much about kinky sex of course. Only what I read once
about an MP with a paper bag and a segment of orange. If Hamilton
mentions either of these I'll know to panic. I pull two mugs from the
cupboard and fiddle with the boxes of tea.

'We have Mint tea, Orange and Ginseng or ...'
Christ, it would be *Orange* and Ginseng wouldn't it? I blush and push
the box to the back of the cupboard.

'Tesco Value and oh, some Earl Grey, but it's been here yonks so I
can't vouch for it,' I say cheerfully producing a tatty box of Twinings
own.
He sighs.

'You don't have any whisky do you?'
I shake my head.

'We're all out of single malt I'm afraid, but it's on my Tesco
shopping list, along with the champagne and caviar,' I say tetchily,
shoving the boxes back into the cupboard.

'I wasn't mocking, I just feel like I need something stronger than
tea.'

'Look, I'm not into kinky sex okay. I don't take money to piss on
people or whatever it is you're going to suggest. I don't take money
for sex, period. In fact, I barely have sex these days. This whole
business is playing havoc with my libido. So I'm really not your girl.'
He backs away in horror.

'Christ,' he groans. I bite my lip.

'I don't want to have sex with you,' he says.
Thanks very much, I'm sure.

'Well that's a relief,' I say. 'I wasn't exactly overwhelmed at the
thought of having sex with you either.'
That was embarrassing. I comfort myself with the fact that I
probably could still sell my body. After all, the people I will be
catering for won't be Hamilton Lancaster types will they? Someone

is bound to find me reasonably appealing aren't they? I could always just hire myself out to the blind and stupid.

He coughs.

'Alistair said you were in a bit of trouble ...'

A bit of trouble, is that what he calls it? If only it was a bit.

'Alistair?' I say spinning round. 'St-st-st-stammering Alistair? Did he tell you my flat had been trashed, and did he tell you where I lived?'

He nods.

'I contacted him. I need, I need ...'

'Yes, well I'm not giving it to you,' I snap.

'I need a future wife,' he finally spits out.

I stare at him.

'Sorry, do you mean you need a future wife, or a wife from the future? I'm confused.'

He flops onto the couch.

'My grandmother has six months to live.'

He seems to ponder this for a second.

'I suppose less now. Anyway, she's threatening to cut us all off. She will sell all her shares to some money-grabbing bastard if one of her grandsons doesn't prove to her that they can be responsible and reliable and will carry on the family name.'

'Oh God, compared to what I'm going through that sounds horrific. I can't imagine anything worse for you,' I say sarcastically.

He runs his hand through his thick dark hair and looks at me pleadingly. I feel a tiny throbbing around my navel area. It's nothing sexual you understand. My new piercing has been itching for days. I think it's the stress. What I need is an evening with a Jo Malone candle, a bottle of Moet and some Michael Buble. Maybe I can borrow Gary's Barclaycard and give myself a little treat. In fact, maybe I can simply borrow Gary's Barclaycard and bugger off.

'Look, I'm really sorry about your grandmother,' I say sincerely, 'but surely someone like you has a girlfriend. It can't be that difficult surely? You said *grandsons*, what about the other one, hasn't he got a girlfriend?'

He lowers his eyes.

'I broke up with my girlfriend. Grandmother hated her. As for my cousin, he couldn't care less about the family business. Look, I just need you to pretend to be my fiancée for a few weekends. She's expecting to see my new girlfriend at our spring break in Scotland. I can't go there without one. I'll make it worth your while. All you have to do is come away for a weekend in Scotland and make the odd visit to the house in Hampstead Heath. Once she thinks I'm engaged she'll change the will and that's it.'

I gape at him.

'That's all is it?'

He nods.

'Oh well, I'm sure I can spare a few weekends and popping up to Scotland shouldn't take long. I mean, honestly what do you take me for? I can't lie to your grandmother, especially if she's dying, that's immoral. And besides I have a boyfriend.'

'Think how happy you'll make her.'

'Think how unhappy I'll make him. And it's still deceiving your grandmother,' I insist. 'And anyway, there is no guarantee I will make your grandmother happy. If how happy I make my mother is anything to go by then it's unlikely. I'm bleeding awful at family stuff, always have been.'

'For pity's sake,' he cries. He tries to get up from the couch, but the springs are so knackered since Diamond's little visit that he falls back down again.

'I could lose everything. Do you have any idea what that will feel like?'

'I've got a vague idea.'

'I'm offering you twenty thousand. My family's future hangs on this.'

Jesus, that's a bit of a responsibility. I stop with my hand on the door handle. Twenty thousand, twenty thousand pounds? That would pay the finance on the van and clear a good part of the bank loan.

'I just have to pretend to be your future wife, that's it?'

He nods eagerly, pushing himself out of the couch.

'I don't have to actually marry you or anything?'

He shakes his head, looking at me expectantly.

'No, by the time she meets you she'll only have four months and she won't be expecting us to get married that quickly. In fact, you don't have to see me ever again.'

This is ridiculous, I can't do that. It would be a complete disaster. I'm all wrong for a start, I wouldn't have a clue how to dress and they would realise right away it was a scam. I don't talk like he does. But if I don't agree to do it what the hell *will* I do. I'm completely exhausted, not to mention freezing. If I stay in this flat I'll die from hypothermia. I look to my goldfish for inspiration. Julian won him at a fair last year. I'm not sure how much longer he will last either. I will probably be driven by starvation to eat the little bugger with some oven chips if I don't sort out my finances soon.

'Okay, I'll make it twenty-five thousand. I can't say fairer than that can I? Half now and the rest when the job is done.'

Does he have to make it sound like we're going to kill his grandmother? I hesitate.

'Okay, thirty thousand, but I can't go any higher than that,' he says urgently. 'You can't tell anyone about this. Everyone has to believe we're engaged and are getting married before the end of the year.'

Holy shit. I wonder if I stay silent long enough he'll offer me fifty thousand. I could pay all the debts and take a holiday.

'But …'

'The spring break is in ten days. I've set up all the people to prime you …'

He is becoming animated and his eyes have lit up.

'Prime me?'

'You'll need to speak better, and dress …'

I raise my eyebrows.

'Differently,' he says quickly.

'I don't know,' I say hesitantly. 'I really can't see something like this working.'

'I assure you it will. Everyone will have to believe it though, and that includes your friends and family, and most importantly my grandmother. She has to love you.'

Bloody hell, even my own grandmother doesn't love me. He's expecting a lot. Mind you, Mum *will* be proud, and it will be one over on Caron's Gary.

'Alistair will know, and Fiona,' I remind him, 'and my mum will think it rather odd that I got over Julian so fast. I may have to tell her.'

He nods thoughtfully.

'Yes, but no one else must know.'

He looks into my eyes.

'Well, what do you think?'

I think it's the maddest idea I have ever heard. Thirty thousand pounds, I bet even Gary couldn't compete with that, I think with a little smile, but what would Julian think about it, me pretending to be engaged to some rich toff? What's wrong with me, why am I giving a toss about Julian? He has left me in a right mess and not even bothered to phone. I could forgive him if they have actually cut out his tongue and he couldn't actually talk. But he still has his tongue and both ears, not to mention my Mini. At that moment there is a knock on the door and before I can stop him Hamilton Lancaster has opened it.

'Bailiffs lady, we've been instructed to take your hi-fi unit and laptops, and any furniture not pertaining to your landlord,' says a ginger-haired man pushing past Hamilton and barging into my lounge.

What is it with these men with ginger hair?

'I've got a gold filling,' I say sarcastically. 'Do you want that too? I can lend you some pliers.'

Hamilton looks horrified while the bailiff considers it.

'Make it thirty-five thousand and it's a deal,' I say.

The bailiff sways.

'You wanna give us thirty-five thousand quid to take out your filling?' he says startled.

'Deal,' Hamilton says holding out a hand. 'Shake on it.'

I clasp his hand. Thirty-five thousand pounds and all I have to do is pretend to be someone else for a weekend. How hard can that be?

* * *

'Are you serious, but this is brilliant news.'

After a week of silence Julian finally phones and I nervously tell him of Hamilton's offer, fully expecting him to go crazy. Instead he is enthusing so much about the plan that I feel depressed. I look around at our dreary kitchen and listen to the dripping tap and feel like screaming. Out of the window I see the yobs teasing my elderly neighbour. I open the window noisily.

'Hey, you little gits leave him alone or I'm calling the police.'

They give me the finger and run off. My neighbour smiles at me and I feel some tension leave my body.

'Thanks sweetheart but I have this nice little spray now which blinds the buggers for a few hours,' he laughs.

'Harry, are you listening to me?' demands Julian.

'When are you coming back?' I ask crossly. 'And why haven't you phoned? I was beginning to think Jack Diamond had cut out your tongue.'

His voice softens.

'I'm sorry babe, you must think me mercenary ...'

'Well ...' I begin.

'The thing is, I have found someone who will invest in the restaurant ...'

This bloody restaurant is driving me to distraction.

'I just need a bit more time and we can get the money together, meanwhile you can pay Diamond with the first half and ...'

Has he gone out of his mind?

'For God's sake Julian, the first half is to pay the back rent, or I'll have nowhere to live, and the loan repayments at the bank. Plus there are all the household bills you didn't pay, or did you forget about those? Then there are the staff at the restaurant, it's not fair not to pay them, it's not their fault, and of course there are the repayments on that bloody van of yours, and there are also my studies. I've never had a bad credit rating in my life and I'm not getting one now.'

'For God's sake Harry, can't you forget the bloody studies? You know you'll never finish it, and you certainly won't be going out to Angola or wherever it is you want to go. You're not Angelina Jolie you know.'

Bloody cheek, is everyone trying to tell me I am plain stupid and ugly.

'Don't I know it? I bet Brad Pitt would be more supportive.'

'I bet Brad Pitt has more sodding money.'

'I bet Brad Pitt doesn't owe money,' I snap back. 'He's certainly more appealing,' I add spitefully, 'and it's South East Asia actually, not Angola.'

'Same thing. Come on Harry, I can't come back yet, you know that. I need to get the money for Diamond or God knows what Babyface Jack and Mad Jack Junior will do.'

'Who are Babyface Jack and Mad Jack Junior? I thought it was Jack Diamond you owed money to?'

Christ, no wonder I could never follow *The Godfather*.

'They're his sons.'

'How can they all be called Jack?'

Julian sighs.

'I don't know. They're bloody insane though. Mad Jack Junior is a total nutcase. He'll kneecap anything that moves. I daren't set foot in Battersea until I have their money.'

'I don't think you dare set foot in Battersea, period. Everyone you owe money to is after you. I would think Jack Diamond, Baby Diamond and Mad Diamond are the least of your worries. I could happily kneecap you myself.'

The dripping tap drums incessantly into a dirty saucepan in the sink.

'For God's sake Harry, you're supposed to be supporting me.'

'Julian, you deceived me. I don't see why I should help you pay back all your debts. They're your problem ...'

'But Harry, they may kill me. I promise to stay in touch and I love you Harry. I appreciate what you're doing for me. I really do. I'm really sorry for what I did. I only did it for us. My only crime was loving you,' he says with a small sob which I'm not sure is real.

'You still love me don't you?' he asks in a self-pitying voice.

I mumble something incoherent which he seems to ignore.

'Well at least the restaurant is still up and running. How many more months can you pay the staff?'

'I'm not sure.'

'If I can get this guy to invest then we can give Diamond his money and get him off our backs for good. I'll have to get rid of this phone, I don't trust them. They may be able to trace me if I keep using it.'

'They're East End gangsters Julian, not the sodding FBI,' I say irritably.

'Still, best to be safe. I'll contact you when I have a new number. I love you Harry, I really am grateful for what you are doing.'

I click off the phone. Angola, when did I ever say I wanted to go to Angola? They have bloody landmines there for Christ's sake. I'm charitable, but not that bloody charitable. Has he ever listened to me? More to the point, has he ever really loved me? What a predicament. I can't very well tell Hamilton that I've now changed my mind can I? I certainly can't wait for Julian either. Bloody men.

Chapter Eight

'This one really becomes you. This is the crème de la crème,' gushes Marcus.

So far I've looked like a prize prat in all of them if you ask me, but who am I to argue with the man who has supposedly dressed Victoria Beckham and the Duchess of York? Mind you, that's not much of a recommendation is it? I mean, have you seen the Duchess of York lately? I go to nervously bite my nails and remember they're not my own any more. I don't mean I've stolen someone else's, just in case you thought I was wearing the Duchess of York's nails. My own bitten nails have been magically replaced by beautiful false ones, which have rendered me totally helpless. I can't hold a knife and fork anymore without looking like someone who's had a stroke. I just about manage to get the fork to my mouth before I lose my grip and drop food down my new designer clothes. I'll be ripping these nails off just so I can eat something. I could be the inventor of the *False Nail Diet*, and will make a fortune writing *The Amazing False Nail Diet Book*. Seriously though, how do women wear these things? If I have an itch I almost scar myself by scratching. As it is I've got injuries on my thighs from pulling up my knickers. I must be the most glamorous laundrette manager ever. Celia Blakely nearly had a fit when she saw me. I told her it was a birthday present from Julian.

'Oh, a makeover,' she had said, 'it must have cost him a fortune.'

He owes a fortune more like. I've had hair waxed from places I didn't know I had hair. My lovely shaggy blonde look is now a neat shoulder length bob, and is so silky that I slip and slide on the pillowcase. I feel like a Barbie doll, and Fiona doesn't help by telling me I look like one. I'm wearing shoes that I've only ever seen transvestites wear and I'm wobbling all over the place in them. I swear roller blades would be easier. I take a peek at myself in the mirror. I look like an oversized ballerina in a tutu. I could seriously be auditioning for a comedy *Strictly Come Dancing* contest. This is a complete disaster. Every dress I try on looks ghastly. Oh, that's a new word I've learnt. Every time I feel myself about to say this is *crap*, I replace it with *ghastly*. It's working so far. I just have to remember not to say *I'm taking a ghastly*. I honestly must have been mad to have agreed to this. I'm having elocution lessons and am constantly chatting away to myself on the bus. I am surprised no one has had me sectioned. Mum barely recognised me when I popped round for tea. Now she is like the cat that got the cream, and double cream at that. Caron's semi has dropped considerably in her estimations, and as for the Platinum card, as soon as I flashed Hamilton's American Express Centurion, Gary was old news. I wasn't strictly honest with Mum, I just said I had met this really nice man who had a bob or two, but he was just a friend. Let's face it she's the one person who will open her mouth and put her foot straight in it.

'Have you gone totally insane? There is no way you can pull this off,' Fiona had said, and I'm starting to think she might just be right. I am going up to Scotland this weekend to meet the family and I am now the proud owner of my own tennis racket, but unfortunately, unless Hamilton can arrange a few private lessons with Steffi Graff, there isn't very much I can do with the damn thing. I look great in my perfect little tennis outfit, although a lot of good that will do me. I've never hit anything with a bat in my life. I'm shit-scared of meeting the grandmother. No, must not say *shit*. Apparently Hamilton's parents abhor swearing, so that's half my vocabulary gone. I'm never going to pull this off. I'm bound to miss my mouth when eating an hors d'oeuvre and send it down my posh frock. I'll just have to starve that's all. I really am digging a grave for myself. If only Julian would call me again. I'm seriously beginning to think that maybe Jack Diamond has had him topped. Oh God, I can't think about it. When I do, I have visions of him at the bottom of the Thames wearing concrete boots. How did we ever get to this? It was only a little French restaurant for Christ's sake. It's no good. I have to stop thinking like this. I have to get through this weekend, whether I want to or not. I've taken half the money now and paid off a lot of the debts. There's a few left but with the other half I'll be able to clear those and have enough for my studies. I look at my reflection in the mirror. I'm totally exhausted. I have been trying on outfit after outfit all morning. I now own inexpensive designer-free corduroys and three very dull-looking sweaters. Not to mention a very smart pair of gumboots.

'One must look as though one spends a great deal of time in the country madam. Clothes need to look used.'

'My own clothes are most certainly used Marcus, so why can't I wear those?'

'Because madam, ladies do not wear Boho ponchos to walk the dogs.'

I've no intention of walking any bleeding dogs, and I've never been called *a lady* in my life. I turn from the mirror and smile wearily at Marcus.

'You don't think I look a little too sparkly in this one? Or a bit too puffy or even a bit ...'

Marcus holds his hands up in horror.

'Puffy? You? My darling, my sweetie, that is not even possible. You always sparkle no matter what you try on but this one my darling, you look fabulous. It is perfect for your first dinner.'

I glance at the price tag and grab a satin-draped chair for support. My God, who pays two thousand pounds for a dress? That would pay the rent and bills for two months. I wish Fiona were here, I so need a second opinion. She promised to be here for this all important fitting. Honestly, I can't rely on anyone. I glance at myself in the mirror and twirl to see the back of the dress. I suppose Marcus knows better than me. He drapes a silk scarf around my neck and sighs.

'You look beautiful madam. Simply stunning.'

There's a snigger from behind

'If you don't mind me saying, you look like an oversized fairy. It might look good on Julian Clary. All you need is a wand and you're sorted,' says a familiar soft voice.

Marcus looks like he may faint on the spot.

'Well really ...' he gasps.

I turn to see Brice Edmunds handing over a silk tie to the assistant. He's wearing khaki trousers and an open necked shirt, and I can see his deep tan. His smile is stunning and he has the loveliest eyes. What a shame I'm a soon-to-be engaged woman. Mind you, he probably isn't good enough for me, with my aristocratic standing and all. Well, I have to keep up the show don't I? Of course, the reality is that he is far too good for me if he buys his ties here. I am surprised he even noticed me. Not many people notice me when I'm trying on clothes in Oxfam, unless you count the old dears who are serving, and they always say everything looks terrific.

'Hello,' I say, blushing in front of him and looking like a huge marshmallow, 'fancy seeing you here.'

I lick my lips and take a deep breath to stop my heart from beating too fast. This is ridiculous. How dare he have such an effect on me? In my whole life I've never turned to jelly when a man looked at me.

'Preparing for another wedding are you? I don't think you'll find anything for a fiver in here,' he smiles.

I shrug.

'I thought I'd give Oxfam a miss this time.'

I look down at the dress and feel myself blush.

'You really think I look like a Christmas decoration?'

He nods solemnly.

'Oh sod it,' I mumble and bite my lip.

He smiles and takes the tie from the assistant.

'Excuse me sir, but this dress is a unique one-off handmade design,' states Marcus, so offended that you'd think he'd designed the awful thing himself.

'Well thank God for that, I'd hate to think there was more than one.'

I try to hide my smile.

'Sir, I can assure you I have undressed and dressed many women in my time. Many titled women in fact. I think I can categorically state that I know what I am talking about,' says Marcus, looking extremely hurt.

'I'm having a hell of time finding a decent dress,' I butt in. 'It's a total nightmare. I've got this fancy dinner you see, do you really think I look like a fairy?'

'It's just my opinion of course, but unless you're planning to sit on top of a Christmas tree I would say this is a reject, but then again I haven't dressed or undressed a titled woman,' he says, raising his eyebrows in an exaggerated manner.

I feel a tingling where I really shouldn't.

'May I point out sir ...' begins Marcus.

'However, I rather think that white one over there might look good on you,' he continues, pointing to a dress.

Marcus gasps.

'That's a Giovanni, not in the least suitable for the occasion. It's far too, too ...'

'Cheap?' says Brice with one of his heart-stopping grins.

'Well really ...' Marcus flicks his hair back in an agitated manner.

'I'll try it on,' I say.

'But I was specifically told ...'

'It's all right Marcus. I'll take full responsibility.'

I spin round to face Brice, whipping him with my tutu as I do so.

'That dress is one dangerous weapon,' he laughs.

'If you think this is dangerous sir, just thank your lucky stars you were not here when we tried on the riding outfit. I thought madam was going to whip us all into shape with her riding crop,' says Marcus dryly.

Brice laughs, his eyes twinkling.

'Looks like I arrived too late,' he says grinning.

I blush.

'It wasn't that bad,' I say.

'Yes, well it's a matter of opinion madam. You were holding the whip while we were at the other end of it. I was only grateful madam didn't have to hold a shotgun while trying on her shooting outfit. I fear there would have been a massacre.'

I sigh and look at Brice.

'He has a tendency to over dramatise,' I say, shrugging. 'Have you got a minute, just to give an opinion? I'm getting a bit desperate.'

Marcus sighs.

'I think *desperate* is a slight exaggeration madam.'

'Sure, it sounds like fun,' Brice says, pulling out a satin-draped chair and reclining back.

I grab the white dress and dive into the cubicle, pulling Marcus in with me as I do so. Two minutes later I reappear with a groaning Marcus trailing behind. Brice raises his eyebrows.

'Better, but still not quite right. How about that purple thing over there?' He points to a rail and Marcus convulses so much that I think he is having an epileptic fit.

'That, that is, well *that is* not the dress of a lady. I really must protest. I cannot possibly allow you to even try that on ...'

Brice removes the floor length strapless dress from the rail and holds it against me. The chiffon feels cool against my skin and the bright colours feel so me.

'It's perfect,' I smile.

Brice takes a shawl from a stand and slides it around my neck and I feel myself shiver. Oh, this is not what I need, not right now. Not with Julian at the bottom of the Thames wearing concrete boots and a soon-to-be pretend fiancé. My life is way too complicated right now, and this is not the time to fancy gorgeous men in an expensive dress shop. Anyway, he is way out of my league.

'This would enhance the dress,' he says, meeting my eyes.

'Really sir, I have to disagree ...'

'Let me just try it Marcus,' I plead, finding myself unable to drag my eyes from Brice's beautiful ones.

'Oh dear oh dear,' mumbles Marcus following me reluctantly into the changing room.

'I know I have to look like a lady Marcus but I have to be comfortable too and feel a bit like me. I'm shit-scared about this weekend,' I whisper.

'Yes madam, but my instructions are to make sure you don't look like *you*. No insult intended.'

I grin.

'None taken.'

I pull the dress over my head and Marcus wraps the shawl around me in an expert manner and appraises me.

'Well, I'm astonished. It actually becomes you madam. The criss-cross ruching really enhances your figure. With the right earrings and accessories, we may have a winner, and you don't resemble the real you at all.'

'Really?' I say, trying to adjust the scarf without tearing it to shreds with my vampire nails.

He sighs.

'You really have to get to grips with the nails madam, or who knows what damage you may cause.'

'You should see my thighs Marcus.'

'I'd rather not madam.'

I step nervously from the fitting room and parade in front of Brice Edmunds.

'Perfect,' he says, nodding appreciatively. 'Not in the least bit suitable for a Christmas tree.'

'Thank God for that,' I sigh, attempt a twirl and sway on my heels.

'Maybe a little less gin though,' he laughs.

'What I wouldn't do for a drop of mother's ruin. It's these bloody heels. I can't cope with them, not to mention ...'

Marcus coughs diplomatically.

'Language madam, now shall we get you undressed, before you tell Mr Brice about your thighs,' whispers Marcus.

Brice raises his eyebrows and grins before offering his hand.

'It was nice meeting you again. I very much enjoyed the fashion show.'

I place my hand in his and feel a small tingle rush through me. Please let him ask me for a coffee or something. Or just ask me for the something. God, right now I'd be so up for it.

'Thank you for your advice,' I say. 'I've got this big weekend coming up and I've got to make a good impression.'

'Madam is meeting her future in-laws,' says Marcus absently, straightening the back of the dress.

Oh great, thanks a lot Marcus. That's the coffee and something out of the window isn't it?

He nods.

'My pleasure, and I think you will make more than a good impression. I would say break a leg except you're likely to if you don't lose those shoes.'

Marcus groans.

'Now he's an expert in shoes. Perhaps you would like a job here?'

'No, the tie will suffice,' he laughs as he opens the door to leave, only to have Fiona walk in.

'Sorry I'm so late. I got on the wrong train, ended up halfway to bloody Croydon. I tried phoning but I just kept getting your voicemail. Jesus, it's posh around here. I've been scared to open my mouth ... oh sorry,' she finishes on seeing Brice.

I shake my head.

'Fiona, this is Brice, he's been helping me choose a dress.'

She widens her eyes and then gives him a big smile.

'That's nice, slightly unusual but nice,' she says.

He shakes her hand warmly and then turns to the door.

'Nice meeting you both. I hope your weekend goes well Harriet.'

The door closes and I open my mouth at her.

'Isn't he gorgeous?'

'And the way he said *Harriet*, ooh didn't it make your legs give way,' she grins.

'Madam's legs have been giving way most of the morning, isn't that right Miss Harriet?' says Marcus, escorting me back to the dressing room.

'Why what have you been doing?' asks Fiona.

'Bloody starving because I can't eat with these, *Nightmare on Elm Street* nails. I've had one stuck in the tumble dryer door. And balancing on these stupid heels is like being on bleeding stilts. I feel like a circus act. I think dancing on ice would be easier. Honestly Fi, I don't think I can get through this.'

I flop onto the couch and lift my legs to take off my shoes but, of course, the nails get in the sodding way and I end up scraping them along my tights, leaving huge ladders.

'Allow me madam, otherwise by the time you get to Scotland you will resemble a character out of *Halloween*,' says Marcus gently.

'I'm dreading the weekend,' I say, rubbing my feet.

'Madam, if I may offer some advice,' he says kindly. 'Clothing excepted, just be yourself and I am sure everyone will love you.'

Five minutes later and I have a bundle of new clothes, and not to mention a Burberry bag for the daytime and a Givenchy for the evening. Fiona sits in a chair, eyes wide and mouth open.

'God, you've got a brilliant riding outfit. I'd die for one of those. I love horse riding.'

'I'll probably die if I have to wear it. No one is getting me on a horse,' I say.

'Right madam, you are ready for the weekend. I shall have everything delivered to your apartment later this afternoon and Claude will collect you in the morning and take you to the heliport.'

'Crikey,' says Fiona. 'You're going to look fab. I'm so excited. I wish I could be there with you.'

'So do I,' I say sadly.

I feel my stomach churn. I may look fab but I also have to sound fab, walk fab, and eat fab. It's going to be a Mission Impossible and I have an awful fear the whole thing will collapse around my ears. The thought of ears immediately makes me think of Julian and the three Jacks. It feels like we are in some kind of horrific nightmare and all we wanted was a French restaurant.

A thought enters my head.

'What day is it?' I ask Fiona.

'Do what?'

'What day is it?' I repeat.

'Friday, why?'

'Come on, I need to do the lottery. Maybe I can win and then I won't have to go through with this charade.'

'Great plan,' she scoffs.

'Marcus said he would get a driver to take me home in his limo. We'll make a quick stop at the newsagents on the way.'

'I'll get Alistair to meet us at the flat; I want him to see me in a limo. We'll get a pizza later shall we?'

Oh, if only life could stay like this.

'First stop newsagents please,' I tell the driver.

Chapter Nine

Jack Diamond is enjoying his favourite dinner. Meatballs and pasta, just the way he likes it. He likes this restaurant. The nice checked tablecloths and the traditional Italian music appeal to him. He fancies himself as a bit of an Italian. With his broad shoulders and toned physique he could pass for a good-looking Italian any day. He likes his Valentino suits. They give him more respect and show he isn't short of a bob or two. They know how to show respect here. They never cause him trouble, not like that little prick Julian Conway. What the stupid bugger thought he was playing at, Jack had no idea. Conway should have known he couldn't get away with not paying on time. Jack considers himself a reasonable man. After all, wasn't he doing Julian a favour, giving him the loan and then offering to keep trouble out of his restaurant? What was five hundred a month to someone like Conway?

'Now, I don't wanna see your lovely little gaff turned over, not now you've put all this money into it Julian. There are some terrible thugs in the old smoke these days. You know what I mean? Now, I'm thinking I can 'elp you out with a little security, think of it like an insurance policy. A monkey will do it, in cash. I'll pop round at the end of each month and collect.'

How much more respectful can a person be? But not that little prick, he doesn't know what the word *respect* means. Well, he would find the little sod and if he didn't have the cash then the little prick would lose just that. And little it most likely is, Jack thought, and chuckles to himself. He'll send it to that pretty girlfriend of his. If he still didn't cough up, then there would be no alternative but to make Julian disappear. Satisfied with his plan he begins to tuck into his tiramisu when Mad Jack Junior bursts in.

Jack Diamond sighs.

'What's the matter with you? Barging in like some kind of thug. What do yer want people to think of us?' snaps Diamond. 'Yer wanna give me indigestion?'

'I've got some news about that Julian loser,' Mad Jack Junior grins.

Jack Diamond wipes his mouth with his serviette and takes a gulp of wine before gesturing to the waiter to refill the glass. Mad Jack fidgets eager to share his news. Jack Diamond looks down to his son's shoes.

'You is still giving me indigestion. Can you bleedin' calm down and eat something. What 'ave I told yer about your shoes. Polished shoes show you are a man to respect.'

'Sorry Dad.'

'Did you get the worm powder for the cat like your mum asked?'

'Babyface Jack is getting that. He likes the pet shop and looking at the animals and stuff.'

Diamond snorts. Unable to contain himself any longer, Mad Jack throws a newspaper at his dad.

'The bloody *Times*,' scoffs Diamond. 'Don't yer think it's a bit late to start reading a rag like that?'

Mad Jack exhales in irritation and turns the pages frantically. He rips out the page he needs and sticks it under his father's nose.

'Sir bleedin' Sebastian Lancaster would like to announce the forthcoming engagement of his son 'amilton Lancaster to none other than 'arriet bleedin' Lawson. Julian's tart 'as got 'erself a rich poncy boyfriend and I mean mega rich. She's paid all the staff at the restaurant. It's still open, but I ain't saw nothin' going on and she's been spending pots of dough in fancy dress shops today. It's funny that though, cos she's still working in that laundrette and that ain't adding up to me, not if she's marrying that ponce. The bitch never offered us nothin',' Mad Jack Junior blurts out, unable to keep the news to himself any longer.

Jack Diamond looks thoughtful. Now that is news. So, the pretty little girlfriend has already found someone new has she? He glances at the newspaper announcement and throws it to one side.

'There's something fishy 'ere and I'm not talking about the menu. Get that snitch Razors on the blower. Tell 'im to do a bit of research. He's as bent as a two bob note. If he can't find out what's going on, no one can.'

'You want me to sort 'er?'

'No, you moron,' Diamond sighs.

'You know give 'er a bell and threaten like?'

Jack Diamond's head snaps up.

'What yer on about?'

'Babyface got 'er number from the prick's phone.'

Diamond thumps his fist down on the table.

'What 'ave I told you about doing stuff like that? That ain't 'ow you get birds.'

'Babyface fancied 'er. Not me. He's been going in that laundrette and stuff.'

'Bugger me,' groans Diamond.

'You really think something is fishy?' asks Mad Jack Junior. 'With 'er suddenly getting a rich poncy boyfriend?'

Jack Diamond laughs.

'I think we should take a trip to 'er flat and talking of fishes …'

Mad Jack Junior laughs.

'Make 'er an offer she can't refuse?'

'Something like that,' grins Jack Diamond while wondering why Julian's girlfriend would stay in such a poxy flat when she has a mega rich boyfriend. Something very fishy indeed is going on and he ain't gonna leave it alone until he finds out what it is. If she knows where that wanker Julian is she'll soon tell them. In the meantime, if she wants to keep that Froggie restaurant open, then she owes him a monkey.

Chapter Ten

Fiona is flushed with excitement by the time we reach Marlborough Mansions. I'm surprised she didn't spend the journey waving like royalty. Our quick stop for a lottery ticket turned into a bit of a disaster. I never imagined it could be so difficult trying to choose six numbers out of forty-nine. For starters you have to ditch the unlucky numbers before you begin, and in my case this is no small feat is it? I didn't want to choose *ten* as that was my birthday, and having the gangsters eat my birthday cake is clearly a bad omen. Everyone chooses seven so I didn't want that one. Obviously thirteen was out of the question, although seriously my luck couldn't get any worse could it? Four is Julian's birthday and he isn't turning out to be a lucky charm is he? So anything with four in it is going to be bad luck, I mean, take fourteen for example. I don't even want to think about that and the Valentine's Day catastrophe at the flat. At one point Fiona asked the shop assistant if he had a chair.

'We're a newsagent, not a dental surgery. I don't have a waiting area,' he had snapped.

Fiona had suggested thirty-one but of course that adds up to four doesn't it, and I couldn't use five as that is the same as fourteen if you add them together. So that also meant I couldn't use number forty-six either, as that makes ten, and that's my birthday again. Honestly, buying a lottery ticket almost gave me a mental breakdown. Eventually Fiona had blown her top and forced me to buy a lucky dip. I ask you with the way my life is spiralling at the moment it is more likely to be the unlucky dip. But I wasn't in the mood to argue and I was beginning to wonder if I would be able to circle the numbers with my Morticia Addams nails anyway.

I feel quite relieved when Claude, the chauffeur, drops us outside the Mansions. Curtains twitch as we pull up and Alistair rushes towards us, the sight of the limousine comforting him no doubt. I spend a full minute trying to open the door but fail miserably and manage to leave a little rip in the upholstery instead. I don't think I need be too concerned about a visit from the Jacks while I am Harriet Scissorhands. Mrs Mollard appears in the doorway, a scarf knotted around her throat and a dustpan and brush in her hand. For a second I think she is going to offer to clean the limo but she just stands there open-mouthed.

Fiona casually nods at Claude as though she has been stepping out of limousines all her life.

'Thank you Claude,' she says in a posh voice.

I give her a startled look. Where did that come from? Sid is at the doorway and so many net curtains are swaying that I am beginning to wonder if there is a small hurricane blowing up in Marlborough Terrace.

'Bucking hell,' says Mrs Mollard.

'Christ, and I thought she was broke,' adds Sid.

'I am,' I say quickly. 'Honestly Sid.'

'Yeah, I can see that. Traded in your old Mini did you? Still, it's your business Harriet. You've paid your rent so I'm not complaining.'

'It's c-c-c-complicated,' says Alistair, his shoulders twitching. Half the street has turned out now and I feel like I should break into song or something. The drug-fuelled yobs begin yelling and rush towards the car.

'Yeah, so is my marriage but I haven't got a car like that,' grins Sid.

'I shall see you tomorrow madam,' Claude says politely.

I nod and the residents of Marlborough Mansions watch the limo drive away.

'Got a rich punter?' asks one of the youths.

'Oh honestly,' groans Alistair.

I begin climbing the stairs with Alistair panting behind me, the aromatic smells of curry and exotic foods emanating from behind the doors.

'Oh yeah, I nearly forgot, your brother Jack came by,' calls Sid.

I turn so fast that my head spins.

'What?' I croak.

'I wouldn't have let him in but he had a key and everything. Nice lad. You never mentioned a brother. We had a laugh ...'

'You did?' I say, finding it hard to breathe.

'God, are you okay?' Fiona asks.

'Nice lad. He left a little something for you. A late birthday present I expect.'

Oh my God. Please let it be Julian's ear. Obviously I don't want it to be any part of his body but if I have to choose then I think the ear is preferable. At least he has another one to hear with. Maybe it can be sewn back on, although, with the NHS waiting lists the way they are these days perhaps not. I should have agreed to that private health insurance that Julian wanted; they would have sewn it back on in a jiffy no doubt. Oh Christ, what if it is his tongue. He'll never be able to speak to me again. I'll never hear him whisper sweet nothings into my ear. Mind you, he never did that much anyway. Jesus, it might be his penis, what the hell do I do with that? A vision of Julian bleeding to death in the gutter appears in front of my eyes and I fly up the stairs with Alistair and Fiona trailing behind me.

'I feel faint, the Jacks have been here,' I say dramatically, fumbling with the key in the lock.

'Oh God,' says Fiona in a hushed tone. 'Do you think they've trashed the place again?'

'It's like being in an episode of *The Sopranos* except it's ten times more sordid,' quips Alistair, walking slowly behind.

'Maybe we shouldn't go in without a weapon,' whispers Fiona.

'Why do we need a weapon?' I whisper back.

'In case they are still in there.'

'I hardly think they would have locked themselves in.'

Then again, Julian did say they were a bit crazy. I'm feeling just a touch crazy myself. What am I doing? In a matter of days my life has gone mad. It isn't my fault that Julian's stupid restaurant has failed is it? I never even wanted the damn place. I was just supporting him. I didn't ask him to borrow money from loan sharks, and I didn't see the need for the sodding van, and now because of all that I have bugger all. I can't even pay the rent because of him and now I am in far too deep. I've already taken half the money and paid off a lot of the debts. I now have just enough to pay the rent and my tuition fees but if I don't see this thing through, Hamilton will demand the money back. God, this is awful. I don't know what is worse, the three Jacks or the Hamilton Lancaster agreement.

The flat looks fine and everything is as it should be. I can't even see the little present that Sid mentioned.

'See, everything is fine,' says Fiona, relief evident in her voice. 'Shall we order pizza? We'll stay with you for a while and then you need to rest, you've got your big day tomorrow.'

I look around the flat nervously, feeling my shoulders tense. I listen to Alistair stuttering our order down the phone and feel sorry for the poor bugger at the other end.

'I'll clear the kitchen table,' Fiona offers as I begin to relax. 'Shall I throw this old paper away?'

I freeze. Fiona is holding up what looks like a crumpled bunch of old newspapers.

'Oh my God,' I cry. 'It's Julian's ear.'

'Holy fuck,' she screams, dropping it to the floor.

We stare at the newspaper in silence.

'How do you know this is it?' she says, looking horrified.

'Yes and how d-d-do you know it's his ear?' asks Alistair.

'Well it isn't going to be an expensive bottle of French perfume is it? And it wasn't here earlier which can only mean ...'

'Who's going to open it?' Fiona asks so quietly that I barely hear her.

'Well I can't, not with these bloody scissors for hands.'

'I c-c-c-can't, I'm not good with b-b-b-b- ...' says Alistair.

'Body parts?' I say helpfully.

'Blood,' he finishes.

Oh God, I hadn't thought about the blood. Well I had, in that I had thought of Julian lying in a pool of it, but not the blood that would come with the dismembered ear/tongue/penis.

'God, this is worse than a Stephen King novel,' groans Fiona. 'Maybe we can pay someone to unwrap it.'

'Oh great idea. Where do you suggest we find someone? I suppose we could look in the yellow pages for 'Specialists in unwrapping severed body parts?' I say cynically.

'Okay, just a thought.'

'I'll get a towel,' I say, rushing to the bathroom.

'Why?' asks Fiona.

'For the blood of course.'

'I'm phoning the p-p-p- ...'

'Christ Alistair, how can you think about pizza now,' snaps Fiona.

'Police,' he blurts out. 'We need to call them.'

'No,' I yell. 'God knows what they'll cut off next. We have to see what's in the parcel. There might be a note.'

I hand Fiona scissors and give her a reassuring nod. We stare mesmerised as she carefully cuts through the newspaper. Alistair can barely watch and stands clutching the pizza menu to his chest. Two layers later and we have still found nothing. I feel myself begin to relax. Maybe it isn't anything after all. Maybe it was sent just to scare us, and God knows it did. Fiona carefully pulls back the next layer and stops.

'I can feel a box,' she says in a trembling voice.

'Is it big enough for a penis or just small enough for a tongue or ...'

'Oh, C-C-C-Christ,' groans Alistair stepping back.

'Shall I put on an apron?' says Fiona. 'You know, for the blood.'

'It isn't going to exactly spurt out at you is it?'

She takes a breath and with shaking hands removes the final layer, and we all stare at the small white box. I swallow and Fiona licks her lips. Alistair clenches his knuckles. The only sound is the bass from someone's stereo thumping in the flat above.

'I'll take the lid off but I can't look,' offers Fiona.

I nod and look to Alistair who turns away. I lift my head, take a deep breath and glance at the goldfish bowl and am about to look back when I realise the goldfish is not in it. Before I can open my mouth Fiona has removed the lid and lying helpless on a box of cotton wool is my goldfish.

'They killed Billy,' I scream. 'They murdered my bleeding goldfish.'

Fiona's eyes snap open and she stares at the fish. Alistair lets out a sigh and says,

'Well at least they didn't leave its head in your b-b-bed.'

'What the hell does that mean?' I say stupidly.

'In *The Godfather* ...'

'Oh sod *The Godfather*, this is bloody Battersea not Sicily.'

I look at little Billy the goldfish and sigh.

'Why kill a goldfish? I mean, it's upsetting but I'm not exactly going to go into mourning am I?'

Alistair claps his hands.

'Of c-c-c-course,' he says excitedly. 'It, m-m-m-means that J-Ju-Ju ...'

'Julian yes,' I interrupt.

'He's getting excited,' says Fiona, stating the obvious yet again.

God, at times like these do I need a friend who stammers?

'Yes, it means what?'

'Sleeps with the fishes.'

Well that was worth waiting for I don't think. What does that mean?

'Oh God, like in *The Godfather*,' whimpers Fiona.

I bloody hate that film.

'It means Julian is sleeping with goldfish, is that what you're saying and where would that be exactly, at the local funfair or should I pop to the nearest pet shop?'

'It means he sleeps with the fishes at the bottom of the Thames,' says Alistair confidently. 'I love *The Godfather*.'

'I didn't know there were goldfish in the Thames,' I say stupidly.

'Mind you,' he adds ignoring me. 'The fish is usually wrapped up in an article of clothing of the person who has been hit or w-w-w-w-...'

'Wiped out,' offers Fiona.

'Washed up,' I mutter.

'Whacked,' finishes Alistair.

'Christ,' I mumble.

'Shall I order the pizza now?' he asks. 'Fi, do you want anchovies?'

God, I think I'm going to be sick. My mobile rings and I grab it, stupidly thinking it might be Julian which is unlikely of course unless he has an underwater phone.

'Ello 'arriet, did you get our little gift. Thoughtful don't yer think? Babyface wrapped it nicely. We wanted to congratulate yer.'

I fall onto the couch and mouth *Jack* to Fiona.

'Congratulate me?' I say. 'Most people send cards and flowers not bleeding dead goldfish.'

Congratulate me on what? Christ, I haven't gone and won the bleeding lottery have I?

'I saw *The Times* announcement of your little engagement to that nice rich snobby bastard, 'amilton Lancaster. You've got taste, I'll give yer that.'

What bleeding announcement? Oh no, what if Celia Blakely sees it, or my boss at the laundrette? Or shit, even worse my mum. Calm down Harriet, what the hell would Celia Blakely be doing with a paper like that unless it has her fish and chips wrapped in it, and the only page of a paper my boss reads is the back page.

'Thought yer might need a little reminder that you and Julian still owe us some dosh, 'specially now you're in with that nice rich family. Don't want yer forgetting us do we?'

Hang on a minute.

'What about your code of honour, what the bleeding hell happened to that?' I say, opening my mouth before engaging my brain.

Alistair winces and shakes his head.

'What code of bleeding 'onour? This ain't the bleeding *Godfather* you know.'

Huh, try telling everyone else that.

'But ...'

''eard from Julian 'ave yer?'

'No,' I say hoarsely while thinking this is a good sign if he's asking me if I've heard from Julian.

'You taking over that Colonel Gaddafi are yer?'

What has Colonel Gaddafi got to do with anything? I suppose that's in *The Godfather* too.

'Colonel Gaddafi?' I mouth to Fiona and Alistair.

They both give me a puzzled look and Fiona shrugs.

'I don't know what you mean,' I say shakily.

'Now, there's me thinking you's a London girl. Colonel Gaddafi, café, get it? Now Julian and I had a little arrangement. I was giving 'im a little security. You know what yobs are these days. Need a bleedin' good 'iding some of 'em. I said as much to Julian. "They'll turn your place over" I said to 'im. So we agreed I'd look after that side of things, save 'im the worry. Know what I mean?'

'But ...' I begin.

'A monkey a month we agreed, in cash. Now, of course ole Julian is well overdue and you 'aving this posh boyfriend and keeping the café open, well I thought to meself who's going to protect it for yer while Julian's away. You don't want that little place burning to the ground now do yer?'

Great, no one is going to invest in an arsoned restaurant are they? God, *I'll* have to rob a bank at this rate.

'But ...' I say again.

'Of course I could ask your poncy future in-laws if ...'

'No,' I scream.

Oh God, this is getting direr by the second.

'So, 'ow 'bout we say you leave it downstairs with that nice landlord of yours and Babyface Jack can collect it tomorrow. A monkey remember, don't you go messin' me around.'

'No,' I cry again before I can stop myself.

I don't want Sid getting pulled into this. There is a heavy silence.

'That's a shame. I was looking forward to popping round, you know, 'aving a cuppa with that nice wife of 'is and those two little nippers. I love kids. I've got two of me own. Little buggers they are though. I've got no control over them ... Well, you know what I'm sayin.'

Oh my God. Julian's investor is bound to pull out if there is any trouble at the restaurant and we'll never get out of this mess.

'No, I understand exactly what you're saying. I can get you the monkey, every month. But I'll, I'll, I'll ...'

Spit it out Harriet for Christ's sake. You're sounding more like Alistair by the minute. Fiona is staring at me wide-eyed.

'I'll deliver it to *you*,' I say quickly.

Have I gone insane? There is silence and I try not to breathe too hard. Don't let them know you're scared, that's the trick. What the hell am I talking about?

'Okay, I'll contact you with a meeting place and 'arriet ...' he says pausing menacingly.

'Yes,' I say breathlessly.

'You'd better answer the phone or Julian suffers.'

Oh, don't worry, Julian will suffer at some point and hopefully at my hands.

'I will, I promise I will. I'll give you a monkey every month, but ...'

Before I can finish the phone goes dead. This is terrible. It's just getting worse and worse. I was beginning to think that maybe, just maybe I could back out of this whole thing with Hamilton Lancaster. I'd even begun to stupidly think that perhaps I could appeal to his compassionate side and ask him to help me. Now I am completely buggered. The last thing I want to do is involve him and his family. The best thing to do is pay Jack Diamond the hundred or is it five hundred? How the hell am I supposed to know how much a monkey is? I'll have to bloody Google it. What if they want the pay-off at the weekend when I am in bleeding Scotland?

'Well?' Fi asks.

I fall onto the couch.

'I've got to deliver a pay-off. They want a monkey every month or they'll do something awful to the restaurant and something even worse to Julian if they find him,' I say, sounding like Bonnie out of *Bonnie and Clyde*.

Fiona looks horrified.

'Every month?' she echoes. 'But where will you get one from and what are they going to do to the little thing. Oh God, they're monsters, first your goldfish and now a monkey.'

Alistair sighs. God help Julian when he does get home. I'll give him monkey all right.

Chapter Eleven

The Lancaster family helicopter makes its turbulent descent into the grounds of the Glenwood estate and I feel like I could throw up at any minute. It's not the bumpy ride that is making me want to gag. I love a good fairground ride, in fact, the scarier the better. It's more that I am shit-scared about what I've let myself in for. I keep telling myself it's only a weekend but we all know how long some weekends can be don't we? Still, once it's over and I've done my bit, I can get back to my life, thirty thousand pounds better off. I need to ask Hamilton about *The Times* announcement. I mean, what if my parents see it? I suppose on reflection that's highly unlikely. I can't imagine Mum walking back from the local Tesco with *The Times* under her arm somehow. *Take a Break* maybe but that's about as highbrow as Mum gets and Dad never reads a newspaper. He prefers News 24 and I don't think I'm going to make it onto there somehow, unless of course Julian's dismembered body is found propping up a flyover somewhere in London or hanging from a meat hook in someone's freezer. Then they might just flash up a picture of yours truly. I can see the headlines now.

Promising young entrepreneur found buried in cement after girlfriend refused to pay East End gangland leaders.

Oh God, don't think about that Harriet. Just study your nice little blue folder and get through the weekend with flying colours, take the money and run. Hamilton sent me a fifteen-page folder with all the details of how we supposedly met, how I started my business, my favourite ice cream, favourite colour and how I like my coffee. I'm surprised it didn't include my inside leg measurement and bra size. Mind you, even I'm not sure what that is anymore since Marcus stuffed me full of silicone enhancers. How women with big breasts cope I shall never know.

I feel like an actor in *Green Card.* What if I mess it up, come to think of it, what if Hamilton messes it up? And I can't begin to tell you the things I read about him. How the other half live, I tell you. He wears only designer underpants it seems, and only briefs. Like I really want to know that. It's not like I'll be popping out to buy some over the weekend is it? I doubt he would be happy with Primark's three pairs for two pounds fifty. He has everything ironed, and I mean everything, from his designer pants to his Marc Jacob socks. I never knew Marc Jacob made socks. He's an expert skier and accomplished horseman as I am too apparently, a horsewoman that is. Seriously, the closest I have come to a horse is when I ate one in a Findus lasagne. Hamilton was an expert rower at Eton and I, hold your breath, was a champion cyclist at school but after the horrific accident (too awful to talk about) I had to give it up. Thank God for that. I only wear Clinique as my skin is sensitive. My cheap Aldi moisturiser was removed from my handbag by Marcus with such precision you would have thought it was a bomb rather than a jar of face cream. It was replaced with numerous jars and bottles of Clinique products which I have to say I am very much enjoying. Oh well, if I bugger it up then I bugger it up. It's not like I'm going to see these people again is it? I can't see them popping round to Marlborough Mansions for a cuppa or dropping their washing off at the laundrette. No, there is very little chance our paths will cross again. They can go off with their jolly hockey sticks and I'll return to my life of drudgery. I just don't want to be made a fool of, that's all. And what if I have to get up all close and personal with Hamilton? No, my relationship with Hamilton will be one of those cold distant types. I'll have to be one of those cool detached type of chicks. In fact they all look like that, these posh birds don't they? I mean just look at Posh Becks, she always looks cold and hard. Mind you, she's from Essex isn't she? I can't do any worse than her can I? I realise part of my nausea is down to hunger and I fish out the pack of Jaffa Cakes I had sneaked into my Burberry. Well, there is no way I can get through this without a chocolate fix. I find my mind wander to Brice Edmunds. If only *he* had asked me to be his soon-to-be fiancée for a weekend, now that would have been a pleasure. I sigh and look down as Glenwood Manor comes into view. It's huge. Hamilton never said it was a Scottish Downton Abbey. I hope I look okay, I feel like bloody Jacqueline Onassis in my tight-fitting pink suit and pearls. I only need a little pillbox hat and I could easily be mistaken for her. I pop another two Jaffa Cakes into my mouth and gasp when I see there is a welcoming party at the side of the heliport. There's seven of them. Not seven welcoming parties, obviously, even I know I'm not that grand. Seven people and bloody hell, two of them are wearing kilts, and one is my soon-to-be pretend fiancé and presumably the other is his father. I hope they're not true Scotsmen. One gust of wind and I would not only see Hamilton's rope and tackle in all its glory but his father's too. It would be far too traumatic an experience. This does not bode well. Even my mum would not be impressed with me dating a man in a skirt. I grab the sides of my seat as the helicopter wobbles as it comes into land and the remaining Jaffa Cakes tumble into my lap. Piss it. The sky is full of threatening rain and the helicopter lurches to the side as a rumble of thunder breaks over the noise of the engine. Christ, talk about the trumpets hailing the arrival of the she-devil. As we go lower and the enormity of the estate becomes apparent, I can practically smell the sweetness of money in the air.

I scramble frantically in my handbag for a tissue to wipe my hands and to check my reflection only to find the sodding clip is stuck. I fiddle desperately with it and my heart pounds with panic. What's wrong with the bloody thing? It opened fine a few seconds ago.

'Come on, open bugger you,' I groan, and like magic it does. I spot my phone and see that little red cross in the corner. You know the cross I mean, the one where usually three lovely bars of signal flash at you. One bar would have been awkward but no bars at all is fatal. Buckery fuck, what if the Jacks phone about the meeting? Surely people with bleeding huge estates have mobiles and phone signal by which to use them? The vibrating of the helicopter comes to a stop and there is silence. The waiting party look like they are lined up waiting to be shot. The door slides open and a frowning Hamilton leans in.

'Are you coming out?' he hisses.

'What the hell were you thinking of taking out an ad in *The Times* announcing our engagement. Why didn't you just shout it from the rooftops?'

'Sorry. My mother's idea, she gets carried away. Are you coming out?'

I smile, grab my new cashmere shawl and nonchalantly brush Jaffa Cake from my skirt. He offers his hand and I reluctantly place my sticky one in his, and feel my right false boob slip. Christ alive, whatever next.

'Don't you have phone signal here?' I whisper.

'Phone signal?' he repeats, looking at me blankly.

Christ, don't tell me he can't speak English now he's in Scotland? I hope they don't speak bleeding Gaelic or something. I've got enough problems trying to talk in my new posh accent without an added language on top.

'My mobile doesn't work,' I say, cautiously stepping from the helicopter.

'You won't get anything here unless you're with Vodafone.'

He might have told me that before I left. What the hell am I supposed to do now? A few drops of rain splatter onto my new suit and I shiver.

'Harriet,' gushes a woman who is hurrying towards me. 'I hope your flight wasn't too arduous. How are your feet, not too swollen I hope?'

She makes it sound like I've flown from Australia rather than London. Everyone looks down at my feet, which are squashed into the Jimmy Choos that Marcus was insistent I wear.

'You've got chocolate all over your face,' whispers Hamilton harshly, handing me a tissue.

A sudden gust of wind lifts up his kilt and I get a quick gander of his designer underpants. Thank God that's all I get a gander of. I dab delicately at my mouth and thank the gods that all eyes are on my feet, and take the opportunity to yank up my right falsie, pinching my own nipple as I do so. Honestly, I should get danger money for doing this. Hamilton leans forward and kisses me softly on the lips. It's not too bad actually. The breath could have been a bit fresher, but overall it's bearable. I rather thought it would be like kissing Hannibal Lecter but it wasn't that bad at all. Not that I know what it's like to kiss Hannibal Lecter of course.

'I'm Lady Melanie Lancaster, Hamilton's mother,' says the gushing woman, hugging me and drowning me in perfume. 'And this is my husband Sir Sebastian Lancaster.'

She pulls an older version of Hamilton towards me. He is the other one wearing a kilt and has a tartan cravat held together with a diamond-encrusted tiepin. Before I can stop the bugger he hugs me and pierces my left silicone breast. There is a little pop and I feel my boob deflate and I begin leaking. Christ, all I need is another hug and

I'll be spraying everywhere like a cat on heat. This is unbearably embarrassing, not to mention sticky.

'Ooh, I'm a little chilly,' I lie, wrapping the cashmere shawl around me.

'Harriet, shall we introduce you to the household staff?' smiles Hamilton.

Oh yes please, anything to put off the moment I have to pretend to be an aristocrat's girlfriend.

'Hello,' I say, looking at the four people lined up. I don't have a clue what you say to household staff. I've never met household staff in my life, not unless you count my mum who used to be a cleaner, but that's sort of different isn't it?

'This is Cedric, he's head butler, and basically Cedric is the man. Isn't that right Cedric?' laughs Hamilton while giving him a slap on the back.

Oh good, he isn't likely to hug me, so hopefully the leakage will stay under control.

'Yes sir,' responds a dour-faced Cedric. His greying hair is swept back making him look a bit like Trevor Eve and his dark brown eyes study me intently.

'Good afternoon madam.'

I nod.

'Good afternoon Cedric, it's nice to meet you,' I say while my breast shrinks by the second and I get stickier and stickier.

'And this is Emily. She's the under maid.'

A young woman in a starched white apron nods at me. She pushes back loose strands of hair which have escaped her neat bun and steps forward.

'Miss Harriet,' she says with a little curtsy.

My God, people really do live like this. It's surreal.

'Hello Emily, nice to meet you too,' I respond, focusing hard on my speech.

'Emily will be your ladies maid while you're here,' adds Lady Lancaster, 'We couldn't cope without a ladies maid could we Harriet?'

Speak for yourself I'm sure.

'Any dress malfunctions just go to Emily, she's very capable.'

I hope that includes tit malfunctions.

'This is Mrs Randall, our cook.'

A stiff-necked woman steps forward and gives a small nod, before saying,

'Good afternoon madam. I hope you have a pleasant stay.'

'And finally, this is Gregory, my valet.'

Gregory gives a weak smile.

'Then of course there is Pa's secretary and Lionel ...'

'Yes, well let's not bombard her with too much information. The poor girl looks shattered. A hot bath is what's needed no doubt. Let's get you to the house,' interrupts Sir Sebastian. Well, he seems quite nice even if he did puncture my tit.

It is a short walk to the manor house. I spot the tennis court and the outdoor swimming pool which is covered with tarpaulin. I'm ushered into the entrance hall of the manor, which is twice the size of my flat, complete with crystal chandelier, bronze statues of Greek gods and a marble staircase, and at the top sitting in a wheelchair, there she is.

'So, she's arrived,' she calls in a clipped clear voice.

'Grandmother,' whispers Hamilton.

Wonderful. I am about to meet the grandmother while I have one deflated breast, Jaffa Cake stuck to my skirt, sweaty palms and apparently, two swollen feet. However, she shows no sign of leaving the wheelchair for the stairlift.

'Freshen up and do whatever it is you businesswomen do and I'll meet you at dinner. Lionel, let's finish our game of gin rummy, and you'd better not beat me again you bugger.'

I stare bemused as a well-dressed man wheels her away from the stairs. I turn to Hamilton.

'But ...'

'Yes, she swears, and it doesn't go down well at all. Emily, please show Harriet to her room. I'll send Cedric up with a drink. What would you like?'

A tankard of red wine would be good.

'A gin and tonic?' suggests Lady Lancaster.

Oh jolly dee. Let's have a tankard of that then.

'We've given you your own room Harriet,' says Melanie softly. 'Obviously it's not far from Hamilton's but well, Margarita is a bit old fashioned ...'

'That's fine isn't it Harriet, I'll just sneak to your room under cover of darkness,' smirks Hamilton.

Just try it mate. I glance away from him and my eyes land on a portrait of Van Gogh. God, it would have to be the one without his ear wouldn't it? It's as if someone is trying to send me a message, like I haven't got enough to contend with?

'Do you like Van Gogh?' asks Melanie.

'Not this particular one,' I say shuddering.

'Yes, pretty awful cutting off your own ear isn't it?'

I bet Julian would prefer to cut off his own ear than have the Jacks do it. In fact I imagine he would prefer not to have it removed at all but you know what I mean.

'Ears are funny things aren't they?' I say, while Hamilton looks at me like I've gone totally insane. 'What I mean is you don't think about them much until you're in danger of losing them.'

Shut up Harriet for God's sake.

'Yes, I imagine Van Gogh felt a bit like that,' she replies, looking confused.

'At least he chose to cut it off,' I say, willing myself to stop. His mother will think her son is with a raving lunatic in a minute. She wouldn't be far wrong would she? Only a raving lunatic would do what I'm doing.

'Yes right, a drink then Harriet,' says Hamilton leading me by the arm to the foot of the stairs.

God, I so need that tankard of gin.

Chapter Twelve

'You have to help me Fi,' I cry down the phone, 'or Julian's toast.'
I'm lounging on my bed in a soft fluffy dressing gown sipping my gin
and tonic. My bedroom has a fantastic view of a loch and some
mountains in the distance, and I've got a phone in the bedroom and
another in the bathroom. How decadent is that? If the Jack thing
wasn't so stressful I could actually enjoy this.

'What are you on about? I thought the reason you were in
Scotland playing Lady Muck was so that Julian *wouldn't* be toast, or
at least earless.'

God, why does no one understand?

'I need to divert my calls to your phone. There is no signal here
and I can't very well arrange the meet using the landline can I? I'll
look like a gangster's moll if I start talking pay-offs and where I'll be
leaving the readies,' I sigh. 'And besides, I don't want the Jacks to get
this number.'

God, these silicone breasts are seriously giving me mastitis.

'Honestly, this is getting out of hand,' I moan. 'My breasts have
deflated thanks to Sir Sebastian's tiepin and ...'

'Blimey Harriet, what was he doing with his tiepin?'

'He hugged me,' I explain.

'Must have been some hug.'

'It was. I swear I've got mastitis. Well? Can I divert to you or not?'
I ask again, trying to keep the desperation out of my voice.

She groans.

'I don't know Harry. I don't want to get involved with these Jacks.
I mean, what if they turn on us. Alistair has enough trouble speaking
as it is without having his tongue cut out.'

'You've got to help me, Fi. All you have to do is take my calls.
When the Jacks phone about the pay-off, just take down the details
and call this number. Say you're my PA, give me the info and it's
done.'

'But I've got to talk to them, then they'll know I exist and ...'

'Just say you're my accountant …'

'What?' she screams. 'If they think you've got an accountant you'll never get them off your back, and a monkey will turn into a grubby hand.'

I choke on my gin and tonic.

'You what?'

'Grubby hand, grand, get it? I've been doing some research on Google. This East End gangster stuff is fascinating; did you know that East End gangsters don't kill innocent victims? Of course, I don't know if Julian is exactly innocent, seeing as he owed them money and all that. Did you know that Reggie Kray …'

'Fiona, what are you now, the new Martina Cole? What are you researching bleeding gangsters for?'

'Sorry,' she mumbles. 'Okay, what do I have to do?'

'When they phone, say I am away for the weekend and have no phone signal. For God's sake don't say where. Tell them I can make the pay-off when I'm back on Monday; I just need to know where and when.'

'Well …' she says hesitatingly.

'Fi, come on,' I urge, 'it's only a bleeding phone call.'

'Okay, but if Alistair gets nailed to the floor, I'm holding you responsible,' she says threateningly.

'Nailed to the floor, bleeding hell Fi, where did you get that from? Even I know that wasn't in *The Godfather*.'

'But it was in *The Long Good Friday,* and that was British,' she says, like that explains everything.

'You've been Googling too much. You'll make yourself go blind doing that,' I say.

'I'm already blind, and it's masturbating that makes you go blind, not Google.'

That explains why I've got 20/20 vision then.

'Thanks Fi. I appreciate it, and honestly, Alistair won't get nailed to the floor but if he does I promise to take full responsibility.'

She laughs.

'Well that's okay then. Anyway what's it like up there?'

'Oh, you know, wall to wall luxury, servants waiting on you hand and foot, that kind of thing.'

'No I don't, but I'm getting a feel, don't stop.'

'I'll probably have Evian water coming out of my ears …'

'I'm surprised you can talk about ears.'

'Grand staircases and balconies, gin and tonic on tap, tell me when to stop.'

'You'll get bored. The grass is always greener on the other side.'

'Well at least there is grass here, there's sod all at Marlborough Mansions or hadn't you noticed.'

'I bet they have beautiful horses. I'd love to ride there. Riding here is not the same is it?'

'I wouldn't know. You're probably more cut out for this than I am. Can't you do it instead of me and then just give me the money?' I ask, hopefully.

'I'm not that great a friend.'

'No, I thought not,' I agree.

She blows a kiss down the phone and hangs up. I sigh with relief. At least I don't have to worry about the Jacks. I sip my gin and tonic. There is a light tap at the door and Cedric enters.

'I thought you might need another G and T Miss Harriet. Are you ready for Emily to dress you for dinner?'

Dress me for dinner? Crikey, do I look that incapable.

'It's the norm to be dressed for dinner Miss Harriet. It may look a little odd if you did it yourself.'

'Right,' I say.

'Good, I'll send her up in about forty-five minutes. Another wee toddy,' he asks, pointing at my glass.

'Ooh yes, another wee toddy indeed, although let's make it less of a wee one shall we?'

I'm not in the habit of saying no to a free drink. He smiles cheekily.

'Of course Miss Harriet, one large wee G and T coming up.'

* * *

I strip off in the bathroom which has to be the size of Fiona's entire semi. Okay, a bit of an exaggeration but crikey. I'm tempted to take some snaps and upload them to Facebook. I'm cocooned for one whole weekend in ankle-deep carpeting and scented air, and what's more, the lighting in the bathroom is very flattering. Note to self: replace light bulbs in Battersea flat with these. I stare longingly at the sunken bath and then at the oversized shower. Maybe I'll have one of each. The shower is one large alcove. I mean, you could seriously get three people in there, not that I'd want to shower with three people. Mind you, the way my finances are going I may have to consider it, if only to save on water. Having to ~~~~ extra five hundred quid hasn't helped. At least I've pa~ the back instalments on the bank loan. I've also m~ decision about Julian. There is no way we can stay toge~ ~er this. Once I have the rest of my money from Hamilton I'll c~ar my debts and try to get my old nursing job back. I'll pay the Jacks this time but once Julian gets his investor he is on his own. If he loses his ears then he loses them. It's not like he ever listened to anyone when he had them. Treating me like this isn't love is it? Not the kind of love that I recognise anyway.

I glance around the bathroom taking everything in. White pristine chenille bath towels hang over a heated towel rail. There are Jo Malone candles around the bath and a whole tray of posh bath products. There is even a music player. I switch on some Michael Buble, fill the bath, and light a candle before sliding into the hot water, pampering myself with Jo Malone Bluebell bath lotion, and all this without Gary's Platinum card. In fact, I'm the one getting paid for the privilege. How much better can it get? I sip from my G and T and let out a relaxed sigh. This is the life. Second note to self, try and bag a rich husband as soon as possible. Preferably not Hamilton as he has slight halitosis. Nothing I couldn't cope with but I'm not sure he is my type. There's a weakness about him and I like my men strong. Oh yes, scoffs a little voice, *that's why you chose that little prick Julian. A fine mess he has got you into*. Hindsight is a wonderful thing. When I first met Julian he was so appealing with his cute baby-face blue eyes and stub nose and of course, his gorgeous sensuous mouth that demanded to be kissed. He seemed so adventurous with lots of vision. Not great hearing but great vision. He had sex appeal too but not such a great libido I learnt later but hey, you can't have everything can you? Michael croons and I'm lost in a whole new world of luxury. I can never stretch out like this in the bath back at the flat without my feet resting on the taps. You never get the full benefit of a Radox bath like that do you? I lean back and massage my breasts. I look at my surroundings again, you know, to convince myself I'm not dreaming and hang on a minute, there is a cat drinking out of the loo with his arse stuck in the air. I leap up, sloshing water onto the floor.

'Oi, you little bugger, what are you doing?' I snap.

The little bugger only turns and hisses at me. I splash it with water but it just hisses more and bares its teeth. It's like the cat from hell.

wouldn't surprise me if it goes for my throat in a minute. God, it's like being trapped with a lion. How do these things happen to me? There is a tap at the door.

'Miss Harriet, it's Emily. Are you okay?'
No I'm not. I've got a bloody demented cat in my bathroom that has obviously had some kind of Stephen King *Pet Sematary* resurrection. I grab the only weapon at hand and hold the Jo Malone candle menacingly near him. I'm at a aristocratic manor for heaven's sake. How can they have demented cats here? I thought these kinds of people had dogs anyway. It's worrying, this. Zilch phone signal and demented cats. The whole family will no doubt turn out to be vampires. Thank God Fiona knows I'm here. When my blood-drained body is found at least she will know who did it.

'There's a bleeding cat in here and it's none too friendly,' I say, sounding every bit *not* like an aristocratic guest.
Emily throws open the door and lurches at the demon. He immediately transforms into a little angel in her arms, all purring and nose rubbing. I fling myself at a chenille towel and wrap it around me.

'Come on Diamond, you know you shouldn't be in here. I'll just take him out and I'll be back, Miss Harriet,' she says calmly.
Diamond? She's got to be kidding me right? Little chance of forgetting Jack Diamond while here then.

'Sorry about that, he's a little b- … terror is Diamond. He's all right once you get to know him. Madam Margarita dotes on him,' smiles Emily shyly, her glance shifting surreptitiously to the silicone breasts sitting on the bed. Ah yes, I'd forgotten about them.

'Sir Sebastian pricked me,' I say, rummaging through my suitcase for a spare pair.
There is a sharp intake of breath and I turn to see she has turned quite white.

'Oh no,' I say quickly. 'Nothing like that …'
Like what? What am I saying exactly?

'His tiepin pricked my breast and …'
She turns even whiter and for a second I think she is in danger of fainting.

'Not my real breast obviously, but one of these,' I say hastily retrieving a spare from the case.

'Oh,' she says with a relieved sigh, 'but why were you wearing those?' She blushes. 'Sorry Miss Harriet.'

'Don't bleeding ask, they're more trouble than they're worth. A bit like balloons they are, one prick and they're gone.'

She nods.

'A bit like losing your virginity but in this case you have spares whereas you can never get that back can you?' she says and bites her lip.

'God, I'm so sorry Miss Harriet, I don't know what came over me.'

I look at her wide-eyed and giggle.

'What are you wearing this evening Miss Harriet?'

That's the million dollar question.

'Buggered if I know. What do most of them wear for dinner?'

She fiddles nervously with my undies.

'I'm sorry madam, what do you mean most of them?'

This is no good. I'll have to tell someone I'm a fraud. I need to trust someone on the inside. God I'm sounding more and more like a gangster by the minute.

'The thing is,' I whisper, pulling her towards me like a conspirator, 'I'm not really one of *them,* you know, a proper lady. I have no idea how to behave … and I've never had a ladies maid in my entire life. In fact, you're the first one I've ever met.'

I think her eyeballs will pop out in disbelief.

'Can I trust you, will you help me?' I ask pleadingly.

She hesitates for a moment and then becomes animated, pulling dresses and scarves from the rails.

'This dress,' she says, picking the one Brice had chosen at Marcus' shop, 'and with these shoes, and this scarf. If I were you I'd have your hair down too. It looks nicer that way, if you don't mind me so saying Miss Harriet?'

'You can say whatever you like but call me *Harriet*. All this Miss Harriet business is making me feel more spinsterish by the minute.'

She studies me intently.

'Let's ditch the silicone, your breasts are perfect.'

Perhaps she can tell Marcus that.

'I can't, the dress only works with them.'

'Bugger,' she blushes. 'Sorry Mi … Harriet.'

'Don't apologise. I'm capable of a lot worse.'

Twenty minutes later she stands me in front of the mirror and I stare transfixed by my own reflection. My skin looks dewy and youthful and my eyes are sparkling. Emily has performed miracles with eye make-up. My hair hangs in soft waves around my face. A look I've never been able to achieve.

'What do you think?' Emily asks proudly.

The sound of an arriving car makes my stomach lurch.

'I think I look stunning. Thanks Emily.'

I glance out of the window.

'I thought it was just family this evening,' I say, trying to hide the panic in my voice.

'Oh it is Mi ... Harriet. They have asked Major Bates ...'

'Major Bates?' I say laughing. 'Is that a grown-up version of Master Bates? He must have done a lot of wanking.'

'He's Madam Margarita's brother-in-law,' Emily says, diverting her eyes.

'Between you and me no one seems that keen on him, if you don't mind me saying Miss Harriet,' she whispers, 'Oh, and of course, Mr Brice will be coming,' she adds with a smile.

My stomach somersaults. Brice? She is kidding me right?

'Brice who?' I say hoarsely.

'Why Mr Hamilton's cousin of course, Mr Brice Edmunds.'

Oh my God. I'm well and truly fucked.

Chapter Thirteen

I have to admit I seriously thought about running out on both Hamilton and Julian after hearing that Brice Edmunds is not only here but is also Hamilton's cousin. Running away from this God-awful crappy weekend, whoops, I mean *ghastly* weekend, must not forget to keep up the posh lingo. I then decide that would be the coward's way out and I'm no coward. So, Brice Edmunds is here, and I have to admit even hearing his name makes my body quiver. Hamilton's cousin, I mean, who has such bad luck? No wonder my lucky dip ticket didn't have one sodding winning number. Well, there is nothing for it. I just have to face him and if he dobs me in then he is dobbing in Hamilton as well. I'm not taking all the blame.

I put on a brave face but I'm sweating like a nun in a field of cucumbers. A light spray of Caroline Herrera perfume and I am ready. Emily looks at me proudly. I take a deep breath and nod for her to open the door. The chiffon feels light and cool against my skin and I drift out onto the landing to the strains of lilting Gaelic music. There is laughter and the clinking of glasses. I reach the top of the stairs and admire the grandeur of the staircase. Portraits adorn the stairwell and seem to follow me with their staring eyes. I see Cedric hanging coats on a rack. He looks up and I shrug nervously. He gives me an encouraging wink and I cling onto the bannister. Well here goes. I shall probably leave claw marks all down it with my long talons. How do women cope with these *Wicked Witch of the East* nails? Do they have someone else tie up the laces on their trainers or what? I am halfway to the bottom when I see Brice walking towards Cedric. He follows Cedric's gaze and our eyes meet and lock. His face breaks into a smile and he acknowledges me with a nod. God, he looks gorgeous. He's wearing a crisp white shirt and the new tie he bought in Marcus's shop. He looks every inch the upper-crust gentleman in his dinner suit. At least he isn't wearing a kilt, although I have to admit a gander at his rope and tackle wouldn't be too distressing. His hair is freshly washed and his eyes twinkle at me. I really would love to drown in those eyes. He frowns slightly when I don't smile back. Oh God, this is awful. He is standing underneath a huge grandfather clock and for a minute it feels a bit like that Titanic under the clock moment, and strangely enough in that exact second it is like something clicks between us, and then he is holding out his arm for me to take. Why do I have this awful feeling that this is going to be the most humiliating night of my life?

'Hello Harriet. The dress is perfect.'

'What are you doing here?' I ask accusingly, forgetting that he has more bloody right to be here than I have.

He takes a step backwards.

'I could ask you the same question.'

'I mean it's lovely seeing you again. It's just everywhere I go you seem to be there,' I add quickly.

Jesus, now I'm almost accusing him of stalking me. But wouldn't that be a dream come true?

'Well, actually I'm here to meet my cousin's new girlfriend. And you?'

I pull an apologetic face.

'I am Hamilton's new girlfriend.'

I'm also thinking of doing a runner but I don't think I'd get very far in these shoes.

'Darling, there you are,' calls Hamilton and my heart sinks.

You know that feeling, the one where you just want the floor to open up and swallow you. I seriously want this whole main hall to disintegrate and devour me. I cannot believe that for the first time in my adult life I finally meet a man who makes my stomach somersault and my legs quiver, and better still actually seems to like me, and who in the next few seconds will be lost to me forever. I pull my shoulders back and turn a bright smile onto Hamilton.

'Sorry darling, you know how long it takes to get ready. I'm so eager to meet your grandmother.'

But not as eager as I am to leg it from this place. Brice is staring intently at me and I tense under his scrutiny, or perhaps squirm might be a better word. It then dawns on me if he is Hamilton's cousin then he is of course the other grandson. Oh no, hells bells, how much deeper in the shit can I get?

'Oh sorry Brice, I should have introduced you two. This is my girlfriend Harriet and this is my cousin Dr Brice Edmunds.'

Doctor? He really is out of my league isn't he? I should have a GP who looks like him. Maybe I should mention my mastitis; he may want to have a look. God, I'm out of control. Get a grip Harriet.

'Brice lives in the old stalkers' lodge when he's home. Not that he's home often,' laughs Hamilton.

He lives here? Jesus, how much worse can this get? If he's not home often why does he have to be home now? Brice doesn't laugh and his eyes continue to bore into mine. I struggle not to lower them and meet his gaze head on.

'So, you're the girlfriend we've heard so much about. Hamilton tells us you are an expert at clay pigeon shooting?'

What the fuck.

'Well I ...'

His soft features harden and his eyes narrow.

'I hope Harriet will be joining us at the shoot tomorrow. It will give us all a chance to get to know her better and she can show us her shooting skills,' he says, his eyes never leaving mine.

The bastard. What is he playing at? I'll show him my shooting skills all right and I'll make sure the first bullet has his name on it and the rest can have Jack, Jack and Jack on them. God I'm losing the plot, or my mind, one or the other, or possibly both.

'Well, I don't know Brice, Harriet has a lot of work to catch up on while she's here. Her jewellery business, you remember I told you about it?'

I nod and reach out to a passing butler who is offering cocktails. I knock back a vodka twist and shudder.

'And of course there is all her charity work,' adds Hamilton.

Jesus Christ. I grab another cocktail quickly before the butler has a chance to move.

'That wouldn't be Oxfam would it?' asks Brice with a sardonic smile and a cursory glance at my false breasts.

Oh no, one hasn't sunk has it? That's all I bloody need. I open my mouth to speak.

'Don't get Brice started on his hobby horse,' Hamilton laughs.

'Actually,' I say in my newly trained voice, 'I'm a huge supporter of Oxfam. I donate much of my earnings to them,' I add pompously.

Well, that certainly isn't an untruth is it? I've probably fed half of Ethiopia in the past two years.

'That's very charitable of you. We should discuss your philanthropy over dinner ...'

'I really don't like ...'

'Shall we go into the drawing room for aperitifs,' says Hamilton, anxiously grabbing my hand. I'm swept from the hallway and led towards the drawing room.

'I met Brice when I was with Marcus. He came to buy a tie,' I whisper.

He stops in his tracks.

'What,' he exclaims loudly and then lowers his voice. 'You weren't yourself were you?'

'Well I wasn't bleeding Pippa Middleton was I? Of course I was myself. He's suspicious of me. We should tell him Hamilton.'

He grips my arm tightly and pulls me into a corner.

'You don't tell Brice anything. He'll think I'm trying to steal his inheritance or something. It's not like that, obviously,' he says glancing quickly behind him. 'He's never here. He's always in Asia or somewhere equally filthy.'

'Asia?' I say admiringly.

'Just don't forget what I've paid in advance and if you mess this up, that's all coming back.'

I swear I will cut off Julian's ear/tongue/penis myself when I next see him. He releases his grip and leads me gently towards the drawing room again, where Brice is standing like a bloody centurion. He is probably going to announce the imposter. God I feel sick. Still it doesn't stop me popping a mini salmon tart into my gob. Well, a girl has got to eat after all. Anyway the way things are escalating here I may not even make it to dinner.

'Well, where is she?' growls a voice.

I glance nervously at the wheelchair which seems to be zooming dangerously towards us. The woman sitting in it is imposing indeed. Her naturally grey hair has been expertly pulled back into a neat bun in a style that makes her look younger than her years. She is stunningly beautiful and for someone very sick her skin glows. Her eyes are sharp and bright and they appraise me thoroughly and finally land on my face. The manic Stephen King cat sits demurely in her lap. She stops the wheelchair by a chaise longue. A hush falls over the room and Hamilton rushes to her side.

'Come here girl,' she says, her voice softening.

'You'd better go,' says Brice. 'I'd yank that right breast up first if I were you. Grandmother hates anything false as do I.'

I look at him sharply and the distrust in his eyes sends a sharp pain through me. He thinks I'm a gold-digger and a liar, and there is no way I can redeem myself. Of all the men to discover I am a fake why did it have to be him?

'It's not what you think?' I say, realising I sound just like Hamilton when he first approached me.

'Isn't it? You're seriously telling me you're not deceiving anyone here?'

Oh hell, if only I could explain.

'Harriet,' calls Hamilton.

I turn from Brice with a sigh and begin to make my way towards Hamilton and his grandmother. Okay, you just to need to remember you're just back from launching your new jewellery collection called *Harriet's* in New York. It has yet to take off here. I of course support the Tories and I read sociology at Cambridge. That's a joke. I'm barely managing to read Social Sciences at Marlborough Mansions with all the stress. I'm an expert horsewoman with a great love of hunting. Yeah right. I'm just getting over the death of my goldfish, I couldn't hunt a poor fox. I'm really not going to pull this off am I? I look behind and my eyes make contact with Brice Edmund's. My heart quickens and for a few seconds I find myself wishing that life could be different. You know, the kind of different where the three Jacks don't exist and the kind of different where I don't work in a laundrette, and the kind of different where I am the Harriet who owns the jewellery business and not the Harriet who in a few minutes will lie to everyone about the woman I really am. Why now? Why now has this man come into my life? And of course the truth is because the three Jacks exist and because I now have to be a different Harriet to get Julian and I out of debt. If the three Jacks hadn't come into Julian's life then Brice Edmunds wouldn't have come into mine. I stop in front of the wheelchair and a hush falls over the room and all that can be heard is the music playing softly in the background. Sebastian approaches us and lays a hand on my shoulder.

'Harriet, what can we tempt you with?' he says, gesturing to Cedric.

'Harriet is a champagne cocktail girl, isn't that right darling?' says Hamilton sliding an arm around my waist.

I feel myself tense and hope he doesn't notice. Right now I'm a *give me anything* with alcohol in it girl. Anything to numb this whole

91

experience but I accept the champagne cocktail gratefully and fight back the urge to knock it back in one.

'I'll have a Bloody Mary,' barks Grandmother, making me jump out of my skin.

No wonder the cat is so bloody demented.

'So you're Harriet, like cats do you?'

Generally, but your one is the exception to the rule.

'Adore them,' I lie, gingerly patting little Diamond who purrs happily. The two-faced little bugger.

She grabs my hand.

'Let's go into dinner. You can sit next to me. MELANIE,' she shouts.

Lady Lancaster practically trips over her dress in her haste to reach Margarita Lancaster's wheelchair.

'Rearrange the seating. I want Harriet next to me and Hamilton the other side. Put Brice opposite and for heaven's sake keep the Major away from me, the man drives me insane.'

She turns back to me.

'Harriet, wheel me in please.'

I look back to see Brice Edmunds watching me intently.

'It's going very well so far,' whispers Hamilton.

Bloody hell, what bleeding planet is he on?

'About as well as executions can go,' I whisper.

He gives me an odd look and follows us into the magnificent dining room. It's terribly impressive with shimmering crystal and candlelight. I've never seen so much crystal in my life. Beautiful chandeliers hang from the ceiling and stuffed stags' heads with antlers adorn each of the four walls. The dining table shimmers under the candlelight and is set out like a banquet. A manservant pulls back a chair for me and I realise all the men are waiting for me to sit. I blush and take my seat. I must try and get a grip and be more positive. Just ignore Brice Edmunds. After all what can he accuse me of? Buying clothes from Oxfam and talking differently the last time he saw me and of course, having slightly larger breasts than at our previous meeting. It's not against the law to have big breasts is it? I mean, it's not a crime. Oh God, what if he mentions Julian though? No, he's probably even forgotten I said my boyfriend's name was Julian. I mean, people don't really listen to what you say do they? I could well have been talking about Hamilton. I sigh with relief. I don't know what I have been worrying about. He can't even accuse me of not having my own business. Hamilton is quite right it is all going very well. I must stop worrying and calm down, otherwise I will blow the whole thing.

'So, we all get to meet you at last Harriet,' booms Hamilton's father. 'Major, you haven't been introduced to Hamilton's girlfriend have you? Harriet this is Major Bates.'

The Major stands up and leans drunkenly across the table towards me. Good grief, he is pissed already and we haven't even started dinner. Margarita Lancaster sniffs loudly.

'Jolly nice to meet you,' he slurs, raising his bushy eyebrows and staring at my breasts. The creep is almost dribbling. I tactfully ignore his outstretched hand and smile politely. He's the ugliest man I have ever met, his nose and cheeks are bright red, and he stinks of wine. How can anyone have a name like Major Bates? It's criminal. He continues to stare at me with his puffy eyes until Sir Sebastian pushes him back into his seat.

'So how is the gout?' he asks as the Major gestures for the butler to refill his wine glass.

'Getting worse I imagine,' snaps Margarita who then tuts as a bowl of soup is placed in front of her.

'What is this?' she demands.

'Cock-a-leekie,' Lady Hamilton says anxiously. 'I thought ...'

'Not the soup, the china. Where's my china? I asked them specifically to put the china out that Garret and I brought back from Asia.'

'Oh, I forgot to ask Lionel, I'll ...' Melanie says getting more flustered by the minute.

'You've been to Asia,' I say unable to hide the excitement in my voice. Has everyone is this family been to Asia?

Margarita turns to me, a half smile on her lips.

'I've been all round the world my dear.'

The Major begins to talk to Brice and the table begins to settle into the meal and I relax a bit more.

'I've always wanted to go to Asia. I have this ...'

Hamilton glares at me.

'Penchant for travel,' he interrupts. 'She's always on a plane. The jewellery business is taking off very well isn't it Harry?'

Shit, that's my first slip up. It's only a matter of time really isn't it? They'll see through me and that will be it for Julian. His bullet-ridden body will be found in the blood-soaked boot of the Pooch. I pick up my roll and go to dip it into my soup when I see Brice Edmunds watching me. I smile at him and break the roll in half and take a small bite before spooning some soup into my mouth. Shit, this is harder than I thought it would be.

'I couldn't stand the place,' mumbles the Major, slurping his soup. 'Everyone eating damn crickets and beetles. Blooming awful place if you ask me. How you do it Brice old man I'll never know.'

I look up at Brice. Blimey, do what exactly? Eat crickets and beetles?

'I agree, and as for that boat ...' begins Hamilton.

'Oh yes, I will be,' bellows Major Bates. 'I rather think that old chap Cameron will get in again. After all we can't have the country run by that other mob. They'll be council houses popping up all over the place.'

He burps loudly and rubs his fat belly. I try not to look too disgusted. What a cheek. My parents live in a very nice council house thank you very much. Not that I am a Labour supporter. Frankly I think they're all as bad as each other. But what's wrong with a council house?

'Boat Major, not vote,' laughs Hamilton, glancing sideways at me.

'There's nothing wrong with the boat actually. It might not be a yacht but it serves its purpose,' says Brice chewing his roll so sensually that it's almost arousing.

'Not everyone can live in a stately home,' I say before I've even realised I've said it.

There is an embarrassing silence and all eyes turn to me. Major Bates looks flustered and peers at me with his bloodshot eyes.

'I suppose you're right. Can't have everyone in mansions can we. Who'd wait at table, what?'

What a snob. I've a good mind to ...

'I imagine having read sociology at Cambridge you have strong opinions on the structure of our society, and politics in general,' says Brice Edmunds with a smirk on his face.

Why is he doing this to me? I feel an overwhelming urge to cry and struggle to hold back my tears. Margarita looks intently at me.

'Don't discuss politics at the table Brice. It raises my blood pressure,' she snaps.

I lean back as Cedric removes my soup bowl. I'm somewhat relieved that's over. Holding a spoon is ten times worse than a knife and fork.

'I'd lose those nails if I were you darling. They're more like claw extensions than false nails, and if you're not careful you're more likely to gouge someone's eyes out and it may well be poor little Diamond's,' Margarita whispers.

Don't give me ideas. Diamond glares at me with evil green eyes. Honestly, if I didn't know better I'd say he was the devil incarnate.

'Besides they make you look predatory rather than glamorous,' she continues.

'I'd love nothing better than to whip the bleeding things off ...' I whisper in return and stop. Her eye catches mine and I pull a face.

Sod it. I just knew I'd bugger it up somewhere. She raises her eyebrows and purses her lips but I can't tell if it's disapproving or not. There is so much noise as the waiters dish up the main course that I feel sure no one else overheard us.

'As for those breasts, well my dear, you could feed half of Africa with those.'

I stop myself from choking on my wine.

'You have a wonderful home,' I say in a feeble attempt to gloss things over.

'Oh,' she says dismissively. 'This is just a small estate my dear. Heavens, when I think of how large Glenwood once was. Of course we gave away a lot of the land. My son is not financially minded and one gets into difficulties.'

Difficulties, is she serious? I can tell her about difficulties. I bet no one has ever threatened Sir Sebastian's ears, or made them an offer they couldn't refuse. That bloody cat would be the first thing to end up in a box if they did. Mind you there isn't any offer they can't refuse is there? Not with all their millions.

'So, do you think we are less of a classless society now Harriet? For instance do you feel the division between the working classes and the upper classes is narrowing or widening?' pushes Brice Edmunds. 'I'd be interested in your expert knowledge.'

'Do we have to talk politics at the table,' smiles Melanie. 'One always argues don't you think.'

I lift my head and meet his stare head on.

'In my expert opinion, to discuss such matters over a family dinner seems not only rude but highly inappropriate in front of those one might offend,' I say inclining my head slightly to Emily and Cedric who stand expressionless at the back of the room.

Christ, did I say all that and in that voice? My elocution teacher would be proud if only she were here. Brice lifts his eyebrows slightly and gives me a small nod. He is so handsome. In fact he looks quite exquisite in candlelight, like some kind of god.

'Quite right Harriet,' says Margarita and in the next breath clicks her fingers at Emily. 'It's time for Diamond's treat, see to it will you?' Emily nods and gives me a cheeky smile.

'Do you have cats?' asks Margarita.

She must be kidding. I can barely feed myself at the moment let alone a stupid cat.

'No, I'm far too busy to give it the love and attention it needs,' I smile.

'They don't take much looking after. Independent creatures are cats. Diamond is an Abyssinian.'

So that's what you call frenzied uncontrolled cats these days is it?

'Yes, how do you find the time to do everything? Hamilton was telling us that you barely get a break from work,' asks Melanie, who had so far only eaten a third of a bread roll, while I'm struggling not to wolf everything down as quickly as possible. After all I'm never going to eat like this again am I? Even with all my debts paid off I won't exactly be feasting on salmon, unless you count salmon fishcakes, which is not quite the same is it? Cedric removes my salmon starter and replaces it with duck in orange sauce, fluffy mashed potatoes, and offers an assortment of vegetables. I've never eaten duck in my life. I've fed them, but never actually eaten them. I feel rather guilty at even considering it.

'Are these from the shoot last week,' bellows Major Bates, spitting bits of bread over Melanie's floral laced bodice.

She brushes herself down delicately and grimaces at Sir Sebastian. I stop with my fork halfway to my mouth. They shot the poor little thing on its home ground? That's just barbaric. Just when the poor little bugger felt safe, they shot the little sod. Oh I hate these people. What am I doing here? I should stand my ground, stick to my principles and all that. Except I'm in no position to have any principles am I? We all sit silently and eat. Just as I start to relax Brice says,

'Harriet is an expert ...'

I swear I shall stuff a roll so far down his throat in a minute.

'I've got an announcement to make,' butts in Hamilton.

'What are you doing?' I say through clenched teeth.

'I was going to wait until after dessert ...'

I so wish he had.

'But for those who didn't see the notice in *The Times*, I wanted to tell everyone here that I asked Harriet to marry me and she has amazingly agreed to take me on.'

Like the fool that I am.

'I bet she has,' says Brice cynically.

Everyone goes silent apart from Major Bates who continues to masticate noisily. Then Melanie suddenly jumps up and enfolds me in a warm hug, covering me in a cloud of perfume. I fight back a sneeze.

'Isn't that just wonderful Margarita? Cedric, Cedric,' she calls. 'You can open that champagne now.'

'Congratulations son,' beams Sir Sebastian 'and welcome to the family Harriet.'

Hamilton grins like a Cheshire cat. I glance sideways to see Margarita looking at me.

'And why would you want to marry my lazy lump of a grandson?' she asks.

Melanie fights back a gasp and Hamilton sighs heavily. Sir Sebastian seems to make a feeble attempt to stand up but Melanie puts a restraining hand on his arm and he sits back down immediately. Cedric approaches with the champagne and Melanie indicates for him to wait. This is it, this is the moment when I am exposed for the fraud that I am. I try to look her in the eye but of course I can't because I know I will be lying. Instead I focus on her dark hair which is peppered with grey and perfectly drawn back into a beautiful knot at the nape of her neck. Her brown watery eyes study me but there is a glint in them. Yes, why would I want to marry Margarita's lazy lump of a grandson? Where do I start? Do I mention my boyfriend's penis/tongue/ears and the fact that he may be hanging upside down in someone's freezer minus all three. Or shall I just give a censored version of Harriet and the three Jacks, or the tale of There once was a little goldfish. No perhaps not. She waits patiently and I feel an awful urge to tell the truth.

'Well, what can I say from the moment he propositioned me ...'

Hamilton's head snaps up with a crack. Major Bates lifts his bushy eyebrows. I was certainly right to have him down as a bucking pervert as Mrs Mollard would say. Margarita cocks her head to one side.

'Harriet,' says Hamilton nervously, 'what are ...'

'With a business offer for some jewellery ...' I add.

Well I can't put the poor sod in it now can I? What a tangled web we weave. Talking about weaving, that bloody Diamond is rolling all around the floor at my feet with the gold chain of my very expensive clutch bag in his mouth. If the little git goes for my dress I swear I shall kick him all the way to the pet cemetery and back. Margarita laughs and Melanie lets out a relieved sigh.

'I knew I couldn't resist him,' I finish with a smile. That's not too far from the truth is it?

Brice stands up abruptly.

'Excuse me. I have to make a phone call,' he says sharply.

'At this very moment?' asks Margarita. 'We're in the middle of dinner.'

He nods.

'Yes, Grandmother at this very moment, will you excuse me.'

He's probably going to phone someone superior to have me thrown out on my ear. Oh Jesus, why is it ears seem to come into everything?

'So, when is this wedding and how much is it going to cost us?' asks Margarita pointedly. 'And talking of jewellery, where is the ring?'

Yes, just where is my ring Hamilton? He puts an arm affectionately around his grandmother's shoulders.

'I was thinking of great grandmother's ring. Do you remember?'

Major Bates tucks his serviette further down his shirt, and gestures to Cedric for a top-up.

'It all seems a bit rushed if you ask me,' he murmurs.

God, how many more hours before the weekend is over? I hope he isn't staying overnight.

'Well, no one asked you did they,' Margarita growls. 'And I think you've drunk more than enough of our best claret don't you?'

He plonks his glass down, scratches his neck self-consciously and mumbles.

'Where's the Eton Mess anyway? I was looking forward to that.'

Like he hasn't made enough of his own mess, and what the hell is Eton Mess when it's at home, and if Hamilton thinks I'm eating something with a name like that he can think again.

'What do you think Sebastian? Your grandmother's ring is, after all, just sitting in a box. Melanie turned her nose up at it ...' grumbles Margarita.

'That's not strictly true,' interjects Melanie.

'And Victoria is so, what's that word ...'

'Bohemian, unconventional, honest, unpretentious,' says Brice returning to the table. 'I think those are the right words for my mother.'

'Yes, all those, she wouldn't be seen dead wearing that ring apparently, so Harriet if it fits, the ring shall be yours.'

'Absolutely,' agrees Sir Sebastian, looking relieved.

I feel like Cinderella, except this is no sodding fairy tale. I'm sitting at a table with a pompous arse named Major Bates and a Sir, who is lovely but has a penchant for shooting his own ducks. A soon-to-be fiancé who wears a skirt and a grandmother who is scarier than all three Jacks put together and that is pretty hard to be let me tell you, not to mention a neurotic soon-to-be mother-in-law and a seriously demented cat. The only consolation is that I have the gorgeous cousin to look at. I smile gratefully.

'Isn't that wonderful darling? An heirloom. That makes it special doesn't it?' gushes Hamilton.

It also makes it cheap for you I think. What is wrong with me, I am beginning to sound so hateful? Hamilton stands and I attempt my most loving look. I allow him to entwine his hand in mine and kiss me on the lips, except the kiss seems to linger longer than it should.

'You lingered,' I whisper.

'Yes, I'm sorry,' he says quietly.

Good God, now what's going on?

'I don't want you lingering again,' I hiss.

'I won't'

I feel Brice's eyes on us and deliberately squeeze Hamilton's hand before he leaves me to return to his seat.

'Cedric, the champagne, and we'll have dessert now,' Margarita orders.

The Major grunts in appreciation, and sneakily pours more wine into his glass. What a pompous ass, honestly. Hamilton blows me a kiss and I nearly fall off the chair. He's going a bit over the top isn't he? I attempt another loving look but the smile is such a strain that I must look like I've been freshly botoxed. To make matters worse bloody Diamond is clawing at my new chiffon dress and the temptation to gouge his eyes out is overwhelming.

'We'll check the ring first thing tomorrow and I'll get Jeremy to come on Monday to prepare for the fitting. Now, what about the engagement party? We'll have the party here, I can't think of a better place. We have our own staff and ...' she takes a breath.

I look at Hamilton with an open mouth. I can't stay here for a ring fitting, why doesn't he say something? Shit, this bleeding cat is driving me bonkers.

'The thing is ...' I begin

'Eton Mess madam?' asks Cedric.

'Well, I ...'

'Raise your glasses to Harriet and Hamilton,' announces Sebastian.

'Harriet and Hamilton,' they chorus.

I smile and clink glasses.

'I don't think Harriet has had Eton Mess before. Isn't that right Harriet?' asks Brice.

He is such an arse. His face will be an Eton Mess if he doesn't shut up, and so will this bloody Diamond's.

'Yes I have,' I say defensively, pulling my dress away from Diamond and hearing a rip.

'And of course we need to arrange a meeting with Chantell about the dress ...' continues Margarita. 'When are we going to meet your parents?'

As late as possible, and who the fuck is Chantell?

'Harriet's family are currently holidaying on St Martha's Vineyard. Obviously we've yet to tell them the good news. They'll be thrilled,' says Hamilton.

What is he saying? The closest my parents have come to a vineyard of any kind is the local offy at the end of their street.

'Harriet, you and I can go over the arrangements and sort out our diaries for next week. Melanie, I trust you'll be around to help. You're not having a facial, manicure or whatever it is you spend your time doing are you?' barks Margarita.

'Well, I ...' Melanie stammers.

'Good. That's settled then. You can then compare diaries with your mother when she returns Harriet.'

Yeah right, as if. I can just see my mum opening her freebie Good Housekeeping diary to jot down notes. Oh, this is becoming too gruesome for words. I pull faces at Hamilton. Why doesn't he say something?

'The thing is Grandmother, we don't want to rush into ...'

Thank God.

'Like I have all the time in the world? You'd begrudge your dying grandmother this last pleasure,' she says placing her champagne glass down with a thud. Good job it's decent crystal.

'The thing is ...' I begin.

'Do you know what is in it exactly?' asks Brice.

What the hell.

'What,' I snap.

'Eton Mess, do you know what's in it?'

I fiddle with my napkin and Diamond dives for it. I give him a little kick and he hisses.

'Oh good heavens, is that Diamond?' says Melanie alarmed.

'Diamond darling, come to Mummy,' calls Margarita.

I lean down and grab the satanic feline by the collar and discreetly throw him towards his mistress.

'Oh dear,' I say sympathetically, 'I think he tangled himself in my bag strap. He looks fine though.'

That's more than can be said for my dress.

'Well?' asks Brice.

I grit my teeth.

'Yes, well of course I do. Everyone knows what Eton Mess is ...'

He waits expectantly and it is all I can do not to slap his face.

'It's a mess of different things isn't it?'

I feel my face turn red.

'Quite right madam, I couldn't have described it better myself,' says Cedric, placing a dish in front of me. 'A nice mess of whipped cream, strawberries and meringue,' he smiles.

I give Brice the finger under the table. That's one up for me.

'The problem is I have to leave on Sunday evening. I've got so much work on.'

Well that's not exactly a lie is it? I have to be back to the laundrette on Monday. Margarita stops with her spoon poised by her mouth. That obviously didn't go down very well.

'Well, that's pretty awful Harriet, if your PA can't cover things for a few days,' says Melanie. 'No wonder you look so drawn and tired.'

I do? I'm not sure if that is a back-bloody-handed compliment or not.

'Tell her to come up for a few days. We've plenty of room. Right that's settled, you can work from here. After all, what is more important than your wedding?' Margarita says firmly her eyes daring me to argue with her.

I scoop a spoon of Eton Mess into my mouth and Cedric winks at me. God, he's on the ball isn't he? He knows I'm a fraud and he loves it. That's two allies.

'Quite right old girl,' says Brice to his grandmother. I nearly choke on my Eton Mess. He calls her old girl?

'Besides we all need to get to know you better. I for one would love to hear about your business and your philanthropy, and what you like to do in your spare time, aside from your Oxfam connection of course.'

He smiles. I give him an evil stare. It is amazing how quickly you can go off people. The Eton Mess comforts me and I eye up Cedric for a bit more. What the hell am I going to do? I now have to explain to the laundrette why I won't be in for half the week and somehow conjure up a PA.

'Now, do you have your diary, or do you use one of those silly Bluebell things?'

'Shall we do this over coffee?' suggests Hamilton.

Before either of us can reply Cedric interjects,

'So sorry to interrupt madam but Miss Lawson's PA is on the phone and she says it is urgent.'

Talk of the devil. But, oh shit, this can only mean bad news.

'Excuse me,' I say as I wobble clumsily from the dining room.

Chapter Fourteen

If the only mess I had in my life was Eton Mess I'd be a happy bunny. I can't believe this is happening. One minute I am swanning off to a posh wedding and the next I am in the middle of a remake of *The Godfather* film, with offers I daren't, let alone can't, refuse. Fiona is in a state, gulping and sobbing so much it is near impossible to hear what she is raving about.

'So what happened?' I ask, not wanting to know.

'It's really bad Harry, I mean these guys aren't messing.'

That reminds me of the Eton Mess. I know I shouldn't dwell on it but I wonder if I can ring a bell or something to get Cedric to bring me seconds.

'What do you mean and can you calm down?'

'Well I'm bloody premenstrual,' she screams, 'so don't tell me to calm down. There's no buggery chocolate in the place either. Why is there never chocolate this time of the month, you would think by now I'd be better prepared ...'

'So what happened Fi?' I probe gently.

'I sent Alistair out to get some.'

'Not the bloody chocolate! What happened with the Jacks?'

'They said they needed a little holiday.'

Oh good, hopefully they'll get a one way ticket to Timbuktu.

'And Scotland seemed as good a place as any,' she sobs.

'Scotland?' I cry. 'How do they know I'm in Scotland?

'I kind of let it slip.'

'What the ...' I groan.

How could she let something like that slip?

'I didn't mean to,' she adds quickly. 'They were going on about their monkey ...'

Shame they don't want a cat.

'And how Jules is going to have to suffer some pain for your oversight. What if they have Julian, we don't know do we? Then he said, *"she's not 'aving a nice 'oliday in Scotland by any chance, is she?"* That's how he speaks.'

'I do know how he speaks Fi.'

'And before I knew it, I'd said "but she couldn't help it" and ...'

'Oh shit Fiona, why didn't you just take out an ad in *The Times*.'

After all, that's what everyone else seems to do. Now I'm right up the creek without a paddle.

'Don't have a go at me, it's not my fault you got involved with East End thugs is it?'

'I didn't, Julian did.'

I stare out of the window at the loch that is shimmering under the light of the moon and curse under my breath. Even a nice long hot bath doesn't feel very appealing unless I can drown in it.

'Okay, tell me everything, slowly and calmly, and please don't speak like the Jacks, it unnerves me.'

She takes a breath and says,

'Okay, so I slipped up and said it wasn't your fault you were in Scotland and that you were keen, I said very keen in fact, to arrange the meet and give them their money. Jack Diamond said *"Well I don't trust anyone who hops it off to bleeding Scotland when they owes me money"*. He said you were taking a *diabolical liberty*, and then he said *"me and the lads ain't"* ...'

I sigh.

'Sorry, *haven't had a holiday in yonks*. They think it's time they did and Scotland is as good a place as any. He said they have friends they can pop and see. I think by friends they meant you. It was sarcasm or something.'

'I know that. Christ, this couldn't get any worse if it tried. I think I need to go to the mattresses.'

'Where's that?'

The only thing I do know about *The Godfather* and no one else does. Yes, well that figures. I exhale.

'Why is it when I need one of those emails from someone in Kenya who has millions to give away, I don't get one?'

'I never get those,' says Fiona thoughtfully. 'I just get the ones offering me a larger penis. Sometimes I do wonder what it would be like having a larger one. I've never measured Alistair's but I imagine it's standard size.'

What is she on about?

'Fiona, they're not offering you a penis. It's for men, to help make their penises bigger.'

God, how did I get into this?

'Oh, that makes more sense,' she says.

How she ever got to be an accountant I'll never know.

'The thing is I've got to stay here for a few more days ...' I say changing the subject.

'What, but you can't ...'

'I've got to plan the wedding with the grandmother. I'm going to try and talk to Hamilton tomorrow, meanwhile I need you to phone the laundrette, I'll have to pull a sickie, tell them I've gone down with shingles or something.'

'But you said it was only going to be a weekend. I don't want to be here on my own next week. Alistair is going away on business.'

I don't think Alistair would be much use. It would take him half an hour to say what emergency services he needed.

'You have to go down with shingles too,' I say quickly.

There is silence and after a few seconds she whispers.

'No Harry.'

'I need a PA and you're the only person I can think of although so far I think your PA skills stink.'

But at least she is with Vodafone. I pull the curtains. Christ the Jacks might be out there. Didn't they shoot through the bedroom window in *Godfather two*, or was it *Godfather three*?

'But, I'll bugger it up.'

Yes most likely.

'You'll be safe though. With all these people here the Jacks wouldn't dare do anything, and you can go riding. You can borrow my riding outfit.'

I can practically hear her brain whirring as she considers it.

'Okay, but how do I get there? And I'm doing this under sufferance. I want you to know that.'

I feel better already. I just need a glass of champagne and a bowl of Eton Mess and I might actually be able to sleep.

'I'll speak to Hamilton and get you here by private helicopter. You said you fancied that?'

'I also fancy Johnny Depp, but I don't expect him to come knocking at the door whereas Jack Diamond, I do.'

I spend five minutes calming her down until Alistair returns with the chocolate. I flop onto my bed and plump the pillows behind my head and exhale loudly. My body begins to relax slowly and I feel the tension ebb away. I need to spend a few minutes going through my folder. I peek through the curtains and look wistfully at the stars. What was I thinking? I should have known this wouldn't go to plan. I must look on the bright side. I'm getting out of debt. My hair is in the best condition ever and it didn't cost me a penny. I'm getting some decent slap-up meals and free Clinique face treatments. I yawn and pull back the satin covered duvet. Oh yes, this is the life. If only I could marry Hamilton. That lingering kiss wasn't so bad, maybe I could grow to love him and perhaps this will turn out to be a fairy tale. There is a light tap at the door and I freeze.

'It's Cedric, Miss Harriet. Lady Lancaster sent you up a nightcap.' I open the door to see him holding a silver tray with a large brandy and a bowl of Eton Mess.

'I hope you don't mind madam, I thought you would like a little dessert before bed.'

This guy is good, he can read my mind. I open the door for him to enter.

'Mr Hamilton said he will see you at breakfast at ten o'clock sharp to discuss things with you, and wishes you a pleasant night.'

'Thank you Cedric,' I say, putting out my hand for the tray.

'May I suggest Miss Harriet that you get out of the habit of helping the staff?'

'Oh, I didn't mean ...'

God, I've offended the bloody domestics now.

'It's fine madam, it's just others may notice. Mr Brice for example might think it odd behaviour for a lady of your means.'

He winks and places the tray by the bed.

'Sleep well Miss Harriet.'

I settle myself back on the bed with the brandy in one hand and spoon Eton Mess into my mouth with the other. I need to get my strength up for tomorrow's shenanigans and I need to yank these stupid nails off.

Chapter Fifteen

I open my bleary eyes and groan. My head feels like Jack Diamond had slipped into my room in the middle of the night and walloped it with a hammer. I attempt to sit up and feel so nauseous that I fall back onto the pillows. Obviously I'm not used to the rich life. All that gin, champagne and brandy, mixed with a large portion of Eton Mess has turned my brain into jelly. I lean gingerly across to the bedside table and pour the contents of an Evian bottle down my throat. My mobile says six a.m. and the room is stiflingly hot. I peel off the satin duvet which is stuck to my sweaty body and fall out of the bed. Why do they have the heating on so high? It's like an oven in here.

'Oh God,' I groan as I crawl to the bathroom and lean my head over the toilet. Fresh air, that's what I need. I step into the shower and stand under the water while it stings my tender body. Finally, I squeeze into my jeans, grab my chunky Aran jumper and scarf, and quietly open my door. Everywhere is still and silent and the only sound is the ticking grandfather clock at the bottom of the stairs. I tiptoe down them, ignoring the snooty portraits, and feeling my head thump with every step. There is clattering emanating from the kitchen. I hesitantly open the door to see the cook kneading bread and Cedric sitting on a rocking chair reading the newspaper. They gape at me and I remember I have damp hair and am wearing no make-up. I must look like I've just escaped from *Shaun of the Dead*.

'Good morning Miss Harriet,' says Cedric, jumping up. 'Shall we bring you breakfast into the dining room?'
Just the word breakfast makes my stomach gurgle and I fight back a gag.

'Is anyone else up?' I ask in a croaky voice.
The cook looks at Cedric and smiles.

'No Miss, no one will be up until well gone ten.'
I look longingly at her steaming mug and sniff at the coffee aroma before moving towards the kettle.

'I'll just make myself a coffee and take it out. I need fresh air,' I say weakly.

I pick up the kettle and cook utters a little cry.

'Cedric,' she says sharply.

'Miss Harriet, you must let us make you coffee. Where would you like it?'

Honestly, can't these toffs make a simple cup of coffee for themselves?

'There is no one else here Cedric. You finish your paper and cook can finish the bread, and I'll make my own coffee. I'm not bleeding helpless. You don't have any aspirin do you?'

They watch bemused as I make a mug of coffee. Cook says cheerfully.

'It's Alka Seltzer you'll be wanting.'

She plops two into a glass of water. Moments later I throw back the fizzing liquid and, with coffee mug in hand, open the door.

'I can't get lost can I?' I ask.

Cedric, stuck for words, shakes his head. It occurs to me that the Jacks may be at large but console myself that they probably don't surface until ten either. I emerge into a beautiful garden. Ahead of me is the loch shimmering in the early morning mist. I hug the coffee mug and walk slowly, breathing in the fresh dew-filled morning air. I stroll leisurely around the loch; it is incredibly beautiful. You don't see this in Battersea at six in the morning. It makes a change from discarded needles, street sleepers huddled in doorways and an assortment of litter from the night before. Mind you, it's bloody freezing here and the clouds are threatening rain again. I sip my coffee and follow the bank of the loch when I see a lodge ahead. It is surrounded by a veranda and through the mist I can make out someone sitting there. As I approach I see that *the someone* is in fact Brice Edmunds, and he is drinking from a cup and studying me. I turn to go back but am stopped by his voice.

'You're an early riser. Can I offer you coffee?'

I hold up my coffee mug.

'I'm fine thank you.'

If I had any hopes of bagging Brice Edmunds I can now most certainly forget it. Suffering from a hangover without any make-up and my hair looking a sight must be the most terrifying thing ever. If this were Loch Ness I would be mistaken for the monster. I should have sought out Diamond before I left the house. That would have put him in his place. The cat that is, not Jack Diamond. I think it will take a lot more than me without make-up and scary hair to frighten him off. To top it all, I realise my Aran jumper has a hole in the sleeve.

'Can I tempt you with a top-up then?' he calls and I can hear laughter in his voice. Actually, a top-up would be rather nice. I edge a little closer to the veranda.

'Well that's it. You're definitely trespassing so you might as well have a top-up and some toast,' he says lifting the cafetiera. The veranda has an awning and although it's a little chilly I can see the attraction of sitting here. The stunning scenery around Glenwood is truly breathtaking.

'Beautiful isn't it? This is the best time of day whatever the season.'

He pushes a chair towards me. I hesitantly sit and wonder why he is being so friendly. He is smiling but the smile doesn't reach his eyes and I can tell he is suspicious of me. He studies me closely and hands me the mug. I take it from him and meet his eyes. His hair is damp and there is a soft smell of soap emanating from him. He's wearing a brown woollen jumper and a pair of faded jeans. He pushes a plate of toast and a jar of marmalade towards me. The walk has made me hungry and I spread a layer of marmalade onto the toast, and am about to take a bite when he says,

'You know, something has been bothering me all night. Do you know what it is?'

Holy shit, I've got a good idea. I shake my head and try to look innocent.

'Why Hamilton didn't introduce you to me at Silvia and Hugh's wedding.'

I sip my coffee and feel my face suffuse with blood. Why didn't my soon-to-be bloody fiancé listen to me yesterday when I said we needed to talk to Brice? I'm such a bloody awful liar.

'Perhaps it slipped his mind,' I say stupidly.

Like your soon-to-be fiancée slips your mind. Although it's not that hard to believe is it? I mean, I seem to have completely slipped Julian's mind, unless of course he really is hanging upside down in someone's freezer and no longer has a mind to slip.

'And, why you don't seem like the same Harriet I met at the wedding and then later at the dress shop.'

His voice is hard and with every word his eyes narrow. Christ, I wish I could think of a snappy answer.

'I don't like people deceiving my grandmother. If I find out that you ...'

At that moment a truck drives manically towards the lodge. Brice jumps from his chair and almost leaps from the veranda. The truck screeches to a halt and a breathless well-built man jumps from the driver's seat.

'Sorry Brice, I would have phoned but I didn't ...'

The man has a thick Scottish accent and wild wiry red hair and a beard to match. Brice rushes round to the passenger side and helps someone out.

'What happened?' he asks sharply.

'I'm not sure. We were sawing the logs and the next minute he stumbled upon us. He passed out and I saw his jacket and all this blood. It looks bad. He wouldn't let us take him to the hospital. He's well drunk. I've seen him in the woods but ...'

'Can you help me Angus, he's fighting me.'

I watch as they struggle with the person in the passenger seat. I then see it is a tramp and the fumes from his breath reach me before they even get him to the veranda and I thought I had a hangover. God, I bet he'll feel pretty rough later. There is a deep gash in his right arm and his old tatty suede jacket is soaked with blood.

'Harriet, would you fetch my medical bag. It's on the floor by the kitchen table. Let's get him into the bedroom and if you're not too squeamish can you bring a bowl of warm water. There's a small bowl in the cupboard under the sink,' he says brusquely.

Bleeding hell, quick with his orders isn't he? Squeamish my backside. What a sodding cheek. Do I look like a stupid squeamish blonde? Honestly, the presumptuous bugger. I fumble around the kitchen cupboard resisting the urge to nosy about, and fill the bowl with warm water before opening the medical bag and removing bandages and tape. I see he has medications too, and find the antibiotics. Squeamish, I'll show him. The other man offers to take the bowl from me but I shake my head and walk to the other side of the bed which is neatly made with sheets, blankets and covered in an ethnic bedspread which he'd obviously brought back with him from abroad. I stare at it enviously for a second and remember all my dreams. I feel a little stab of loss knowing that now those dreams are just that and are unlikely to become a reality for some time now, thanks to Julian's irresponsibility. The room stinks of alcohol and the man's unwashed body. Brice has removed the man's jacket and now rips at the sleeve of his shirt. At the sight of the wound Angus gasps and turns to the door. The wound looks a few days old and is already turning septic. I soak cotton wool in the water and hand it to Brice. He begins cleaning the wound gently and I watch fascinated as his large hands work swiftly and deftly.

'It will need ...'

'Suturing,' I finish for him.

His head snaps up and his eyes meet mine. He nods at me. Ah, a bit of respect at last. About bloody time too. Just because I don't talk posh and didn't go a fancy school doesn't mean I am plain Jane with no brain thank you very much.

'Can you pass the scissors from the bag?' he asks softly.

I remove the scissors but instead of handing them to him I begin to gently cut away at the dead skin. I feel his eyes on me. The man groans. The stench of urine reaches my nostril and I fight the urge to throw up the toast I'd just eaten. I lean over him and the fumes from his breath practically knock me out. I wouldn't like to be his liver and he certainly couldn't sell his kidneys.

'It's okay,' I say quietly. 'We need to clean the wound and then we'll close it up.'

I look up at Brice.

'He should go to hospital,' I say. 'He'll need a tetanus jab.'

'He won't go. I can give him that,' he says, closely watching me at work.

'Where did you learn to do that?' he asks.

'During my nursing training,' I snap.

He raises his eyebrows, bites his lips and then gently places his hand on mine.

'That's fine, I'll close it up.'

My body shivers and I feel sure he must feel it. His hand seems to linger on mine longer than it should.

'You and I should have a proper talk,' he says quietly.

I slide my hand away from under his and stand up.

'Actually, seeing as you're capable, perhaps you could fetch the tetanus vial from the fridge.'

'I think I can find it,' I say confidently.

The kitchen is a bit messy with a few unwashed mugs in the sink and a scattering of newspapers over the small kitchen table but the fridge is scrupulously clean. The top shelf has several boxes of vials and I search for a tetanus and take it to the bedroom. He takes it from me and nods.

'He has a small gash on his foot, perhaps you can clean and dress that,' he says abruptly without looking at me. I nod and check the foot. Ten minutes later after cleaning and dressing the wound I go out to the veranda.

'Thanks, I appreciate your help,' he mumbles. Angus is sitting nursing a mug of coffee. He turns sharply.

'Is he okay?'

'I'm sure he'll be fine. Brice seems to know exactly what he's doing.'

He smiles.

'Yes, he's brilliant. He never turns anyone away.'

Oh, I think he would like to turn me away pretty quickly if he could. He taps his head with his hand.

'I'm sorry, I'm being very rude. I'm Angus. I have a place along the road there. Are you here from London?'

'Yes, I'm visiting the family,' I say.

I take his outstretched hand.

'Nice to meet you,' I say politely.

Brice walks out onto the veranda and gives me a curious look.

'I've given him a sedative. He can sleep here for a few hours. I'll try and talk him into going to the hospital when he wakes up.'

Angus stands to leave. I take my cue and walk towards the steps leading down from the veranda.

'I'd better get back,' says Angus. 'Thanks Brice, I appreciate it.'

I go to follow when Brice's hand stops me and his eyes, sharp and bright lock onto mine. There is something raw and powerful about him and he almost commands me with his eyes not to turn away from him. I feel a mild throbbing between my thighs and fight back a gasp. God, what's happening to me? He removes his hand and I fall into the nearest chair. Surely he felt something too, but his eyes give nothing away.

'I'll make some fresh coffee,' he says calm and controlled.

'I'm fine,' I mutter but he obviously doesn't hear me. *I'm fine?* Blimey, that's a bloody understatement. I feel drawn to him like a magnet. I need to get this under control and quickly.

I fan myself with his newspaper. I feel like I'm on fire and the chilly morning air is doing nothing to dampen my flames. He returns with the coffee and pours us both a mug.

'So you're a nurse?' he says casually.

'Not any more. I was. I gave it up for ...'

'Oh yes, the jewellery business,' he says cynically. 'Quite a leap from nursing isn't it?'

I sip from the coffee and nod. He continues to look at me and I shift uncomfortably under his gaze.

'So you and Hamilton are madly in love are you?'

Right that's enough. If I stay here much longer and he keeps appraising me with those beautiful eyes of his I shall either reveal everything or throw myself wantonly onto his very desirable body. Both options best to be avoided I think. I stand up abruptly and knock my coffee mug over, spilling coffee across the table.

'I'm sorry,' I say, rushing into the house for something to clean it up. He moves towards the door at the same time and we collide and I find myself imprisoned in the doorway by his lean muscular body.

'I'll get it,' he says quietly, his shoulder lightly brushing my breasts. I fight back the small gasp that threatens to escape and squeeze myself away from him. I need to leave and soon, otherwise I won't be responsible for my actions. He is back before I have barely moved.

'I ought to get back,' I say trying to hide the tremble in my voice.

'Yes, back to your loving fiancé,' he says in that cynical tone I'm coming to know so well. Any thought I had of trying to explain the truth to him is instantly curtailed. He would never understand, in fact, he probably wouldn't even believe me. He has already formed an opinion of me and nothing I say will change that.

'Thank you for the coffee,' I say walking towards the steps.

'Thanks for your help.'

I nod and begin walking back to Glenwood Manor. Hopefully Fi will arrive this afternoon and I can relax a bit. I'm becoming an absolute bag of nerves. I'm not sure I can take much more of this.

Chapter Sixteen

Jack Diamond and Mad Jack Junior sit on a tartan rug overlooking a babbling stream. The thundering traffic of the M6 motorway, just a stone's throw away, spoils the otherwise tranquil Lakeland countryside. It's chilly, and Mad Jack shivers even though he is wearing the new leather jacket he bought at Petticoat Lane market.

'Don't yer think it's a bit taters to sit out 'ere Dad? Can't we go to a posh hotel for dinner? We've been on the road since five this morning,' he whines, throwing a stick in the water.

'What's a matter with yer? You a bleedin' man or mouse?' snaps Diamond.

He's not in a good mood. This prick Julian is beginning to get on his tits and his bloody girlfriend even more so. What the hell are they playing at? The prick vanishes and she finds herself a rich ponce and is now getting married. What's the world coming to? You don't owe punters money and then shove it in their mush that you've got plenty. That Julian's taking a diabolical liberty. Everyone is ripping everyone off these days; things ain't what they used to be. Well, no one messes with the firm and gets away with it.

'I bought this lovely new rug, all Scottish looking, and I thought we could 'ave a nice picnic on it. No gratitude you two, 'ave yer?'

Babyface Jack struggles with an oversized picnic basket and drops it onto the rug.

'Be bleedin' careful with that will yer?' snaps Diamond.

'You got a body in 'ere?' quips Babyface.

'I wish. That little prick Julian's will do. I'm telling yer, when I find him I'll 'ave more than a few verbals with the little shit.'

Mad Jack Junior dons some gloves and looks around.

'It's bloody taters 'ere, that's all I know. Ain't there anywhere round 'ere that does 'ot dogs or somethin'?' he asks scratching his arms.

Diamond shakes his head in exasperation.

'Yeah of course there is, and right around the corner is an ice cream stall an all.'

Babyface Jack's face lights up.

'Yeah really? I could kill a Raspberry Ripple,' he says getting up.

Diamond pulls him roughly onto the blanket.

'Sit on the bleedin' blanket you pair of sissies. We've come all this way and I said we'd 'ave a picnic when we got 'alfway, and a sodding picnic we're 'aving. Got it?'

Both men fall onto the blanket with heavy sighs.

'What about the 'ot dog?' asks Mad Jack.

'Don't be a bloody moron all your life. Do you see an 'ot dog van anywhere?'

He opens the basket and takes out a large foil wrapped parcel.

'What's this?' he asks, wrinkling his nose.

'That's me pilchard sarnies. You said I could bring 'em as long as I didn't put 'em near the other stuff.'

Diamond pulls a face and hands the parcel to Babyface.

'I'll 'ave a pork pie and scratchings. I suppose you packed them didn't yer?' asks Mad Jack rubbing his leg.

Two minutes later and the blanket is covered with pork pies, pilchard sandwiches, hard boiled eggs, pickled gherkins and crisps. Diamond uncorks a bottle of expensive wine and pours himself a glass.

'Why did yer get sodding Worcester Sauce crisps, Babyface? You thick or something? I said *Barbeque* didn't I?' groans Mad Jack Junior.

'I thought it was Barbeque. The bags look the same, it's not my fault,' mumbles Babyface as he struggles to open a bottle of Sprite. Diamond recoils as Sprite sprays from the loosened top over the picnic and splashes his white shirt.

'For Christ's sake, what the 'ell is wrong with you. You're like a bleedin' spastic sometimes. Pass those pickled gherkins before I bleedin' pickle you.'

'I don't know why we even 'ad to come to stupid Scotland anyway. I 'ate foreign people and foreign food,' moans Babyface. 'I bet there's no pie and mash shop 'ere either.'

He fidgets on the blanket next to Mad Jack.

'What the 'ells wrong with you two? Can't you sit bloody still for five sodding minutes?'

'I'm itching everywhere,' says Babyface, scratching his neck.

Diamond sighs. What the hell did he do wrong? He gave his boys everything and look at them now. This is what comes of spoiling. No bloody gratitude.

'We're 'ere because ole Julian's tart is 'ere remember? And if she thinks she can get away with just paying me a monkey she can think again.'

Mad Jack belches after drinking some Sprite and says,

'I 'ad Razor on the blower and he said it's a put up job. The old dear with all the money 'as given them an ult ... ulta ...well somethin' anyway, or she gives all her money and stuff to some bloke who isn't even family. I mean, that's bang out of order ain't it? You don't give outside family right? So this 'amilton's got to prove he's kosher by marrying a good 'un and showing himself all good and proper to run the family firm. That's what Razor said.'

'She is a good 'un,' says Babyface, going doe eyed. 'I really like 'er.'

'So be bloody grateful I've bought you 'ere for an 'oliday. I booked us into a nice B and B too. I want you lads to behave yourselves. No nicking from the old girl who owns it, you got that?' says Diamond leaning forward to scratch his ankles.

'Yes Dad,' says Babyface, tucking into a pilchard sandwich.

'Ow the 'ell you can eat that stuff I'll never know, and I asked you to get pork pie with egg. You can't get anythin' bloody right can yer?' Babyface shakes his head.

'No I can't.'

Mad Jack Junior laughs as Diamond clouts Babyface around the head. Stuffing two olives into his mouth he thinks of Harriet. She's also taking a diabolical liberty swanning off up here to Scotland. They're all bloody poofters up here, wearing their tartan skirts and whatnot? What kind of man would do that? If she really thought she could get away with this then she's got another think coming. In fact, after all this traipsing around after her he is beginning to think a monkey is not enough. After all, she can afford a bit more now she has a rich geezer for a boyfriend.

'There ain't even a bleedin' boozer 'ere,' sighs Mad Jack. 'We could 'ave 'ad a nice dinner if there was. After all we've been up since five. I thought we were stopping to 'ave a nice dinner somewhere.'

Diamond pulls up his sock and curses.

'You pair of pillocks; you only put the bleedin' blanket over an ants nest.'

Mad Jack jumps up and starts dancing around like a maniac.

'Right,' yells Diamond. 'Clear this lot and get in the bloody motor. You ungrateful little arses. You ain't got my blood in yer that's for sure,' he says, angrily kicking over the Sprite bottle.

'Well it ain't the bleedin' milkman's is it?' retorts Mad Jack Junior. 'He's as soft as a marshmallow he is.'

Babyface laughs.

'Let's get going,' Diamond orders. He ignores Babyface as he struggles with the picnic basket and the ants running up his leg. 'And shake the bloody blanket. I don't want the buggers in the motor.'

'Can I drive the motor the rest of the way?' asks Mad Jack Junior.

Diamond throws him the keys and grins as he looks at the shiny new van. Oh yes, he is going to get a lot out of old Julian and his bird before the week is out.

Chapter Seventeen

I watch the helicopter descend and a sense of relief envelopes me. I couldn't feel more secure if Daniel Craig were on board. By the time everyone had finished breakfast I had helped Brice with the tramp, visited the stables, checked out the tennis court and curiously wandered around the gun room. Honestly, there were enough guns in there to equip an army. At least I know where the weapons are if I bump into Jack Diamond. No way is he cutting off my ears or the ears of anyone in this house while I'm around and there is a gun room not far away. I think Jack Diamond may have bitten off more than he can chew this time. I'd done some serious thinking on my walk and I really don't see why I should let Julian, Diamond, Hamilton Lancaster or Brice Edmunds, come to that, interfere with my dreams. Let Brice expose me, ooh I rather wish he would. I don't remember ever getting this aroused with Julian. I only have to look at Brice Edmund's hands and I go all a tremor. The wind from the approaching helicopter whips at my hair and the engine noise deafens me. I step back and find myself in Brice Edmunds arms.

'Your PA is it? Is that the one who couldn't find her way to posh St John's Wood?' he says sarcastically.

Talk about blowing hot and cold. He seemed quite nice when I was helping him with the tramp. I turn on him angrily.

'Look, will you stop judging me. You don't know anything about me ...'

'Now isn't that just the truth.'

His eyes blaze and his gorgeous lips have turned a dark shade of pink. He's very sexy when he's angry. Correction, he is very sexy; period. Heavens, are those my nipples tingling, my real nipples that is? It's probably the mastitis. Maybe I should ask him to have a look. I don't want to get an infection from those falsies do I? I've chucked the things back in my suitcase along with the Morticia Adams nails. After all, there is a good chance I might gouge someone's eyes out like Margarita said, and most likely my own. I'm sure Marcus meant well but hopefully there won't be too many big dinners now.

'The padding is disappearing I see, who knows what we will be left with in the end,' he shouts above the roar of the helicopter while blatantly staring at my boobs. Jesus, I hope he doesn't see my erect nipples. That's a clear giveaway. I stop myself from looking down to see if he is giving anything away. Honestly, this is obscene, what am I thinking? Someone like Brice Edmunds, correction, Doctor Brice Edmunds is bound to have a girlfriend. She is most likely some top heart surgeon, who is at this very moment in the middle of some lifesaving heart operation, which is no doubt being filmed for some medical programme. Whereas I am a simple ex-nurse and barely even that. I'm just a laundrette manager and at the rate I'm going I'll be lucky if I keep that job. You do actually have to be at your job to keep it don't you? He leans close to me and for one terrifying moment I wonder what on earth he is going to do.

'You know, I just can't quite figure you out. You don't seem dishonest but something's not right here. How did you go from a NHS career in nursing to setting up an international jewellery business?'

I can smell the freshness of him and the memory returns of his closeness to me back at his lodge and my breath catches in my throat. I lower my head, open my mouth and almost blurt out everything when Fi yells,

'Harry, I'm so pleased to see you.'

It's just as well. Brice will no doubt have gone to his grandmother and I would have been thrown out on my ear, which I am grateful to still have I might add. The money would have to be given back and I'd be again in debt, probably homeless, and with the Jacks after me. I do, after all, have an agreement with Hamilton so why doesn't this Brice Edmunds go and do some doctoring somewhere and leave me alone?

'Shouldn't you be in Asia or Africa, or on your boat, or whatever it is you do? Can't you go and be a flying doctor somewhere, like Australia?' I snap, annoyed with my shaking hands and fluttering heart.

'And miss all the fun. No I'll stick around a bit longer, thanks Harriet. By the way is that your real name or is it Sharon or Tracey or ...'

I spin round to face him.

'You bastard, how dare you. You're the bloody rudest man I have ever met and I've met a bleeding lot of them let me tell you.'

'Now that's the Harriet I recognise,' he smiles.

Fiona coughs.

'Harriet hi, everything okay?' she says nervously.

Does it look bloody okay? The silly cow hasn't got her glasses on and is squinting to see Brice, and Brice is standing with his hands in his pockets and has a stupid smirk on his face. God, he is winding me up.

'Hello, we meet again,' he smiles at Fiona. Fiona's eyes dart all over the place, finally landing on me. I raise my eyebrows and give a despairing look.

'Hello,' she says, her teeth chattering. 'It's very cold here isn't it?'

'Cold and wet I'm afraid, but you can always rely on the weather here. It is always cold and wet. So you're Harriet's PA? How is the business going? Doing well is it?'

Her eyes dash to me and then back to Brice.

'Yes, it is doing very well actually. I have brought the figures with me Harriet, so we can go over them, and also there are some forms you need to fill in. Tax purposes you understand,' she smiles at Brice. 'It's a bugger the tax system but we find a way round it.'

She smiles at me. Good old Fi. When it comes to money she knows her stuff. I only wish I could say the same for Julian, the little git. I'm getting closer and closer to cutting the little sod's penis off myself.

'It will be sunny later for our shoot. I hope you'll come. We're all looking forward to seeing Harriet's expertise at clay pigeon shooting.'

'Oh yes, she's fabulous,' she gushes.

I glare at her. What the hell.

'I hope you'll come too. Do you shoot?'

Does she shoot? Saints alive, Fiona, a shotgun and no contacts? Jesus, there'd be a massacre in minutes. I'm not letting Fiona near a shotgun. God, what I wouldn't do to wipe that smirk off his handsome face but there is fat chance of that.

'I well, I ...,' fumbles Fiona looking at me for help.

'Fiona doesn't shoot,' I say, taking her overnight bag and pushing past Brice Edmunds. 'Come on Fi.'

'See you later at the shoot. I'm looking forward to it,' he says with humour in his voice

'Bastard,' I mumble, 'and what the hell was all that? *Oh yes, she's fabulous?*' I mimic.

'Well, I just thought that's what you told them. I don't know do I? What's he doing here anyway?' she asks breathlessly struggling to keep up with me in her high heels.

'Don't bloody ask. He's only Hamilton's bleeding cousin isn't he? The other grandson of all things, I mean honestly, you couldn't write this stuff,' I grumble and then realise she is no longer with me but has stopped in her tracks and is staring ahead at the house. Her hair blows in the wind and the grass sways in the background from the helicopter taking off. I swear all she needs is a Cadbury's Flake in her hand and she would be a commercial. Cedric hurries to take the bag from my hands.

'Is madam coming in?' he asks, looking at Fiona who is fumbling with her glasses.

'I'm not sure. I think she's stuck.'

I walk back to Fiona who gulps and shudders.

'Holy shit, you might have said it was Buckingham bloody Palace. I'll never fit in here.'

I sigh.

'And you think I do. Come on.'

She pulls off her glasses and follows me.

'This is Cedric, he's the head butler. But it seems to me he's the head everything. Isn't that right Cedric?' I say grinning.

The only time I ever feel at home is when I am with the domestic staff. I guess that says a lot about me doesn't it?

'Come on let's get you a cuppa,' I say dragging her into the entrance hall, only to be met by Margarita and Lionel.

'We're off for our constitutional,' she says, looking at Fiona with interest. 'Although, it's more a constitutional for Lionel than me as I just sit in this damn thing. Has that dreadful wind dropped? It's supposed to be sunny and still around four. Good for clay pigeon shooting. Do you shoot Miss ...?'

'Clayton, Fiona Clayton. No, I've never shot anything, well maybe once at a funfair but ...'

'Ah, your PA is here,' bellows Hamilton.

To my horror he kisses me fully on the lips. Aware that Margarita is sitting right in front of us I slide my arm around his waist.

'Hello Hamilton,' says Fiona, blushing. 'How are you?'

'Yah great, just off for a ride, but I'll see you later.'

'I want to see you two in the library after the shoot this afternoon. We need to make arrangements and check the ring fitting.'

We both nod obediently.

'Good, that's settled. Let's go Lionel. Get this over and done with.'

'Come on Fi,' I say dragging her towards the kitchen.

'She's a bit of a witch,' comments Fiona.

'You should meet the cat.'

I open the kitchen door.

'Oh my God, this is f ...' she begins and stops on seeing Mrs Randall, 'fabulously decorated,' she finishes.

'This is cook,' I say filling the kettle only to have Cedric take it off me.

'Miss Harriet, have we not had this conversation several times now.'

Oh God, this is getting tedious.

'Sorry Cedric.'

Fiona is gawping like she has never seen a kitchen before. I pull her by the arm and take her upstairs to her room. Once inside she puts on her glasses and gasps.

'Have you heard from the Jacks?' I ask.

'This must be how royalty live. Is this all mine? You must be paying me a helluva salary.'

I starfish myself on her bed and twiddle my toes.

'Well, have you?'

She shakes her head.

'Not yet, maybe they've given up, found bigger fish to fry.'

I shoot her a dirty look.

'Sorry, I forgot about your goldfish.'

'What am I going to do? I feel like my life is falling apart. Brice is on to me and it is just a matter of time before he exposes me to his grandmother. This afternoon is the bloody clay pigeon shoot. Hamilton has told them all I'm an expert. Apart from breaking my arm in the next hour I have no idea how to get out of it. I don't even know what a clay pigeon is.'

'A pigeon made of clay obviously. They fire it into the air and you have to shoot it like a real pigeon I suppose. It can't be that hard surely? Just pull the trigger.'

She strolls into the bathroom.

'Holy shit, I feel like Cameron Diaz. Is it okay if I have a bath?'

'If you can indulge in luxury knowing I'm facing the worst dilemma of my life.'

'It's not that bad, at least you're getting the bills paid,' she calls over the sound of the running taps.

'What did you tell them at the laundrette?' I ask anxiously. After all, I can't afford to lose that job.

'Oh yeah, I said you have chickenpox and it's highly contagious. They've said take the week off. Maud will look after things. She said you'll get sick pay. Of course, thanks to you I've got it too. I've got the week off. Alistair thinks you're fucking mad doing this. His words, not mine. Well, actually his words were, "she is f-f-f-fucking m-m-"...'

'Yes, I get the gist,' I say, breaking in quickly.

Her mobile trills and I stare at her bag.

'The Jacks,' she cries rushing into the room in her bra and panties. I rummage through her bag but can't find the phone.

'Shit, shit, where is it? Why is your bag so huge?'

There is a soft tapping at the door and Cedric enters with the tea. Fiona flies into the bathroom while I continue throwing everything from the handbag.

'Your tea madam,' says Cedric placing the tray onto a small table and turning to expertly catch a flying tampon.

I pull a face.

'Sorry,' I mumble, reaching the phone just as it stops.

'Bollocks,' I groan.

'Cock it,' mumbles Fi from the bathroom.

Cedric blinks several times, hands me the tampon and retrieves a lipstick from the floor.

'Is there anything else madam?'

Yes, you couldn't make a pay-off for me could you?

'That's great, thanks Cedric.'

The door closes and I sit miserably holding Fiona's Blackberry. She peeks round the bathroom door.

'Was it them?'

'I don't know the number was withheld.'

The phone rings again and we both jump.

'Hello,' I say breathlessly.

'Well well, it's 'arriet 'erself. Enjoying your bit of snobbery with them upper classes are yer? I bet yer thought you could get away from me didn't yer?'

It did cross my mind.

'Nice gaff is it? Maybe me and the boys should do it over.'

'I haven't forgotten the monkey,' I say. 'It's just there is no phone signal here.'

'Thing is, I 'ad to bring me boys down 'ere. An agreement is an agreement after all, you know what I mean? 'olidays are bloody expensive buggers ain't they? I've had to book a B&B and take the boys out for dinner. It all adds up. So I figured if it wasn't for that bleeding 'arriet, I wouldn't be in Scotland freezing me fricking bollocks off would I?'

I suppose he has a point.

'So, I've been thinking maybe a monkey's not much for someone of your standing ...'

'I still don't have any money,' I argue.

'Yeah right and I'm a monkey's uncle. Talking of monkeys, you owes me one and let's say another ton on top. I'll be 'appy with that.'

Oh God almighty, how much is a ton. It sounds a bloody lot. I'll be mugging the grandmother next.

A ton, I mouth to Fiona, the gangster expert.

'One hundred,' she mouths back.

Blimey she's good. I'll give her that. Oh, that's not so bad then. I thought it would be worse than that.

'The meet will be tonight. I 'ave a friend of a friend who 'as a friend that's a friend of mine. He owns an old disused ware'ouse. Be there at eight, at eight sharp. I'll text details. Don't let me down 'arriet. Jules is relying on you, and put it in a nice little bag and I don't mean a bleedin' Sainsbury's carrier bag. Got it?'

The phone goes dead.

'When's the meeting,' Fiona asks sniffing from a bottle of bath oil.

'Tonight at eight. His friend, that's a friend of a friend, that's a friend of his.'

What the hell am I saying?

'Anyway, someone's friend has a disused warehouse and it's to be there,' I say shakily, while wondering how the hell we are going to find the place. I barely know my way around the other side of the grounds here. How will I ever find the destination for the meeting? Jesus, I need to find a bank too and quickly. My head begins to spin.

'That gives us plenty of time then,' Fiona says vaguely, pouring oil into the bath.

'How much money can you take out of the hole in the wall in one go?' I ask.

She turns and stares at me, her hand poised over the bath. Oil pours from the bottle and the overpowering smell of lavender fills the room.

'You mean you don't have the money?' she says aghast.

'Of course not, I thought it would be Monday. Do you think they will take a cheque?' I say hopefully.

Her face tells me this is clearly not acceptable, and who am I to argue with a leading authority on East End gangland?

'Jesus, Mary Mother of God, have you gone insane? These people hack off limbs and then go and eat their dinner, and you want to give them a cheque? Christ, why didn't you just ask if they took MasterCard?'

'Do you think they do?'

'Oh for Christ's sake.'

'Crikey, keep your bleeding hair on.'

'What do you have in the bank?'

'Enough but I don't know where the nearest bank is. Anyway, I think you can only take three hundred quid out at one time. They want an extra hundred too. Can you get the rest on your card?'

'I don't believe this,' she mumbles, turning the taps off. 'Isn't there a bell you can pull to get that Cedric guy up here? He can tell us where we can find a bank.'

'This isn't *Upstairs Downstairs* you know,' I quip, picking up the phone and dialling the kitchen.

'Yes Miss Harriet?' Cedric answers.

'I need to get some money. Is there a bank near here?'

'There is one in the village, not far from here Miss Harriet. Should I ask James to come round with the car?'

I sigh with relief.

'That would be wonderful Cedric, thank you. I have to go with Fiona to sort out some things and sign some boring papers,' I say with a forced yawn.

'Yes, of course Miss Harriet. I'll be sure to have Emily ready for when you return, to dress you for the shoot.'

Oh shit, I'd happily forgotten about the bloody clay pigeon thing.

'Let's go,' I say briskly.

Fiona looks longingly at the bath. Mumbles something about things being too good to be true and pulls out the bath plug.

Chapter Eighteen

Fortunately the bank isn't that far away. I drag Fiona to the cash machine, whip out my debit card, punch in the numbers and withdraw three hundred pounds. I hold the notes tightly in my hand and wonder if I will actually be able to part with them when the time comes. I silently curse Julian and turn to Fiona who is fumbling in her purse.

'It's here somewhere,' she mutters. I try hard not to sigh, and yank her glasses from her handbag.
She reluctantly puts them on and finally pulls out a debit card. A small queue is beginning to form behind us and I urge her to hurry up.

'Damn,' she mumbles.
I follow her gaze to the machine's screen.
Incorrect pin, please try again.
I put my head in my hands.

'How can you not know your pin number?' I say accusingly.
She runs her hand through her hair.

'Okay, don't nag me. I just have to think. Debit card, debit card,' she mumbles. 'I've not used the thing for about a year. Right, if it's not my birthday then it must be Alistair's. I'll try that.'
I cross my fingers and hold my breath as she punches in the numbers and groans when the message flags up again.

'Oh God Fi, this is your last chance,' I say panic punching me in the stomach. Jack Diamond is already decidedly pissed off with me. I somehow don't think he will take kindly to me telling him I don't have the money because Fiona couldn't remember her pin number.

'Jesus, the pressure,' she groans, biting her nails.

'Think,' I say, adding to the pressure. 'What numbers do you usually use for these things?'

'Well obviously they're all different aren't they? That's what they tell you to do isn't it? Have different passwords and things, so you don't get hacked.'

'Someone will get hacked alright, if we don't give them the money.'

Her face lights up.

'I remember now. It's the date Alistair and I met.'

I scoff.

'No wonder you couldn't remember it.'

'You're cruel sometimes, do you know that?' she says in a hurt voice.

I decide only to apologise if it accepts the number. She taps it in and hallelujah, she gets it right.

'I'm sorry,' I say.

'Oh God,' says Fiona.

I look reluctantly at the screen, *'Your withdrawal has been declined due to insufficient funds.'*

'I take that apology back. How can you have insufficient funds?' I say accusingly.

She stamps her foot angrily.

'Okay, so I don't have enough. You're a fine one to talk. You've not always been so flush, remember. I'll take out a hundred on this and the rest on my credit card.'

A man behind us grunts and we pretend not to hear him. She tries again and manages successfully to withdraw one hundred pounds.

'Right, that gives us four hundred,' she says gleefully.

'Keep your voice down,' I whisper.

She fumbles through a wad of cards. She must have at least twenty of the things

'Hau much longer will yer be,' asks a woman behind us. 'I've got wee bairns.'

'Sorry,' I say politely.

'Hurry up,' I say not so politely to Fiona. 'The lady's got wee burns.'

Fiona turns to glance at the woman.

'How do you get those?' she whispers.

'How the hell do I know, now hurry up for God's sake.'

'Okay, okay, I have to think this through. The Barclaycard Gold is no good. I'm up to the limit on that. My standard Halifax has been blocked. I lost it, well at least I thought I'd lost it but then I found it in my make-up bag, but I'd cancelled it by then and the new one hasn't come yet.'

'Fiona, you're giving me a migraine.'

'Okay, sorry, I'll try my other Halifax card I should be able to get fifty on that.'

'You've got two?'

'It's a long story, and I don't think ...'

'No, you're right. Just do it Fi.'

Jesus, we're going to be here all night and I don't even have a mobile to let Hamilton know I may be late back for the shoot. See what happens when you try to deceive people. It all comes back on you in the end. The Halifax card gives us another fifty with still another one hundred and fifty to go. I'm thinking it would be easier and quicker to mug someone.

'Bugger it,' sighs Fiona rummaging through her bag and spilling half the contents.

'I've got a Creation card somewhere. I know the pin for that one and I have credit. I feel sure I have,' she says desperately.

I look behind at the queue and give everyone an apologetic smile as I diplomatically retrieve her spare undies that have attached themselves to someone's leg.

'Are yer leaving anything in that there machine lass?' asks one woman.

'Got it,' Fi shouts, and everyone applauds.

God, this is dead embarrassing. The machine accepts her pin and surprisingly allows her to withdraw another one hundred.

'Shit, we still need fifty,' I say.

Fiona begins another bag search and I hear a group sigh from the queue behind us.

'Whit if we all gie 'em a fiver?' calls someone. 'I'm already saxty sieven. I don't want to still be standing here when I'm saxty aicht.'

'What did he say?' asks Fiona.

'A'm already late for the bairns, I'll gie a fiver.'

'If it means we don't see her knickers again, I'm happy to give a fiver.'

'It's okay,' says Fiona nicely. 'I have another one I can use.'

There is a groan as she pushes yet another card into the machine only to get the pin number wrong again.

'Why don't you know the pin numbers,' I say, so exasperated at this point that I could scream.

'Because I don't usually use these cards for buying things,' she retorts.

'What the hell do you use them for then?'

'Scraping her windscreen probably,' someone quips.

'I pay off my Barclaycard with them. So I don't need a pin when I pay over the phone.'

I can't believe she is an accountant. When it comes to her own money she is as useless. The second try results in another decline and with a shaking hand she taps into her Blackberry to search for the pin number.

'I'm sure I put it in here under Creation or something.'

'It's most likely under pin,' I say cynically.

A few more grunts from the queue and she hiccups back a little sob.

'I can't find anything. I'll just have to try again.'

A last ditch effort and a small hissing sound from the machine tells us it has swallowed the card.

'Oh no,' she cries. 'It will all be my fault if they chop something off. I feel so guilty.'

She begins to sob. I grab her and pull her towards the limo.

'Thank you for your patience,' I say politely as we pass the long line of people.

'Well a'll be foocked,' I hear one say as James opens the door for us.

'They say those with money are the worst,' mumbles the burns woman.

'I'll try and borrow it from Hamilton,' I say, knowing full well I won't. There is no way he will give me any more money. I'll just have to write a little apologetic note to the Jacks explaining the pay-off is short by fifty quid. I'm sure they'll understand.

'Oh yeah, sure they will,' says Fiona when I tell her my plan. 'And that's a pig I just saw fly by. We're foocked.'

I think she means I'm foocked.

* * *

Diamond waltzes past me in the hallway, panting tuna fish breath as she goes. I have left Fiona to her luxurious bath and have quickly changed. I decide to take a stroll to work off my frustration, or I'll end up shooting a lot more than bloody clay pigeons. The grounds are immaculate and I pass the gardener tending a flower bed.

'The gardens are lovely,' I say casually. 'I don't have a garden where I live. Well, you can't really can you, not when you're on the third floor. I tried to grow some hyacinths once but they just kept sort of flopping, do you know what I mean?'

God, I must be seriously losing the plot if I'm discussing my hyacinths with the gardener. I see Melanie watching me from a window and continue walking. I think of my little flat at Marlborough Mansions. If only I was there now and none of this had ever happened. I could be poring over my study books while the spag bol bubbled away nicely. Okay, so we never had champagne, and there wasn't much luxury and I slapped on Aldi's cheap face cream, but I was happy wasn't I? The Clinique is doing bugger all. I've aged overnight from all the stress anyway. I didn't mind cheap plonk. It fact, if you ask me it tastes better than the posh stuff we have here. Okay, so I mixed it with lemonade but so what. Just goes to show I'm not meant for this kind of life am I? I have to constantly remind myself not to add lemonade to the wine. My mind wanders to the Jacks and my heart sinks. I look around expecting to see them pop up from behind a rhododendron bush any minute. How could I be fifty quid short? Diamond will go bananas. It occurs to me I could kidnap Diamond, not Jack Diamond, of course, I'm not that daft. Diamond the cat obviously. Margarita would no doubt pay a small fortune to get her back. I'd only have to hold the little demon for a few hours and then I could miraculously find her and claim the reward. I sigh. No, that wouldn't work. I don't imagine for one second the reward will be more than a thousand. Oh, if only a thousand was all I needed. Mind you, fifty pounds right now would be good. Jesus, the thought of having a shotgun in my hand shortly is a bit disconcerting. I'm seriously beginning to feel I could mow everyone down. How could Julian have abandoned me like this? He must have been deceiving me the whole time we had been together, and because of him my future has been shot to pieces. As you can see I'm trying to stay in shooting mode. The Jacks are going to bleed us dry, or should I say bleed *me* dry. I wonder if Julian has tried to call.

'Penny for your thoughts.'

I look up to see Brice Edmunds walking towards me. I sigh. Wanky tit basket, this is all I need.

'Make it fifty quid and I'll consider it,' I say wryly.

He gives me a quizzical look. Actually, on reflection maybe it is time I gave him a piece of my mind and a large piece at that. He's wearing a brown Lambswool pullover with a zip-neck. Beneath it I can just see a checked green shirt. His hair is tousled from where the wind has blown it. He approaches with a smile; I return it with a scowl. I've had as much as I can take from him. He is carrying a waterproof jacket and wears wellingtons over his corduroys. I march towards him feeling my face flush with anger. Ahead, in the distance, I can see Stalkers Lodge, and the memory of his hand on mine when we were treating the tramp floods into my mind.

'How dare you judge me,' I say angrily, feeling my jaw tighten. 'You know nothing about me, nothing at all. You're arrogant, rude, and disrespectful.'

He stops smiling and bites his lip. God, what's happening to me? I'm getting aroused just by watching him biting his lip. Christ, I've been too long without sex, that's my problem. It wasn't a case of not wanting it with Julian you understand. It was more a case of staying awake to have it. I actually didn't, in fact, stay awake that is. I fell asleep in the middle. How embarrassing is that? I look at Brice Edmunds and find myself thinking *no way would I fall asleep in the middle of anything with you*.

'I apologise for earlier. You're quite right, I was rude,' he says quietly.

'Oh,' I say, taken aback.

'You're very attractive when you're angry,' he smiles. 'You have a very open face. Your eyes blaze when you're angry and you lower them when you're hiding something.'

I feel my jaw tighten.

'How dare ...'

'And your nose gives a little twitch when you feel uncomfortable.'

Christ, what is he doing, some kind of human study on me? I'll also show him how quickly my knee can jerk in a minute if he's not careful.

'Or maybe it just twitches when I'm casting a spell,' I say, 'so be careful I don't turn you into a frog.'

He smiles.

'I presume you're not clay shooting in that outfit, as nice as it is.'

I look down at my silk shirt and jeans and pull my cardigan together.

'Of course not,' I snap.

'Marcus sorted you out a nice little outfit did he? Oh yes, of course,' he says, tapping his head. 'I remember now, didn't he say something about being grateful you didn't have a shotgun in your hand, that the riding crop had been quite an ordeal. Odd thing to say don't you think, to someone's who's an expert?'

'I'm rather wishing I had the riding crop in my hand at this moment.'

He gives me a smile so sensual and says in a voice that I'm sure would bring most women to orgasm,

'I didn't have you down as the kinky type. You're full of nice surprises.'

I struggle to control my breathing.

'Look, I know you don't like me ...'

He raises his eyebrows.

'I never said that. I've actually always liked you.'

My heart dances in my chest and the words *tell him, tell him now* shout in my head. But I can't. I can't tell him that Hamilton has paid me a lot of money to lie to his grandmother can I? Well I can, but then I'd have to explain about Julian and the Jacks, and then he'll know how poor I really am and that I only work in a laundrette and he'll then hate me. At least he actually likes me at the moment. *Go on take a chance,* whispers a voice in my head, *what is the worst that can happen*? Well actually the worst that can happen is that Hamilton will demand the money back, which means the Jacks won't get their monkey short of fifty quid, and they will burn down the restaurant, which in turn means Julian won't get his backer and that of course means Julian will be toast, that is if he isn't already. But seeing as I don't know if he is toast I can't take the risk can I? God, my head is spinning.

'I'm thinking you might like to come for a boat trip across the loch with me tomorrow,' he says casually.

'And what on earth do you think would possess me to go on a boat trip across the loch with you?' I say disdainfully while thinking what a lovely, if not dangerous, idea it is.

'Because I'm presuming you may prefer it to the stag stalk my grandmother has planned for tomorrow. You don't look much like a stag stalker to me. Personally I detest it.'

Oh dear God, stag stalking. I hate killing anything but to kill a poor little deer would be awful. I try to hide the distaste from my face but fail miserably.

'That's settled then. I'll be leaving at ten.'

He turns and strides away from me.

'No, hang on a minute. I'll just stay at the house and ...' I say, following like a power walker.

He smirks.

'And you think Grandmother will fall for that? You'll have a convenient migraine will you? I should tell you, Grandmother doesn't warm to women with failing health. Far better if you say you had agreed to come on the trip with me to see something of the estate. At least that way I'll know the family silver is safe while everyone is out.'

I gape at him. What a wanking, pissing, bastard.

'That's slander,' I snap, pushing past him.

'So take me to court.'

'Go to hell,' I say viciously and march to the house almost falling over Diamond in the process.

'Bollocking cat,' I mumble and stomp up the stairs. Fiona meets me on the landing, dressed in shooting gear. She tips her cap.

'Where have you been? Emily has been waiting to dress you. What do you think?' she asks gaily, giving a twirl.

'Fiona, have you forgotten why we are here? Where did you get that? And if you think I am letting you near a gun without contacts then forget it. Murder at the manor we do not need.'

'Christ,' she grumbles, 'who rattled your cage?'

Emily greets me with a wide smile.

'Oh Miss Harriet, it's good you are here, I have everything laid out for you. The shoot is about to start and Cedric is setting everything up. Now, how shall we dress you?'

I think I shall have to give up trying to get her to call me just plain Harriet. A tray of oatcakes sits on the table with a pot of tea. I stare at them with a feeling of doom.

'How do you usually dress the condemned?' I mumble.

'Bloody hell you're cheerful,' says Fiona. 'Here,' she passes me an oatcake, 'your last supper madam.'

'Are you coming down for the shoot?' Calls Hamilton in that whiney voice that makes me cringe.

'We're coming,' shouts Fiona.

Oh well, I've only got to fire a gun at a stupid clay pigeon. That can't be too hard can it? So let's get it over with.

Chapter Nineteen

Brice Edmunds doesn't take his eyes off me and I can assure you it isn't because he finds me captivating, at least I don't think that is the reason. The bugger is just waiting for me to make a mistake.

'The bastard wind has dropped at last,' states Margarita bluntly. Melanie winces and Sebastian follows suit. Blimey they *are* sensitive. They could never live with me, that's for sure. I personally am rather hoping that bastard wind may just whip up again and we can all return to the house. I feel like a prize prat in my moleskin breeks, and I only know they're called breeks because Emily told me. They feel as uncomfortable as buggery and I would have been just as happy in my jeans. Topped with my country tweed jacket and Compton cap, I must resemble someone out of a P G Wodehouse novel. Frankly I think we all look like twats. Margarita looks like she could have stepped out of the film *The Queen*. As for Melanie, everything is just drowned in that God-awful perfume that she wears. I hate to say it but Fiona looks the most aristocratic out of all us and God knows she is far from that. I rather think with a shotgun in her hand that may drastically change however and she is then more likely to resemble the daughter of Al Capone. As for pigeons, well there isn't one to be seen for dust, clay or otherwise. Oh, I so wish Julian would walk across the field like Sir Galahad and tell me that everything is now okay, that the Jacks are now sorted and we can just go home and life will be as it used to be. The question is do I want life to be as it used to be? I remove Fiona's phone from my jacket pocket to see if Jack Diamond has sent instructions but there is nothing. I switch it to vibrate and slip it back. Cedric hands me a shotgun and I freeze.

'I've given you a twenty bore Miss Harriet,' he says.
I hate to tell him that it wouldn't matter if he had given me a two bore. I'm still going to do as much damage.

'And your cartridges Miss Harriet,' he adds politely, placing a box in my hands.

Oh no, please don't give me these.

'Well let's get on with the damn thing,' grumbles Margarita. 'I didn't come out here for the fresh air and pneumonia. Who's going first?'

You're more likely to get shot than catch pneumonia I think and if you're waiting for me to go first, you can think again.

'Why don't you go first old girl and wrap that scarf around you instead of holding it,' says Brice good-humouredly, walking towards her and wrapping it around her neck himself. Good, that means he has forgotten me for a time at least. I study her closely as she opens the gun and inserts the cartridges. Okay, that looked easy. I'm still watching when I feel a warm hand stroke my neck.

'I'd wear these if I were you,' says Brice quietly slipping earmuffs over my head. 'We don't want you to go deaf do we?'

'If it means I don't have to listen to your twaddle any more it sounds like a great idea to me,' I whisper.

He smiles and drops them over my ears as Margarita shouts *pull*. I watch as a clay disc flies through the air. She fires and the disc explodes into dust. I wonder if I can feign a dizzy spell to get out of taking my turn. Melanie misses hers and I wildly imagine if I can do the same. Fiona is looking at me earnestly. At least I think she is looking at me. It's always hard to know where she is looking when she hasn't got her contacts in. Sebastian fires next and the smart bugger hits his as well. This does not bode well for me. Why Hamilton isn't coming forward to guide me I do not know. I give him an appealing look but he just shakes his head. What was the stupid arse thinking when he told everyone I was an expert shot? Margarita raises her finger in a way that indicates she needs a drink.

'A hot toddy please Cedric,' she says.

Thankfully we all take a break. As Cedric pours from a flask Fiona edges close to me.

'Do you know what to do?' she asks.

'Not a bleeding clue.'

She nods.

'I thought not. I'll stand well clear when it's your go then.'

'Oh, thanks a lot.'

'Would you like brandy or coffee Miss Harriet?' asks Cedric.

'Brandy please Cedric, anything that will calm my trembling knees,' I smile.

'Just remember to cock it Miss Harriet ...'

I widen my eyes.

'I've cocked a few things up Cedric, what do you actually propose I cock up this time?'

'The shotgun might be a good idea Miss. Then insert your cartridges. Release the safety catch and aim.'

I suppose he couldn't write that down.

'Be careful of the recoil.'

'I'm fully expecting everyone to recoil Cedric,' I say nervously.

'I'm talking about the recoil from the shot Miss Harriet.'

'Yes of course,' I say grabbing his flask and pouring more brandy into my glass. I walk over to Hamilton trying to look casual while I'm sure my trembling knees can be seen a mile off.

'Get me out of this. There is no way I can pull it off,' I say firmly.

'If you can't shoot she'll know something's up. Just aim, hold the gun firmly and if you miss, you miss. We'll say you've hurt your hand but we didn't want to ruin the shoot by saying anything.'

What the fuck.

'Just tell them I've hurt my hand now,' I hiss.

'Harriet, it's your turn. Are you ready dear?' asks Sebastian kindly.

I most certainly am not. Brice edges close to me and takes the drink from my hand.

'Load the gun, slide the safety catch, aim, shout pull and squeeze the trigger halfway for the first shot. Pull it back for your second shot,' he whispers. 'But of course you know all that, being an expert and all.'

I turn to look at him but he avoids my eyes. Why is he suddenly helping me?

'Come on girl, do you want me to die from hypothermia,' bellows Margarita.

I'd rather that than you die from a gunshot wound. I pull my earmuffs back on, open the shotgun which is amazingly easy, remove the cartridges from the box and insert them. I glance at Brice and his nod is practically imperceptible but I recognise it and know I have at least got them in the right way. I cock the gun, release the safety catch and lift it to my shoulder in the same way I saw Margarita do. I feel perspiration run between my breasts and my heart is beating so fast I'm finding it hard to breathe. My hands slip on the barrel and I quickly wipe them on my breeks. I take a deep breath and shout *pull*. The disk flies into the air and I follow it with my eye and pull the trigger halfway and the bleeding phone vibrates in my pocket making me jump out of my skin. I fall back, firing God knows where. Cedric was right about the recoil, the force spun me around like a spinning top and before I know what I'm doing I have fired my second shot at the house. Everyone turns horror-stricken towards Glenwood. I pull off my earmuffs to the sound of shattering glass and screams from the house.

'Good Lord, she's shot the servants. Quick Hamilton,' shouts Melanie.

Oh my God, please don't say I've gone and killed Emily. Sweet lovely Emily, oh my God, how can I live with myself? Emily comes running out all a fluster and my legs almost give way.

'It's alright,' she shouts. 'Just the landing window was hit.'

'Good shot though,' says Hamilton stupidly.

'I'm so sorry Margarita. My mobile vibrated in my pocket and made me jump.'

She meets my eyes and studies me intently.

'I would suggest leaving the phone back at the house in future,' grins Sebastian. 'Another round Mother?' he suggests.

'Yes why not. Harriet?'

Oh God, no really? I take the toddy Cedric offers me and throw it back. My shirt is soaked in perspiration.

'I think I'll take a rain check if that's okay. That's rather shaken me up. It's never happened to me before,' I say feeling more confident with the drink in me. Maybe I could have another go. No, Harriet, don't push your luck.

'No, I'm sure it hasn't,' says Brice with that familiar sarcasm.

'No, you're normally a brilliant shot, can't think what possessed you to carry your mobile darling,' says Hamilton draping an arm around my shoulder.

'You all carry on. Harriet can take me back to the house. Come along Harriet,' orders Margarita.

I look to Hamilton who nods and begins to follow.

'You stay here Hamilton. I want to have a little chat with Harriet.'

Uh oh, this doesn't sound promising. I look pleadingly at Fiona and mouth 'Jack's text' but she has been sidetracked by Sebastian.

'How about you Fiona, do you want to have a try?' he asks.

'Well, I could,' she says hesitantly taking a gun from Cedric. I decide it is time for a hasty retreat and start pushing Margarita's wheelchair to the house as fast as I can before Fiona starts spraying bullets everywhere. I struggle up the ramp breathing heavily. Christ I'm likely to die before Margarita at this rate.

'Take me to the library,' she says abruptly and I do as I am bidden. I'm having serious doubts about Margarita Lancaster. If this woman has only got six months to live then I'm a monkey's uncle. Talking of monkeys, I discreetly check the text message on Fiona's phone.

Lower Glen, ten miles from Glenwood. Get a map. Disused warehouse at the back of Glengarry estate. Don't be late Harriet.

Get a map? From where exactly? Margarita orders Lionel to bring us another brandy and gestures for me to sit in the leather armchair opposite her and I slyly look around to see if there are maps lying about. Her cheeks are pink and her eyes animated. She's pretty robust for someone who is dying. There is something very odd going on with Margarita Lancaster and I can't quite put my finger on it. My heart is beating normally but I'm perspiring even more now we are in the stifling hot library, and it's not helping knowing Fiona has a gun in her hand. I expect stray bullets to shatter the library window any second. With a bit of luck one will hit me and it will all be over. I stretch my neck to see the time on the small mantelpiece clock. It is almost five. It will take us forty minutes to drive to this Lower Glen place and I've still got to organise transport, then we've got to find the warehouse. We'll have to leave by six-thirty which also means I've got to get us out of dinner as well as hire a car and somehow get a map.

'Bring the ring,' she orders Lionel.

Oh no, and now I have to try *The Ring*. My life resembles a horror film by the minute. Lionel doesn't flinch but produces a box and hands it to her.

'You're very pretty,' she says looking at me intently. 'You have a natural beauty, not like Melanie,' she grimaces. 'It's all smoke and mirrors with her. Nothing's real.'

Best not to comment I think sensibly and sip from the brandy. She points a finger in my direction.

'You remind me of myself when I was your age. You're strong and independent which is why ...' she stops to sip her brandy.

I bite my lip and try not to give myself away.

'I can't get my head around the fact you want to be with that useless lump of a grandson of mine.'

'He gives me everything I need,' I say simply.

Well, that's not lying is it? Thirty thousand pounds is exactly what I need.

'That surprises me,' she says with heavy cynicism as she opens the box.

I gasp at the sight of the ring. It is a huge sapphire surrounded by single diamonds. I can't accept this. I can't deceive this woman. This is getting out of hand. The sound of a gunshot makes me jump and I gulp the brandy.

'Margarita ...' I begin.

'Try it on and if it needs adjusting Jeremy can do it on Monday.'

I remove the ring from the box and stare at it.

'Brice tells me you've declined to come on the stag shoot tomorrow. He seems to think you have distaste for it as he does. He's taking you across the loch instead.'

I nod uncomfortably.

'I hope you don't mind. I'm slightly uncomfortable with any kind of hunting,' I say truthfully.

She flicks a hand irritably.

'It's not everyone sport. How's your tennis?'

If watching Wimbledon every year counts for anything, I'm an expert. I have played badminton with Julian on the odd occasion. I guess that's the same isn't it? Except it's a ball instead of a shuttlecock and of course, with different rackets and a different court too. So, I guess, in theory, it isn't anywhere near the same is it?

'Rusty,' I say finally.

'Brice is very good. What do you think of Brice?' she asks suddenly and the ring slips from my fingers and clatters on the oak floor. Diamond rushes in and sniffs around it. I reluctantly lean down to pick it up and meet the demon's eyes. If I didn't know better I'd swear the little git was human and what's more, related to *the* Jack Diamond. Maybe if I kill the cat Jack Diamond will die too.

'I don't really know him that well,' I say, avoiding her eyes.

I actually think he is the sexiest man I have ever laid eyes on but I can't tell her that, can I?

'He seems to approve of you.'

Bloody hell, are we talking about the same Brice?

'Try it on girl, it won't bite you.'

I slip the ring onto my finger and like Cinder-sodding-rella it only bleeding fits doesn't it? It glitters so much I need sunglasses. I've never in my entire life been near such a huge bling, let alone worn one. She claps her hands.

'Excellent, a perfect fit, almost as if it were made for you. What do you think? Being in the jewellery business you surely have an opinion. How many carats do you think?'

'More than I can count. It's beautiful.'

I've got to get myself out of this and quick. I'm getting deeper and deeper and deceiving people more and more. I can't do this. She gestures to Lionel.

'Some grapes would go nice with this brandy. Yes, I know. Don't give me that look. Would you please ask Cedric if he has any?'

Lionel sighs and for the first time ever I hear him speak.

'They'll play havoc with your ulcer so don't go blaming me later.'

'You have an ulcer?' I ask.

'So the doctor's say. What do they know? Between you and me, this lot here,' she waves towards the window, 'would have me in a nursing home tomorrow if I wasn't so overpowering. A weaker woman wouldn't have survived.'

She makes them sound like the family from hell.

'Except Brice of course,' she says, her voice softening. 'That's if he's around when they do it and not in the depths of the jungle somewhere seeing to some war chief's wounds,' she sighs.

When they do it? God, she makes it sound like they're planning to knock her off. Mind you, I'd put nothing past that Hamilton. No wonder she's got a manic cat. It's probably her only protection. I twiddle the ring around my finger and it then occurs to me that it's odd to talk about nursing homes when you only have a few months to live.

'Right then my dear,' she says brightening. 'I think next weekend would be good for the engagement party, what do you think? You're not tied up with anything are you?'

'Well ...' I begin. Hopefully I'll be tied to several washing machines and tumble driers doing what I do best and catching up on my studies.

'We can discuss it over dinner. Ah good,' she says on seeing the bowl of grapes in Lionel's hand.

Holy shit, I'm going to need a bloody miracle to get me out of this. A great deal of laughter and shouts tells us everyone has returned from the shoot. The door flies open and Fiona glides in.

'Sorry to disturb,' she says in that posh smoky voice she has now well developed. Hell, she's turning into one of them. 'Would you mind awfully if I missed dinner. I'm desperately sorry Harriet but we have a problem at the New York office and you'll need to sign some papers urgently to be faxed over to Dudley. I've arranged an urgent appointment with a local solicitor.'

You'll appreciate that I don't have a bleeding clue what she's on about so just look at her blankly, anticipation prickling at my nerves. Who is Dudley when he's at home? Brice stands behind her and his effect on me is unnerving. I feel he can see right through me.

'Our family lawyer can sort this out for you surely,' says Margarita. 'Lionel, get Parker on the phone ...'

'No,' I say quickly. 'I couldn't possibly impose. Anyway it sounds like Fiona has everything set up.'

'I'm very sorry. It was actually my fault. We have a seven-thirty appointment Harriet, I'm sorry for the inconvenience.'

I drain my glass, attempt to regain my composure and with trembling hands replace the ring back into the box.

'You'll need James,' says Brice.

'Oh no really, I feel awful as it is. Maybe we can hire a car,' Fiona says quickly.

'You can take my Porsche,' says Hamilton, looking confused.

'Fabulous, thanks so much,' smiles Fiona.

Blimey she's good. Bloody good in fact. I follow her out.

'Thank God you're a better liar than me,' I whisper.

I'm on the bottom stair when Hamilton's arm encircles my waist.

'What's going on?' he asks quietly.

'It's complicated,' I say, feeling all my senses on fire as Brice scrutinises me over the rim of his brandy glass.

'Those tiresome gangsters aren't hassling you here are they?'

Tiresome? Oh, what different worlds we live in.

'Kind of, I'll just sign the papers and I'll be back before you can say Jack Robinson,' I say loudly.

It would have to be Jack wouldn't it?

Chapter Twenty

'You can't be serious,' says Fiona, shaking her head in disbelief.

'What do you suggest then? He said not a bleeding Sainsbury's carrier bag and apart from this, a Sainsbury's carrier bag is all I have,' I mumble, studying the map that Cedric had lent me.

'How are we supposed to leave the house carrying a suitcase? If Hamilton sees you he'll think you're doing a runner.'

I so wish I was.

'What about my Cath Kidston holdall?' she says genuinely.

I feel nauseous with nerves.

'You think a pink floral holdall is more appropriate do you?' I say, not even attempting to hide my irritation.

'Well it's that or your pink suitcase. We're supposed to be going to a meeting not a bloody spa weekend. How do we explain why we're taking a suitcase?'

'Paperwork,' I suggest.

She shakes her head. I scrape my hair back into a ponytail and look at her.

'Well, what do you suggest, we don't have anything else?' I snap, pulling the pink Primark case from under the bed.

Silently we drop five hundred and fifty pounds into the case along with a note written on Glenwood Manor personalised notepaper. Fiona reads it aloud.

Dear Jack Diamond, I'm sorry but we could only get five hundred and fifty pounds from the cash machine. So please accept this as an IOU.

'Jesus Christ Harry.'

I shrug.

'You said they wouldn't take a cheque.'

'I don't think they will take kindly to an IOU either.'

I zip up the suitcase and peek outside the door. I drop Fiona's phone into my handbag, push my old woollen hat in there too and nod at her.

'Let's go,' I say feeling myself buoyed up with adrenalin.

Fiona opens the door slowly, peeks round it and then closes it again.

'Do you think we should take a gun or something?'

'Crikey, Fiona, what the hell are you going to do with a gun?'

'Well, obviously to shoot them if they turn out to be psychos.'

I suppose she has a point. I check the time on her phone.

'We don't have time to sneak into the gun room. I'll grab a tin of hairspray.'

'What use is that? Are you going to threaten them with a wash and blow dry?'

She stands with her hand on the doorknob.

'Harriet, I'm not sure this is a good idea. Maybe you should tell Hamilton's family the truth. Or tell Brice, he seems nice.'

I shake my head.

'I can't. Hamilton will want back all the money he's given me. I've got to get out of this debt Fiona. Otherwise my life will be ruined.'

'I fucking hate Julian,' she says her voice cracking with emotion. 'You don't deserve this.'

I fight back the tears that prick my eyelids and gesture to the door. She opens it cautiously.

'Okay, all clear.'

I'm beginning to feel like we are off to pull a heist. Actually that's not such a bad idea is it? We can borrow the guns from the gun room. It would be easy to buy balaclavas and then all we'd have to do is hold up a bank. No one need know it's us. I mean, seriously, who would ever suspect the two women staying at Glenwood's aristocratic estate? I'm about to suggest the idea to Fiona when I see Sebastian mounting the stairs and I begin to sweat for all I'm worth.

'Oh shit,' mumbles Fiona.

'You girls just off?' he asks smiling.

I nod mutely, trying to discreetly push the suitcase behind me but it's too late and he points to it.

'Are you staying overnight there?' he asks suspiciously.

Fiona laughs and shakes back her hair in the manner of a sex goddess but she obviously shakes it too much and wobbles on her wedges.

'It's all the paperwork. I feel so bad that I thought it would be better to have everything with us,' she says, grabbing the bannister for support. 'It would be Sod's Law that we'll get there and the one document we need, will be the one I left behind,' she says, stressing each word with extreme hand gestures and shakes of her head.

Wow, doesn't she sound like one efficient PA, not!

'I prefer to have everything at hand at any important meeting,' I add.

'Well, let me carry it down the stairs for you. We don't want you ladies doing yourselves an injury do we?'

'No really it's fine,' I say quickly.

'Good muscle exercise,' says Fiona flexing her arm. Oh God, I do wish she would shut up. He looks at her oddly.

'I'd be no gentleman if I let you carry this heavy thing all the way down the stairs,' he says inclining his head towards the case. If only he knew. Then, before I can stop him, he crouches down beside the case and prepares himself to lift it. I pull a face at Fiona. He takes a breath and lifts the handles with such force that he reels backwards.

'Good heavens, it's as light as a feather,' he says in a puzzled voice.

'It's just you're awfully strong Sir Sebastian,' purrs Fiona fluttering her eyelashes.

Good God, what is she playing at?

'I'll put it into the Porsche for you,' he says, flustered.

'Sebastian, thank you so much,' she says huskily.

I gawp at them like an imbecile and then quickly follow. Two minutes later Fiona is waving gratefully from the Porsche while Sebastian stares after us with a bemused look on his face.

* * *

'Holy shit,' says Fi.

Fiona and I sit in the Porsche staring at Glengarry estate in a state of shock. I'm not sure what Fi and I expected but it certainly wasn't this.

'I need a drink,' Fi says eventually.

I stare at the run-down houses which make the Mardyke Estate look like luxury apartments. The buildings look like they will fall down if you so much as blow on them. At that moment a couple of youths wearing leather jackets begin to stroll towards the Porsche and I pull my hat lower over my eyes.

'Oh shit, I told you we should have brought guns,' moans Fiona.

'You can't shoot everyone that approaches us,' I say, not taking my eyes off the youths whose numbers seem to have doubled.

'Oh God,' says Fiona in a shaky voice. 'Do they look like the type that would bang gang us?'

'What?'

'I mean gang-bang us,' she says wringing her hands.

I start the engine again and continue on. They give us a two finger salute as we pass, and Fiona takes a deep breath. We pass dirty faced children playing in the streets, burnt out cars and women in aprons smoking as their kids kick footballs at parked cars. But there is no sign of a disused warehouse. Fiona points eagerly and I follow her finger to a run-down off-licence where several youths stand around swigging from a whisky bottle. What I wouldn't do for a quick swig too.

'God, this is not the place to bring a Porsche,' says Fiona, stating the bloody obvious as only Fiona can.

She has a point though. If we leave the car for so much as five seconds it will be pounced upon and then how the hell do I explain to everyone that Hamilton's car no longer has tyres, hubcaps or a radio? In fact how do I explain that Hamilton no longer has a car? Fiona is right. This not the place to bring a Porsche. In fact, it's not a place to bring a car, period. It's certainly not the place for two aristocratic women either. I miserably think it is probably the right place for a laundrette manager though.

'You'll have to stay in the car while I meet Jack Diamond.'

'No way,' she squeals. 'I'm not going to be the centre of rape and pillage thank you very much. Not unless they all look like Colin Firth, which is highly unlikely.'

'Can't you fantasise?' I joke. 'Just think of *Pride and Prejudice*.'

'How can you make fun at a time like this?' she cries.

'You meet Diamond and I'll stay in the car then.'

'You must be joking. I want to hang onto my ears, thank you very much.'

I bring the car to a screeching halt when I spot a disused warehouse ahead of us. We both peer through the windscreen.

'This must be it,' whispers Fiona. 'We can both go. We can easily see the car from the warehouse.'

Adrenalin is pumping madly though my body. My shoulders are tense and my head thumps.

'Supposing they have Julian and he's all beaten and battered,' I say anxiously.

'You make him sound like a piece of cod,' quakes Fiona.

I unlock the car and step out cautiously. Thank God it's still light. I lift the suitcase from the boot and begin walking towards the warehouse.

'Wait for me,' squeals Fiona, struggling with her glasses.

The door of the warehouse creaks open and a well-dressed man appears in the doorway. I drop the case in fear when two other men appear from the shadows.

"ello 'arriet, who's yer friend?'

'Oh my God, he has a finger missing,' she whispers.

'Don't draw attention to it,' I whisper back.

'These are seriously hard Harry. I told you we should have brought a gun.'

'Who are *your* friends,' I say trying to sound cocky but my voice shakes.

He looks at the suitcase.

'What the 'ell is that?'

I lift up my pink Primark suitcase and clutch it tightly to my hip.

'It's the money you asked for.'

'The monkey,' adds Fiona.

I cock my head at her.

'Sorry,' she mumbles.

'You brought it in a *pink* suitcase?' he asks, his eyes widening. 'And why's it so big, you taking the piss 'arriet?'

I struggle to see the other two men whom I presume are Mad Jack Junior and Babyface Jack but they stay in the shadows.

'You said not to bring it in a Sainsbury's carrier bag. If you had a favourite colour you should have told me,' I snap, feeling irritated as well as anxious.

'Ouch,' whispers Fiona hanging onto my arm and I feel the trembling of her body.

He gestures to one of the men who steps forward to take the suitcase and both Fiona and I jump back. The other man ventures out of the shadows and averts his face but I recognise him immediately and step forward.

'Harry, what are you doing?' trembles Fiona.

'Is that you Jack?' I ask.

He bows his head and looks uncomfortable.

'Me lad Babyface,' says Jack Diamond, pulling the man forward. I gasp. I know him. He comes into the laundrette. I stare into his eyes and he looks away.

'But I know you, we've chatted in the laundrette. I've always been nice to you. I thought you were a decent person,' I yell. 'Do you have any idea what you've done?'

'Harry,' Fiona quakes, 'don't upset them. Do you want a Valium?' Don't upset them? How about the way they have upset me?

'I folded your shirts and paired your socks. I should have strung them all together and bleeding throttled you,' I say feeling my anger well over.

'Oh dear, oh dear,' groans Fiona, frantically shaking Valium from a bottle. 'God Harry, we'll lose more than our ears if you go on like this.'
I let out a long sigh.

'My sons are spoilt. I blame their mother, yer know what I mean. Now, let's get back to business,' says Jack Diamond with a jerk of his head and a twitch of his shoulders. Sod this for a game of soldiers. I've paid their monkey and the ton.

'I'm not talking business with you or your stupid sons. You killed my goldfish,' I say accusingly to Babyface Jack.
Mad Jack Junior takes a step forward and Fiona lets out a small moan and tries to pull me towards the car.

'It was business 'arriet, not personal,' says Diamond lifting his palms upwards.
Not personal, not bleeding personal. It was *my* goldfish wasn't it? Not Mrs Mollard's on the second floor. How much more personal can you get?

'That's the last I'm paying you. If you want any more you'll have to get it from Julian. That money should keep the restaurant safe for one month unless of course you don't keep your word.'

'Don't keep me word?' Diamond pulls at the lapels of his jacket. 'What kind of bleedin' respect is that?'

'Oh God, we're going to die here, I just know we are,' mumbles Fiona shakily. 'Alistair will never forgive me if I die in this slum. Why can't you just be nice to them?'

'I'm sorry 'arriet,' says Babyface. 'I didn't mean any 'arm.'

'Shut up whining. How many times do I 'ave to tell yer that ain't 'ow yer get birds,' Diamond says angrily walloping Babyface around the head before turning back to me.

'I suggest you get me another monkey by the end of this month, else ole Julian's little gaff will be a pile of ash,' says Diamond menacingly.

'I'm not getting you a monkey, a goldfish or anything else.'
Although I could offer a cat I suppose. No, Harriet, think how distraught Margarita would be.

'She'll get it, I promise there won't be a problem,' says Fiona, popping a Valium into her mouth. 'Isn't that right Harry?' she finishes looking at me hopefully.
No, it's not right. I've had it with everyone now. I was really nice to young Jack and look what he did to me. I was a good girlfriend to Julian and look what he has done to me. No, enough is enough. My whole life has been ruined because of all this. To top it all I meet someone who I actually really like and he can't stand me and all because of Julian and the bloody Jacks. I am going to avoid all people whose name begins with a J in future, unless it's Johnny Depp, of course. I'll make an exception then. If I didn't have all this debt hanging over me I would tell Brice the truth. What a mess.

'You bloody get it if you're so keen,' I snap at Fiona, turning on my heel towards the Porsche.

'Nice motor. You like them porches don't yer Mad Jack?' he says turning to his son.

'Get yourself a builder then if you like porches so much,' I say sarcastically.

'Oh God,' groans Fiona.

'You're getting nothing else from me,' I say firmly and grab Fiona who seems rooted to the spot. I practically drag her to the car and shove her trembling body into it. The Jacks watch me open-mouthed like three stooges. I fumble shakily with the key in the ignition and then with a screech, zoom off back the way we had come.

'Oh dear, oh dear, oh dear me,' groans Fiona.

'Do shut up Fiona.'

'Do you realise what you've done,' she says, trying to tip pills from the bottle as I take a corner on two wheels.

'Holy fuck Harriet, are you losing your mind. I certainly lost all my Valium when you took that turning.'
I ignore her and pull up sharply outside the off-licence. I check the rear-view mirror to see if the Jacks are following us. Reassured that they aren't and feeling quite sure that the youths standing outside the offy are a lot less intimidating than the Jacks, I climb from the car

with Fiona yelling at me. I buy a bottle of whisky and stroll back to the car feeling surprisingly calm. I find Fiona fumbling around the floor crying and picking up pills.

'I think you've lost your mind,' she says throwing two Valium into her mouth and chasing them down with the whisky.

'No I think I've finally come to my senses,' I say, snatching the whisky bottle from her and taking a gulp from it.

She drops her head into her hands.

'I don't know why you're getting so upset,' I say, taking a swig from the bottle. 'I don't care about Julian, after all, he doesn't care about me. I've given them what they want. There's no reason why they should bother me again. I'll do my bit here with Hamilton, take the money, pay my debts and get a nursing job. I've got a sneaky feeling I won't see Julian again.'

'You mean they've ...' she lowers her voice to a whisper, 'topped him.'

'I don't know but if they have, he bloody deserved it. I prefer to think he's laying low until I've paid off all the debts. Well, he can lay low his whole life because I'm not doing it. I'm getting my life back after this is over.'

She sighs and pops the pills back into the bottle.

'You've forgotten haven't you?' she says with a resigned sigh.

'Forgotten what?'

'We were fifty quid short 'arriet, remember,' she says mimicking Jack Diamond.

Oh shit. I'd completely forgotten about that.

She whips the bottle out of my hand.

'They'll probably want more than a monkey next time and they won't even consider an *Ant and Dec*. You should have listened to me. It will be a *grubby hand* and they'll expect *sausage and mash*, and it serves you right. I kept saying to be nice.'

Bloody hell, I think the whisky and Valium have scrambled her brain. Oh my God, she's not had a stroke has she? She was in a bit of a state back there.

'Fiona, I think maybe you're in shock ...'

Perhaps I should take her to see Brice, after all, any excuse to see his gorgeous eyes and tanned body again.

'For God's sake,' she screams and I almost drop the whisky. '*Sausage and mash* is cash, *Ant and Dec* is cheque and a *grubby hand* is a grand. I already told you this. You've messed them around

Harriet and you got stroppy. Christ, you'll be lucky if you escape being found in a back alley somewhere.'

I shiver.

'Aren't you exaggerating a bit? It's only fifty quid,' I say nervously.

'It's business 'arriet, not personal,' she says. Crikey she's beginning to sound like one of them.

Oh God, how could I have been so stupid. I wonder if they'll be happy with the cat until I can get the fifty quid sorted. Fiona sighs and I start the engine again.

'Oh, I miss Alistair and I never thought I'd say that,' she says miserably.

That is a bad sign.

Chapter Twenty-One

I barely slept a wink that night. My dreams were full of stags with pleading eyes, which turned into Julian's eyes, and the stag's head became Julian's head minus both ears. I have to say he looked okay in the dream but everything looks okay in dreams doesn't it. Brice Edmunds muscled himself into it too, but all I could see was my reflection in his beautiful deep brown eyes. He smiled and leaned close until his lips were only a fraction from mine, and then he became Jack Diamond holding up the pink suitcase and shouting,

'Where's me fifty quid 'arriet?'

I woke covered in perspiration and with a severely itchy navel. It had taken me ages to get back to sleep and I tossed and turned until light streamed through the bedroom curtains. I shower, dress and blow dry my hair. I slip on my own filigree earrings in preference to those Marcus had lent me and wander downstairs. Everyone, including Fiona, is assembled in the dining room, dressed in hunting gear. The only exception is Melanie who is wearing the most ridiculous kimono I have ever seen. She is devoid of make-up and for a brief second I didn't recognise her. Fiona is wearing my riding breeches with a white blouse and checked waistcoat. Blimey, she really is taking to the high life.

'Ah Harriet, there you are,' cries Margarita, clicking open a Filofax.

Crikey, I thought those things went out with car phones.

'I've drawn up a list of guests for the party next weekend. Your parents will be back from St Martha's Vineyard won't they?'

Yes, I feel quite certain they will be. After all, their vineyard is only five minutes up the road and is known as Threshers, but I'm not going to tell Margarita that am I?

'I think so,' I say hesitantly.

I see a cafeteria on the sideboard and walk over to it.

'What are you doing dear?' asks Melanie.

I stop as Cedric approaches me.

'Can I get you croissants and coffee Miss Harriet?' he asks, gesturing to a chair. 'Or would madam prefer kippers, or perhaps porridge, or eggs benedict with toast?'

Blimey, breakfast is fast becoming a three course meal.

'Just a croissant and coffee please,' I say.

I reluctantly return to the table. Thank goodness Brice isn't here to make his usual cutting remarks.

'Can you give me your guest list by this evening?' demands Margarita.

Fiona fidgets with some egg on her plate. I look pleadingly at Hamilton, although I'm not sure why the hell I bother. He just shrugs.

'Actually, it will only be Fiona and her partner, and of course my parents,' I say, biting into a croissant and showering crumbs down my top.

'What about your friends?' asks Margarita. 'You surely have friends you wish to ask?'

I lift my eyes to Hamilton.

'All Harry's friends are in New York, and we were thinking we'd do something there a bit later, isn't that right honey?' he says.

Thank God. Why does it always take the bugger so long to help me out?

'Yes,' I mumble.

'We were discussing it only last night weren't we?' he rambles on. 'Everyone being so busy and everything and what with it being a bit last minute and well, we thought just family would be nice,' he says sounding like a complete moron.

'Yes, just family,' I repeat, sounding even more moronic than him.

I feel all eyes on me.

'Oh,' says Margarita slamming closed the Filofax. 'That won't take much organising will it? Don't you have work colleagues here, or old university friends? You surely have brothers and sisters? What about your grandparents?'

Heavens, talk about a cross examination. Can I use my fifty-fifty, or call a friend?

'Grandmother is in a home, and she rarely ventures out, and my other grandparents are dead ...'

'Who's going to be your maid of honour, and what about the bridesmaids?' she snaps.

I'm actually hoping there won't be a bride, let alone bridesmaids.

'Her sister ...' Hamilton begins. He stops at my piercing glare.

What is he saying? Caron and Gary can't come here. Caron with her purple pineapple hair and him with his shaved head and tattoos, it will be like *Big Fat Gypsy Wedding* meets *Downton Abbey*. He'll be swigging a Becks from the bottle and she'll be knocking back white wine spritzers. It's bad enough that my mum has to come. She will no doubt ask for her port and lemon, and my dad is bound to dunk his bread in the soup. He's done that for years so they'll be no stopping him. It's too painful to think about. I've only got four days to prime them. I'm never going to knock forty years of habit out of them in four days am I? It would be easier to kill them all. God Harriet, what are you thinking of? This is what comes of owing money. It makes you consider matricide and patricide. And if you include my sister and her boyfriend it is more like genocide. This situation is turning into my personal hell. Hamilton returns my look with a grimace. I know he's paying me a hell of a lot of money but does he have to make me work so bloody hard to earn it?

'She's surely coming then?' says Margarita while Melanie and Sebastian continue to eat their eggs benedict in an uncomfortable silence.

'Of course, of course, that goes without saying,' says Hamilton.

Margarita opens the Filofax and at that moment the door swings open and Brice glides in with an air of confidence. He looks so sexy and appealing that I have to avert my eyes.

'Ah Brice, we're just discussing the guest list for the engagement party at the weekend. Who will you be bringing?'

Yes, who will you be bringing I think, pricking up my ears.

'Why do I have to be bringing anyone? Can't I come alone?' he grins at his grandmother.

'Don't be ridiculous. I just thought there might be a special someone you might wish to invite.'

Yes, surely there is someone special isn't there? How can he be so handsome, confident and sexy and there not be someone special in his life? I hate the bitch whoever she is.

'No just me, but if you're really insistent on it I'm sure I could drag someone along. Why don't you be my date old girl, and give Lionel a rest that night.'

There is no earthly way this guy is available. It's not possible. Oh God, don't tell me he's bleeding gay, that would so be my luck wouldn't it? He leans over me to the toast rack and I inhale the fresh smell of him. Margarita looks at the list she's just written and sighs.

'I suppose we'd better invite the Major and of course Lady Sophie Henderson. What about your mother, do you think she'll make some kind of effort to get here for her nephew's engagement party?' she asks Brice, pushing the jam towards him which sadly stops him leaning over me.

'I doubt it, after all it's a ridiculously long way to come for a party,' he replies, accepting a cup of coffee from Cedric.

'A ridiculously long way to come and visit her dying mother too, it would seem.'

'You look perfectly okay to me,' he grins, 'but we should take your blood pressure before you go on the stalk.'

She waves her hand dismissively.

'Nonsense,' she says.

'I'm still going to take it.'

She looks down to her Filofax but I detect a little smile on her lips.

'Right, that's the guest list organised. Jeremy is coming this afternoon to clean the ring ready for the weekend and I've contacted Grayson's to do the catering ...'

'Oh,' says Hamilton lifting his hand. We wait expectantly while he finishes chewing his kipper. To think I am supposed to be marrying this creep.

'Grayson's are the best,' says Margarita in a tone that clearly indicates she has no intention of debating it.

'It's just, well,' struggles Hamilton.

'It's just well what?' I snap, surprising myself.

He glares at me and says 'It's just Grayson's are rather pricey Grandma.'

'Exactly. Why do you think they're the best, boy?'

Melanie stands up, wobbles and leans on my chair for support.

'Are you alright?' I ask, jumping up to steady her.

'Just a migraine. I'll retire to my room I think,' she says softly.

'Can I bring you something? Would you like a hot drink and some painkillers?'

I feel Margarita's eyes on me and Hamilton taps me lightly on the arm.

'Emily will see to anything Mother needs, but I'm sure Mother is grateful for the offer,' he says sternly.

I pull my arm away and I see Fiona cringe.

'I'll help your mother to her room,' I say sharply, leading Melanie gently towards the door.

'I'll send Emily up,' he says.

'We won't need Emily,' I say firmly.

Melanie looks about to faint and I'm not sure if it's the migraine or the fact that I am escorting her to her room. Once there she falls onto her bed and I look around in awe. This isn't a bedroom it's a full-size apartment. I run the cold tap and soak a towel under it. She accepts it gratefully and takes a painkiller.

'Margarita will be cross I'm not with the family for the stalk,' she says anxiously.

I wonder if this is a real migraine, or if she also is making an excuse to get out of the thing. I would invite her on the boat trip but it seems a shame to share Brice doesn't it? I pull the curtains and quietly leave the room. I look over the bannister to see everyone heading out. Fiona sees me and rushes up the stairs.

'Aren't you coming on the stalk?' she asks.

I shake my head. 'Not unless you're stalking Jack Diamond.'

She pulls a face.

'I'm surprised he hasn't texted about the fifty pounds. He must have noticed by now.'

That's all I need. A silent Jack Diamond is much worse than a chatty Jack Diamond. She hands me her phone and dashes down the stairs.

'If Alistair calls, tell him I'm out stalking stags. Just so he knows he isn't the only one having fun.'

Fun? Christ, she has a warped idea of fun. She skips down the stairs waving a hand at me and almost collides with a sour-faced Hamilton on his way up.

'Sorry,' she mumbles. 'No contacts.'

'What are you doing? I thought you were coming on the stalk,' he hisses.

I step back as his kipper breath suffocates me. God, he really needs to do something about that halitosis.

'I'm not the stalking type,' I retort.

'I couldn't give a shit. What does it look like you going off with Brice in the boat? You're making a bloody fool out of me.'

That's a joke. He doesn't need my help to make a fool of himself.

'He said your grandmother wouldn't fall for a migraine. He told her the truth, I'm not a stalking person and neither is he so he offered to take me out on the boat, and besides I really think you should back me up more. You know how I hate lying.'

He huffs.

'This business is one big lie, or hadn't you noticed? Anyway, I'm not sure you should go with Brice, it doesn't look good on me.'

'I don't want to go,' I say, lying through my teeth.

'Just watch what you say,' he snaps before storming off.

I click my heels.

'Yes sir,' I retort primly.

Bloody hell, what a Nazi. I watch the hunting party from the landing window as they pack their weapons into the back of the stalker's Range Rover. What a relief to be free from them for a few hours. To my surprise I see Margarita not only out of her wheelchair, but leading a horse. Well I never. I hope I'm that fit when I'm three months from dying.

'I'm leaving in ten minutes,' says Brice behind me. I spin round to face him and something clutches tightly at my belly. He is composed and carrying his coffee cup.

'Meet me on the jetty, you can't miss it.'

I nod mutely and watch him stroll out of the house. I frantically think of what I can wear. I fly back upstairs and throw everything from the wardrobe onto the bed. There is absolutely nothing I feel comfortable wearing. I finally rummage through my suitcase and pull out one of my woollen sweaters and throw it over a silk shirt, and then don my jeans and boots and pull my Boho poncho over everything. I grab my handbag and force myself to walk to the loch as calmly as I can. In the distance I can see him loading things into the little rowing boat. I try to imagine my parents up here. I will have to keep a constant check on Mum otherwise she will be getting out the hoover or clearing everyone's dishes to do the washing up. It really does not bear thinking about. It's hard enough keeping up this farce without them here. And what the hell is wrong with Hamilton? This isn't at all what we agreed. It was only supposed to be a bleeding weekend. Before I know where I am I'll be bloody marrying the wet dishcloth. Yes, that's about right. I'll find myself at the altar and Mum will be handing around cheese and pineapple sticks to all and sundry. They're her favourites, that and port and lemon. I'll have to jump on Margarita's horse like *The Runaway Bride*. I seriously cannot believe I have let things go this far. And now I'm about to step into a boat with Mr Drop Dead Gorgeous and I don't like to say I can't swim. I've always meant to learn and I have tried a few times but I just can't manage to get that other foot off the bottom of the pool. Do you know what I mean? I kind of skip along the pool from one end to the other and make it look good but if anyone so much as attempts to get that other foot off the bottom, I'm flapping away like a bloody penguin. I only hope this bleeding boat is safe. Didn't they mention a boat at dinner the other night, and if I remember both Hamilton and the Major were not very complimentary. Maybe I'll end up drowning. I suppose that will save Jack Diamond from chopping me into little pieces. My heart lurches at the thought of Diamond. Fiona is quite right. It is very odd of Diamond not to mention the missing fifty quid. He must have read my note. What if he is planning something terrible, something to take me totally by surprise? They will probably zoom up to us in the middle of the loch and board the boat like Somali pirates, and hold us at gunpoint until I pay the fifty quid. They always seem to know my next move. My blood turns cold. Jesus, how can I get in the boat now? Brice turns and the intensity of his stare is almost mesmerising. He looks at me in amazement as I drag my hair back and tie it with a band.

'You look completely different with your hair like that,' he says, gently smoothing back a loose strand that has escaped.
I shiver under his touch. I step gingerly onto the jetty. It seems to dip under my weight and doesn't feel very safe. I climb into the boat and send it reeling to one side and almost fall out. My legs give way and I fall onto the narrow bench and grasp it for all I'm worth. I must look a right plonker. Brice stares at me with a little smirk on his face.

'Is it safe?' I ask, trying to hide my anxiety.

'Why wouldn't it be?' he says, untying the rope from the mooring.

'It's just Hamilton and Major Bates said ...'
He laughs and leans over me to push a basket to the back of the boat.

'They meant my rickety boat in Laos. Now that isn't safe,' he smiles.

'Why do you have a boat in Laos?' I ask.

'It's more of a floating clinic. I go up and down the Mekong River and give medical help to those who can't afford to travel to a hospital. I find it rewarding.'
I so much want to ask him about his life in Laos but of course I daren't. I might end up telling him my dreams, which hardly match

up to that of a successful businesswoman with her own jewellery business.

'Don't you have life jackets?' I ask, looking under the seat.

'We're only going across the loch,' he says with a tinge of amusement in his voice. 'Although I brought my rope and tackle in case you fancied a bit,' he says licking his lips, and then not missing a beat adds, 'of fishing that is.'

I feel my face grow hot. Is he flirting with me? Has he forgotten I am supposed to be his cousin's fiancée? It occurs to me that I actually don't have to stay for the weekend. I could book a flight to Mexico, or is it Brazil? Didn't a train robber go to Brazil? I could do that. Hamilton would never find me. I needn't pay back the debts and I could sun myself on the beach and get a job in a beach bar. But I won't do that because I'm too damn honest. The cold wind whips me in the face and I huddle beneath my poncho and lift my eyes to take a sneaky look at him. He has on a thick woollen jumper and beneath I can see signs of a grey shirt. His jeans are tight and I can barely take my eyes off his lean thighs. His beautiful eyes meet mine and I find myself blinking rapidly. He pushes the boat out using an oar and I grip the sides and try to stop my knees from trembling. The sun shimmers on the loch and I relax. The muscles in his biceps seem to ripple with the water as he pulls the oars. This is all playing havoc with my navel, and a few other places. He stares at me as he rows.

'You're staring at me,' I say. 'It's very unnerving and not to mention bloody rude.'

'That's because you're extremely attractive,' he says in a matter-of-fact tone that leaves me quite speechless.

I can't even find the words to thank him. He stops rowing and casually leans back. I feel myself tense.

'You don't like boats do you? Either that, or it's the water you're not fond of.'

'I'm fine with both as long as they don't get too intimate with each other.'

He laughs and I marvel at his sparkling white teeth.

'The only water we'll have in this boat is this,' he says, reaching behind me. One hand slides sensually and deliberately, I am sure, over one of my knees. He returns with a bottle of Evian water and two plastic cups.

'Sorry it's nothing stronger. I thought we could have the wine later.'

I could do with it now as I need something to calm the stirring in my loins. I'm finding his warmth and friendliness disconcerting. It's like he is trying to lull me into a false sense of security and then he'll turn on me. I need to keep my wits about me. I'm struggling to keep my eyes off him, he is enthralling. His voice fascinates me. It is so smooth and soft. His eyes are worldly and his body lean and muscular. He is so self-possessed and animal sexuality oozes from him. I swear he could have any woman he wanted, so why doesn't there seem to be one? I wish my pulse would slow down. He continues rowing and points things out in the hills surrounding the loch but apart from that we are silent. The gentle rhythmic movements of the boat make me quite sleepy.

'You don't seem Hamilton's type,' he says abruptly.

God, you've got that one right. I snap my eyes open to see him sitting opposite me, his questioning eyes meeting mine. I struggle not to flinch. I knew I shouldn't have let my guard down. The sky is darkening and threatening rain. I take my scarf from my bag and wrap it around my neck.

'There is going to be a storm,' I say worriedly, acutely aware we are in the middle of the loch and surrounded by nothing but water.

'You're too honest for a start,' he says, ignoring me, 'and you're kind. It's something in you that you can't control. So, I am asking myself, what would someone like you see in Hamilton and you know what?'

A clap of thunder crashes above us.

'You're either madly in love with him, which I find hard to believe or ...'

A flash of lightning and another rumble of thunder stop him. He looks at the sky. I feel the first drops of rain and pull the scarf over my head.

'We'd better head for the boathouse,' he says, calmly picking up the oars while I feel my knees tremble and my heart race as a strong gust of wind rocks the boat. I grasp the sides. How can he not have life jackets? The light raindrops turn into a heavy shower and the wind and rain slap at my face. I feel sure the boat will tip over any second. I squeeze my bag between my knees and watch anxiously as he rows effortlessly through the storm. My shoulders ache from hunching and my fingers are numb from gripping the sides of the boat.

'How much further?' I ask in a shaky voice.

I am too afraid to look in case I send the whole thing tits up.

'Not far. Don't worry, nothing will happen to you while you're with me,' he says, casually throwing a waterproof over his head. He shakes wet hair out of his eyes and smiles at me in such a way that my heart flutters. Coming from anybody else I would have thought them an arrogant pig, but not so from Brice. In fact, he is probably quite right. Still, I'd be much happier if this bastard wind, as Margarita calls it, would drop. I focus on his rowing to keep my mind from the rocking boat, the bastard wind, and the hellish hailstones.

'Here,' he shouts over the wind and throws a waterproof mac my way. I cautiously pull it over my head. I'm too afraid to move in case I rock the boat and tip it over. He would then find out I can't swim. I don't know which is worse, Brice knowing I can't swim or me drowning in the loch. It's a no-brainer isn't it? I don't want Brice to know I can't swim. He manoeuvres the boat to the mooring under the boathouse and without a word, leaps out. I look around but it is impossible to see anything through the mist of heavy rain. Brice struggles to tie the boat and I stand unsteadily in an attempt to step off it. A strong gust of wind knocks me sideways. I feel myself lurch backwards as I lose my footing. A tiny scream escapes my lips as my foot twists under me and a searing pain shoots through it. Brice jumps back into the boat in a flash and steady's me with his strong arms.

'I've got you,' he says gently.

Oh yes, don't I know it. His firm body presses against mine and I feel dizzy with longing. The wind whistles and the rain pounds our bodies but I am only aware of his body touching mine and the heat that emanates from us both. It's like the cold wind can't reach us. His eyes meet mine and something flashes in them, but before I have time to recognise it he has pulled me from the boat. He points to the steps ahead.

'We'll shelter in there,' he says.

He takes my hand and guides me as I limp across to the steps of the boathouse. He pushes open the door, lays the basket down and walks towards the large open fireplace.

'I'll get the fire going and then have a look at that foot. The bathroom is through there if you want to get your clothes off.'

Blimey he doesn't waste time does he? I should be so lucky. The living area is sparse with two opposing couches draped in colourful throws, and an old oak coffee table between them. A sink and a tiny work surface with kettle and microwave constitute a kitchen area, and a large fireplace takes pride of place along one wall. The fireplace dominates the room and a large basket of logs sits to one side of it. The mantelpiece is covered in an assortment of candles. I follow his direction to the bathroom, passing a window that has a spectacular view of the loch. I can't believe Brice didn't check the weather before we left. He doesn't strike me as the irresponsible type. It then occurs to me he deliberately brought me here knowing full well we would get stuck. Oh my God, he probably plans to tie me to the rafters and whip me until I confess the truth. Ooh, I would have brought my *Bound To Tease Suede Flogger* if I'd known. I'm hopeful if nothing else. I peer through the rain at something in the water and blink several times to make sure my imagination isn't playing tricks on me, but no, our little rowing boat is now drifting aimlessly towards the middle of the loch.

Chapter Twenty-Two

I hobble back into the living room where Brice is stoking a blazing fire.

'The boat ...' I stutter pointing to the window.

He follows my finger and groans.

'Damn it,' he says and throws another log on the fire.

'Aren't you going to get it?' I demand.

He shrugs.

'Have you seen the weather?'

'But ...'

'We have food and drink, a warm place, cosy couches, a lovely fire. What more could you want?'

What more could I want? A bleeding boat to take me back from whence I came is what I want.

'But how do we get back?'

'Ah, haven't you heard of *Brice Luck*. We'll be fine.'

What is *Brice Luck* when it's at home?

'But Hamilton,' I begin.

He gives a mischievous grin.

'Ah yes Hamilton. Don't worry, you won't have to miss him too long. They'll most likely come back early from the shoot although, I think, the weather will break in an hour. They'll realise we've sheltered from the rain and won't worry about us until about five. Then they'll send someone to look for us.'

I gape at him. There was me thinking he was intelligent when he is obviously as moronic as his cousin.

'Haven't you heard of telephones?' I say sarcastically.

He raises his eyebrows.

'Are you using the bathroom? If you're not then I will. Although I think you would be more comfortable out of those clothes.'

His eyes travel over my body and I beg myself not to blush.

'There's a couple of towelling robes in the bathroom. The brown one is mine. You can have the other one.'

I snatch my bag from the couch and pull out Fiona's mobile. I don't believe it, no bleeding signal.

'Bleeding Scotland. It will be the buggery death of me,' I mumble as I limp to the bathroom. I hear him laugh as I slam the door. Hanging on the back are the towelling robes and I lift his off the hook and smell it. The familiar scent of him sends an electric shock through my body. I replace it and take the other one. I pull off my poncho and peel off my wet shirt and jeans. My foot is turning a shade of purple and blowing up like a balloon. Bloody wonderful. Still, on the bright side it will be the perfect excuse to get me out of the next round of stalks, shoots and tennis matches. The bathroom is very masculine. There is no bath, just a shower, a sink, a small bathroom cabinet and a toilet. There are towels piled up on a stool. I check the door is locked and plop myself on the loo. Taking my compact mirror from my handbag I check my reflection to see my hair is one straggly mess. I pull it out of the hair band and rub it with a towel until it is dry. I imagine a hairdryer would be too much to ask? After tying the towel robe around me I limp back to the living room where two steaming mugs of tea sit on the coffee table. He takes my wet clothes and lays them over a chair in front of the fire. The sight of the blazing fire doesn't stop me from shivering and I'm grateful for the blanket he offers. He has a change of clothes for himself on the couch. That's a relief. I rather felt the sight of him in a dressing gown might have tipped me over the edge.

'Here,' he says abruptly handing me a mug of tea. 'I won't be long.'

He stops to get a wash bag and another blanket from a tiny cupboard. I wonder if there is also a hairdryer in that little Tardis. My clothes steam in front of the fire and after a couple of sips of tea I feel much warmer. This is ridiculous and I need to tell him so. We can't just wait for his so-called *Brice Luck* can we? I don't know what he expects his Brice Luck to do, unless it is going to magically turn the boat around and send it cruising back to us. Maybe the Brice Luck may even tie it securely to the mooring. Mind you, if the real Brice can't do that how can you expect the Brice Luck to do any better? I glance down reluctantly at my foot to see it is swollen. Damn it. I've obviously sprained the bleeding thing. I'm seriously buggered if I have to sprint away from the Jacks. My stomach churns when I think they may be trying to phone me. They'll be well pissed at getting Fiona's voicemail. I imagine Alistair will be rather pissed too if he is calling it. I lift my throbbing ankle onto a footstool and curse. I'm just considering a peek into the Tardis when he steps out of the bathroom wearing a grey sweatshirt over jeans. He throws another log onto the fire and flops onto the couch opposite me. I sigh.

'Look, I don't want you to think I'm dissing the Brice Luck or anything, but I can't help wondering how we're going to get back. Aren't you even slightly anxious?'

He shakes his head.

'What's the point of getting anxious?'

'But we need to get back ...'

'Not at this exact moment we don't. It's eleven-thirty, it's pouring with rain, so why are you worrying about getting back now? That's a problem for later. The important thing right now is to look at that foot and check you haven't broken anything.'

For someone who thinks I may have broken something he's taking his time looking at it. If he was any more laid back he'll fall over. He finishes his tea, God forbid I should come before that, and then crouches down on the floor. I feel my stomach wobble and my heart skip a bit as his hand touches my foot. He strokes it carefully, making it seem more like a caress, and I have to control the shiver that runs through me. This is ridiculous. I'm not the type of woman who falls at the feet of a good-looking man. I don't go all soppy in front of a man, no matter how attractive he is. Mind you, most attractive men are arrogant so-and-sos aren't they? But heavens, I can't deny the slightest touch from this man has me aroused, in fact, just the promise of a touch has me aroused. I'm worried that if he begins to bandage my foot I'm likely to have an earth-shattering orgasm. That would be dead embarrassing wouldn't it? Fortunately he turns it slightly and an earth-shattering pain shoots through my foot and up my leg, quickly dispelling any thoughts of orgasms. I recoil immediately.

'That bloody hurt,' I say without thinking.

'I'm sure it did,' he says, frowning and lifting my foot into his lap. I'm acutely conscious that it sits on his thigh and can't get his joke about his rope and tackle out of my mind. I make a determined effort to look everywhere but at my swollen foot that sits just inches from his rope and tackle, and I find myself wondering if that is swollen too by any chance. God, this man is turning me into a nympho.

'Does that hurt?' he asks, pushing at my ankle. I nod and bite my lip.

He places my foot gently onto the footstool.

'Fortunately you haven't broken anything, but you've sprained it quite badly. It will get better in a few days. It will throb less once the bruise is out but presumably you know all that. I'll put something on to encourage the bruising.'

Oh no, that means he will have to massage it and I really don't know how much more of his hands my loins can take. He disappears into the bathroom and I take the opportunity to fan my hot face. He returns with a tube of cream. I take a deep breath to prepare myself. His hands are gentle and they caress my foot in the most sensual way.

'I realise I have been a bit rude to you,' he says softly.

A bit rude, crikey, that's an understatement.

'The truth is, I don't have the best opinion of Hamilton,' his eyes meet mine and I feel uncomfortable. 'I don't expect you to understand. It's just I worry about my grandmother. I know you most probably think she is a tough old bird, but she's vulnerable and not as tough as she seems. And she's getting older. I'm not here as much as I'd like but I feel when I am the least I can do is look out for her.'

'What is wrong with her exactly?' I ask softly.

'Aside from her blood pressure? To be honest I don't really know. She's sworn the doctors to secrecy. She's a mischievous madam but for all that I love her and I care about her welfare. I don't want her to be hurt or deceived.'

One hand rests on my foot and the other on his knee. I feel tears sting my eyes and curse him for making me feel guiltier than ever. What the hell am I supposed to do now? He's a fine one to talk. Like he just said, he's barely here so what would he do with the shares if they were left to him? My brain spins. This is the worst dilemma of my life. It was one thing for Julian to let me down but to make me compromise all my principles is unforgiveable. I've never been dishonest in my life. This whole business is agony for me, and I can see no way out. If I tell Hamilton I want 'out' he'll want his money returned and I'll be back where I started. I could declare myself bankrupt but then I'll never be able to rent a flat again, and the thought of living with my parents drives me to distraction. Just the thought of bankruptcy makes my heart sink. Would I still get a nursing job? Jesus, if Julian thinks the Jacks are scary just wait till he sees me. I'll bleeding kill the little git.

'Harriet?' asks Brice.

I pull my mind from Julian and back to the most gorgeous man I have ever met, and raise my eyebrows.

'I said, do you think some wine, French bread and brie would help the pain?'

It will certainly dull my thought that's for sure. I nod.

'Is it hurting? Would a couple of painkillers help?'

Do you have morphine? That and the wine should knock me out until this is all over. I'll talk to Hamilton, explain my predicament. That's the best thing. I'll tell him I feel awful about his grandmother. Maybe we can both talk to her and explain Hamilton's fears about being cut off without a penny. God forbid he would have to get a job and earn a living like the rest of us.

'Yes, that would be great. Thank you,' I say.

'The wine will help,' he says and strokes a hand down my cheek affectionately.

The wind whistles under the door. A loud crack of thunder makes me jump and I pull the blanket closer. If only wine was the answer to this hellish muddle I am in. I'm relieved when he moves his irresistible body away from me and I can tell you, it isn't only my foot that is throbbing. A voice inside my head whispers *tell him, tell him now, he will help you, w*hile another argues *oh yes, go on tell him and then see if you enjoy wine, brie and French bread.* He's just told you how protective he is of his grandmother. Oh God, it's all I can do not to drop my head in my hands and tell him my story. I watch as he silently cuts the bread and uncorks the wine. I make a feeble effort to stand up and hobble towards him.

'What are you doing?' he says abruptly.

'Coming to help. I feel useless sitting there, and it's all my fault the boat has drifted and I, I ...'

And then damn it, I start crying. Me, Harriet bleeding Lawson who hasn't cried since my pet rabbit, Bernard, died, and even then just a few hiccups. Before I can turn away he has wrapped his arms around me and that just sets me off even more. Before I know it, I am sobbing in his arms and clinging to his muscular body. I feel his hand stroking my back and his breath on my neck.

'It's okay, it's not that bad,' he says quietly.

His voice is raspy. He doesn't know the half of it. This is terrible, I swear I can feel things I shouldn't be feeling and I push myself away gently.

'I never cry,' I hiccup.

His hand continues to clasp mine. I look into his eyes and feel him lean towards me. He smells wonderful and I feel drunk on the essence of him. A gust of wind flings the door open and he releases me to close it. I take the opportunity to calm my beating heart.

'You rest that foot. You should know better as a nurse than to keep putting weight on it like that,' he says, but I hear a shake in his voice.

I nod, sensing that he wishes to put a distance between us. I hobble back to the couch and flop down. I so wish Fiona was here so I could ask her what I should do. *Don't drink too much* would be her advice no doubt. Yes, that's good advice. *I must not drink too much* I say to myself as I accept a large glass of Chardonnay. It couldn't be a more romantic setting if it tried. A storm outside and a roaring log fire, a glass of wine and a gorgeous hunk; it all makes for the best kissing scenario doesn't it? It is bloody typical of my life that there also has to be an arse of an ex-boyfriend, three wanking gangsters and a corrupt aristocrat with a filthy-rich grandmother. I'd best not drink too much Chardonnay. Julian said wine makes me randy. Mind you, I don't need much encouragement to feel randy with Brice Edmunds just a few inches away. He places a piece of bread onto my plate and pops open a jar of olives.

'So why did you give up nursing?' he asks casually.

I take a sip of wine and say honestly,

'My then boyfriend was starting up a French restaurant, and he, well we both felt we wouldn't see that much of each other if I continued working shifts.'

Not that we bloody saw much of each other when I stopped. Ooh that little bugger. Just thinking of Julian makes my blood boil. He nods, but I can see his brain whirring. The room is hot and I unwrap myself from the blanket and drop it to the floor. He stares at me and I look down to see the towelling robe is gaping slightly. I pull it together and hide behind my glass.

'So you met Hamilton after that presumably?' he asks, but there is no hostility in his voice.

'Brice, I really don't feel comfortable talking about my relationship with Hamilton.'

He cuts through the bread roughly.

'I can understand that,' he says sarcastically, placing another piece of bread onto my plate. His gaze is hypnotic and I can't take my eyes off him.

'Do you remember when we met at the wedding,' he smiles, his eyes twinkling.

I nod and sip the wine. I'm already feeling a little light-headed. A croissant for breakfast and a slice of French bread are all I've eaten all day, and I've almost emptied a large glass of Chardonnay. He lights the candles on the mantelpiece.

'You were wearing that lovely dress,' he says, topping up my glass before I can stop him.

'It wasn't that lovely,' I mumble.

'I thought it was,' he refills his glass and sits next to me. I tighten the belt of the towelling robe. Good God Harriet, he isn't going to rape you.

'I remember you saying that Alistair always thinks you look crap.' I smile. Well, that's true isn't it?

'And I remember thinking how fresh and lovely you were,' he says glancing at me over the rim of his glass. 'I looked for you later but you had already left.'

I swallow. The memory of my return to Marlborough Mansions with Fiona and Alistair makes me shudder. I take another gulp of wine.

'Then I saw you again in the dress shop and I was so pleased. I was beginning to think I'd dreamt you up.'

I look into his eyes which are intent on mine. I suppress a gasp at what I read on his face. It is pure desire, naked, raw, hot and pulsating and I have to lean back against the couch as the breath is knocked out of me.

'When I saw you again at Glenwood, and you were telling me you were Hamilton's girlfriend, I felt like someone had just whacked me with a cricket bat and nothing made any sense.'

'Brice, I really think ...'

I sense him leaning towards me and my hand goes to his chest. I allow him to take the glass from my hand and push me back on the couch. My pulse quickens and I can't breathe. I feel sure once his lips touch mine I shall die from the desire. He tastes delicious, his kiss hard and hot. I wrap one arm around his neck and push my other hand under his sweater. His hand searches inside my robe. I gasp as his fingers stroke my nipple. His lips ravage mine until the ache in my loins is unbearable. The kiss deepens and the scent of him drives me wild. His passion is overwhelming and threatens to take me over. The burning desire deep inside me is battling with my sensible need to be in control. As his lips travel slowly down my neck and towards my breast I reach down to feel the hardness of him. He groans beneath my touch and the need to have him inside me is too much to bear. I push against his chest.

'Brice wait, please wait,' I say, my breath shuddering.

His lips reluctantly leave my breast and with trembling hands I pull the robe together.

'I'm sorry,' he says huskily, moving away and I avert my eyes from the noticeable bulge in his jeans. As if not trusting himself he moves to the other couch.

'Brice, I'm ...'

God, I can't speak, I'm so overcome with desire. If things get any more complicated I'm likely to forget who I am. He reaches for his wine glass, his eyes avoiding mine. Neither of us speaks and all that can be heard is the rain hammering on the roof, and the crackling of the logs in the fire. He takes a deep shuddering breath. After what seems like an eternity he stands up and walks over to the Tardis cupboard. After rummaging through the contents he retrieves a shoebox.

'Let's see if anybody is on the air shall we?' he says simply as he lifts an old looking radio from the box. I feel all my emotions tip over into anger. The bastard had a sodding CB radio in the cupboard all the time and never even mentioned it. I feel horribly deceived and go to storm into the bathroom forgetting about my injured foot. It bends under me and he is instantly at my side.

'Didn't I tell you not to put weight on that foot,' he barks, his arms holding me. I grab the table for support and gently remove myself from his arms. The radio squeaks and crackles and a voice launches itself at us.

'Blue Yonder Blue Yonder, anyone else on the air?'

He turns back to the radio.

'Scooby Doo here, is that you Hamish?'

Scooby Doo? God give me strength.

'Yes, Brice old chap, how are you?'

'I'm good thanks Hamish, how are you doing?'

'Same old, same old, nothing changes here in bonnie Scotland as you know. How's that beautiful girlfriend of yours?'

I shoot him a sharp look.

'Oh, she's gone back to South Africa, she couldn't hack the life in Asia. Listen Hamish, I'm stuck at the boathouse with a friend. I didn't moor the boat properly and she's drifted off. Could you phone Angus and see if he could do us a favour and come out with his boat?'

'Of course mate, no problem. We should get together for a wee dram.'

I hobble past him to the loo and mumble.

'You deceived me.'

'That makes two of us then,' he says, putting a hand over the microphone.

I turn huffily and slam the bathroom door. What a pig, he had deliberately exposed my weakness. In that moment I hate him even more than I hate Julian.

Chapter Twenty-Three

Jack Diamond paces back and forth past the bench where his sons sit drinking cider. Mad Jack Junior rubs his hands exaggeratingly to let his father know how cold he is, but Diamond doesn't give a shit. All he can think about is that Harriet tart and her useless boyfriend Julian. What the hell was going on? How could she drop him fifty quid short?

'Can we go back to the B and B now Dad?' asks Babyface. 'I'm bleedin' freezing.'

'Yeah, bleedin' taters up 'ere in Scotland. I dunno 'ow the buggers live 'ere. They should get a bleedin' medal, that's what I think,' adds Mad Jack, rubbing his hands together.

'Yeah, well I don't give a diddlyshit what yer think, so just shut up,' snaps Diamond. 'We ain't going 'ome yet.

It wasn't so much the fifty quid, it was more her bleeding attitude that had irritated him. The little wanker Julian had pissed off and now she has got a rich poncy boyfriend she couldn't care less it seems. He takes a gulp of cider and slams the glass on the table, making both boys jump.

'Right, we're gonna stake out that 'ouse. I reckon we can turn that over easy enough. We just 'ave to watch their movements and go in when the time's right.'

Both lads stare at him with wide eyes.

'But we never stake out big 'ouses,' protests Mad Jack.

'Yeah, remember what Mum says bout alarms and stuff,' agrees Babyface.

'What does yer mum know? What are yer now, bloody mummy's boys?'

'I just want to go 'ome and get some decent grub. That bleedin' 'aggis we 'ad last night an 'alf affected me bowels. You know me bowels ain't good,' groans Mad Jack. 'I need a plate of pie and mash, decent bleeding grub.'

'Bloody hell,' mumbles Diamond.

'I've 'ad to take them Imodium otherwise I'd be on the bog all bleedin' day. This bag of crisps is the first thing I've eaten.'

'You'll be like a bleedin' constipated duck if you keep taking those sodding pills,' snorts Diamond.

'Yeah, I ain't feeling so good neither. It ain't natural eatin' that stuff,' says Babyface.

'Will you shut the piss up before I have to run again,' groans Mad Jack.

'We ain't going nowhere until we get something back from that 'arriet,' says Diamond firmly.

'I reckon I bloody will be,' moans Mad Jack holding his stomach.

'She took us for idiots and we're far from that, right?' says Diamond, looking to them for confirmation.

Mad Jack nods in agreement.

'Yeah, she proper cut off her nose to spite 'er face and shot 'erself in the foot.'

'What the 'ell you talking about?' asks Diamond.

'Well it's a saying ain't it. She didn't do 'erself no favours like, so she cut off 'er nose ...'

'I know that you stupid plonker, but it can't be both can it? She can't cut off her nose to spite her face *and* bleedin' shoot 'erself in the foot. It's one or the other ain't it? Jesus, I really can't think yer can be me boys.'

'I think we should go 'ome and think this through,' says Babyface quietly. 'It's a big 'ouse and they'll be security and guards and all sorts. They may 'ave guards with guns and stuff.'

'Don't be bloody stupid. It'll be a piece of piss, and we only have to steal a few bits to make it worthwhile. We'll start staking out tonight. We'll need those balaclavas from the boot.'

Mad Jack bangs his glass on the table.

'I bloody 'ate them. They always give me a bloody rash and I've got enough with this stomach,' he says farting loudly.

'Jesus Christ,' mumbles Diamond. 'You're a bloody girl's blouse.' He hits Mad Jack round the head. 'I thought you were a man. You'll be wearing a bloody skirt like this lot up 'ere next.'

Babyface laughs until Mad Jack punches him in the stomach.

'Christ Mad Jack, that hurt.'

'Good. See how you like having sore guts.'

Jack Diamond sighs. Thank Christ he's not retiring yet. The firm would not last five minutes without him.

Chapter Twenty-Four

'God, what happened to your foot? It's all black and swollen,' says Fiona, stating the obvious as only Fiona can.

'I slipped getting off the stupid boat. I had to take the bleeding stairlift to get up the stairs. I felt a right wally.'

I'm lying on the bed feeling very sorry for myself. Just the sight of Fiona all flushed and excited, and in my riding outfit, almost has me in tears. I don't know what's wrong with me, I don't even cry around period time. I'm really good with the monthlies, except once when I pinned Julian against the wall with a breadknife at his throat, but I figure he probably asked for it. In fact, if he walked in the door right now I would have no hesitation in holding a knife to his throat and my period is ages away.

'It's a peculiar colour. Don't you think you should see a doctor?'

'I've seen a doctor,' I say.

'Oh,' she says, sitting beside me on the bed. 'Hamilton said he'll be up in a minute.'

'Did you have a good time?' I ask, knowing she is bursting to tell me all about it.

She jumps up excitedly.

'God, it's amazing riding here Harry. It's so freeing with the mountains and the open spaces, it releases so much stress. The shooting bit was gross and I feel a bit sick just thinking about it, but the riding was fantastic. I thought the rain would never stop, and we're having the deer for dinner.'

'Fan-bloody-tastic,' I say scornfully.

She flops back onto the bed.

'Yes, I know what you mean. But oh, being on a horse and Sebastian was so helpful. You have to admit he is pretty appealing. I've worn my contacts all day just so I could get a good look at him.'

Oh my God, what's happening here?

'You do know he's married? He is Hamilton's father remember, and like, old enough to be your dad?'

She tuts and twists her hair before knotting it with a hairband.

'I know that but it's common knowledge that the marriage is shaky, what with her,' she leans forward like a conspirator, 'little liaison.'

'What, Melanie?' I say, trying not to squeal.

She nods, glances at the door and says quickly,

'With Gregory the valet, didn't you know? It's common knowledge in the servant's quarters. I feel so sorry for Seb.'

Seb? Jesus Christ, how could all this have been going on under my nose? Maybe I'm the one who needs the glasses.

'Bleeding hell Fiona, you've only been here a few hours,' I mutter. 'What about Alistair?'

'Yes, well Alistair is not as nice as you might think,' she says defensively.

'I never thought he was,' I say honestly.

'And anyway, I wanted to make the most of it. When will I ever stay in a house like this again?'

Perhaps she'd like to get engaged to Hamilton.

'But Melanie and a servant, crikey, it's like something out of Downtown Abbey.'

'What do you think that migraine was all about?' she says, dropping the contacts from her eyes.

God almighty, everyone is at it except me, although I did come close earlier.

'So has there been any news? Did the Jacks phone?' she asks, dropping her voice to a whisper.

I shake my head.

'Shit, you're joking?'

'I kid you not. There has been nothing from them.'

'God, that's worrying.'

'You had two voicemail messages from Alistair. Something along the lines of j-j-j-just c-c-c-calling t-t-t-t- ... I kind of gave up after the third word. I didn't really have an hour to spare.'

'Don't mock.'

'He's never nice to me so I don't see why I should make an effort.'

'Two messages, that's even more worrying,' she grumbles.

Not as worrying as the state of my mind.

'I'm telling Hamilton I'm leaving,' I say, making a sudden decision.

She almost falls off the bed.

'You can't do that, what about the grandmother?'

'Yes, what about the grandmother?' I say, struggling to get up. 'How did she cope with the stalk? I take it she didn't collapse or anything then?'

'We had to stop for a while because she felt tired, but ...' she looks thoughtful. 'I have to say for someone who doesn't have long, she is doing incredibly well.'

I nod knowingly.

'Exactly, there is something very fishy going on here and I'm going to find out what it is.'

There is a knock and Fiona ventures to open the door. But not before she has crashed into the dressing table and opened the bathroom door by mistake.

'Fiona, put your glasses on,' I snap.

'Hello Hamilton,' she says to Brice as he strolls in with a pair of crutches tucked under his arm.

'It's Brice actually,' he smiles.

'Sorry,' she apologises, 'no contacts.'

'Oh, it's Scooby Doo,' I say nastily. 'Don't worry Fi, easy mistake, after all they are cousins and they're both deceitful buggers,' I add nastily.

'Harriet,' admonishes Fi.

Brice gives me a heart-stopping smile and offers me his hand.

'I brought you these. You'll probably need them for a few days. It's best not to put your weight on the injury.'

I ignore his hand and pull myself up with the end of the bed. I grab a crutch, support myself and then take the other one from him, the whole time being careful not to touch any part of his body.

'Are you having a party?'

We all turn to see Hamilton in the doorway.

'Harriet had a little accident on the boat, nothing serious. I brought her some crutches. I'll see you all at dinner,' Brice says in his matter-of-fact voice before strolling from the room.

'I must get cleaned up,' says Fiona as she stumbles into the wall.

'And put some contacts in before you fall down the bleeding stairs.'

'Language,' snaps Hamilton.

I turn angrily on him.

'In the next few minutes Hamilton-bloody-Lancaster I believe you'll hear a lot worse.'

'Have you lost your mind?' he hisses. 'Keep your voice down.'
He is wearing a jumper similar to the one Brice had on earlier but the effect on me is the exact opposite.

'I'm leaving, and I'm telling your grandmother the truth. This is all getting out of hand,' I say and turn to the door.
He grabs my arm roughly.

'You're not telling Grandmother anything Harriet. Not now we've come this far.'
I pull my arm out of his grasp and steady myself on the crutches.

'Hamilton, this has gone further than we agreed,' I say, struggling to keep my voice down. 'At the rate we're going I can see myself on a bleeding honeymoon with you.'

'It's only until the weekend,' he pleads.
If I remember it was only going to be a weekend in the first place, and that weekend has long gone.

'I can't do it Hamilton. I'm lying more and more. I really don't see how I can get through this engagement party, I'll have to ask my sister and my parents and ...'

'I'm warning you Harriet, if you pull out now you'll have to pay back every penny.'
Oh bugger this for a game of soldiers.

'You can have it all back, every single penny of it. I'll go back to nursing and I'll take out a loan if I have to, but I'll give you back everything you've paid me.'
Knowing my bloody awful luck I will most likely have to borrow it from the Jacks. I don't believe that Babyface Jack, I thought he was a nice lad. Honestly, you can't trust anyone these days. I put my hand on the door handle and stop when he says,

'I don't think you'll be returning to nursing because I assure you, if you go to my grandmother, I'll make sure you never nurse again.'
A shiver runs down my spine like a cold caress. I spin round to face him and feel my body shake.

'Are you threatening me Hamilton?'

'My whole family could end up penniless if I let you do this. Do you understand what I'm saying Harriet? I can't let that happen. Don't underestimate my power. I can see to it that you never work again and if you think anything of Fiona ...'

'Don't you dare drag her into this,' I say loudly.

'Don't raise your voice,' he says, stepping towards me.

'Fiona has got nothing to do with this,' I hiss.

'You brought her here and I'll have no qualms telling my grandmother that she was a bit light-fingered, you know what I mean? You're from Battersea you should know what I'm talking about.'

I gasp.

'You're such a bastard. What's to stop me telling your grandmother everything? I'll tell her how you just threatened me and all because you want her money.'

'I'll tell her that she was absolutely right when she suggested you were nothing but a gold-digger. I'll say you've only come to her because I've broken off the engagement after discovering you weren't who you said you were, and that in fact, you work in a laundrette. I don't think that would be very hard to prove would it?'

I stare at him totally appalled at the sudden change in his personality.

'And while we're at it, make sure your parents keep their fingers away from the silver.'

My hand comes up instinctively and slaps him so hard across the face that he loses his balance. I open the door as he cowers from me.

'Get the fuck out of my room you no good piece of scum.'

'Now that sounds like Harriet the washerwoman. Now if I were you I would think through this crazy decision of yours and get dressed for dinner,' he mumbles, rubbing his cheek. 'Oh, and Grandmother wants to go clay pigeon shooting tomorrow. She's keen to see how well you do your second time around. Try not to bugger it up again.'

'I'd stay clear then if I were you Hamilton, I may well be tempted to aim the gun up your arse, and don't underestimate my anger,' I say darkly.

He gives me a mean glance and heads out of the room. The temptation to whack him with a crutch is curtailed only when I see Brice walking towards us. Hamilton nods at him and strides to the stairs. I'm about to close my door when he passes.

'Lovers' tiff?' he enquires with a smile.

'Oh bugger off,' I snap and slam the door.

I struggle to control my tears of anger. What the hell am I going to do? I find myself seriously considering shooting Hamilton tomorrow. The little git certainly deserves it. That kind of thing must happen at these posh dos all the time, there is no health and safety malarkey so what the heck. No way are my parents coming here to mix with these lunatics. I debate whether to go to Margarita's room but I know Hamilton has me by the short and curlies. There is no way Margarita is going to believe me over him. After all, I'm a total stranger, and I do work in a laundrette and I'm not ashamed of it. Bloody men, how did I manage to get tied up with two of the world's worst?

Chapter Twenty-Five

You could cut the tension at dinner with a knife. Melanie looks more strung than a violin. She always looks edgy but tonight even more so. She spends the first course wringing her hands. Sebastian has great difficulty keeping his eyes off Fiona, who, I have to say looks sensational in a long Monsoon Indian-style dress. Her face glows and her thick chestnut hair hangs in delicious waves behind her ears from which hang large ethnic earrings, giving her an oriental look. She looks stunning, and I can understand Sebastian being mesmerised. Hamilton is spending most of his time giving me piercing looks which I ignore, and Brice gives me an occasional sideways glance. He is sitting beside me and it is making me feel decidedly uncomfortable.

'How's the foot?' he asks. 'You're very quiet, is it painful?'

'The foot is fine thank you. Something else is giving me a pain,' I say looking pointedly at Hamilton. Margarita sits beside him and looks like a woman in the first flush of youth rather than one at death's door. God, she looks better than me. I'd like to know what she's up to. She meets my eyes and nods.

'Nice dress Harriet. Black suits you,' she says. 'I have a beautiful set of pearls that would complement that dress perfectly,' she adds clicking her fingers for Emily.

'Fetch them would you dear?'

'Yes madam,' says Emily, giving me a sly wink.

Hamilton looks appalled and turns to his grandmother.

'Really Grandma, that's not necessary. Harry wouldn't want to take family pearls would you Harry? I'll buy her a nice set for the wedding.'

I stroke my forehead with my middle finger while looking at Hamilton in the manner of *up yours you wanker*. His mouth tightens.

'Actually, that would be lovely Margarita, thank you so much. It means a lot to wear something that has been in Ham's family for years.'

'Ham?' questions Sebastian, his eyes widening.

'It's my little pet name for Hamilton, isn't that right sweetheart?' I say, kicking his shin under the table.

'Yes, it's quaint, don't you think?' he says through gritted teeth.

'Makes you sound like a leg of meat,' says Brice leaning across me for a bread roll.

'Be careful you don't kick him with the wrong foot,' he whispers. 'You want *him* to feel the pain.'

I stifle a gasp as his hand with the bread roll *accidently* strokes my arm.

'Your father gave me these after your birth,' she says to Sebastian as she takes the pearls from Emily. 'They should be around a young woman's throat, don't you agree?'

'Absolutely,' replies Sebastian with his eyes fixed on Fiona.

I watch fascinated as Gregory steps forward with a silver platter of venison. He places it carefully onto the table and strokes Melanie's neck as he pulls back. It is almost imperceptible but it definitely happened. Oh my God. She picks up her glass with a trembling hand. Talk about *carry on with the aristocrats.* How have I managed to miss this stuff?

'Meat from the stalk, excellent,' cries Margarita, seemingly oblivious of the tension at the dinner table.

'By the way Fiona, excellent horse riding today, do you not agree Sebastian?'

'Outstanding. You look splendid on horseback,' he says dreamily.

Melanie's head snaps up. She glances at Fiona curiously before resuming the picking at her bread roll. Jesus Christ, these people are unbelievable. How the other half live or what?

'Are you joining us for the shoot tomorrow?' asks Sebastian.

'Oh yes,' says Fiona.

She is practically panting. If only it was Sebastian who needed the future wife and Alistair the one in debt. Ignoring the fact that Sebastian is old enough to be her father, but how easily that could have been sorted. I could go back to my nice little life as a laundrette manager and finish my studies, and perhaps just perhaps I could one day follow my dream and do charity work in a third-world country.

'Will you be able to manage the shoot with that foot?' Margarita says grimacing.

'Absolutely,' I say. 'I hope to hit something this time.'

I glance casually at Hamilton. Margarita pushes the pearls across the table to me.

'Wear them at the party on Friday,' she says casually.

I glare at Hamilton. What the hell? When did the party get to be on Friday?

'Didn't he tell you?' barks Margarita, seeing the surprise on my face.

'Actually, no he didn't,' I say angrily. 'Ham sweetie, did you forget to mention it?'

'Oh dear,' says Brice under his breath.

'You can zip it too,' I hiss.

He laughs.

'I can assure you madam it isn't unzipped yet,' he whispers. 'But just say the word.'

I feel myself blush.

'Grandmother thought it would be good to have the engagement party on Friday. We always have a ball the last Friday before we leave so …'

'So you and your grandmother decide to change the date without telling me,' I say angrily banging my glass onto the table.

'Well …' begins Hamilton.

'Shut up Hamilton unless you have something worth saying, which I doubt you have. Margarita, don't you think you should have asked, rather than told me?' I say, meeting her steely unfaltering eyes.

'I rarely discuss things my dear because I'm always right.'

Fiona shifts in her seat and says softly, 'Harriet, don't overreact.'

'Overreact?' I snap. 'You haven't seen me anywhere near overreact yet.'

'Harriet darling, we all realise you're in pain but it isn't like you to get so upset,' says Hamilton in that lovey-dovey voice that I'm growing to detest.

I push my plate away.

'If you'll excuse me, I really don't think I can eat anything. Thank you for the pearls Margarita,' I say, snatching them before Hamilton can grab them. 'We can discuss Friday's engagement party sometime tomorrow, and we can then see if you have made the right decision,' I finish firmly. I don't give a damn if the old girl is on her last legs. Frankly, I hope I have her bleeding legs when I get to her age.

'Yes of course dear,' interjects Melanie. 'You go and have a rest. We can all chat over breakfast. Isn't that right Hamilton?'

Hamilton forces a weak smile but his eyes are cursing me. Fiona grasps my hand as I pass.

'Do you need me?' she asks quietly.

'I'll be fine.'

'Let me give you something for the pain,' adds Brice.

'Oh really, this is ridiculous,' moans Margarita. 'We have decent venison here.'

'It can be kept hot. I'll be back. Don't get your blood pressure up over a piece of venison old girl,' he smiles. 'I'll just give Harriet something to help her feel better and I'll be back.'

There's only one thing he can give me to help me feel better, and if he's that quick maybe it's not worth it. Oh well, I at least still have my sense of humour. I hobble on my crutches. As I reach the foot of the stairs his hand touches my arm.

'Let's go for a hobble outside shall we?' he says pleasantly. 'There's a bench by the rose garden. We can sit there.'

'Weren't you ordered to get back to the venison as soon as possible?'

'Grandma knows I don't obey her or anyone else's orders come to that,' he says, offering his arm.

I exhale and accept his offer feeling that little tingle of pleasure as soon as I touch him. We walk slowly to the bench and he takes one of the crutches before helping me sit down. The sky is clear and the stars twinkle above us. He drops my shawl around my shoulders and lets his hand rest there for a few seconds before taking the pearls from my hand and sliding them sensually around my throat before clipping them at the back.

'She's quite right,' he says softly. 'They go perfectly with that dress.'

I stroke my neck and look up at the stars. We are silent for a while and I stretch my foot out and study the bruise. I've never felt so helpless in my whole life. I feel so angry with this stupid foot and knowing Hamilton has got me over a barrel makes me fume. I really cannot believe how foolish I have been. Trusting Julian was the biggest mistake of my life. What in God's name made me sign things without reading them? How could I have been so easily deceived? I always thought of myself as a sensible person. How did this ever happen. I'd kick myself but it would hurt twice as much. Fuck it all. If trusting Julian wasn't bad enough I then went and trusted that bugger Hamilton Lancaster, and now look at the mess I am in. I feel Brice's eyes on me and sigh heavily.

'So, you had a girlfriend that couldn't hack your life in Laos,' I say, just as something to shift the thought of wanking Hamilton and cocking Julian from my mind.

I feel him nod beside me.

'She didn't get off on *rickety boats and maggot-infested open wounds,* her words not mine. She didn't like exposing herself to the sun too much either, and considering the sun is always out and always hot, it got a bit awkward.'

'She sounds just your type,' I smile.

He nods.

'She pretended to be but when she came to Laos wearing her Christian Dior swimsuit and Jimmy Choo sandals I felt the first stirrings of doubt.'

I laugh and turn to see him looking at me and my heart flutters at the naked desire that flashes in his eyes.

'I'd like to go to Laos,' I say quickly turning away. 'I always wanted to nurse abroad and help those less privileged than myself.'

Oh God, what am I saying now? Blood suffuses my body and I feel on fire. I so wish I had brought my vibrator. There is a lot to be said for BOBs. Although a battery operated boyfriend I feel would be no substitute for Brice Edmunds. With a fierce determination I push the image of Brice Edmunds in my bed from my mind and attempt to stand up, but my feet seem rooted to the spot.

'We should get back,' I stammer, making another fruitless effort to get off the bench.

'Why?' he says, raising his eyebrows. 'Are you afraid of something?'

I shake my head and push my hand onto the bench to lever myself up and find I am leaning on his knee.

'Maybe this,' he whispers huskily, leaning towards me. I let out a shuddering breath as his body connects with mine.

'This thing between us that we're both trying to ignore?' he whispers into my ear.

His eyes travel flirtatiously over my body before his lips reach hungrily for mine.

'Brice we mustn't, we can't.'

A deep instinct tells me I have to pull away, but I'm not able. As his body moulds against mine I lose all resistance and meet his tongue with my own. I feel sure I hear all the stars burst above me. My heart pounds in my ears and his lips taste like honey. My breath becomes ragged gasps. God, I have no control when this man touches me. I feel his hand slip down the front of my dress and gently cup my breast, and I fight the urge to call out. I need to think clearly but the scent of him is invading my nostrils and numbing my brain. My breasts ache for his touch and I arch myself towards him. At that moment there is the sound of a door slamming and reality strikes me like a bolt of lightning and I push him away from me roughly.

'What are we doing? I'm engaged to your cousin and and ...' I say breathlessly.

'You're not really with Hamilton. If I believed that for one minute I wouldn't be sitting here now. I don't flirt with other people's fiancées, it really isn't my style. I believe you have a boyfriend. If I remember correctly his name is Julian, and I think somehow he has got you into this fix. I could be wrong. You could just be a gold-digger and a con woman. But I don't think I could feel this for someone like that. I believe you are a genuinely nice person and that's why I wish you would tell me what's going on. I'm drawn like a magnet to you. I have been since Hugh's wedding. There is something special happening between us, don't you feel it?'

'I can't,' I whisper, tears springing to my eyes. Damn and blast Julian and his goddam stupid restaurant.

'I'm not good enough for you.'

'That's rubbish. You're perfect for me. Just tell me what's going on.'

His hand clasps mine.

'You'll hate me,' I say pushing myself up onto my trembling legs.

'Just stop it all now Harry. It can't be that difficult surely?'

I take a deep breath. Maybe I can tell him the truth.

'Brice.'

We turn and see Sebastian running towards us.

'Quick, it's Mother.'

Christ, she hasn't gone and croaked it has she? I suppose Hamilton will blame me for this too. I can't win can I?

Chapter Twenty-Six

'Caron and I will pop to Debenhams tomorrow and buy something special. Oh I'm that excited Harry.'

'It's nothing special,' I say, still holding out hope that I may get out of all this before Friday arrives. 'This thing with Hamilton is, well ...'

'Nothing special,' she shrieks. 'You're getting engaged and you say it's nothing special. Bleeding hell, I'll have to get your dad a new shirt that's how bleeding special it is. You and some rich bloke, well that's special all right.'

'It's just families getting together that's all Mum, don't get carried away. The thing is ...'

'Carried away? My daughter is only getting engaged to bleeding royalty.'

I sigh. Why won't she ever let me get a word in?

'Not quite,' I correct.

'Well, as close as buggery.'

The last thing I want to do is put my parents through the ordeal of meeting Hamilton and his parents, and I really cannot bear the thought of putting Hamilton and his parents through the ordeal of meeting my parents. I mean, what the fuck will they have to talk about? Mum no doubt will start helping Cedric, and Caron will want to talk fashion and trust me, Caron's idea of fashion is whatever is the latest rage down Carnaby Street. I don't somehow imagine Hamilton, or any of his family, has ever frequented that part of London, but then again knowing Hamilton I wouldn't like to guess where he has frequented.

'Don't swear though will you, not when you're here. Hamilton's parents hate swearing.'

'Oh goodness, how are you coping then?'

'I don't swear that much,' I say indignantly.

'Well, I'm buying a new two piece and I'll get me hair permed properly at the hairdressers,' chatters Mum. 'I thought I'd have that mahogany colour again. You remember you said it suited me?'

Bleeding hell.

'Yes it did, but maybe a more conservative colour would be better for coming here,' I say carefully.

Shit, this is awful. Why shouldn't my mum have her hair mahogany if she wants? Maybe I should wear more of my own clothes. Yes, that's one way of bringing this to a head. Maybe I'll drop all this posh talk too.

'Well, whatever you think best,' she says hesitantly. 'I could just be plain brown. Anyway, I'll get Dad to get the coach tickets; I don't want your dad driving all that way. He's bound to get lost. I'll let you know what time we'll get there and maybe you can pick us up?'

'Right,' I say in a depressed tone.

She lets out a little gasp.

'Oh Lord, do we have to curtsy to them? I mean you said his father is titled and everything. What does your dad do, I mean he and Gary can't curtsy now can they? They'll look right daft ha'p'orths if they do.'

It's not too late for me to run away. I could sell the pearls couldn't I? They are no doubt worth a few bob, and then I could bugger off to Brazil. Maybe I can do a Shirley Valentine and meet some lovely foreign bloke. What I'd really like to do is walk in front of the bullets at the shoot today. Preferably Hamilton's, just so he'll feel guilty. After assuring Mum that no one has to curtsy I hang up and flop onto the bed. I swallow two of the painkillers Brice had given me. The thought of Brice sends a shiver down my spine and a lovely tingle up my thighs and beyond. It also produces a stab in my stomach. How can I meet someone like him now? How bleeding unfair is that? He thinks I'm perfect for him, me, Harriet bleeding Lawson. He likes me for exactly who I am. Every woman's dream right? My body aches at the thought of him. To think I came close to telling him everything and if Sebastian hadn't come out at that moment I would have revealed all. Fortunately Margarita hadn't snuffed it but had just got a rather tough piece of venison stuck in her throat as if the poor stag was taking his final revenge. Brice had quickly lifted her correctly and it had flown straight out of her mouth and landed in Hamilton's lap. All very fitting I like to think.

Breakfast was a farce. Melanie was laid up with another migraine and Gregory was resting with a virus. Very bloody convenient I found myself thinking. Fiona and Sebastian had gone to check the horses, but I bet they spent more time checking the hay. Honestly, it seems like everyone is at it except Hamilton and I. Although knowing him, I wouldn't be surprised if he was at it somewhere too. Breakfast was attended by me, Hamilton, Brice and Margarita, and the conversation was dominated by the sodding engagement party which Margarita wants on Friday so everyone can travel home on Sunday.

'We'll need Saturday to recover,' she had said.

As for me, I'll need the rest of my bleeding life to recover. I sigh. Honestly, I have never sighed so much in my life. Emily quietly enters the room.

'How do you feel Miss Harriet? Is your foot any better today?'

I open one eye to look at her.

'If I asked you to kill me would you? I mean, do you do everything you're told?'

She giggles.

'Almost everything, but I stop at murder.'

'Think of it as euthanasia, you'd be putting me out of my misery.'

'Come on Miss, you have the shoot this afternoon. Think how much you'll enjoy that.'

'You like torturing me don't you?' I say as Fiona's mobile starts to ring. Please don't let it be the Jacks. I pick it up and see Alistair's name flashing on the screen. Not as bad but bad enough.

'Hello Alistair, Fiona isn't here I'm afraid she's, she's ...' Christ, what exactly is she doing?

'How's the business trip going?' I say to distract him.

'I'm b-b-b- ...'

'Bored?' I offer.

'B-back,' he says.

I sit up.

'Back,' I echo, 'but I thought you were away all week?'

'W-w-w- ...'

'I said I thought you were away all week.'

'You d-d-don't have to repeat yourself.'

'I thought you were trying to say *what*.'

'W-we got everything done early so I thought I'd j-j-j- ...'

'Jump ship?'

Emily gives me a strange look.

'He stammers,' I whisper. 'I'm trying to help.'

Where the hell is Fiona when her boyfriend calls?

'J-j-jump on a plane to Scotland. I have a b-b-b- ...'

'Christ,' I say, jumping up and standing on my bad foot. 'Shit, bleeding foot.'

Emily winces.

'Business proposal for Hamilton and ...'

Shit and double shit.

'Can you ask F-Fiona to call me? I'll be there sometime tomorrow afternoon.'

I may have to beg Emily to kill me. I could offer her the pearls as payment.

'Alistair, I don't think that is a good idea.'

'Of c-c-course it is. Have you heard from the Jacks?'

I sigh.

'Kind of, but Alistair ...'

'Did J-J-J-J- ...'

Oh for pity's sake.

'Yes, Jack Diamond has contacted us but we have it ...'

'No Julian, did he phone you? He called me and ...'

'What,' I yell, grabbing the dressing table for support and pointing to my crutches for Emily to fetch.

'He said he's been t-t-t-t- ...' he sighs.

'Tied up?' I ask feeling a knot in my stomach.

'T-t-tr-tr-trying to reach you on your m-m-mobile.'

'Yeah well, that doesn't work.'

'He's got a backer and is c-c-c-c- ...'

'Calmer?'

It's more than I bloody am.

'C-coming home. Are you engaged to Hamilton yet?'

Christ, this is a farce and I'm the main character. Fiona tumbles in all flushed and happy and I throw the mobile at her.

'Your boyfriend,' I say. 'He's coming here tomorrow. Do you want me to shoot you first or after I have shot myself?'

'Shit,' she grumbles.

'Yes, we're in it quite deep actually.'

I hobble into the bathroom and fall onto the loo. I don't believe this. It's bad enough my parents, and Gary and Caron coming here, without stuttering Alistair too. I'm a nice person, honest I am. None of this is my fault. I don't care about money, or restaurants or fancy houses. I just want to be debt free and with a nice boyfriend. On reflection forget the boyfriend. Men are just nothing but trouble.

Chapter Twenty-Seven

'I don't like this,' mumbles Babyface. 'Mum wouldn't 'alf be cross if she knew.'

'What yer mumbling about?' snaps Jack Diamond.

'Us being 'ere, it ain't right, and yer know it ain't. We ain't never done nothin' like this before.'

'Put a bleedin' sock in it,' snarls Mad Jack Junior. 'Just cos you're a wimp.'

'I ain't no wimp,' protests Babyface. 'It just ain't right and I know Mum would be cross.'

'What's yer bleedin' mum got to do with anythin'? I'm the boss of this family,' barks Jack Diamond.

Mad Jack sniggers.

'One more snigger from you and I'll knock you from 'ere to kingdom come, got it?' snarls Diamond.

'Yes Dad.'

They're sitting crouched in the undergrowth. In the distance they can see Glenwood in all its glory. Diamond stares fascinated. He likes tasteful homes and this is certainly one of those.

'I still don't think we should be on private property,' moans Babyface.

'You're always on sodding private property you knobhead,' sighs Diamond. 'When you go to collect protection money you're on private property ain't yer?'

Babyface sighs impatiently.

'Yeah but this is different somehow ain't it? They've probably got bleedin' dogs and everything. They could go for our bleedin' throats,' he says shakily.

Mad Jack fidgets nervously.

'What if Babyface is right Dad? What if they 'ave vicious dogs?'

Diamond lifts his binoculars to his eyes and studies the house.

'I ain't seen no dogs,' he says focusing the lens onto Fiona and Sebastian who have just come out of the house. Jesus bloody Christ, did that pervert just stroke her arse? Honestly these bleedin' ponces are the worst.

'That don't mean there ain't any does it?' argues Babyface.

Jack turns to his sons.

'Christ, how can I concentrate with all this moaning going on? Now listen, you two knobheads. You do as I tells yer, got that?'

They nod.

'Now, we stay here a bit longer and case the joint, yer both got that? When we think things are cushty we go in. They're bound to all go out crocheting or to play polio, or whatever the bloody rich and privileged do. When they do we go in.'

'Don't you mean croqueting,' corrects Mad Jack. 'And ain't it Polo? Polio is an illness Dad.'

'I'll give you a bloody illness if yer don't shut it.'

'Well, I don't like it,' moans Babyface.

'I told yer, it will be a piece of piss.'

'Yeah, I think Dad's right. It will be a piece of piss,' agrees Mad Jack.

'I still don't like it.'

'What's a matter with you these days?' snaps Diamond.

'I just don't want no Rottweiler tearing at me throat,' argues Babyface.

Diamond shakes his head.

'I got someone interested in the silver and it ain't old Mick either. I don't want me pants pulled down over the price. This time I got us a good deal. So we go for the silver first, got it? Then we leave a nice little note like, thanking old 'arriet for all 'er 'elp.'

'That ain't fair,' argues Babyface.

'What yer on about now?' asks Diamond.

'Christ Babyface, who the 'ell 'ad the jam out of your doughnut?' groans Mad Jack.

'It ain't 'arriet's fault.'

'It ain't 'arriet's fault,' mimics Mad Jack. 'Not bleedin' much.'

'You need to find yourself a proper slapper, and stop 'ankering over those you can't 'ave,' says Diamond, lifting the binoculars again. Yeah, this should make him a nice little packet. All they've got to do is go in when they're all out doing whatever it is they do. Most likely the servants have a kip or something. Yeah, that's it. They'll go in, nick the silver, leave the note and leg it. They'll make a few grand on that lot. Not bad for a day's work. That will teach that prick and his girlfriend to muck Jack Diamond about.

Chapter Twenty-Eight

'I don't believe it. I just don't believe it,' repeats Fiona. 'He's never home early from a business trip. Talk about Sod's Law.'
I hobble to the table and take a glass of champagne.

'We're having cocktails after the shoot Miss Harriet. Is there anything in particular you and Miss Fiona would like?' asks Cedric.

'Harriet is a champagne cocktail girl, isn't that right?' puffs Hamilton, pushing Margarita in her wheelchair towards us.
God, why does he keep saying that? It's like the only bloody thing he knows about me is what I drink.

'What I'd love is a Screaming Orgasm,' I say.
Isn't that the truth? I bet Brice Edmunds could cope with that. Hamilton's jaw drops and Fiona lowers her eyes.

'No need to tell the whole world dear, maybe just a little word in Hamilton's ear,' suggests Margarita as she wheels herself away.

'Of course Miss Harriet, I can do that for you,' says Cedric calmly, wiping a glass. 'One part vodka, one and half parts Kahlua and one and a half parts Bailey's. Does that sound right Miss Harriet?'

'You know how to give a perfect Screaming Orgasm to a woman Cedric,' I laugh.
Hamilton shifts uncomfortably and coughs nervously. He takes my arm and pulls me into an embrace.

'Did you phone your parents?'
I nod.

'Don't worry Harriet, after Friday you'll never see me again,' he hisses nastily.

'Really? Margarita due to pop her clogs at the weekend is she? Or are you knocking her off yourself? Oh, talking of knocking off, did you know Gregory was knocking off your mother, not to mention the fact that your father would knock off Fiona at the drop of a hat, or her knickers come to that. That's if he hasn't already. I don't like to ask.'

'How dare you,' he snarls, his face turning beetroot.

'No wonder your grandmother doesn't want to leave the family business to you lot. You'd be too shagging busy to get any work done.'

'Just watch your mouth Harriet, you're getting too cocky.'

I'm getting cocky? I'm the only one not getting any cock if you ask me.

'I'm warning you,' whispers Hamilton, pulling me in closer. 'We're getting engaged in three days. You're madly in love with me, remember?'

I stroke his bum.

'How could I forget,' I reply. 'Nice arse Ham, pity you're the arsehole that goes with it.'

I pinch his bum and his grip loosens. I seize the opportunity to step away. Sebastian and Brice stroll down the steps from the rear of the house. Brice looks gorgeous in a white Aran jumper, khaki trousers and a grey scarf. I could rip the whole lot off him right here, right now.

'I'll have to tell Alistair won't I?' says Fiona, making me jump. I was miles away in my little fantasy world of Brice's naked body.

'Tell him what?'

'That's it over,' she says with a sigh.

Bloody hell, that seems a bit drastic.

'Because of Sebastian?' I say shocked, I mean, she barely knows the guy.

'No, because he just isn't caring or loving. We haven't done it in months.'

Join the club.

'That's not a reason to end it surely? At least he hasn't forced you to get engaged to someone else and had your goldfish killed, not to mention killing all your dreams and practically bankrupting you. I think you've got it quite good with Alistair, all things considered.'

She sighs.

'Cedric, can I have a Screaming Orgasm too? I'm in desperate need.'

Brice raises his eyebrows.

'What's this about screaming orgasms?' he laughs.

'I'm preparing them sir, may I offer you one?'

'Well, I'll never say no to an orgasm, screaming or otherwise,' he grins.

His eyes meet mine. My legs tremble and I thank God for the crutches.

'Good heavens, what is the world coming to?' grumbles Margarita.

'It's only a cocktail old girl. Maybe you should try one.'

'I've had more than my fair share of orgasms dear boy, all very overrated.'

'I've sure you have, you naughty madam,' he laughs and I want to do everything filthy under the sun with him. I feel my face and neck turn red and I avert my eyes.

'I hear your partner is coming,' Margarita says to Fiona.

Sebastian inclines his head to Fiona who shrugs.

'Yes. Apparently his business trip came to an end earlier than planned. I hope it won't be an inconvenience Sir Sebastian,' she says fluttering her eyelashes.

He lays a hand on her arm and she visibly swoons.

'Of course not, after all he was coming for the engagement party. We'll have to monopolise you before he gets here.'

'So you're partial to Screaming Orgasms,' Brice teases.

I bite my lip.

'Yes, I am.'

'Why am I not surprised?' he says, offering me a plate of sandwiches.

The sun shines brightly on us and I watch as Cedric prepares for the shoot. Brice looks down at my foot.

'I thought you were about to tell me something last night,' he whispers.

'I wasn't,' I whisper back.

'Oh bugger, who asked that old fart to the shoot,' says Margarita as Major Bates ambles towards us.

'Afternoon all, spiffing day for a shoot. Thanks for asking me old man,' he says, slapping a hand onto Sebastian's shoulder.

'Make mine a Chablis old boy, a nice large one if you would,' he says to Cedric.

'Well let's get on with it or this old bugger will be as drunk as a skunk before we've got one pigeon in the air,' says Margarita.

I hobble forward and give Hamilton a nod.

'Keep clear,' I say as I pass him.

'Fiona, are you participating or observing?' asks Margarita.

'I'll just watch. I don't want to shoot myself in the foot. One of us hobbling around is enough I think.'

Not by the time I've finished.

'Is the trap ready Cedric?' calls Sebastian, lifting his gun.

I pull on my earmuffs and watch Sebastian aim and miss. I am about to turn to Brice when I see he is cocking his gun. Seconds later he has a clear hit.

'Brilliant,' yells Margarita, 'a good kill, well done.'

Brice calls to Cedric to pull and aims again, getting another direct hit. Margarita gestures to Cedric for cartridges. Brice lifts my earmuffs off and smiles.

'Good shot,' I say. 'I expect you're an expert horseman too.'

Whereas I am bleeding useless at everything. Honestly, I can't think what the fuck I've been doing with my time.

'I'm still looking forward to seeing you in your riding outfit,' he whispers. 'I'm particularly interested in that riding crop of yours.'

I go weak at the knees and grab his arm for support.

'I wouldn't have a clue what to do with it,' I say huskily.

'I'm sure I could find a use,' he says provocatively.

God, I'm going to have a screaming orgasm right here and now if he carries on like this. He pats my earmuffs down as Margarita shouts *pull*. I grab my champagne glass and down the remains. Emily, in her starched white apron, refills my glass. I drink half and realise everyone is looking at me. It's my go. Here we go again. Let's hope this time I hit the sodding pigeon. I load the gun more confidently and the feel of the metal in my hands gives me a strange sense of power. I could go mad for a moment and turn it on all of them couldn't I? I could make them all listen while I tell them what a bastard Julian is and how horrible Hamilton has been. Yes, I could easily do that. Except standing behind a loaded shotgun while you force people to listen doesn't make you look very sane does it? I slide forward the catch and shout *pull*. I aim carefully with my finger on the trigger and get the pigeon in my sight. Something catches my eye in the woods on the other side of the rose garden. I lower the shotgun and the bleeding thing goes off. I gasp as I see something drop.

'Oh my God, I've hit something,' I cry, pulling off the muffs.

'What in buggeration was that?' asks the Major pouring another glass of Chablis.

'My God, was that someone out there?' says Hamilton shakily.

'Could have been a deer,' says Sebastian.

'Did you say someone? Good grief, why would there be someone out there?' says the Major.

'Oh God, it's not Alistair is it?' cries Fiona, frozen in fear.

'Someone go and damn well see. Bloody fools whoever they are. Bloody trespassers no doubt, and idiots on top of that. They must have seen we were having a shoot,' snorts Margarita who I'm beginning to think should take a trip along the yellow brick road to find herself a heart.

I drop the gun and hobble after Brice who is sprinting ahead. I cross the lawn to the woods and look for Brice, but he is nowhere to be seen.

'Brice,' I call. 'Where are you?'

'Come in a bit further and we're on the left,' he shouts.

Oh my God, who's *we*? I've shot someone. I hear a groan and my stomach churns. Please don't let it be Alistair, Fiona will never forgive me. God, I hope it's not Julian, then again ... No Harriet, you mustn't think like that. No matter what Julian has done he doesn't deserve to be killed. Jesus, I could go to prison. I don't believe this. Ever since Silvia's wedding, life has turned into a nightmare, and it just gets worse and worse. I shake my head and forge ahead until I see Brice leaning over a man on the ground. I put my hand to my mouth.

'Is he dead?' I whisper.

Brice looks up.

'Of course not, it's just a graze. He's in shock more than anything. He must have been poaching. Honestly, no sense these people.'

I hobble closer and look down at the man on the ground and fight back a cry when I see it is Babyface Jack. Jesus Christ, I'd only gone and shot one of the bleeding Jacks. And I thought they would be upset with me owing them the fifty quid, but this has got to be worse. I'm in deep shit now.

'I'll need to get him back to the house to dress the wound,' Brice says calmly.

If Babyface is here then Jack Diamond and Mad Jack can't be far away. I'm seriously debating whether to go back for the gun when Brice asks,

'Harriet, are you okay? Did you hear me?'

I nod dumbly.

'You'll need to get Hamilton to help me carry him to the house. He's in a severe state of shock.'

I nod but don't move. Diamond could be hiding behind a tree right next to us

'It was an accident,' I say loudly.

'Yes, that's right. He shouldn't have been here. Can you fetch Hamilton?'

I nod and hobble back to the house.

'It's a man,' I say. 'He's okay, it's just a graze but he's in shock. Brice asked if you can help carry him to the house. He needs to dress the wound.'

'It's one of the Jacks,' I whisper to Fiona.

'Fuck,' she mouths.

I nod.

'They're going to cut off more than your ear,' she mumbles.

We watch as Hamilton and Brice carry Babyface across the lawn.

'Who in damnation is that?' asks the Major.

'Have another drink Bates,' snaps Margarita.

'I'm going to help,' I say and follow Brice and Hamilton to the house. Babyface is taken to a bedroom. I wait until Hamilton comes out before venturing in.

'Don't you think you've caused enough damage?' Hamilton says nastily. 'No one has ever shot a poacher on our land before.'

I lower my eyes and hobble into the bedroom. Brice is filling a bowl of water from the en suite bathroom, and Babyface looks at me with fear in his eyes.

'I'm sorry,' I whisper. 'It was an accident.'

He whimpers something but I don't quite catch it. Brice emerges from the bathroom and his eyes light up on seeing me.

'Oh good, you're here. As you can see it's just a graze.'

I look at Babyface Jack's leg and breathe a sigh of relief when I see it is just a scratch. Babyface is shaking so much that I think he will fall off the bed.

'He's in a terrible state of shock. I'm going to have to sedate him. Odd though, he wasn't this bad before you came in.'

I look into Babyface Jack's eyes.

'You're going to be fine, it isn't serious,' I say kindly.

'I'm sorry 'arriet,' he moans.

Brice's head snaps up and he stares at me.

'Do you know him?'

I bite my lip. He looks at me for a few seconds and then reaches down to his bag.

'I'm giving you an injection. It will relax you and make you sleep. I'm then going to dress your wound. Do you understand?'

Babyface nods. I watch silently as Brice gives the injection and Babyface Jack's eyes slowly close.

'Do you want to tell me how you know him?' Brice asks as he cleans the wound.

'Yes,' I whisper, 'but not here. I don't want anyone else to know.'

'Not even Hamilton, your fiancé?' he says, lifting his eyes to meet mine.

'Hamilton isn't going to be my fiancé,' I say quietly, averting my eyes from his.

He nods.

'I kind of guessed that right from the start. Come to Stalkers Lodge for dinner. Bring on a migraine, after all, everyone else does, and excuse yourself from supper. You can tell me everything then. Is it a deal?'

'It's a deal.'

'Dress casual. Come as 'arriet, you know what I mean.'

I hide my smile and nod, but anxiety clutches at my stomach. The relief of being able to tell someone the truth at last is overwhelming but the fear that he will hate me for it is unbearable.

Chapter Twenty-Nine

With Fiona's help I sneak down the stairs and out the back door.

'I'll tell everyone your migraine is improving but you can't eat,' she says while hugging me. 'I hope it goes okay.'

I nervously make my way to Stalkers Lodge. The moon is bright and I follow the path around the loch. I am wearing jeans, a black vest and an oversize top. I'd washed my hair and blow dried it into my usual shaggy look. Apart from a small amount of blusher I am make-up free. My heart races as it occurs to me that Jack Diamond could spring out from the undergrowth at any moment and it is a huge relief when I finally reach the lodge. Brice greets me in a short sleeved white shirt which is open at the neck. He looks so sexy. My breath catches in my throat when I say hello. His hair is ruffled and his eyes are sparkling. His jeans hug his backside and I fight the urge to squeeze it. The fragrant aroma of spices makes my mouth water and I sniff in appreciation.

'I hope you like curry,' he says nervously.

I enter the living room and pull off my poncho. The table is laid and there are candles everywhere. The candlelight and blazing fire cast flickering shadows around the room.

'It's almost ready,' he says, walking to the kitchen. I follow and accept a glass of wine from him.

'What kind of doctor are you?' I ask curiously.

'I trained as a GP and then I spent a year doing voluntary work in South East Asia. I loved it and when I came back I studied tropical diseases. I went out again and set up my own charity.'

He hands me two plates of rice and points to the table. I take them and he follows with a bowl of curry.

'Do you live there?' I ask.

I know he will ask how I know Babyface and I'm trying to put that off for as long as possible.

'For about six months of the year, and then I come back here where I shamefully work in private practice. I like to use my own money for my work in Laos. Money isn't really an issue. I have an allowance from Grandma. In that way I'm not much different to Hamilton.'

'Oh, you're very different to Hamilton,' I protest.

He passes the curry dish and I take a large spoonful.

'God, I'm so hungry I could eat a horse.'

The curry is delicious.

'This is really good,' I say. 'Almost as good as the curries down Brick Lane, and they're the dog's bollocks.'

I bite my lip when I realise what I've said. He laughs heartily and dips a piece of naan bread into his curry. I take a sip of wine and struggle not to blush.

'You did say come as 'arriet,' I mumble.

He laughs softly.

'So, how did Hamilton find you?' he asks, avoiding my eyes.

'At Silva's wedding,' I say quietly.

He nods and his mouth tightens.

'Why did you accept?'

I put down my fork and lift my glass.

'My boyfriend Julian, you got that bit right by the way, never turned up for the wedding. He was ragging it down the A40 in my car. That night I found out that he had taken more from me than just my car. He owes thousands of pounds, most of it connected to the French restaurant he started. Some of his debts had my name on them too. I was a stupid bitch. I trusted him.'

I pause and sip the wine. God, this is harder than I thought it would be. No matter how I tell it I still sound like a bloody fool. He looks at me over the rim of his glass and gives an encouraging smile.

'So, Hamilton offered you a way to pay off those debts did he?'

I nod.

'Julian borrowed money from this loan shark named Jack Diamond. Babyface Jack, the guy back at the house ...'

He nods, his brows knitted together.

'That's Diamond's son. He has two, Babyface Jack and Mad Jack Junior.'

'That's one way of not forgetting your kids' names,' he laughs.

I can't laugh with him. Just talking about the Jacks' makes me feel depressed. I take more curry but feel I have lost my appetite.

'How much do you owe?' he asks, spooning more curry onto my plate. I put out a hand to stop him and it brushes his. I see a spark in his eyes and that familiar tingle runs through me.

'Thirty-eight thousand,' I say bluntly. 'Julian bought a new van and the loan for it was in my name. I must have signed something. He was always putting things in front of me but I thought they were connected to the Barclays loan of seven thousand, which of course turned out to be a hell of a lot more than that. Jack Diamond has the van now.'

'Sounds like you've been very naive,' he says, topping up my wine glass.

What a cheek.

'I don't need you bleeding reminding me thank you very much,' I say angrily. 'I trusted a man, that was my bloody problem and it seems like I've made the same mistake again.'

I stand up abruptly and hobble towards the door. He doesn't move from the table and I feel stupidly disappointed that he doesn't try and stop me.

'If you think trusting me was a mistake then leave. I'm not going to stop you. All I'm saying is maybe you were stupid to have trusted Julian. He's sounds like an idiot and frankly you deserve better. So, sit back down and enjoy the dinner. I personally think it's the dog's bollocks.'

I lower my eyes and walk back to the table. Honestly, this man can do anything he likes with me. Oh, what a delicious thought.

'I'm only staying because the dinner *is* the dog's bollocks,' I say.

'That's a good enough reason.'

We eat in silence for a while and he replenishes our glasses.

'So Jack Diamond is blackmailing you?' he asks finally, pushing his plate away.

'Everyone is blackmailing me,' I say miserably, 'except you, but I suppose you will after dinner is over. I'll tell you now you might as well forget it as I haven't got a pot to piss in. Hamilton has promised me I won't work again if I don't do what he says, and the Jacks have threatened to burn down the restaurant. I paid the protection money but I'm not doing it any more. Sod Julian and sod his restaurant, but I underpaid Jack Diamond by fifty quid,' I groan.

I finish the wine and feel my head spin. He doesn't comment but opens another bottle. I know I shouldn't drink any more but the wine is giving me the courage I wouldn't otherwise have.

'Anyway, the Jacks must have come here and I accidently shot Babyface. That's it in a nutshell really. I've left out loads like my dead goldfish, Julian's ears or the lack of them. Basically I'm a Battersea girl,' I shrug. 'I'm not a posh toff like you. I went to uni but that's it. I was studying but I had to chuck that in to do all this crap to get the money to pay the bills.'

'I knew Hamilton was up to something, that little creep. He's trying to get the shares isn't he? He is as corrupt as his father.'

Oh dear, I really should warn Fi.

'We can sort this out Harriet but you have to trust me. Can you do that?'

My heart skips a beat. Can I trust him? I trusted Julian didn't I and look where that got me. Then I trusted Hamilton. No, if I'm honest I never trusted Hamilton. I find it hard to answer.

'I'm no good at desserts,' he says, changing the subject. 'So I bought a couple of tubs of ice cream. I hope that's okay. You're not one of those silly women who don't eat ice cream because of the calories are you?'

Not bloody likely. I stand up and help with the dishes.

'I'll do that,' he says gently. 'You're my guest and I like to please my guests.'

His hand strokes my arm before taking a plate from me and I sway slightly, grasping the table for support.

'So,' he says softly, 'you're not in love with Hamilton?'

I shake my head and shiver as he his fingers trace the curve of my shoulder slowly upwards to my neck.

'And you're no longer in love with Julian?'

His fingers are moving slowly downwards now to the swell of my breast and I restrain a gasp.

'No, no longer in love,' I say huskily, the ache in my loins unbearable.

He puts the plate down and encircles my waist with one hand while the other cups my breast. Just the warmth of his breath in my ear makes my nipple harden in his palm. I'm pushed back against the table and I feel its hardness press into the low of my back.

'You drive me mad Harriet,' he whispers.

Oh good. At least I drive him mad in a nice way. I should have brought my riding crop. After all, it's a shame not to find a use for it after Hamilton spent all that money. His lips brush mine gently and my body goes limp. He groans beneath my lips and grinds himself against my hips. It was never like this with Julian. I don't think Julian ever had me up against a table. The closest we ever came to a table together was making them at the restaurant or eating from one at home. But hip grinding against one ... No we never did that. I'm not sure we ever hip grinded anywhere. Julian was more a *wham bam thank you mam* type of bloke. That was okay because I was always too bloody tired to give it much myself. This past year, the quicker the wham bam, the better I liked it. I guess that says a lot about us in the past few months. My breasts are now so swollen I feel sure they will burst out of my bra if he doesn't release them soon. His lips leave mine and travel slowly down my neck. I stretch one hand behind to steady myself and squeeze his buttocks with the other. I feel my legs will soon give way and I'm engulfed by so many emotions that I can't think straight. The only thing I know is that I never want to lose this man now I have found him. A loud rapping noise sounds in my head and Brice suddenly releases me. Someone is at the door.

'Damn it. Who in God's name?' he says brusquely.

I open my eyes and it takes a while for me to remember where I am.

'Angus, is everything okay?' he asks on opening the door.

I fall into a chair and quickly tidy my hair. My face feels hot and I fan myself with my hand.

'Sorry Brice, it isn't a bad time is it?'

'Of course not, come in. Harriet's here, she came for dinner.'

Oh God, I hope I don't have that 'about to be fucked' look on my face.

'I'm sorry to be a pest but the pickup has broken down just outside Glenwood. I've got jump leads but ...'

Jump leads that's bloody appropriate isn't it? Honestly, bad timing or what.

'Actually Angus, you're just the man.'

Oh really? And there was me thinking it was *me* he wanted to see. I'm grateful for the dim lighting but I can see Angus is uncomfortable.

'I'm sorry guys, the wee pickup just conked out. Look, I'm in the way I'll scoot up to the house and get Cedric to jump start me.'

'Don't be ridiculous,' says Brice. 'You couldn't have timed it better.'

I give him a sharp look. What the hell does that mean?

'Harriet and I have a little problem with a man named Jack Diamond and as an ex-policeman I think you can help us. What do you say to a wee dram and we can discuss it?'

Brice winks at me and Angus grins.

'Am I going to enjoy this?' he asks.

'Oh indeed you are,' laughs Brice, pouring whisky into three glasses.

I look longingly towards the bedroom. Bloody Jack Diamond is becoming a real thorn in my side. It's a bit much when he interferes with my sex life.

'Tell me all about it,' says Angus.

I relax in my chair and listen as Brice recounts my story.

Chapter Thirty

'Christ,' moans Fiona as she crashes into the door.

'Keep your voice down,' I hiss. 'Don't you have your contacts in?' She shakes her head.

'For God's sake Fiona,' I say irritably. 'Who the hell is going to see you at this time of night?'

'Alright, keep your hair on. I'll put my glasses on. Can we put this thing down for a minute, I can barely lift it.'

Fiona's timing is priceless. We carefully lower the rolled up carpet and I wait until she has her glasses on. I prick my ears for any sounds of movement but the house is quiet. It's two o'clock in the morning and the only sound I can hear is the distant hoot from an owl.

'I can't believe we are doing this. What if something goes wrong?' she says worriedly.

'Nothing is going to go wrong,' I say, my jaw tightening in determination. 'Anyway, what choice do we have?'

'Speak for yourself. I don't know why the hell I'm getting involved. God, I'll get a hernia lifting this,' she complains as we each lift an end of the carpet.

'This could only happen to us,' she says miserably as she gingerly steps through the doorway into the moonlit night. I'm thankful for the full moon. At least we will be able to spot anyone lurking outside. I look down at the carpet and my heart pounds like a bongo drum. I've never been so scared in my life.

'You've got it haven't you?' I ask anxiously.

'Yes, but I'm not happy about this. Dumping bodies in lochs isn't quite what I imagined we'd be doing when I came up here.'

'It's for the best,' I say, struggling to catch my breath. Christ, I'm hyperventilating, that's all we need.

'Brice had better be there,' she mumbles sidestepping something on the ground. 'Fuck,' she cries. 'What the hell was that?'

'What?' I ask.

'Shit, I don't know but it moved bloody fast. Jesus Harry, do we have to do this? These sodding midges are eating me to death, bloody vampire things, and God knows what that was at my feet.'
I look down and spot Diamond wandering towards the rose garden.

'It was Diamond,' I say, feeling an ache in my shoulders.

'Oh Christ,' she says a look of horror on her face. 'Where is he, can you see him? Oh shit Harry, what if he jumps out and cuts off our ears?'
I sigh.

'Diamond the *cat* Fiona, not Jack bleeding Diamond.'
She groans and lowers her shoulders.

'You might have said.'

'Can you just stop moaning and keep walking,' I snap.

'I'm doing you a favour you know, so don't snap at me. Anyway, you don't know what kind of creepy-crawlies they have out here do you?'

'It's Scotland, not the bleeding jungle.'

'All the same.'

'Do you want me to go backwards?' I offer.

'It won't matter if I'm going forwards or backwards, I'm still not going to be happy.'

'I'm thinking you'll be happier if you know where you're going and what you're doing.'

'I know what I'm doing and I'm not happy about it at all.'
I sigh. The sooner we dump this thing the better.

'But on reflection, yes I think I'd prefer to go forwards. That way you can walk into Jack Diamond if he jumps out on us,' she says.

'I wish you'd said this when we had the light from the house. Okay, start turning clockwise,' I say.

'Your clockwise or my clockwise?'
I stare at her.

'What?'

'Well, if you're thinking clockwise your way I need to go anti-clockwise and vice versa if you meant the other way round.'
Bleeding hell, it's two in the morning and she wants to play mind games.

'I'll go clockwise and you follow me, right?' I hiss, wishing my foot would stop throbbing.

'No need to get huffy. I'm just trying to help.'

'Yes, well it would have been more helpful if you had mentioned this earlier. Right are you ready to turn?'

At that moment we are bathed in light and Fiona squeals and drops her end of the carpet with a thud. She really has to be the worst partner in crime anyone ever had. I squint against the light and see Cedric in the shadows. God almighty, what is he doing up at this time of night?

'Jesus,' Fiona groans.

'Good evening madam, may I be of assistance?'

'Fuck me Cedric, are you trying to give me a heart attack?' I say feeling the perspiration trickle between my breasts.

'I rather think trying to carry that ...'

'Oh God,' Fiona moans.

'Carpet,' I say.

'Yes madam. I rather think trying to carry a heavy carpet in the dead of night might possibly give *you* a heart attack. It certainly won't help your foot.'

It's knocking pounds off me that's for sure. I lower my end carefully and try to breathe normally.

'Madam, may I enquire why you would be removing a carpet in the dead of night?'

Fiona stifles a little cry.

'We're not stealing it,' she says.

'The truth is Cedric, we have something inside it that we need to dump in the loch.'

Fiona gasps.

'Harry, what are you saying?'

'Who's out there?' Emily appears in the doorway in her nightie.

Oh for pity's sake. Why don't we just blow the hunting horn and get everyone out here.

'Miss Harriet and Miss Fiona are disposing of something in a carpet,' says Cedric in a matter-of-fact voice.

'Don't you lot sleep?' I ask, stifling a yawn.

'Not when people are banging and shuffling around next to the servants' quarters,' replies Cedric.

'Do you need a torch?' asks Emily.

Sweet Jesus, why don't they just play some wee bagpipes and dance the Highland fling while they're at it.

'Emily could help carry my end,' suggests Fiona. 'It is bloody heavy and I think my arms may fall off before I make it to the loch.'

The carpet sags heavily in the middle and even I have to agree it feels heavier by the second.

'Okay,' says Emily, jumping forward and tying her shawl around her shoulders.

'I'll lift the middle and we can get this over and done with, and we can all return to our beds,' says Cedric.

I nod in agreement. After all, what else can I do? Cedric counts to three and we all lift the carpet together.

'Bloody hell, it's heavy. Have you got a body in here?' quips Emily.

Fiona's eyes meet mine and I quickly turn away.

'Language please Emily,' admonishes Cedric.

'Can you please keep your voices down? We don't want someone calling the police,' I say.

'Good God no,' groans Fiona.

Cedric is quite right however, and we reach the jetty in no time and without incident. Brice and Angus widen their eyes at the sight of the four of us.

'Good evening Mr Brice,' says Cedric. 'Do you require this on the boat?'

'Indeed, well done Cedric. Of course it goes without saying doesn't it that this will all be forgotten by the morning.'

'It's already forgotten sir, isn't that right Emily?'

Emily's cheeks glow in the moonlight. This is probably the most excitement she has had in years.

'Oh yes, of course sir,' she smiles.

Angus and Brice haul the carpet onto the boat and lower it gently. Fiona and I stand panting while Cedric and Emily look at us.

'Thank you Cedric, that's all I think,' I say looking at Brice.

He nods.

'That's fabulous guys,' he says, as though hauling a rolled up carpet onto a boat in the dead of night happens every day. Cedric gives a nod and takes Emily's hand.

'Well, goodnight sir, madam,' says Cedric.

We watch them walk away and as soon as they are out of sight Fiona groans.

'I really cannot believe we are doing this. Do you think Jack Diamond is out there?'

'I think it very likely he is,' smiles Brice.

I sincerely hope so otherwise this has all been a waste of time.

Chapter Thirty-One

'What we gonna do about it?' asks Mad Jack Junior as he kicks the trunk of a tree.

'I'm not sure. But you don't tell yer mum nothing, not yet anyway.'

Mad Jack stares in disbelief.

'But we've got to tell her that they shot Babyface and dumped ...' he falters.

'We can't get emotional, it ain't professional,' snaps Diamond, staring at the loch.

Their plan to rob the place had certainly gone tits up. He'd thought they would come here, find Babyface outside the house and nick some of the good stuff. But there was no sign of Babyface. The truth is they have no proof that Babyface Jack's body was rolled up in the carpet but what else could it have been? You're not going to dump a rolled up carpet in the early hours of the morning are you, not unless there is something fishy inside it? He really underestimated that Harriet all right. Julian is a weak wanker but bleedin' hell, she is something else altogether.

'What we gonna do then?' Mad Jack asks again, giving the tree another kick.

'I need to think about it,' replies Diamond.

The truth is the whole thing has shaken him up more than he wants to admit. He'd seen a few things in his time and was convinced Babyface had not been badly injured. He'd never have left him otherwise. In fact, he had expected him to come limping back to the B&B later that night. When he hadn't they had crept back to the house to try and get an idea of what was going on but apart from seeing Harriet sneak into Stalker Lodge everything was quiet. At first he had thought that perhaps they had taken him to hospital but there was no record of him there.

'Think about bleedin' what?' asks Mad Jack angrily.

Diamond glares at his son.

'Do yer really think I'm going to let them kill Babyface and dump him in the loch? What kind of father do you take me for?' snaps Diamond.

'I dunno,' mumbles Mad Jack.

'It all depends whether it was business or personal,' says Diamond thoughtfully.

Mad Jack kicks the tree again.

'Will you leave that bleedin' tree alone?'

'It's personal ain't it, I mean that's obvious. He was your son, that's personal ain't it?'

'Yeah but we killed 'arriet's goldfish and that weren't personal.'

Mad Jack Junior gapes at his dad.

'Babyface is a bit different to a goldfish.'

Diamond shrugs.

'I know that and you know that but,' he widens his hands expressively. 'It was her goldfish, so it was personal to her.'

Mad Jack shakes his head.

'I don't believe this. We're comparing Babyface to a bleedin' goldfish. Somethin' ain't right 'ere,' he mumbles. 'We didn't dump the stupid goldfish in a loch though did we?'

Jack exhales.

'It don't matter what we did with the goldfish. Okay, it just don't matter. We might have to accept a life for a life, right?'

'Babyface's life for a goldfish? I don't believe I'm 'earing this.'

Diamond bites his lip.

'But then again, maybe you're right. They should perhaps pay for what they've done.'

Mad Jack jumps up and down in excitement.

'Yeah that's more like it. Get some dosh out of the buggers.'

Diamond scratches his head. Yeah, maybe Mad Jack is right. They could make a little packet out of all this and all because old Harriet got it all wrong. Maybe she did them a favour. Shame Babyface got whacked in the process. Still, business is business. You can't let emotions get in the way.

'Let's go back and get the plan in motion,' says Diamond.

Mad Jack nods happily.

'Yeah, let's sort the bastards.'

Chapter Thirty-Two

'I don't know what you're up to,' Hamilton had hissed over breakfast. 'But you'd better be careful. If you put one foot wrong now I'm warning you, you'll never work again. You'll end up homeless.'

'Why Ham, you say the nicest things,' I had responded, only to receive a piercing glare from him. Melanie was bustling around giving the servants orders while Margarita took to her room for a nap. Fiona had gone riding with Sebastian and no one had batted an eyelid.

And then Alistair turns up. He bursts into my room, eyes blazing and cheeks red.

'Harriet, I g-g-g got an earlier flight. I thought I'd surprise Fiona.'
Oh she'll be surprised all right.

'She thought you were coming this evening.'

'W-w-w- ...'

'I said, she thought you were coming this evening.'
He takes a deep breath.

'I'm not deaf,' he says, dropping his suitcase onto the bed.

'Shall I get Cedric to show you to her room?' I say. I don't want him making himself too comfortable in mine

'W-w-w- ...'
Oh he doesn't give up does he?

'She's out riding,' I say.

'Nothing new then,' he says dismissively, looking around my room. 'W-w-what happened to your f-f-f-f- ...'

'Flat? I say helpfully, 'I think it's still there. I've been paying the rent. I don't think Diamond wants to burn that down.'

'F-f-f-f- ...'
Yes fuck, I know exactly what he's going through.

'Foot,' he blurts out.

'Oh that,' I smile. 'I kind of fell out of a boat.'

He nods knowingly, like falling out of boats is what you do when you live this kind of life.

'I say, this is grand isn't it? I bet you're enjoying being Hamilton's b-b-b-b- ...'

I shake my head.

'Bitch?' I say questioningly.

Well, let's be honest that's how Hamilton views me.

'Bride to be,' he finishes.

I pull a face. He has no idea. There is a knock at the door and before I can answer, Hamilton has strolled in. What a bloody cheek.

'Do come in,' I say sarcastically.

'Hello darling. Alistair old man, how are you? The servants told me you were here.'

How bleeding pompous is that?

'What, all of them at once?' I say putting on a shocked expression. 'Blimey that's bleeding amazing.'

'Watch your language Harriet,' Hamilton barks.

I storm out of my room and leave them to it. At the top of the stairs I hear the sound of a woman's voice.

'Don't be ridiculous Cedric. He can't be upstairs with his fiancée. I am marrying Hamilton.'

Her voice is soft, cultured, and terribly posh. I feel my stomach churn. Who the bleeding hell is this? I turn back and hurry to my room. Hamilton and Alistair start at my entrance.

'It is *my* room,' I say irritably, 'and by the way, there is a woman downstairs saying she is your fiancée.'

'My fiancée?' says Alistair knitting his brows together.

'No not you Alistair, Hamilton's fiancée.'

'But you're Hamilton's fiancée.'

I roll my eyes.

'Oh Good heavens, what is she doing here?' says Hamilton looking anxiously around the room.

'I don't have a panic room if that's what you're looking for,' I say sarcastically.

'Christ, are you absolutely sure?'

'Believe me if there was one I would have been in it days ago.'

'Are you absolutely sure she is my fiancée?' he asks crossly.

'No I'm not sure. She's bleeding sure though. Don't you know if you have a fiancée?' I snap.

'Harriet language.'

'Piss off Hamilton.'

'C-c-c-can I do anything?' stammers Alistair.

'Like what exactly?' I say.

He shrugs helplessly.

'Oh God, why did Phoebe have to turn up now?' groans Hamilton.

Phoebe? Who the hell is Phoebe? We all leave the bedroom together and I'm grateful no one is around to see that. It looks like I've just had a threesome. The fact that someone may think I've had a threesome doesn't bother me so much, but a threesome with Alistair and Hamilton would be dead embarrassing. I feel nauseous at the thought of it and push it from my mind. I reluctantly sit on the stairlift and begin my descent. What a ridiculous entrance this is. She looks up at me and I meet her eyes. She's very beautiful, I mean, seriously beautiful in a celebrity kind of way, whereas I'm kind of pretty in a very non-celebrity kind of way, if you catch my drift. The way people are arriving at the moment I wouldn't bat an eyelid if Angelina Jolie and Brad Pitt turned up. She wears a green Armani suit which flatters her trim body perfectly. I know it's Armani because I recognise it as one Marcus wanted to dress me in. Her make-up is immaculate and she is far more Hamilton's type than I could ever be. *This is Phoebe, a friend of the family*, I hear myself introduce her to Caron and Gary. The thought of Caron and Gary, and my parents, makes me feel sick. What will this woman make of Gary with his shaved head and neck tattoos, and Caron with her pineapple-style hair. Talk about opposite ends of the fashion spectrum. I don't want my parents ridiculed and they really won't fit in. I don't bleeding fit in, so I know they won't.

'Hamilton honey, what the hell is going on?' she says in a high-pitched voice that echoes in the hall. She turns her head to me and nods, 'who is that?'

'I sent you a text, several in fact. Why didn't you respond?' Hamilton hisses.

The stairlift comes to a juddering halt and I slide off and lean on my crutches for support.

'What texts darling? You know I've been in New York. I don't use my Blackberry when I'm there. I flew straight here and that stupid butler tells me you have a fiancée. You really should get better staff.'

'Cedric is excellent,' I say, trying to hide my London accent. She gives me a scathing look and eyes me up and down in a disdainful manner. I don't know why she's giving me such a snotty stare, I'm wearing leggings and the baggy woollen jumper that Marcus had found for me, it's designer. Don't ask me which designer mind you.

'Christ Phoebe, I'd wish you'd seen the bloody texts,' snaps Hamilton.

'Who are you?' she asks pointedly.

'Hello, I'm Harriet,' I say, extending a hand and ignoring Hamilton's filthy look.

'Who's arrived?' calls Margarita from the library. 'Is that Harriet's sister?'

She wheels herself into the long hall and stops abruptly on seeing Phoebe. She is wearing a glorious multi-coloured silk robe which hangs to her perfectly manicured bare feet.

'Hamilton, explain yourself,' she barks.

'Phoebe is here for the party Grandma. She came to wish us well, isn't that right Phoebe? Let me show you to your room.'

'Hello Mrs Lancaster, how are you?' asks Phoebe.

'I've been better,' she says sharply.

'What do you mean *my room*, I'll be with you Hamilton,' Phoebe says looking flustered.

'Let me get some tea,' he says, hastily dragging her away.

'And who are you young man?' demands Margarita of Alistair.

'Oh, I'm F-F-F- ...'

She continues to stare at him.

'F-Fiona's boyfriend, I g-g-g-got an earlier f-f-f-flight.'

'Do you have a stutter?'

Good God, what an obvious question to ask.

'Yes, I have actually.'

'Yes I noticed. Can't you get that fixed?'

'Well, n-n-n- ...'

'Are you trying to say *No*?'

'N-not really.'

'So you can get it fixed?'

'No, not really. I mean, not really I can't get it f-f-f-fixed.'

She shakes her head.

'Good Lord boy, how can anyone ever understand you?'

'Are your parents here yet Harriet?' she says, turning to me and not waiting for Alistair's reply.

No, thank God. I watch as Phoebe's green Armani suit disappears into the kitchen.

'They're arriving tomorrow.'

'Well, I certainly hope they make more sense than this lot,' she says, wheeling herself to the library.

'I thought she w-w-was supposed to b-b-be on her deathbed,' says Alistair, staring wide-eyed.

'Yep, she's amazing isn't she?'

The house is alive with activity. Cedric is on a stepladder hanging fairy lights from the ceiling with Emily's help, and there is a crashing of pots and pans from the kitchen. Party preparations are in full swing it would seem. The ballroom has been decorated with glittering hearts, and balloons hang from the antlers of the stags' heads. It would all be wonderfully romantic if it was true and I was getting engaged, but the decorations make me feel a cheat and a liar. In the middle of the room is a statue of cupid. He certainly shot the wrong arrow this time.

'Hello you must be Fiona's Alistair,' Melanie calls as she breezes into the hall. 'Someone mentioned you had arrived. I'm Lady Melanie Lancaster, Hamilton's mother. Have you been shown to your room?'

'I presume I'm with F-F-Fi,' he replies.

'Margarita doesn't approve of ...' she breaks off with a blush. 'But your room is very close to Fiona's, let me show you.'

I hobble to the kitchen where Phoebe and Hamilton are having a heated argument.

'Don't mind me,' I say with a smirk. 'Do carry on. I've just come for some water.'

'I hope Hamilton has made it very clear that this is a business arrangement,' she snaps. 'I happen to find the whole thing distasteful. How you can even lower yourself to such degradation is beyond me but I guess women like you don't know any better and will do anything for money.'

Her hair has come loose from her bun and her face is flushed. I almost feel sorry for her.

'I've been called worse by better people than you,' I retort, pouring water into a glass. I fight the urge to throw it over her, after all, she needs cooling down.

She shakes with rage and if Cedric had not walked in at that moment I wouldn't like to think what Phoebe would have done next.

'Miss Harriet, there is a phone call for you. Would you like to take it in the drawing room?'

I turn angrily.

'If you want to stop our little arrangement Hamilton, just let me know,' I snap. 'I'd be happy to tell Margarita for you.'

'Phoebe's upset. You won't be telling Grandma anything, will you Harriet?'

'You'll have to wait and see, won't you Hamilton?' I say threateningly as I make my exit from the kitchen.

I wonder who the hell would be phoning me at Glenwood, unless of course it is Jack Diamond. I tremble at the thought and by the time I pick up the phone my hands are shaking. I hadn't expected him to phone this soon.

'Hello,' I say timidly.

'Harry, it's me Julian.'

I grasp the back of an armchair and slowly lower myself into it. Jeez Louise, whatever next?

'Harry are you still there? I have tried your mobile but it always goes to Fiona's voicemail. I didn't want to leave a message on her phone.'

'How did you get this number?'

'Easily. Hamilton Lancaster is all over the Internet. It wasn't hard to find his summer retreat.'

'Spring,' I correct.

'Whatever, it doesn't matter. I've got good news Harry. I've got a backer for the restaurant.'

Oh, excuse me while I do a little jig. I let out a long lingering sigh.

'Great news isn't it? The thing is, his money will help with some of the debts but I was thinking maybe Hamilton could throw some money in too and ...'

'What?' I say.

I can't believe I'm hearing this.

'I've worked it all out. He's loaded Harriet, the family have money to throw away.'

Yes, but not necessarily in your direction.

'We can get ourselves out of this mess and get our lives back to normal,' he continues. 'I can't wait to see you babe, I've missed you so much.'

He's got to be joking. And what does he mean *we can get ourselves out of this mess*, doesn't he mean *his* mess?

'Julian, I hate to burst your bubble but I haven't missed you at all, and I don't want to see you. I'm not helping you pay your bills. I'm only paying what I owe. You lied to me.'

'Come on babe, I love you and you love me, we have a flat together.'

He makes it sound like we've had a child together.

'It's my flat, and I'm not sharing it with you or anyone. I'm livid with you Julian. I've had to lie to my parents and to Caron. You completely shattered my dreams,' I say and much to my annoyance I feel tears well up. Oh great, all I need is for Julian to hear me cry.

'Come on Harry, don't overreact. You know you would never have gone to Angola ...'

'It wasn't bloody Angola,' I shout. 'Why do you keep saying that?'

'Okay, okay. Does it matter? The thing is, we have the restaurant and the flat and well, the rest of our lives together. We just need to get these debts and the Jacks sorted and we'll be the way we used to be.'

'I don't want to be the way we used to be.'

I hear him sigh.

'Harriet, I'm coming to Glenwood. I need to ask Hamilton for some money.'

'He won't give it to you,' I say bluntly.

'He will, especially when I threaten to tell his grandmother you're not really his girlfriend, but mine.'

I gasp in horror.

'Julian, don't you dare.'

'I'm doing this for us babe. I'm in Scotland and I'm coming to Glenwood. We've got to get our lives back to normal.'

'Christ Julian, life with you was far from normal, and don't you dare come here. I'm warning you Julian, I won't be responsible for my actions if you do,' I say, recalling my expertise with a shotgun.

I slam the phone down in anger and realise I didn't tell him that the Jacks are in Scotland too. Oh bugger it. Bugger Julian, bugger the Jacks and bugger Hamilton bleeding Lancaster. I'll be glad when Saturday arrives. I'll be out of here faster than a whippet.

Chapter Thirty-Three

I've been to many cringe-worthy dinner parties in my time but never one where I have been so drunk that I could barely see the dinner table. I'm living my worst nightmare, a dinner with Hamilton's family and my parents, along with Caron and Gary and the shadow of Julian hanging over me like a bloody shroud. It wouldn't have been so bad if it had just been Hamilton's family, but Hamilton's family in full Scottish regalia is a little too much. Both Sebastian and Hamilton are wearing kilts. Blessings of blessings though, they are both wearing black tights underneath. Hamilton hasn't stopped pointing out the pattern on his sporran. Caron blushes every time she looks at it, and I can see Gary does not know what to make of men who wear skirts to dinner. Melanie is wearing a tartan sash over her dress, and Margarita has been sporting a very fashionable tartan shawl all day. I expect them to launch into a Highland fling at any moment. I've had so much champagne that even Hamilton is beginning to look appealing. Not as appealing as Brice however, who is wearing the same dinner suit he wore at Silvia's wedding, and I'm struggling to keep my eyes off him.

'You're getting drunk,' hisses Hamilton as he takes my arm. 'Don't do anything stupid.'
Well I couldn't look any more stupid than him in his bleeding kilt could I? I pull myself away and sway towards Caron.

'Hamilton's lovely,' she whispers. 'You're so lucky Harriet.'
Bleeding hell, which part of Hamilton has she found lovely? I'm obviously looking in all the wrong places.

'He is isn't he?' I lie.
Phoebe glides in wearing a black strapless dress that hangs to her ankles. Sparkling on her wrist is a diamond-studded bracelet. Her hair has been freed from the earlier bun and hangs loosely around her shoulders. She looks amazing and I find myself wondering why Hamilton didn't just get engaged to her. She is surely more suited to this life than me.

'Who is that? She's stunning,' asks Caron, staring wide-eyed.

'A friend of the family,' I slur, 'but she's no friend of mine.'

Phoebe glides towards us on a cloud of Chanel perfume.

'Hello, this must be your family Harriet, how quaint. Interesting hair,' she says looking at Caron. 'Oh, and I love this little thing,' she adds, fingering Caron's cocktail dress.

'Where did you get it? I've seen nothing like it,' she purrs.

'Mum and I went to Debenhams,' Caron says proudly.

Phoebe wrinkles her nose.

'Debenhams? I had no idea they sold clothes.'

'You'd be surprised what goes on outside the confines of Harrods Phoebe,' interjects Brice, taking my empty glass as he does so. 'Enough, don't you think?' he whispers.

What a sodding cheek. I beckon to Gregory who is carrying a tray of champagne flutes.

'Another please?' I say, avoiding Brice's raised eyebrows.

'Brice, how are you? I thought you'd be on that rickety boat of yours. How is darling Lara?' Phoebe says, seductively pushing her breasts towards him. God, they look as huge as my falsies except these are the real McCoy. I feel decidedly flat-chested compared to her, and decidedly dowdy in my River Island chenille dress. He steps back to avoid being assaulted by her Dolly Parton breasts.

'Back home in South Africa, I imagine,' he responds.

I wander away from Phoebe and Brice but not before I hear Melanie say quietly,

'Phoebe, such bad timing dear.'

'I'm sorry Melanie. I didn't get Hamilton's texts. I have to say this whole thing disgusts me.'

I down my champagne and try to digest what I have just heard. Has Melanie known about Hamilton's deceit all along? Does this mean that Brice has known too? What the fuck is going on? Is he just playing with the common girl from Battersea? What a bloody diabolical liberty, I feel my cheeks flame and join my parents. Dad is looking extremely uncomfortable in his old suit, which is now at least one size too small, and he constantly tugs at his tie. Fiona stands beside him, looking as gorgeous as ever. Her eyes are riveted on Sebastian and anyone who had been in doubt that she fancied him is unlikely to be any longer.

'Fi, you're really transparent. Where's Alistair?'

'Alistair's having a wonderful time looking at whiskies with Major Bates. Talk about bloody boring.'

'What do they want to look at them for? Alcohol is for drinking, not for looking at, that's what I say,' says Gary from behind us. 'I have to say the booze here is fan-bloody-tastic.'

'Enjoying your lager are you?' I say. 'Tastes just as good out of a glass does it?'

'Harriet,' admonishes Mum.

'Yes I know. I'm sorry.'

Yes Harriet, what is wrong with you? I've felt angry ever since Julian phoned, and I've not been able to tell anyone, not even Fiona. There just hasn't been time.

Cedric approaches with a tray and Mum pulls a face.

'What can I get you madam?'

'Can I have a port and lemon love? Caron, do you want another wine spritzer?'

I try to hide my cringe.

'Would that be port with a slice of lemon madam?'

Mum laughs.

'No darling, port with lemonade. Douglas do you want another shandy?'

Oh this is just too gruesome to bear.

'Yes madam, one shandy, one spritzer and a port and lemon coming up.'

They'll be asking for bleeding pork scratchings next.

'It is dead posh here dear,' Mum says nervously. 'I really didn't know whether to get in the bath or to take a photo of it. Everything in our room looks much too good to use.'

'Don't be silly Mum, think of it as a posh hotel,' I say. 'Mum I really need to talk to you about Hamilton ...'

'Are our clothes okay do you think?'

'Well at least I'm wearing men's clothes,' says Dad, yanking at his tie again.

'Will you leave that alone Douglas, anyone would think you'd never worn a tie before.'

'I normally only wear them for funerals, and this suit's a bit on the tight side. I've never felt so trussed up in my life.'

'Well, this isn't a funeral is it?' snaps Mum.

'I don't know what it is. Men in skirts, I've seen nothing like it.'

I stifle my giggle.

'Are you pissed young lady, whatever will Hamilton think?'
I don't give a flying fig what Hamilton bloody thinks.

'About Hamilton,' I try again.

'Is Hamilton giving you the ring tomorrow?' interrupts Caron sipping from her white wine spritzer.

'Yes, it was his great grandmother's. It's an antique, but the thing is …'
Mum shrieks.

'Oh my giddy aunt, why that's just bleeding marvellous.'

'You won't have to worry about that debt Julian got you into,' adds Caron.

'No, it's more complicated than you think …'

'Does Jules know?' asks Gary.

'Yes, obviously he's not happy …'

'Hamilton's a far better catch dear,' says Dad.

'Oh absolutely,' agrees Mum.
Oh God, I can't get a word in edgewise.

'Julian might come here,' I say without thinking.

'What, well you'll just have to tell him to leave,' says Mum.

'The thing is, this engagement with Hamilton is just …'

'Just what dear?' asks Mum, her cheeks rosy from the champagne.

'Well you remember those gangsters and …'
There is a sudden hush as everyone stops talking, everyone except me, and my *well, you remember those gangsters and,* seem to reverberate around the hall. Don't you just hate it when that happens? I turn to see Margarita standing in the doorway.

'It's Margarita,' I say in way of explanation, 'Hamilton's grandmother.'

'Anyone would think she was the queen,' whispers Caron.
Margarita walks stiffly towards us, leaning heavily on her stick, with Lionel following closely behind.

'So these are your parents,' she says, studying my mother closely.
No, they're two aliens from the planet Vogon actually, I want to say but fight back the impulse.

'Yes Margarita, this is my mum, Lillian, and my dad, Douglas.'
Mum hovers between a curtsy and a bow and finally decides to do neither but simply holds out a shaky hand.

'It's an honour to meet you …' she says hesitantly and looks to me for guidance.

'Margarita or Mrs Lancaster whatever you prefer. Unfortunately I was not graced with a title. Those are given to people who rarely deserve them I think,' Margarita says looking at her son.

'Was it a good journey for you?'

'Very nice thank you,' says Dad in his best posh voice.

'Cedric, get Hamilton's parents a drink. You don't have to drink champagne just because it's being offered. I'll have a Bloody Mary please Cedric. How about you Mrs Lawson? What can Cedric get you?'

'Well I was going to have a port and lemon but maybe I'll have a bloody Margarita too. I've never had one of those,' says Mum.

I don't think anyone has had one of those. I cringe and Phoebe hides a snigger.

'Do you really think you have the breeding to marry someone like Hamilton?' whispers Phoebe. 'I hope you realise you're making a complete fool of yourself.'

I glance at Brice as he chats to Sebastian. He has one hand in the pocket of his trousers and looks completely relaxed. I realise that Phoebe is of course quite right and I really don't fit in here. I must be out of my mind to think that Brice actually likes me, for me. I suppose I am just a distraction. I must be to him, and all of these upper-class toffs, a circus freak, a clown for their amusement. What a fool I've been. I turn away from Phoebe without answering and am relieved when Cedric rings the bell for us to take our places at the table. Damn and double damn, I've lost my chance to explain to Mum about Hamilton, the Jacks and that the engagement is not for real. I grab another champagne flute and make my way to the table. Mum gasps.

'What a lovely spread, all that work,' she mumbles.

'Allow me,' says Brice, pulling out a chair for her. He waits until the women are seated before taking his place between us.

'Scotch broth to start,' says Melanie. 'It is cook's speciality. I don't think anyone makes it quite like her.'

'Heinz don't do a bad job,' mumbles Gary.

'Is it tr-tr-tr-tr- ...' stutters Alistair.

Fiona rolls her eyes

'True?' asks Margarita. 'Of course it's true, why would Melanie lie?'

'No, I was asking if it is tr-tr-tradition to wear kilts for dinner?' finishes a red-faced Alistair.

'We like to when entertaining,' says Hamilton with a smug smile. I find him more repugnant by the minute.

'Is it the L-L-La-La- ...'

'Jesus,' mumbles Fiona.

'Lamb?' I offer.

'We're having Scottish beef aren't we Melanie?' questions Margarita.

'Or trout, but if you would prefer lamb Alistair, I'm sure we can arrange something,' Melanie says gesturing to Cedric.

Alistair sighs.

'L-Lancaster tartan that you wear?' he asks.

'Don't be ridiculous young man, there is no such thing.' Margarita barks.

Melanie dismisses Cedric and Alistair returns to his soup.

'How do you like Scotland?' Margarita asks my parents.

'We really only saw it from the coach, didn't we dear,' says Dad as he dunks a roll in the soup.

I reach for a wine bottle but Brice stops my hand, sending a tingle through me

'Why are you so nervous?'

'I'm not nervous,' I say, draining the last drop of champagne from the flute.

'White wine madam?' asks Gregory.

'Yes please,' I say, shaking off Brice's hand.

'Yes,' says Mum, looking at the roll each side of her. 'But what we saw was lovely, and of course your home is beautiful.'

Brice picks up his roll and bites into it and Mum gives him a relieved smile.

'I'll get Cedric to give you a tour. We're having the engagement party in the ballroom. Of course if the weather had been decent we could have hired a marquee, but one has to think of the servants carrying everything in the rain,' replies Margarita.

'We're so excited about the party aren't we Douglas?'

'I think you'll find it interesting,' says Hamilton condescendingly.

'Mum and Dad have been to engagement parties before, you know,' says Caron with an edge to her voice.

'We don't have servants,' says Dad. 'Lillian does everything in our home, don't you love?'

'Yes, well it is smaller Dad,' chips in Caron.

Oh God, I want to die. I wonder if I crawl under the table anyone will miss me. Perhaps I can pop to the kitchen and help cook with the food. I just pray Mum doesn't offer to do the washing up.

'You must have help of some kind. Don't you have a cleaner?' asks Margarita as she gives a piece of bread to Diamond.

'Oh yes she has a cleaner. I bought you a new Henry for Christmas didn't I Lil?' says Dad proudly.

I suppose I could dunk my head into my soup as a distraction. I down half a glass of wine and debate whether I should ask Alistair if he has his Valium with him.

'You do your own cleaning?' says a stunned Margarita.

'It's not unknown old girl. Not everyone has domestic staff,' smiles Brice.

'Well you young man,' she says affectionately, 'could do with some staff at Stalkers Lodge.'

'I'm perfectly happy cleaning it myself,' he grins.

I feel myself slide from the chair and grab his knee to stop myself falling. One hand covers mine while the other helps me back into my seat.

'Sorry,' I slur.

'I'm very happy to hold your delectable body, but not throughout the whole of dinner,' he whispers while moving my wine glass out of reach.

'Spoilsport,' I mumble.

'For withholding the wine or not holding your delectable body throughout dinner?'

'Both,' I whisper, trying to sound seductive but sounding more like a lush.

'Douglas does the garden,' Mum adds.

'Oh good heavens,' exclaims Phoebe. 'You mean you don't have a gardener? But that's just absurd.'

Oh sod this for a game of soldiers.

'No more absurd than your enormous tits,' I say drunkenly. 'I'd like to see Sebastian prick those with his tiepin.'

Phoebe gasps. Oh God, I must be pissed. I never say things like that.

'How dare you. Really Lady Lancaster, this is just too common ...' she says turning to Melanie.

'You were being rather toffee nosed Phoebe,' remarks Brice.

'Too right,' adds Caron.

Brice gives my hand a reassuring squeeze. The touch of his hand has my body on fire immediately and I feel quite bereft when he moves it. True to form, Mum starts collecting the soup bowls. Brice places his hand gently on hers.

'Don't worry about that. Emily will collect the dishes. We lead a privileged life as you can see.'

'We have Scottish beef for the main course, or trout, I do hope you're all happy with that,' says Melanie cheerfully in an attempt to ease the tension.

'I've never had Scottish beef,' says Caron. 'We get ours from Tesco, don't we Gary?'

'It's rather good,' says Cedric, offering a slice to Gary. In response, Gary hands his plate to Cedric,

'I'll try anything once,' he says.

'Damn fine cows they are too the Aberdeen Angus, and I assume the trout is from the loch?' says Major Bates. 'Will you be back for grouse season old man?' he adds, looking at Sebastian.

Caron catches my eye and gestures to the door with a tip of her head. I stand up and Caron follows suit.

'If you'll excuse us,' I say, leading Caron to the door.

She closes it behind us and sighs.

'Christ Harriet, how can you stand this lot? You're not seriously getting engaged to that plonker Hamilton are you? I know Julian put you in the shit but Christ, this lot are so up their own arses it's untrue. God, I need fresh air.'

She yanks open the front door and I follow her out. The chilly air hits us and I feel myself sway.

'Christ, how much have I drunk?' I groan, feeling my head pound.

'Is there something going on Harry, something that Mum and Dad should know about? And who is that obnoxious Phoebe? Just who is she a friend of?'

'Oh God, Caron, the thing is ...'

God have I drunk that much that I am beginning to hear things? My heart beats faster when I hear that distinctive whining sound that says *Harriet's Mini*? I see a car turning into the estate driveway. I strain my eyes but everything just blurs.

'Do you see that?' I ask paranoia in my voice.

'Yes, who is that?' Caron replies walking towards the figure that has emerged from the car. Oh Jesus, what if it is Jack Diamond?

'Caron, come back,' I say, hobbling after her.

'Good heaven's Julian, is that you?' she cries.

Dear God, I can't think which is worse, Julian or Jack Diamond.

'Hello Harriet. So this is Glenwood,' he says and plonks a wet kiss on my cheek.

Chapter Thirty-Four

It seems to take forever to get my brain in gear and even longer to get my tongue to work.

'Julian, I told you not to come here,' I slur.

He ignores me and smiles at Caron.

'Does he know?' she whispers.

'That Harriet is getting engaged to another man?' asks Julian.

'Well I ...' stammers Caron.

'That's why I'm here. Perhaps you could give us a few minutes Caron?'

Shit, this is all I need.

'I'll be in the dining room. Don't be too long, it's chilly out here.'

'I won't keep her long,' he smiles. 'What happened to your foot?'

'Like you care Julian, I mean, please don't insult me.'

He moves towards me and I take a step backwards, swaying ungainly as I do so. His arm reaches out and encircles my waist and I am pulled towards him.

'Why are you being like this Harry? I made a mistake, I'm sorry. But I'm trying to get us out of the mess.'

I pull myself from his arms and scoff.

'By blackmailing Hamilton?' I say.

'It's not like that. I'll only tell his grandmother if he doesn't make a small investment in the restaurant. Come on Harry, he's loaded. It's a drop in the ocean for him, you could have asked for a lot more than thirty-five thousand.'

'I think you have a nerve coming here,' snaps a voice behind us.

I turn to see Mum striding towards us. For one awful minute I think she may clip him round the ear, and I'm pleased to see he still has both ears for her to clip. Is this my mum talking or has she been possessed by the Antichrist? It must be the bloody Scottish beef. My placid mum is now a force to be reckoned with.

'Mrs Lawson, I think this is a matter between Harriet and I. Whatever you may think, I happen to know that Harriet loves me and we'll get this mess sorted.'

'I rather think you have let her down something awful Julian. Harriet has a chance for happiness now and I don't think you should get in the way of that.'

'Mum, the thing with Hamilton is ...'

'Be quiet Harriet,' she says forcefully. 'You've put my daughter right in the bleeding shit. When I got to your flat she was a wreck, sitting there holding a sodding vibrator. You left her without a pot to piss in or a window to throw it out of. You're a selfish bleeder and she's better off without you.'

Holy shit. Her cheeks are flushed and in the moonlight she looks quite angelic. I can't say the same for her language. Julian's eyes widen.

'Why were you holding a vibrator?'

I don't believe this is happening.

'Well, she wasn't having an earth-shattering orgasm thinking about you, if that's what you're thinking.'

Christ almighty.

'Mum,' I say reaching the doorpost for support. 'Don't get all worked up.'

'Hello there, I'm Sir Sebastian Lancaster, can I help you?'

Mum and I look at Julian as Sebastian joins us.

'This is my son Julian,' says Mum quickly.

What the fuck. Has she taken leave of her senses?

'Come in, come in,' Sebastian waves.

I force a smile.

'Sorry I'm late,' says Julian, acting the part perfectly. 'I drove down. Hit traffic I'm afraid.'

Hamilton stands in the doorway and I try to ignore his piercing eyes.

'My son Julian, just in time for dinner,' says Mum on seeing Hamilton. She pulls Julian into the hall and strides to the dining room. No doubt she is hurrying to warn Dad and Caron. God, everyone has gone mad. My heart drops as it occurs to me that Brice is bound to remember who Julian is.

'I'm warning you,' I hiss.

Julian ignores me and walks ahead to the dining room. Thoughts of stabbing him in the back fleetingly cross my mind.

'What the hell is going on?' Hamilton asks blocking my way.

'You'll have to ask Julian,' I say nervously.

'I'm warning you Harriet ...'

'Oh Hamilton, do stop warning me. It's becoming quite tedious now,' I snap, hobbling to the dinner table.

'Cedric, lay a place for Mr Lawson,' Melanie says as she shakes Julian's hand and welcomes him to Glenwood. Mr Lawson my arse. Fiona stares in shock and Alistair stutters something, which thankfully everyone ignores. I sit down and finish what is left in my wine glass. I feel Brice's eyes on me and try to ignore him. The tension from his body is almost tangible, and when his knee brushes mine it feels like an electric current shoots through me. Julian arrogantly shakes hands with Hamilton and congratulates him on his engagement. Gary looks baffled and is about to open his mouth when Caron nudges him sharply in the ribs.

'I must say you don't resemble your parents at all,' says Margarita, studying him.

'Christ, why don't we invite the Jacks too,' mumbles Fiona.

'What was that dear?' asks Mum.

Gregory sidles up to me with a silver platter and looking at my glass of white wine asks,

'Are you the trout madam?'

'Most certainly not,' I smile. 'You must mean Phoebe.'

Phoebe looks at Hamilton who tactfully turns his head away.

'Well, this is nice isn't it?' says Melanie, 'All your family here.'

I can't think of anything worse.

'Yes,' I say with a forced smile.

'We're a very close family, aren't we Harry,' Julian says with a half smile. Phoebe looks at him appraisingly and I sigh. He is good looking in a smarmy kind of way. He is wearing a smart suit and white shirt. It was his good looks that attracted me to him in the first place, that and his ambition. I now feel nothing but loathing for him.

'So what do you do Julian?' asks Brice, his tone hard and his eyes focused entirely on him.

'The beef is superb,' says Hamilton.

I am grateful for the change of subject.

'Yes excellent,' agrees Phoebe. 'As always the food is outstanding Margarita.'

Margarita gives Phoebe a scathing look.

'But of course. I'm surprised you need to say so. We'd never serve anything but superb food,' she says sharply.

Phoebe gives her a tight smile. Brice's eyes continue to bore into Julian and I wait for his response with bated breath. Julian opens his mouth to reply as Brice holds up a hand to stop him.

'No, I remember now. Harriet mentioned something about you trying to set up a French restaurant. How's that going? I imagine you need a lot of finance for something like that?'

'I'm not *trying* anything,' says Julian, an undercurrent of anger in his voice. 'I *own* a French restaurant and it's doing very well actually.'

He meets Brice's stare head on. Oh no, please don't let there be a scene.

'I love French food,' says Phoebe. 'Do you speak French to your customers?'

Speak French? That's a laugh. The only 'French' to come out of Julian's mouth are curses.

'I did try,' he says arrogantly, 'but the customers prefer English.'

What a little liar. She giggles flirtatiously,

'What a shame, I love a man who speaks French.'

'I speak French,' says Hamilton, looking hurt.

'I do too,' says Alistair.

'When you can get it out,' adds Fiona.

'I don't stammer in F-F-F-French,' he argues.

'Why not?' I ask.

'Probably because no one can understand him,' quips Fiona.

'Foreign languages are so romantic aren't they?' says Julian, smiling at Phoebe.

Good God is he flirting with her, and right under my nose. Well, that takes the biscuit doesn't it? Cedric and Gregory remove our plates, and I hear Julian say,

'By the way Hamilton, I wonder if I could have a little chat with you about the restaurant. You're a businessman. I could do with a few tips.'

Hamilton looks uneasy.

'I don't know much about restaurants,' he says cautiously.

'It's more financial advice I was looking for,' Julian says, taking a roll.

Fiona looks wide-eyed at me. I shake my head miserably and knock back some wine.

'Madam, what would you like for dessert, we have lemon tart or Scottish trifle,' offers Gregory.

'Scottish trifle is also known as *Tipsy Laird,*' laughs Sebastian.

'I would think the tart is more you,' says Phoebe spitefully.

I study her over the rim of the wine glass.

'It takes one to know one,' I snap. 'I'll have the Scottish trifle please. Nothing like a tipsy laird to finish the evening.'

'Touché,' Brice laughs.

I blush and pick up my spoon.

'I'll be your tipsy laird any night,' he whispers huskily and I feel an urge to cross my legs to stop the unbearable ache between them. I see Julian staring at us and I give him a weak smile.

'You tease me sir,' I whisper back.

'I tease not m'lady and why pray, do I behold your boyfriend here?'

I lower my spoon and turn to face him. Everyone is chatting about the desserts and I feel sure I won't be overheard.

'He's here to get money from Hamilton,' I say honestly.

'And you didn't know he was coming?'

I shake my head.

'I hope you're not flirting with the bride to be,' says Julian loudly. Brice lifts a glass of wine to his lips.

'Yes I was. Last chance before she has that ring on her finger,' he smiles.

There is an uncomfortable silence until Sebastian says,

'Who's for a game of charades?'

I hate to tell him we've been playing that all evening.

Chapter Thirty-Five

I feel imprisoned. Yes I know, it's pretty hard to feel imprisoned in a mansion, but believe me, that is exactly how I feel. The corset Emily had suggested I wear is not helping. I can barely breathe. I think Major Bates thought I was panting over him earlier. The damn thing is rubbing my navel so badly that it has almost taken my breath away. I discreetly pull at the front of my Givenchy white dress to gain some relief, but only succeed in pinching myself. I watch Diamond and the shocking scene of unbridled carnage the other side of the French doors as he devours a rabbit. A friend of Melanie's stands around smoking, while her daughter looks on mesmerised. I suppose I should rescue her before she is damaged for life, the child that is, not the mother, who seems totally oblivious to the carnage in front of her. Today is my engagement party, the happiest day of any woman's life, and I have never felt more miserable. There seems to be hundreds of people here, although in reality it is more like fifty. Etta James' smooth voice croons over the loudspeakers and everyone is jolly. The ballroom is impressive. There is shimmering crystal everywhere. Hired staff bustling amongst guests with drinks and titbits and Hamilton's family looking as pleased as punch. Fiona is positively glowing and Phoebe looks amazing in a backless satin dress. She is flirting outrageously with Brice and it's all I can do not to look at them. She fans herself seductively with an oriental fan and glances at me. I turn away and sip from my glass of coke. Hamilton has said I'm not to drink.

'I don't want you messing things up, not today of all days. Let's face it you have a habit of messing things up.'
I have no idea what he means. I see him watching me from across the room and lift my glass of coke in salute. That's the thing about vodka. No one can tell it is in your glass can they? I've had three vodkas so far and I still feel tense. I see Julian approach Hamilton and my heart sinks. I really could do with some fresh air, but fresh air coupled with dead rabbit just doesn't appeal. I turn back to the

French doors and see Diamond now has a mouse and is shaking it in his mouth like a rag doll. I swear that animal is evil. I'd best stay indoors else he'll be at my throat next. I swear the little sod is giving me the evil eye through the doors.

'He's having fun is he?' says Margarita from behind me.

'I'm not so sure the rabbit is,' I reply breathlessly, trying to avoid the sight of the bloodbath.

'You look very lovely tonight,' she compliments me. 'Far better without those *feed half of Africa breasts.*'

'Yes, I donated them to Comic Relief.'

She laughs and wanders towards a group of guests as the music changes to a more upbeat tune.

'You're bearing up well,' says Alistair, sidling up to me.

'Hello Alistair,' I say checking his flies.

'These are g-g-good trousers,' he smiles.

'Excellent,' I say, trying to pull the corset away from my navel.

'Are you okay?' he asks.

'Oh yes, fab, after all this is my engagement party isn't it?' I clench my teeth to make a false smile.

'Everyone seems to be having a good time. I'm surprised you haven't c-c-c-c- …'

'Cocked it up?' I offer.

He shakes his head.

'No, I'm surprised you haven't c-c-cracked up under the pressure.'

So am I.

'Are you taking something?' he asks curiously.

'Coke,' I reply.

His eyes widen.

'The drink not the drug but with a touch of vodka, but don't tell Hamilton.'

We glance at the said Hamilton who is chatting animatedly with Julian, and then our eyes scroll to Fiona and Sebastian who are talking intently.

'Is there something wrong with that Major chap?' he asks.

I look at Major Bates as he convulses around the dance floor like someone having an epileptic fit.

'He c-c-c-can't keep still,' says Alistair.

'Someone mentioned he had restless legs syndrome,' I say, transfixed by the Major's dancing.

'Do you think Sebastian is f-f-f-f- ...'

'What?' I say turning my attention to Fiona and Sebastian.

'Do you think he is f-f-f-f- ...'

Oh God, how do I know?

'I don't know. Is that what you're thinking?'

He looks at me.

'What do you think I'm thinking?'

Is Fiona fucking Sebastian is what I think he's thinking but of course he could be thinking something entirely different. Stammers are buggers aren't they?

'I'm not sure,' I say struggling to breathe.

'Do you find him f-f-f- ...'

Fuckable? Most certainly not.

'Not in the least,' I say.

'Really, you wouldn't f-f-f-find ...'

Good God no.

'Christ, of course not.'

'I don't think he's funny either,' he mutters.

Oh funny, of course. Why didn't I think of that? The music changes and Van Morrison's Brown Eyed Girl blasts out, and before I know it I am being whisked around the floor by Brice Edmunds.

'Enjoying your engagement party?' he asks twirling me, obviously forgetting my bad foot. I wince.

'I was until this torturous dance began,' I reply.

'Sorry,' he smiles and lifts me off the ground.

The room spins with me as my vodka and coke takes effect.

'You look very lovely in this dress,' he says into my ear.

'You look rather good yourself,' I say feeling the drink loosen my tongue. My hands slide around his neck and his cheek brushes mine.

'Are you ready for tonight?' he asks softly.

'I think so,' I say, knowing full well I am nowhere near ready.

I see Hamilton striding towards us and the music changes as he reaches me.

'Here we go,' whispers Brice, releasing me.

Hamilton grabs me roughly and drags me to the middle of the floor. He pulls me tightly to him and I feel the breath squeezed out of me.

'What the hell do you and your thieving little boyfriend think you're up to?' he grunts angrily as he whips me around the dance floor. Faces spin past me and I begin to feel dizzy.

'I asked Julian not to come,' I gasp.

'He's asking for twenty thousand pounds. Where do you think I'm going to get that kind of money from?'

He squeezes me roughly and I feel the corset pinch me.

'Hamilton, you're hurting me,' I protest.

'Smile and look happy. In just a few weeks the old girl won't know what's going on. Tell your thieving boyfriend to back off, do you hear me.'

'Hamilton,' I say breathlessly, 'I just want the other half of the money as we agreed. I came here and I pretended to be your girlfriend. I did more, in fact. I just want the remaining fifteen thousand you promised, nothing else.'

He drags me towards his grandmother and we stop with a skid in front of her. My foot is throbbing and my face flushed.

'Good Lord boy, I've heard of sweeping a woman off her feet, but this is ridiculous.'

'Harriet loves to dance don't you Harriet?'

'Oh yes,' I say breathlessly. 'Being dragged around a dance floor is my ultimate pleasure.'

She looks at me suspiciously and then back to Hamilton.

'Grandma, Harriet and I were wondering if you would give us an early wedding present. With you being sick and everything, we want to be sure you see how we use it. We've seen a nice house and we want to get something for it to remind us of you,' he lies. 'We'd be so happy. Harriet wants to name the house *Margarita*, don't you darling?'

As if. I barely know the woman, so why would I want to name my semi after her. God, he is such a wally, but I nod all the same.

'We were thinking fifteen thousand,' he says boldly.

I fight back my gasp. My God, he doesn't have the money to give me. All this time he has been leading me on when he's as broke as I am. I feel my heart sink. All this hassle and I'm not even going to get myself out of debt. I feel tears smart my eyes. Margarita looks at me closely and I try to meet her eyes but I can't.

'That sounds marvellous Hamilton. Let's get the ring ceremony over shall we, and I shall announce my plans.'

'Thank you Grandma,' he says kissing her.

It's all I can do not to slap him across the face. I force a smile for Margarita and excuse myself saying my foot is painful. I need air. How could he have deceived me like that? I push past the guests and make my way to the kitchen where Emily, Cedric and Cook are bustling about frantically preparing food.

'Miss Harriet, can we help?' asks Cedric, seeing my crumpled face. I rush through the kitchen and out the back door, only stopping when I reach the bench in the rose garden. I flop onto it and sigh loudly.

'Bastard, bastard,' I mumble.

This must be some kind of divine punishment. What for I do not know. Maybe I'm being punished because I stole a ring from Woolworths when I was five. It all seems a bit extreme, especially considering I took it back after my mum found out and threatened to call the police. Or perhaps it is because I bought all those things in Oxfam. Perhaps God thinks I'm supporting starving children and benefiting from their misfortune. Well I am in a way. Not supporting them starving, obviously not, I mean that goes without saying. I'm feeding them in a roundabout way, so why punish me for that? Blimey, this is a bizarre evening. I'd phone the Samaritans for advice except I don't have any signal. I pull the corset from my navel and take a long shuddering breath. Maybe it is time to tell the truth. Instead of waiting for the shit to hit the fan maybe I'll just throw the shit straight at it, get it over and done with. I begin to walk back to the house when I see Brice and my mouth goes dry. Before I know what's happening I've fallen back onto the bench and he is beside me, his arms wrapped around me and I am snuggled against his chest, a mixture of emotions flooding through my body. I push weakly against him but it is useless and his lips are firm and demanding of mine. I respond passionately, feeling if I am to be punished it might as well be for something worthwhile.

'Harriet, what are you doing to me? I have no control when with you,' he growls into my ear.

The throbbing in my loins is unbearable now and I feel he could have me right here on the bench and I really wouldn't care. My breasts are throbbing and begging for release. My head is spinning and there is a loud buzzing in my ears. Suddenly Brice is torn away from me and the only face I can see is Julian's angry one.

'What the fuck do you think you're doing with my girlfriend? How dare you force yourself on her,' he yells. 'You ponces think everything is yours for the bloody taking don't you?'

'Julian, he wasn't ...' I begin.

Julian glares at me.

'Shut up Harriet. Just because I agreed to the Hamilton thing doesn't mean I don't care about other men manhandling you.'

'Julian ...'

'Just stay out of the way,' he barks, pushing me roughly onto the bench.

'That's enough,' says Brice menacingly. His eyes are dark and hard and I shudder. 'Don't touch her.'

'Who do you think you are telling me I can't touch my own girlfriend?' asks Julian with a sneer.

Brice shakes his head.

'You have no idea how to treat women. You've treated Harriet abominably. You ran off and left her with all your debts and you call yourself a man.'

I nod, that's a good point actually.

'He is right,' I say.

Julian glares at me.

'Whose bloody side are you on?'

Brice's actually, but I think it best if I don't voice that. I have to say I feel terribly flattered at having men fight over me. A shame there has to be blood and everything though.

'A real man doesn't desert a woman,' Brice says provocatively with a gleam in his eye.

Julian's face turns red with anger and he whips off his jacket in one fast furious movement.

'Right,' he says determinedly, and drapes it over my arm like I'm a coat hanger. 'I'm not having him talk about you like that.'

Like what? Did I miss something? Oh Christ, don't tell me he's fighting for me now. I look down at the jacket and sigh. What is it with men and this macho thing off pulling off their jackets?

'You stuck up pompous bastard,' he yells, lashing out with his fist. I close my eyes and wince in anticipation.

'What's happening?' calls Fiona. I open my eyes to see her running towards us in her silk red dress, Sebastian close behind her. Brice has caught the flying fist and with his other hand aims a punch to Julian's stomach sending him staggering back.

'Oh God,' I squeal.

'Why is Brice beating the shit out of Julian?' cries Caron, rushing out with Mum.

Julian slowly scrambles up from the ground and looks around. There's a big audience now.

'Brice, please don't,' I beg.

'Don't what? Don't stand up for you?' he demands breathlessly, perspiration running from his forehead. Perhaps I should take his jacket too.

Well, when he puts it like that obviously I want him to stand up for me. I just wish he didn't have to beat Julian to a pulp in the process.

'No, I didn't mean that, I meant,' I say flustered.

'Meant what?' he asks looking at me. Julian, seeing his opportunity throws a fist at Brice's chin. I scream and Fiona covers her eyes.

'Oh God,' groans Caron.

'Never thought I'd see a bleeding toff fighting,' says Gary excitedly. 'This is great.'

Brice tumbles back onto his haunches and Julian lashes out with his foot.

'Dirty f-f-f-f-f- ...'

'Yes, *dirty fucker*,' shouts Caron.

Oh God, I could die with embarrassment.

'Dirty fighter,' finishes Alistair.

Brice grabs Julian's foot and twists it, before pulling Julian up by his collar and shoving him into the rose bushes.

'*Yes!*' shouts Fiona.

'Fiona for God's sake,' I snap.

'Sorry, aren't we on Brice's side?'

'Yes of course but ...'

Oh God, this is just awful. The sound of a lone piper playing in the ballroom makes the whole thing seem surreal. It feels like that moment the Titanic went down, only this time I feel sure the person going under is me. Julian dives headfirst for Brice and I cover my face with my hands.

'What the bleeding hell is going on?' asks Mum as she hurries towards me.

'Brice is standing up for me,' I say.

Although now he isn't as such because Julian has sent him sprawling into the rose bushes and they are both scrambling around amongst the shrubs. Julian's lip is swelling up and his eyebrow looks cut.

'Dad, can't you do something?' I beg.

'Stop two men fighting? I don't think so dear.'

Julian crashes out of the rose bushes and lands at our feet. Brice strolls out and stands over him.

'*Kill him, kill him*,' shouts Mum.

'For God's sake Mum, it's not a bleeding boxing match.'

Brice's lip is also bleeding and I don't know who to run to first.

'What in buggeration is going on here?'

We all turn at Margarita's strong firm voice.

'Hello old girl. I was teaching this young man here the right way to treat a woman,' says Brice casually, offering Julian his hand. Julian grasps it roughly while aiming his foot at Brice's groin. I flinch and Fiona squeals.

'Oh dirty play,' yells Gary.

'Quite,' agrees Alistair as Brice goes sprawling, clutching his groin. Julian grins proudly at me. We all watch with our breath held as Brice recovers and sends a punch to Julian's stomach.

'Good God Brice, stop this at once. We have guests. If I had wanted entertainment I would have paid for it. Just what woman are you standing up for?'

'Me,' I say stepping forward timidly.

'Well aren't you the popular one.'

Hamilton stands behind her giving me daggers.

'I really think we all should go inside. It is time for the engagement ring ceremony and I have an announcement to make.'

She turns on her heel with all the spirit of a fifty year old.

'If your grandmother is dying then I'm a monkey's uncle,' I say to Hamilton.

'What?' he asks looking puzzled.

'You heard me,' I say, walking towards Julian who is slumped on the ground.

'Harriet,' he says looking at me longingly. 'I did it for you. I love you.'

'You're lucky he didn't beat you to a pulp,' I say. 'God knows you deserved it.'

I ignore his outstretched hand and walk to the house feeling Brice's eyes boring into my back. Phoebe stops me in the doorway.

'You don't really think that was about you do you? That's just men's pride. Really Harriet, if you think Brice would ever take a woman like you seriously you must be mad. He's way out of your league. You're just a novelty.'

I turn away from her and walk into the house. As much as I don't want to believe what she says I can't help feeling she may be right. If only I could just run away but I really think I should hear Margarita's announcement. I have a terrible feeling Hamilton is not going to like what she has to say.

Chapter Thirty-Six

I stare mesmerised at the sparkling engagement ring as Hamilton pushes it over my finger to loud applause and whistles. This is surreal. I'm engaged to one of the richest men in England but it turns out he has no money at all. I am destined to attract men with bad financial sense, not that I attracted Hamilton but you know what I mean. Phoebe looks enviously at the ring and then angrily at me as Hamilton leans towards me and kisses me full on the lips. I'm overwhelmed for a moment, although this is more because of Hamilton's halitosis than his kissing expertise. Phoebe is welcome to this if she can stand it. God, his breath is enough to knock you dead. Perhaps he should just breathe over Margarita, she will drop dead, Hamilton will get his inheritance and we can all go home.

'Well,' says Margarita with some kind of finality.

She gestures to Cedric to pour the champagne.

'I would like to propose a toast to the happy couple,' she says, raising her glass. Hamilton takes my hand and raises his glass to me.

'Well done,' he says gleefully.

'Why didn't you tell me you had no money?' I hiss angrily.

'I do but it's all tied up, that's all. I'll get it. After tonight you'll never have to see me again. I'll tell Grandma you've gone to New York to wrap up the business, she'll believe that. The next big event will be her funeral no doubt.'

'You're such a bastard,' I say disdainfully.

'Yes. And you've not done too badly out of it either.'

'To Hamilton and Harriet,' says Margarita loudly.

'To Hamilton and Harriet,' everyone repeats.

'And to a long marriage,' she says, eyeing us both. 'I have to say Hamilton you have surprised me, and surpassed my expectations.'

'Thank you Grandma,' Hamilton smiles, looking pleased with himself.

'I never thought you would go through with it,' she adds, settling herself into the wheelchair.

Hamilton looks confused, and I knock back my champagne. I have a bad feeling about this and I quickly grab another glass.

'I knew you would go to extremes to get the shares but I never thought you would go so far as to marry someone you barely knew. I'm quite amazed you would go to such lengths to get your own way. Your deceit is almost admirable in its planning. Such scheming Hamilton, you have quite surpassed yourself.'

Melanie gasps and falls into a chair. Sebastian turns white and Hamilton looks as if he will collapse at any moment. Julian glares at me like this is all my fault. Honestly, I'm the innocent victim here. I look at the engagement ring. Well, I might as well get a little pleasure from it. I imagine they will whip it off me before long.

'Bloody hell,' gasps Gary.

'Grandma ... I can ...' Hamilton begins but she quickly dismisses him.

'The Lancaster business has been in the family for generations,' she begins. 'Its success has been due to the way the business has been run, with honesty and integrity. I had hoped, with my little test, that you would have taken one last opportunity to prove yourself, but you have only shown yourself to be purely mercenary. I have decided to make Brice the majority shareholder. And don't get into a state thinking you're going to lose everything. I'll keep my word. I have some integrity even if you don't. You'll get a substantial share of the business too.'

Hamilton sighs with relief. I don't suppose she is going to say I'll get my share. This is bloody awful. Julian is the prick who got me into this, and Hamilton is the second prick who led me down the garden path letting me think he could get me out of it. Bleeding men, I swear they'll be the sodding death of me. I wonder if they'll forget about the ring. Well, you never know, maybe I could forget it too and wander off home with it on my finger.

'Brice, you'll receive yours when I complete the paperwork next month and Hamilton you will receive yours on the tenth anniversary of your marriage to Harriet.'

Good God. There is no way on earth I'm going to marry this little shit. As for spending ten years with him, Christ, I'd rather cover myself in jam and sit in a wasps' nest. Hamilton sways on his feet and Melanie looks about to faint. Sebastian freezes, and for a moment resembles the bronze statues in the hall, without the bronze of course. I've never seen anyone so white. Some of the guests lower their heads in embarrassment while others make a discreet exit to the hall.

'Perhaps after ten years you will have learnt some sense of responsibility,' she adds ignoring the potent affect her words are having.

'What do you mean *little test*,' he asks.

Oh, the penny has finally dropped has it?

'She's not dying Hamilton, at least not in the next few weeks,' I say calmly.

'Quite right my dear, I am not.'

'I'm glad,' I say, removing the ring. Well, I couldn't really sneak out with this huge rock on my finger could I?

The news that Margarita isn't about to pop her clogs stuns everyone into silence. After the calm comes the storm, and the hall bursts into commotion.

'Ten years?' cries Phoebe. 'How can you make him do that? That's unbearably cruel to make him stay with *her* for ten years. You forced him to take her as his wife. He wouldn't have looked twice at her otherwise.'

She rushes to his side and clasps his hand.

'It's okay honey,' she whispers softly.

'You can always be my Camilla,' he says thoughtlessly.

I suppose I should be flattered to be the Princess Diana in this scenario, and I give Phoebe a smug smile.

'Oh well, it's much better to be the consolation prize than to be ignored altogether isn't it?' I say.

She looks about to slap me. I have to admit to rather enjoying this. A shame I will leave penniless, but what the hell, it is what I have been used to all my life.

'What's going on?' Mum asks Fiona.

'Are they engaged or not?' asks Dad.

'I'm bleeding confused,' says Caron.

'You lied,' yells Hamilton, snatching the ring from me. 'You said you were dying, you lying old witch. You deliberately made us all desperate.'

Sebastian steps forward, his face deathly white.

'You're not going to die in the next few weeks?' he says with frustration evident in his voice. This family are unbelievable.

'Sorry to be a disappointment to you Sebastian,' she retorts haughtily. 'I hope you haven't gone to too much trouble with the funeral arrangements.'

Melanie is so overcome that she cannot stop trembling.

'Do you realise how much this whole thing has cost us,' she says, seething with anger. 'The engagement cake alone was two hundred pounds.'

My God, two hundred pounds, Christ, is it full of hash? Maybe I should have a slice now and ease some of this tension. On reflection it might be a good idea to force feed it all to Hamilton.

'That was an obscene thing to do Mother,' Sebastian says through gritted teeth.

'And your behaviour hasn't been?' she snaps.

'That's enough abuse,' says Brice, stepping forward. 'Grandma has the right to do whatever she wishes. They are her shares after all.'

'You would say that wouldn't you,' Sebastian says angrily.

Fiona quietly slips her arm through Alistair's.

'I think you are all incorrigible,' she says. 'You are vultures, the lot of you'.

'Hamilton is such a w-w-w-w- ...'

'Wanker,' says Fiona.

'Waste of space,' finishes Alistair.

'I think wanker was more fitting,' I say.

Julian sighs and downs a glass of champagne.

'You're a wicked lying old witch,' repeats Hamilton. 'You'll end up alone and miserable and may it serve you right.'

She reels at his words and I put a restraining hand on his chest.

'Hamilton, try to calm down.'

'Don't tell me to calm down you common little tart. You knew, you knew she wasn't dying. What did she pay you to play along? You can sling your hook and crawl back to the gutter where you belong.'

'Watch your bleeding mouth young man,' shouts Mum.

'Yes, you bloody upstart, who do you think you're calling a tart,' cries Caron, edging towards him.

'Yeah, bloody toffs. You think money can buy everything don't you?' joins in Gary.

I roll my eyes. This is all I need. The Montagues and the Capulets in the grand ballroom. I'll be knocking back the poison next. Perhaps I'll just slip out when all the mayhem starts. I can sneak Gary's

Barclaycard Platinum into my bag and bugger off somewhere nice. Hamilton steps towards his grandmother and she wheels herself backwards. I put a restraining hand on his chest yet again. I'm a glutton for punishment that's for sure. I'm about to beg him to think about his actions when there is a loud rapping on the front door.

'Open up,' shouts an all too familiar voice.

I look at Brice who nods and pulls out his mobile.

'This is Scooby Doo,' he says with a grin. 'Let's rock and roll.'

Chapter Thirty-Seven

Meanwhile, at the Boathouse ...

Babyface Jack paces back and forth, anxiously looking across the loch as he does so. Hamish had radioed to say they were on their way. He has been dreading this moment. He knew it would come but he hadn't expected to feel so sick at the prospect. He is tempted to leg it but he knows he can't. He has promised Harriet and he can't go back on that promise. He finds his mind wandering back to the events of the last two days ...

'What's 'appening now?' Mad Jack Junior asks, biting into a Scotch egg.

'How the 'ell do I know,' answers Diamond.

'Christ, they ain't going to shoot things are they?' asks a nervous Mad Jack spotting a rifle in Sebastian's hands.

'I think we should go,' says Babyface in a nervous voice.

'Will yer stop being such a pansy,' snaps Diamond. 'If they're all out 'ere it's a good time for us to go in, ain't it?'

'Not with 'em all in the bleedin' back garden,' says Mad Jack, scratching his leg. 'These bleedin' midgets are a pain in the arse.'

'They're not out yet, what's the matter with yer,' sighs Diamond. They all jump at the sound of a shotgun.

'Jesus Christ Dad, this is bleedin' dangerous,' says Mad Jack, dropping his egg.

'They're shooting in the air you wally, not firing at us.'
Several more shots sound and echo round the glen making Babyface tremble.

'I think Mad Jack is right, I think we should leg it,' he says shakily.

'Yeah,' agrees Mad Jack. 'Come on, let's go. I think ...'
He stops in mid-sentence as another shot sounds and Babyface drops to the ground.

'What the fuck?' squeals Mad Jack

'Oh my God, they shot him, they shot Babyface,' he screams.

Diamond stares at his son and then back to the house where someone is running towards them. He looks at Babyface lying still on the ground.

'The bastards 'ave only gone and killed 'im,' says Mad Jack with a sob.

Jack Diamond grabs his eldest son and pushes him forward.

'We can't do nothin' for him now, come on let's go.'

Mad Jack freezes.

'We can't leave him.'

'Don't be a plonker all your life. What's to stop them shooting the both of us too? Leg it now.'

Babyface hears them running away but is too stunned to call them. He's shaking so much that he wonders if the ground is moving beneath him. A man leans over him and he feels his hand on his leg. A sharp pain shoots through his knee and he groans.

'You're okay, it's not a serious wound,' says the man. 'What are you doing here?'

He tries to answer but nothing seems to come from his mouth.

'Is he dead?' He recognises Harriet's voice and tries to turn his head to see her.

'Of course not, it's just a graze. He's in shock more than anything. He must have been poaching. Honestly, no sense these people.'

He wishes he could get away. It won't be long before Harriet recognises him. He tries to speak but the trembling stops him. He feels himself carried to the house and then he is lying on a bed and Harriet is apologising to him. That's all wrong ain't it? He should be apologising to her. He struggles to find a voice and finally says,

'I'm sorry 'arriet.'

There is some commotion around him and then a prick in his arm and he knows nothing until the morning when the doctor and Harriet have a long chat with him. He knows he shouldn't have told them everything, that it was disrespect to his dad who he knows is big on respect. Not just big, bleeding huge. But what else was he to do? He didn't agree with his dad, and all he ever wanted to be was clever like Harriet. He found himself telling her and Brice all this. How he'd always wanted to study like she was doing. He wanted to be a proper car mechanic and own his own garage one day. She was nice, was Harriet, she listened. Brice said they could get Harriet out of this *mess. He wasn't sure what they were suggesting about playing his dad at his own game but Harriet said it would mean he could study and his dad wouldn't end up in the slammer. As it was now, he could be done for all sorts, blackmail, extortion, trespassing and threatening behaviour. The doctor said the list was endless. Babyface said yes for his dad really. Although he hated pretending he was dead all this time. Being carried in the carpet was a bit hairy and he'd been relieved when the copper and Brice, the doctor, had taken over. He'd had the shock of his life when he'd heard that Cedric's voice. He'd had visions of rolling out of the carpet and having to face that toffee nosed woman with the barking voice. But they'd made it to the boat. He knew his dad would be watching. Dad always did the one-to-five shift whenever they staked a place out. Mad Jack was useless at night shifts, he always dozed off. That's what he told Harriet.*

'If you want my dad to see yer, then yer 'ave to do it about two o'clock, otherwise by three he'll be asleep. You should make some noise with the boat just in case.'

And so he had rolled out of the carpet once it was on the boat and then Brice and the copper had chucked it into the loch shortly afterwards. Dad would think it was his body for sure. That was how bodies were disposed of his dad had always said, that and other ways that Babyface didn't even want to think about. His dad weren't bad, not really. He ain't never killed anyone. But he knew people who had and how they had disposed of the body in a rolled up carpet. He was a bit crooked his dad, but that was all. That's why Babyface told them a rolled up carpet was best. He knew his dad would come to the house, and now he has. He'll miss this little boathouse, it had been nice for his short stay and Brice had given him some interesting books to read. He likes Brice. He hears the boat in the distance and collects the books before opening the door to meet Angus.

Chapter Thirty-Eight

'Excuse me madam, there is a … erm gentleman at the door asking for you. At least I think he is asking for you,' says Cedric, blushing slightly.

Heavens I don't think I have ever seen Cedric blush.

'Did he ask for me by name?' asks Margarita.

'In a manner of speaking,' replies Cedric.

'Oh for God's sake man, who did he ask for?'

'The old battleaxe madam. I couldn't fit that description to anyone else,' he replies poker-faced.

'Who is this person, and are you sure it is me he wants to see?' she replies, seemingly not in the least put out to be termed the old battleaxe.

'I think it may well be you old girl,' says Brice.

'And what would you know about it young man?'

The interruption couldn't have come at a better time. I rather felt had it not, that Sebastian or Hamilton may well have murdered Margarita themselves. Honestly, I've never known a family like this one. I'm thinking I should buy them all self-help books as leaving presents. You know, along the lines of Louise Hay *You can heal your life*. Before Brice can reply the ballroom door is flung open and Jack Diamond and his son stride in arrogantly. They stop at the opulent sight in front of them and Mad Jack opens his mouth in shock.

'Good evening,' Jack Diamond says, taking everyone in. A hush descends upon the room and all that can be heard are the bagpipes slowly grinding to a halt.

'Bleeding 'ell, this is fan-bloody-tastic,' Mad Jack Junior gasps.

Jack Diamond looks around and nods in agreement.

'Don't stop on my account,' Diamond says to the piper. 'We like a bit of music don't we Mad Jack? Me missus loves all that old-fashioned stuff.'

Mad Jack nods. They are both wearing suits, complete with ties and shiny shoes. Diamond's hair is greased back with gel and the smell of his aftershave permeates the room. Fiona pulls Alistair closer to her and whispers,

'It's the Jacks, well two of them at least.'

Alistair's mouth drops open. Julian backs slowly away from them until he is at the ballroom doors. His attempt to slip through them is thwarted by Brice who pushes him back. Jack Diamond walks towards the tray of champagne that Emily is holding and takes two glasses.

'Thanks darlin'. You're looking pretty tonight. 'ere Mad Jack, 'ave one of these. I bet you ain't had champagne like this.'

'Now look here …' begins Sebastian.

Jack Diamond stops him with his hand.

'Business after pleasure, mate, what do yer say? Let's all enjoy the champers shall we? 'aving a celebration are yer? Let me guess, it's an engagement party right?'

'I don't know who you are but if you don't leave right now you'll leave me with no option but to phone the police,' says Sebastian confidently.

'Oh, I wouldn't go doing that if I was you,' smiles Diamond. 'You ain't begrudging me 'avin' a little toast for old 'arriet and 'amilton are yer?'

Melanie lets out a little cry.

'How did you know about that?' demands Sebastian.

'I think you should call the police Dad,' says Hamilton.

'Mate, we know everythin', ain't that right 'arriet?' says Mad Jack looking at me.

'What the hell Harry?' says Julian.

'Friends of yours are they Harriet?' sniggers Phoebe. 'Well that figures doesn't it? Or are they extended family?'

Margarita wheels herself in front of Diamond and knocks the champagne out of his hand.

'Alright young man, you may be able to frighten everyone else here but you don't frighten me. Now, you wanted to speak to the old battleaxe and here I am. Spit it out. I'm presuming people like you are good at spitting.'

'Bleedin' cheek,' says Mad Jack Junior putting his glass down.

Jack Diamond calmly brushes down the front of his shirt.

'I think you get the message,' says Sebastian arrogantly. 'Now leave our house. By the back door if you would. Cedric, show these gentlemen out, and I use that term loosely.'

Diamond laughs.

'Cocky ain't we? But I don't think you cut the mustard me ole mate. Now let's get down to brass tacks shall we?'

'I have no idea what this man is talking about,' barks Margarita. 'What does he mean *brass tacks*? And what is this about the mustard? Does cook know about this Cedric?'

I reluctantly step forward. Desperate times call for desperate measures. God, I'm sounding like Diamond, it must be catching. Margarita looks across the room and shouts,

'Diamond, what do you think you're doing?'

Jack Diamond's head snaps up.

'What,' he says.

'Stop that at once, you bad girl.'

Mad Jack Junior fidgets nervously.

'She called you a bad girl Dad,' he says, looking at Margarita with wide eyes.

'Now, hang on Mrs ...' says Diamond looking thrown.

I point to the cat that is licking the engagement cake.

'That is Diamond,' I say. 'He's just a dumb animal with the same name, but still, if the name fits.'

Diamond looks at me with distaste.

'I think it's time for a few home truths, don't you 'arriet?'

I shrug.

'I'll cut to the chase shall I? First of all, she,' he says cockily pointing at me, 'is no more 'amilton's fiancée than I am. She's just after the money.'

'I wonder why?' chips in Brice.

Jack Diamond ignores him and points at Margarita.

'And this old battleaxe would like you all to think she's dying. Well, I can tell yer now, she ain't.'

'Yeah,' says Mad Jack, smugly. 'You've all been conned.'

We all stare at them with bored expressions on our faces.

'Is that it?' asks Sebastian.

'Yes, is that everything?' encourages Brice.

'Do you want to tell us something we don't know?' adds Sebastian.

Jack Diamond and Mad Jack look around puzzled.

'I'm afraid you're a bit late. The shit hit the fan ten minutes ago,' I say. 'It's kind of old news.'

Diamond shakes with anger and turns a red face towards Margarita.

'Right,' he says loudly, 'I want ten grand up front and a grubby hand every month after that.'

'A grubby hand?' she repeats distastefully.

'A grand,' says Fi helpfully.

'How d-d-d-did you know that?' asks Alistair impressed.

'I picked it up somewhere,' she says proudly, squeezing his arm.

I shake my head. Honestly, those two, what are they like? One minute Fiona can't stand him and the next she's all over him like a rash.

'Have you gone stark staring mad young man, no one is going to give you that,' says a shocked Margarita.

'Then, I'll call the old bill shall I? Ask them to search that lake of yours.'

Margarita looks puzzled.

'He means the loch,' adds Brice helpfully.

'Why would anyone want to search the loch?' she asks.

Jack Diamond slaps his hand to his head.

'Of course, none of yer know do yer? I got to paint a bleeding portrait for you ain't I? When they search your loch they'll find my son, cos she killed 'im,' he says, dramatically pointing to me. 'And he 'elped dispose of the body, and so did she?' He reels around and points first to Brice and then Fiona.

There are gasps and murmurs from around the ballroom. Phoebe claps her hand to her mouth and Alistair's eyes widen. His mouth gapes and all he can articulate is,

'F-f-f-f-f- ...'

'Fiddlesticks,' I say.

'Fuck,' he finishes.

'Oh,' I say, 'it never normally is that.'

'Shut up Harry,' snaps Fiona.

'I knew you were a nasty piece of work but I didn't think you were that nasty,' cries Phoebe.

I give her an evil look.

'Christ Harry, you bloody killed Babyface Jack. Were you out of your mind?' says Julian,

'Have you gone stark staring mad? My grandson is a doctor. He makes people well, he doesn't kill them,' Margarita says with disbelief etched on her face.

'Oh, I get it now,' says Caron excitedly. 'Is it one of them murder mystery things?'

Gary claps his hands.

'Blimey, you've planned this bloody well. Are they actors?' he asks nodding towards the Jacks. 'And he's got a finger missing, this is cool, huh Caron?'

She nods.

'Is this a game Brice?' Margarita asks.

Jack Diamond bangs his fist on the table.

'Right, listen up will yer? There ain't no bleedin' mystery 'ere. 'arriet shot my son Babyface Jack, and she and that friend of 'ers carried him to a boat in a rolled up carpet. I saw it with me own eyes. In the dead of bleeding night they did it. I saw me son Babyface Jack, dead on the ground he was, ain't that right Mad Jack Junior.'

'Oh yeah, as if,' laughs Gary.

'Oh God,' cries Emily softly.

Cedric looks from Diamond to me.

'Is this true madam?' he asks. 'Did you shoot this baby Jackface?'

'Babyface Jack,' corrects Fiona.

'It was an accident,' I say.

Well it was wasn't it? There is a stunned silence. Mum and Dad are looking incredulous along with everyone else.

'You murdered someone?' says Dad.

There are shocked cries from the guests.

'Shouldn't someone call the police? This is highly irregular,' says one stepping forward to face Diamond.

'On your way young man while you can,' he says in his upper-crust voice.

Diamond surveys him and grins.

'And who the 'ell are you?'

'I'm the Honourable Lord Maycroft and you are very much upsetting my wife, Lady Annabel Maycroft.'

'Ooh I say,' says Mad Jack imitating Lord Maycroft's accent.

'Well we're the Honourable Diamonds and we ain't going nowhere. Now, there ain't no good crying over spilt milk is there, I mean what's done is done. I just think you should pay a little compensation for it. I ain't going to the filth as long as you pay up,' says Diamond his eyes hard as steel.

He walks calmly past Margarita to the table. Several guests back away nervously and he smiles before taking another glass of champagne. 'Of course, if you don't pay up I'll have to pay the old bill a visit, and I guess old 'arriet and your doctor grandson will rot away in prison.'

'Are you seriously threatening us?' asks Brice. 'There are a lot of very respectable witnesses in this room.'

I hold my breath.

'I think a few crates of this nice champers would go down a treat too. Shall we say a crate a month? Put it this way, I can't guarantee anything if you don't 'elp yourself. Yer know what I mean? There are villains around who wouldn't think twice about robbing an old dear like your Gran 'ere or torching them barns outside. You know what I'm saying? Little bleeders some of these villains but me, well I've got a bit of class.'

Brice steps forward and Margarita looks at him hopefully.

'If it's all the same I think we'll decline your whole offer as fair as it seems to be,' he says calmly. 'Do you agree old girl,' he adds looking towards Margarita.

'Well, I don't know. I don't want you going to prison Brice,' she says anxiously.

I wait for her to mention me but there is nothing, nothing from her at all. It's okay for me to rot in jail then. Mad Jack looks uncomfortable but forces a laugh.

'I think you would be going up a blind alley mate if you don't pay me,' says Diamond with a hint of menace in his tone.

'I can't agree with you Diamond. You see, the thing is, I don't know what you're talking about when you say Babyface is dead. Harriet shot him in error yes, but we took good care of him. I rather think your blackmailing of Harriet is something of a bigger crime,' says Brice, helping himself to a glass of champagne.

'What yer talking about?' asks Diamond. 'I saw the carpet with me own bleedin' eyes.'

'Indeed you did,' smiles Brice. 'And he was in it. But we never dumped him in the loch. We dumped the carpet, but your son was not in it.'

'I don't believe this. You're all bleedin' mad. I'll go to the old bill, I'm telling yer. Give me the money or I'll do it.'

Brice nods to me and I open the French doors to allow Babyface and Angus into the ballroom.

'Allow us to bring the police to you,' says Brice with a smile.

'Evening all,' nods Angus in his police uniform. The uniform is just a bit tight and Angus's chest strains against the fabric and his hair spills out from under his hat. I fight back my smile. He looks a most unlikely police officer.

'Good God Angus, why are you dressed ...' blurts out Margarita.

'Shall we hear what people have to say old girl,' butts in Brice.

I take a deep breath and send out a silent prayer. Please please let this go according to plan, otherwise I'm in shit street good and proper. Julian looks like he is about to keel over any minute. Gary is jumping around in excitement. The poor bugger still thinks it is a murder mystery evening. He'll be devastated when he finds out there are no prizes. Jack Diamond looks at Babyface and his face widens in a huge grin.

'Where the bastard 'ell have you been?' he demands.

Melanie sighs.

'Oh honestly, do we have to listen to this?' asks Sebastian. 'God knows haven't we had enough shocks for one evening?'

Margarita scoffs.

'Do shut up Sebastian and for once in your life listen to someone else. Now, what on earth is this all about Brice?'

I step forward.

'It's all about me really,' I say.

'Isn't that a surprise,' snaps Phoebe. There is pleasure written all over her face.

'Harriet, careful what you say,' warns Julian.

'I think you would be wise to stay out of this,' says Brice firmly.

'I'm sorry Dad,' says Babyface. 'I know it was wrong to let yer think I was dead. But the thing is I was getting scared about you doing bird. I mean, what would Mum do with you inside? And ...'

'What did he just say?' asks a perplexed Margarita.

'Yer mum has sod all to do with this boy. Now, just keep yer mouth shut.'

Babyface looks worriedly at Brice and then to me.

'We've got a small problem here Jack,' Brice says pointing to Diamond. 'We know about your blackmailing of Harriet, extorting money from her, threatening to burn down the restaurant if she didn't pay, and of course I'm conveniently forgetting you were trespassing on private property, and I'm not even mentioning how you blackmailed Harriet's boyfriend Julian, over there,' he says pointing to a nervous Julian. 'Although I'm sure *he* deserved everything he got. But you made the big mistake of coming here and blackmailing my grandmother. The problem is Sergeant Tweedy here heard everything outside the door.'

Diamond looks wide-eyed at Angus.

'Sergeant Angus Tweedy at your disposal,' Angus grins.

'God, this is fan-bloody-tastic,' cries Gary. 'I bet it was in the library with the lead piping. Am I right?'

'It's sheer bloody madness,' says Phoebe. 'Hamilton why are you allowing such common behaviour in your home?'

'I'll have you know this is my home, young lady,' barks Margarita. 'None of this belongs to Hamilton and if I have my way, it never will. As for you Angus, I have no idea what you're playing at but I'm willing to see this charade to its conclusion.'

Angus nods politely.

'What the hell is going on Babyface?' Mad Jack Junior shouts. 'You're a bloody traitor you are. Letting the firm down, where's your respect?'

'Shut your mush Mad Jack,' says Diamond, taking a sip from his glass.

'I don't wanna keep me mouth shut,' says Babyface proudly. 'I 'ave got respect, so you just shut it Mad Jack. I don't want Dad in the clink and you shouldn't want that neither and the other thing Dad, is I don't wanna be a ... a ...'

'Yeah a what?' laughs Mad Jack. 'A bleedin' retard ...'

'I'm not a retard,' shouts Babyface. 'I've been studying ...'

'You've been what?' shouts Diamond, spitting out his drink.

Gary waves his hand in the air.

'When do we start guessing who did it?' he asks, gesturing to Cedric. 'Another lager mate.'

I roll my eyes.

'This isn't bloody Columbo,' I snap.

'Be quiet Gary love,' says Mum. 'I'm sure Harry will tell us when we can join in.'

'Studying what?' laughs Mad Jack. 'How to be a bleedin' idiot? Cos I can tell yer it worked.'

'Shut your mush I told yer?' snaps Diamond. 'What yer been studying?' he asks Babyface.

'Car mechanics, I like it. I ain't done much but I like it and I don't wanna be in the firm.'

Julian steps forward cockily, obviously not so fearful of losing his ear/tongue/penis with a room full of witnesses.

'I'm not paying you any more either,' he says with a little quiver in his voice.

Diamond shoves him aside roughly.

'Obviously I'm happy to discuss it,' adds Julian nervously.

'Do shut up Julian. Amazingly enough this isn't about you,' I snap. Angus takes a pair of handcuffs from his pocket.

'Okay, let's go shall we?' he says, stepping towards Diamond.

'Just a minute,' I say taking my cue.

'If these men are sorry and promise not to bother us again we don't have to press charges do we?'

'I rather think we do young lady,' says Margarita.

'I think Grandmother is right,' Hamilton adds. 'I'm with you all the way Grandma. We can't have people like this threatening you. The thing is it wouldn't surprise me if Harriet knows these men. In fact, I'm starting to wonder if she is involved. I didn't want to tell you this but she actually forced me to deceive you. I didn't want to,' he says stepping close to her and warming to his theme. 'But, I got involved with her and when I tried to break it off she threatened me saying she'd go to the papers, tell them how I demanded kinky sex and …'

What the fuck. Several of the guests gasp in amazement and make their way to the French doors.

'That's enough Hamilton. I think we get the picture,' interrupts Sebastian.

'Hamilton, I wouldn't have sex, bleeding kinky or otherwise, with you. As for telling the papers, well really, you don't honestly think I would admit to anyone that we had sex, do you? Unless you sort out that halitosis of yours I really can't imagine anyone wanting sex with you.'

Margarita laughs.

'She does have a point boy. What is your reason for not pressing charges against these men Harriet?'

'Because everyone deserves a second chance,' I say, praying she agrees.

'That's my feeling,' agrees Hamilton. 'Everyone deserves a second chance.'

'It's not mine,' says Julian.

'I totally agree. I think Babyface is the killer and the body is in the kitchen,' pipes up Gary.

For Christ's sake.

'Second chances,' barks Margarita. 'Not fourth and fifth chances, Hamilton. You have well passed your second chance. You never stop lying. Now let me get this straight. Mr Diamond here was blackmailing Julian, who I now understand is your boyfriend?'

'Ex-boyfriend,' I correct.

'Harriet, come on,' pleads Julian.

'Shut up you bleeding idiot. If my Harriet says you're her ex, that's exactly what you are,' snaps Mum.

'And you got left with the debts. Am I correct so far?'

I nod.

'So my darling grandson here offered you money to pretend to be his girlfriend so I'd be pleased.'

'No no ...' begins Hamilton.

She gives him a sharp look and he stops immediately.

'Brice, what are your thoughts? You seem to be getting somewhat involved I notice.'

Phoebe laughs.

'This is a joke of the most ridiculous magnitude. She's just a washerwoman. Brice isn't interested in her. He told me so. She works in a laundrette, I ask you, and she swans down here and thinks all the men want her. You're a novelty, you and your family. Everyone here is just enjoying the farce of your little working-class family. Let's face it, this is the first time we've seen someone drinking lager from a can. You can't possibly take anything she says seriously.'

I look at Brice who lowers his eyes. Gary's shoulders twitch and he puts his can down. I feel both anger and pity for him. Caron walks towards Phoebe and before anyone has a chance to stop her she slaps Phoebe across the face.

'I imagine you've never had anyone do that either,' she yells.

'Oh my giddy aunt,' cries Mum.

'How dare you speak about people like that in my home. Harriet and her family are here at my invitation which is more than can be said for you,' growls Margarita.

Brice steps towards me but I give him a warning glance. How dare he discuss me with that horrible Phoebe?

'I think we should leave this in the hands of Angus,' Brice says simply.

'I agree. Take them away Angus.'

He nods and ushers the Jacks into the hall. Noise breaks out in the ballroom the minute we close the door.

'So she agrees,' says Angus.

'I knew she would,' smiles Brice looking at me. I turn away. Somewhere at the back of my mind is the notion that Phoebe was right. Brice is enjoying all of this. It has probably been good entertainment for him. What a fool I am. You'd think I'd have learnt something from Julian's lies wouldn't you?

Diamond shrugs off Angus's arm.

'What the bleedin' hell is going on?' he asks nervously.

'Let's just say it's your lucky day shall we,' Angus says, rubbing his hands. 'Now, I'm getting old, you know what I mean? All this hassle, it's too much for me. The police force doesn't pay what it used to, know what I mean? I'm sure you do. Now, how about you give me six hundred pounds, in cash mind you, and we forget everything, saves me the hassle of taking you and your boys in and all the paperwork I'd have to do. Of course, if you go near Harriet again I'll come after you with all guns blazing. You got that?'

'Pay him Dad,' says Mad Jack his eyes wild and bright.

Babyface winks at me and I give a half smile.

'Wait a minute, you saying we can just go if I pay yer six hundred smackers?'

'And promise never to go near Harriet again. If you do I'll have you for everything, and I mean everything, blackmail, extortion, trespassing, threatening behaviour, and of course theft.'

'I ain't stole nothing,' says Diamond confidently as he fishes in his wallet.

He hands over the cash reluctantly.

'Come on Dad, let's go while we can. Get in the motor Babyface,' orders Mad Jack.

'Oh yes, one more thing if you want me off your back. We want to see Babyface studying, isn't that right Harriet?'

I nod and give Babyface a smile.

'Jesus Christ, she'll be wantin' to bleedin' adopt him next.'

'And of course we'll want the van back. You know the one you stole.'

'I ain't stole nothin', that motor's mine. Julian gave it to me.'

I feel Brice's eyes on me. I struggle not to look at him. I'm dead grateful for everything he has done but I cannot forgive him for talking about me to Phoebe. How could he do such a thing? I trusted him and he told her, of all people, that he wasn't interested in me.

'Julian had no right to give it to you because it belongs to Harriet.'

'Like 'ell it does.'

Brice pulls the loan agreement for the van from his pocket and points to the signature on the form.

'If you drive off in that van Diamond, I'll have you for everything.'

Jack Diamond gives the papers a cursory glance.

'I've got to give it to yer, your 'ead's screwed on all right. You're too good for that prick Julian.'

Diamond gives me an approving nod. I rather think he is right. I watch as Angus escorts them down the drive to where a taxi is waiting. Brice reaches out for me and I back away.

'I think you've made it very clear I'm not your type. I and my embarrassing family will be gone by the morning,' I say, forcing hardness to my voice.

'Harry, wait a minute,' he says, 'you surely don't believe those things Phoebe said?'

'I saw your face when she said I was a washerwoman. We live different lives Brice. You're a highfalutin doctor with a highfalutin family and I'm just the common girl from Battersea. It will never work.'

'You think I am that shallow do you?' he responds sharply.

Well no, I don't actually, but what if it were true? What if he had told Phoebe he didn't really fancy me? What if in a few months he regrets it all. The thing is I can't go through all this hurt again.

'Yes, I do,' I say.

Pain crosses his face and he turns away from me. I give him one last look and rush inside the house. I've had enough of men making a fool out of me. I'll shall pack my things immediately and leave. The thought of returning to my little flat and my job at the laundrette fills me with some comfort. I feel like a weight has been lifted, at last I can stop all this pretending and deceit.

Chapter Thirty-Nine

The smartly dressed woman from *Medical Aiders* looks over her spectacles at me.

'We only have three placements we can offer. Because of your lack of experience working abroad it does limit us quite considerably.'

Oh dear. I really can't tell her my only reason for not wanting to go to South East Asia is a good-looking, well-to-do doctor, can I? I imagine that would be the driving force for most young single nurses.

'It's just South East Asia, I don't mind anywhere else,' I say, trying not to sound too fussy.

She pushes her thick-rimmed glasses up the bridge of her nose, reminding me of Fiona. God, I'm going to miss her so much. Still, it is only for six months. The woman looks back to the screen and sighs.

'Right, let me see. Your college has suggested the placement. You're behind with your studies I understand.'

Christ, does she have to rub it in.

'Yes, but I'm doing tropical medicine when I get back.'

'Well like I said, there is an ideal placement in Laos. They have a temporary doctor who needs an extra pair of hands, at least until the regular doctor comes back. It will be very good experience for you,' she says, looking at me eagerly.

I lower my eyes. I can't do it. I just can't go where Brice may be. I haven't seen him since the morning after the party. I know I should have given him a chance to explain, but the truth is I had always known he was too good for me. I saw him blanch when Phoebe had referred to me as the washerwoman. I can't even think back to that moment without feeling total humiliation. I'd just wanted to escape from Glenwood as quickly as possible. I sometimes imagine their conversation. Did they laugh about me? It doesn't bear thinking about. No way can I see him again and have him scoff at my dream of working in a third-world country. But for all that, I can't seem to stop thinking about him. He did try to visit me at the flat but I told Fiona to say I didn't want to see him. That had been six weeks ago. I've heard nothing since.

'Thank you, but I really can't work in Laos, or any part of South East Asia,' I say firmly.

'It says here that was your first choice,' she says, trying to hide the irritation from her voice.

'It was originally, but that was before ...'

She raises her eyebrows, then clicks the mouse and says with a grimace.

'All I have to offer you is Angola. There is a mud hut outpost,' she says wrinkling her nose. 'It's called, let me see, ah yes, Montamo. It's a war-ravaged country. Not as civilised as South East Asia. They need someone next week, and it's only for five months, you'll be replacing an experienced nurse who is leaving to marry. It's your choice. It's not the best placement, and with your lack of experience ...'

Holy shit, how ironic is that? I bet Julian will have a good laugh when he hears this. Angola of all places, I ask you. I'll probably get blown up by a landmine. I hope that makes Brice Edmunds happy. The Major thought Laos was primitive, this sounds even worse. I smile at the memory and strangely find myself missing Margarita and her demented cat. I sip from a cup of lukewarm tea and sigh. The cheque from Margarita had been a big surprise. It had arrived three days after I got home. There was nothing with it, no note, no explanation but I wouldn't have expected there to be. A day later Cedric had visited with all the clothes I had left behind and the six hundred quid from Angus.

'Madam said you have to take them Miss Harriet as they fit no one else, and that she hoped you got her little message.'

Her ten thousand pound cheque and the sale of the van had completely cleared my debts and I was now officially in the black. I even managed to get an extra fifty quid from the Jacks thanks to Angus's Oscar prizewinning performance. I had asked Cedric how Hamilton was faring and he straightaway knew what I'd meant.

'Mr Hamilton is getting engaged to Miss Phoebe,' he had smiled. 'Of course, there had to be some adjustments regarding finance. I think they will be happy enough.'

So, Margarita had given in on that one then? Pity she couldn't have done it sooner. I smile at the memory of the old girl staring at my false breasts. God, I can't believe I did that. My mind is pulled back to the present by the sharp voice of the woman sitting in front of me.

'Well?' she asks. 'Do you want it? You'll be under a doctor ...' she squints at the screen. 'Doctor Beadu. The other staff are Angolan.'

I bite my lip. It sounds really isolated. Even the doctor is foreign. Christ, I hope I can understand him.

'Does Dr Beadu speak English?' I ask nervously.

'It says he does here. There is no mention of his nationality. He may be Norwegian.'

At least I'll be as far from Brice Edmunds as anyone can be. Actually, I'll be as far away as I can be from just about everyone. That seems like a good idea to me.

'I'll take the position,' I hear myself say.

'Rather you than me,' she says, handing me the forms to complete.

* * *

I zip up my suitcase and glance at the boxes covering the floor of my living room. It's hard to believe that Julian and I once shared this flat and were so happy. Well okay, reasonably happy.

'I can't believe you're doing this,' says Fiona, scooping papers into a neat pile.

Mum pops her head around the kitchen door.

'Well the kitchen is as bright as a new pin. If that landlord tries to hold back your deposit he'll have me to deal with.'

'Thanks Mum,' I smile.

'Are you sure you know what you're doing?' she asks earnestly.

'She'll be co-co-co- ...'

'Cocking it up again?' offers Mum. 'That's what she usually does, isn't that right love?'

'Congo dancing like a native,' says Alistair.

'You've got that mosquito net I gave you haven't you?' says Caron stepping from the bathroom with the loo brush in her hand. 'We don't want you getting malaria.'

'Yes I have and will you lot stop cleaning this flat. It's bleeding spotless.'

Fiona laughs. Oh God, I am so going to miss everyone. Even I am beginning to think I must be mad. Of all the places to end up it has to be Angola.

'Let's hope the doctor is nice,' says Fiona.

'I hope you know what you're doing,' says Gary.

All the same, I'm feeling quite proud of myself. I've got a placement, and I've managed to change my course to Third-World Medicine. I'm actually feeling life is opening up a world of new opportunities for me. At least I won't go falling in love, not with a Norwegian doctor anyway. Even I couldn't marry a man with a name like Beadu, *Harriet Beadu* sounds like a brand of face cream.

'Either that or the whole thing with Hamilton has turned her insane,' sighs Fiona. 'Don't think I'm visiting you there. I don't have a death wish.'

'Maybe Julian would like to visit me,' I laugh.

'I think she has gone insane. I mean, who goes to sodding Angola unless they're off their trolley,' quips Mum.

'I'll tell him,' grins Alistair.

Julian's restaurant is apparently doing very well with the new backer, and Julian has moved into the flat above it. It's a mess so Alistair tells me, but Julian is getting in an interior designer. I don't even want to ask where the money for that is coming from, but a Leopard can't change his spots, so they say. As for the Jacks, I have no idea what happened to them and I prefer it that way. I check the time on my phone and look at Fiona.

'Nearly time to go. Enjoy your last cup of decent tea and bourbon biscuits. Who the hell knows what you'll get out there,' she says smiling but I see the tears forming in her eyes.

'Dysentery most likely,' says Dad, hugging me.

'I've had my jabs,' I laugh.

'I expect this will be the last time you'll see a white person,' says Mum. 'God, can you bleeding imagine it Caron?'

'Mum honestly,' I laugh.

'We're all going to miss you,' says Fiona, holding back the tears.

'I'll miss your c-c-c-c- ...' begins Alistair.

Fiona sighs.

'Cooking?' I suggest.

'Cock-ups,' he laughs, 'and not to mention your outrageous clothes.'

'And I won't miss your stammer,' I grin.

I hug Mum and Caron, before kissing Gary and Alistair. Angola here I come. How ironic is that? I somehow think it is fate and who knows, maybe I will meet Mr Right out there. You never know.

Chapter Forty

Brice

I look at the crowded waiting area and gesture to the toddlers in linen harnesses. My translator Akua nods and explains what the problem is. Rachel, my American nurse rubs her head to soothe her hangover. I smile. It had been something of a party last night. The homemade cocktails here are something else. The most lethal thing I've ever drunk. Akua's wife had made the food and I hate to tell him that I had spent most of the night in the loo. He had after all slaughtered a goat in Rachel's honour, so it would be an insult to tell him that it had not agreed with me. I shall miss Rachel terribly. I've become close to her over the past four weeks, I must have shared everything with her. That's the thing with being isolated like this. Other English speaking colleagues become your closest friends in next to no time. She walks towards me and I smile. The heat beats down onto my neck and I shield it with my hat. The humidity is high and the desire to jump under the shower again overwhelms me.

'A little hung-over are we Doctor Edmunds?' she laughs.

'I blame you. If you weren't leaving to marry that handsome surgeon I wouldn't be in this state.'

She laughs. I envy her leaving and I never thought I'd say that. My four weeks here have been gruelling and I crave the tranquillity of Laos.

'The children first I agree, but we have a man in a serious condition from a snake bite that should take priority,' she says professionally.

I turn back to the hospital, a single-storey building, tatty from the outside but clean and neat inside. Inadequate in so many areas, but it is all I have.

'I'm going to miss you so much,' I say, draping an arm around her shoulder.

'You've only got five months here. It will fly by, and I want you to know Brice, that your acceptance of this post was the best thing that happened to Montamo. I know you will make a difference.'

'Not without a damn nurse I won't.'

We step into the outpatient department where the doors are flimsy and the roof leaks. The power cuts out as we enter and I curse. Akua sets about getting the generator working. I look at the snake bite first. Rachel calls for antivenin and has a bag of IV fluid attached to him before I have even examined him.

'I don't know how you can leave me,' I say miserably.

'You'll be pleased to know there is a new nurse arriving tomorrow,' she says. I can tell from her eyes she is smiling even though a mask covers her mouth. 'Travis told me this morning.'

'Where is the old bugger?'

'In his office with a worse hangover than you.'

'Poor old bugger then,' I laugh.

I kneel beside the man and struggle to find a spot on his arm for the injection. I finally find a vein and inject him with the antivenin.

'Let's hope she is as good as you,' I mumble.

'Oh I think you'll like her very much.'

I run the fluid into the patient as fast as possible and hang a second bag.

'We'll need anti-tetanus from the cupboard,' I yell to an Angolan nurse, throwing him the keys to the cupboard.

'I doubt that,' I say.

'Her name is Harriet Lawson,' she says nodding at me over the bed.

I stop with one hand on the fluid bag.

'What?' I say looking at her in disbelief. Surely not, it must be a joke.

'Of course it may not be *your* Harriet Lawson but everything indicates it is. Harvey interviewed her. She's from Battersea and has an excellent nursing degree. She is booked to do tropical diseases on her return. Apparently her first choice was South East Asia but for reasons she wouldn't go in to she changed her mind and chose Angola.'

Akua hands me a hypodermic with the anti-tetanus. I feel my hands shake and Rachel takes the hypodermic from me.

'It has to be fate Brice.'

'Or *Brice Luck*,' I say, not believing that Brice Luck could stretch even this far. Maybe Rachel is right. Maybe it is fate. After all, what were the chances of me being in Angola? I imagine they were her thoughts too. If Dannie had not been struck down with malaria he would have been here instead of me. I hate to feel glad he was. His downfall is my last chance. I look at my watch.

'She arrives in just over twenty-four hours,' smiles Rachel. 'Plenty of time to make this place look romantic.'

I'll need more than twenty-four hours.

'She'll probably get the next flight out,' I say realistically. 'Anyway, as soon as she knows I'm the doctor she'll back out.'

With that thought in mind I take back the needle and inject the patient. Memories suddenly unleashing themselves of the night I had injected Babyface Jack. Phoebe's scheming face launches itself at me and I feel myself shake with anger.

'Brice,' Rachel asks concerned.

'It's okay,' I assure her, wiping the man's wounds with antiseptic. The bitch had really stirred it up. How could I explain to Harriet that I *had* told Phoebe that Harriet was not my type? I didn't want that evil bitch to know my true feelings.

'Well, the notification came for a Doctor Sku Beadu. So, either they have your name wrong, or you've been having a little joke with the volunteers.'

'You're kidding,' I say, unable to hide my surprise. 'I'd forgotten all about that. It was a bit of fun.'

She laughs.

'God Brice, you're bloody mad.'

'I can't believe she's coming. She'll want to kill me you know that? She'll say I deceived her all over again.'

She shakes her head.

'I told Harvey to give you a fighting chance. So no one has told her your real name. Okay, so she may not stay the full five months but she'll have to stay twenty-four hours. How long do you need?'

I feel the excitement building up in me. I hadn't seen Harriet for five weeks but I hadn't forgotten the smell and taste of her, and the way her nose twitched. I can't believe she is coming here.

'How the hell am I supposed to make this place romantic?' I groan.

'Akua and I have already thought about that.'

I smile. As much as I will miss Rachel I'm really rather glad she is going. Her replacement sounds far more appealing.

Chapter Forty-One

The little Cessna aeroplane rattles and shakes so much that I feel it may fall apart before we arrive. I sit next to the pilot whose name is Jose. His shirt is unbuttoned and in broken English he has been trying to chat me up since take-off from Luanda an hour ago. If his flying skills are anything like his seduction skills I'll be lucky if I make it to the hospital. I feel a bit like a female Bob Geldof. Off to do my bit. Although, my bit won't be quite as impressive as his bit was. I'm feeling really scared. Maybe my decision not to go to Asia was a bit rash. I could have given it a go. After all, the chances of Brice Edmunds being the doctor on my placement were pretty slim. God, Harriet, it's a bit late to be thinking that now isn't it? I'd had two briefings with the voluntary organisation and Montamo had seemed like a dream then. Two flights later and I find myself boarding the most rickety plane I have ever seen. The intoxicating fumes from it make my stomach turn over. I look out of the window and see just flatness. I'm so tired but fear of the plane crashing or falling apart keeps me awake.

'We land,' says Jose.

I look at him in horror.

'What already? But there is nothing down there.'

The truth is the thought of landing this plane is scaring the shit out of me. I was bloody surprised when we got the thing off the ground and I'm beginning to feel that getting it back onto the ground is going to be something of a feat.

He nods.

'Yes, we land now.'

'But where?' I ask, looking for an airfield.

I look down and see a few little huts. Good God, what have I done? What if this doctor Beadu is a cruel twisted misogynist? That would be so my luck wouldn't it, or what if he's an axe-wielding mad eccentric, or even worse, a ghastly bucking pervert?

'There.'

He points to a dirt runway and I see a small group of men watching the plane eagerly. They're undoubtedly waiting for it to crash. It is probably their only entertainment. Then I see the hospital and a small flutter of excitement rushes through me. Suddenly it all seems worth it. At last my dreams are coming true. Julian and his irresponsibility is now far behind me, as are the Jacks. I needn't fear bumping into Brice Edmunds. I imagine what he would think of me volunteering to work in Angola. I find myself thinking how wonderful it would have been to have worked with him but quickly push it from my mind as the plane descends. I close my eyes and grip the seat. The little aeroplane lurches up and down as Jose fiddles with the knobs. My mind flashes back to the helicopter descent at Glenwood. We hit the runway with a bump and bounce up before going down again. Jesus, I feel the sweat run from under my armpits and my knuckles turn white. Only when the plane finally comes to a halt do I release my grip. I step from the plane into scorching heat, and am so relieved to be back on terra firma I have to stop myself from kneeling down to kiss the ground. A sea of black faces stare at me and I smile nervously. A young white man pushes through the crowd and waves to me. Thank God for a white face, not that I'm racist or anything.

'Harriet Lawson?' he shouts.

I nod, relieved that he speaks English.

'Hello I'm Travis, coordinator for Medical Aiders. Fantastic, you're on time. That doesn't happen very often.'

I try not to show my disappointment. I had hoped he was Dr Beadu.

'Where's Doctor Beadu?' I ask.

He takes my cases and tips the pilot.

'We've had an emergency. I say emergency, to be honest that's pretty routine around here, but he said he does hope you will join him for dinner. Let's get you to your room shall we? Sorry to seem in a rush. I'm getting the plane back. We need some supplies and you can't trust anyone around here. I know it doesn't look like much but it is one of the best compounds.'

He smiles apologetically. My bedroom is cool and furnished with a single bed and a small dressing table. There is a door to a bathroom.

'I'll get someone to send coffee over,' he says.

I look around and fall onto the bed. I cannot believe I have done this. I stretch back and before I know it I am asleep.

Chapter Forty-Two

A light tapping on the door wakes me. I open it bleary eyed and with wild hair to see a boy standing there.

'Missy, doctor said please come for dinner in fifteen minutes.'

The sun is setting and I calculate that I must have slept for three hours. I rub my eyes.

'Yes of course, where do I go?'

He points to a building at the far end of the hospital. I throw things out of my suitcase and find a suitable summer dress. The bathroom has a bucket of lukewarm water and a bowl, and I rinse my hair and quickly wash. I towel dry my hair when I realise there are no mains to plug in my hairdryer. I use my handbag mirror to apply my make-up. It will be wasted on this Belgium, or was it Danish doctor, but first impressions and all that. I try to check my dress in the little handbag mirror but it's impossible. Picking up my bag I head to the building that the boy pointed at. The only lights are those from the hospital and the outbuildings. The one I'm heading to seems to be well lit and I walk carefully, looking around as I do. No doubt there are worse things to be had here than demented cats. Why is it everything I do somehow reminds me of Glenwood and Brice? The door is open and soft music reaches my ears. I push it open further and gasp. The room is filled with candles. The boy I had seen earlier ushers me in.

'Has there been a power cut?' I ask. 'Does this happen often?'

He pushes me further into the room. A table is beautifully laid. There are two plates and a small stove in the middle.

'It's not homemade curry but I did my best. Hi I'm Dr Beadu, but you can call me Sku,' he says.

I gasp and grab one of the chairs for support. Oh my God, why didn't I realise, *Scooby Doo*. What a bastard.

'But you're in Laos,' I say stupidly.

'Is that man impersonating me again?'

I can't take my eyes off him. I want to but I just can't. He's looks so gorgeous I feel like I may faint. He is wearing a white shirt and knee-length linen trousers which show off his deep tan. His warm hazel eyes are shining and I feel hypnotised by them. His hair is damp, like mine, and I desperately want to run my hands through it. He pulls a chair out for me and I fall into it.

'I'm surprised you of all people didn't get the Scooby Doo bit.'

'I'm not staying,' I say in a shaky voice.

My body is trembling so much that I'm afraid to lift even a glass to my lips.

'I didn't think you would,' he replies calmly, placing a casserole dish onto the table.

'It looks like the dogs bollocks,' I say before I can stop myself.

'No, they were sold out of those at the market this morning,' he smiles cheekily. 'It's chicken, with an assortment of vegetables, sorry it isn't grander but things are sparse around here and ...'

He stops and I look up at him.

'God, it's good to see you. Amazing in fact,' he says softly.

'I wanted to go to Asia,' I say stupidly, holding a glass of water, 'but I didn't want to see you. Isn't that ironic?'

'Don't you just love irony,' he smiles.

'Jane Austen might, but I'm not so keen,' I say, struggling to breathe. This is terrible. I can't even walk out, not that I really want to. I look around at the candles and realise there hasn't been a power cut at all.

'How can this happen?' I say.

'Brice Luck,' he grins, sitting opposite me.

I don't know whether to laugh or cry, to be angry or to be happy.

'I've missed you,' he says softly and I feel my knees tremble.

'You told Phoebe you weren't interested in me and besides we have nothing in common. I'll fly home tomorrow,' I say, knowing the last thing I want to do is fly anywhere except, maybe, into his bedroom.

'Harriet, you never fail to make me laugh. We have nothing in common? We're both sitting in the middle of nowhere, surrounded by mud huts because we both want to help the needy, and you say we have nothing in common. There aren't many women who would be here. As for Phoebe ...' he breaks off and leaves the table and returns with a bottle of wine.

'Homemade, not by me I hasten to add. My translator enjoys doing it. It's a bit potent. Phoebe is,' he says pouring the liquid into the glasses, 'an interfering, stuck up little cow who likes to cause trouble. I wasn't going to tell her my feelings for you. She is the last person on earth I would share my intimate feelings with. I'm disappointed you would think me so shallow.'

My body aches to touch him, to feel his lips on mine, his hands on my breasts. I take a sharp breath as he moves towards me.

'Harry, there isn't another woman on earth that could have more in common with me. From the moment we met outside the church I knew you were something special.'

I feel tears prick my eyes.

'I don't think you're shallow. I just can't imagine what you see in me.'

'Fishing for compliments are you?' he smiles. 'Well, I see your lovely nose which twitches at certain times. I see your fabulous sense of humour which matches mine. I see your honesty and your beauty. I see a woman I want to spend every day and every night with. I see a woman I can work with. A woman who not only understands my work but one that can also help with it, in fact I see my perfect woman.'

'Oh,' I say feeling my body tremble. 'I'm out of debt,' I add stupidly.

'I'm more interested in whether you're available,' he says, desire hanging thick between us.

'Oh yes,' I say feeling my breath becoming more ragged by the second.

I'm in his arms with no idea how I got there. His lips cover my cheeks, chin and neck before landing urgently on my lips. His hands grasp my buttocks and I sigh heavily, feeling my legs give way.

'If you don't mind Miss Lawson, I think I shall have you for a starter,' he says huskily, his hands sliding down the front of my dress. 'Or maybe I shall just make you my three course meal.'

'Oh yes please,' I moan as my hands circle his hardness.

'Don't you just love *Brice Luck*?' he whispers into my ear as he lifts me from the ground and carries me across the compound. 'Or do you want to diss it again.'

'Just shut up,' I laugh, kicking open the door of his room.

Pink Wellies and Flat Caps

Alice Lane has everything; a wonderful fiancé, a responsible job and a lovely flat in Chelsea, but after she has a bra fitting her life goes tits up. Homeless, and with just a sparkling engagement ring as a memory of her previous life Alice accepts a live-in farm manager's job and discovers that things actually can get worse. Come with Alice as she makes her hilarious career change and struggles to cope with her moody employer, Edward. But can Alice turn her back on romance and resist the dashing Dominic or will the past come back to surprise her?

Coconuts and Wonderbras

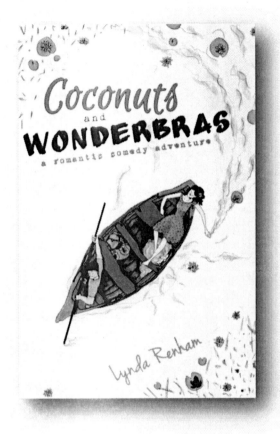

Literary agent Libby Holmes is desperate for her boyfriend, Toby, to propose to her and will do anything for him and if that means dieting for England then she'll have a go. However, when Libby's boss introduces her to her new client, Alex Bryant, her life is turned upside down. Alex Bryant, ex-SAS officer and British hero, insists Libby accompany him to Cambodia for a book fair. What she hadn't bargained for was a country in revolt. Libby finds herself in the middle of an uprising with only Alex Bryant to protect her, that is, until Toby flies out to win back her affections. Come with Libby on her romantic comedy adventure to see if love blossoms in the warm Cambodian sunshine or if, in the heat of the day, emotions get just too hot to handle.